Sign up for our newsletter to hear
about new and upcoming releases.

www.ylva-publishing.com

Other Books by Jess Lea

Looking for Trouble

Murder Under the Gum Trees
A Curious Woman
A Curious Visit

Anthology
The Taste of Her – Vol 1 (e-book)
The Taste of Her – Vol 2 (e-book)
The Taste of Her – A Collection of Ten Erotic Short Stories (paperback)

A Curious Visit

JESS LEA

Acknowledgements

Thanks to everyone at Ylva, especially Astrid, Lee, Julie, Jenny, and Daniela, who were so supportive of this sequel. Thanks to Rach for demanding more of "maritime Margaret"! And thanks especially to my partner, Sam, for reading the drafts with such care and enthusiasm, talking me through my dilemmas, and refusing to hear any notion of quitting.

Dedication

For Jenny and David, who made us very welcome in Tasmania.

Chapter 1

BESS CAMPBELL ADJUSTED HER RAINBOW coat made of recycled plastics, then pulled on her emerald-green woolly hat. She'd knitted it herself in the shape of a Viking's helmet, and it made a striking contrast with her red hair. If there were spirits haunting this place, why not give them some colour to enjoy? They spent enough time in darkness.

She said that to the guide leading the ghost tour, but he gave her a funny look.

The guide shone his lantern at the display wall. It was engraved with names: *Martha. Maria. Susannah. Eliza. Ann.* Few other details were known. She wondered what it said on the women's tombstones, if they had them.

Shivering, Bess thrust her hands into her coat pockets and stamped her feet against the flagstones. No moon tonight. Icy breezes whipped across the yard, plastering her skirt to her legs. Normally, Bess liked being outdoors; she loved nature, found it invigorating. But she wasn't sure about this place.

The prison walls were high, made of rugged sandstone. Weeds grew through the cracks. Behind her was the site of the old punishment cells. They had no windows, just small, rough vents too high to see out. Women condemned to those cells had to climb down underground, into the earth.

"That was a lesson," the guide explained, "to show them where they were headed in the next life if they kept breaking the rules."

There had been a lot of rules in the women's penitentiary built here in Tasmania in the 1820s, back when the island off Australia's mainland was still called Van Diemen's Land: an infamously wild, cold, and dangerous prison colony at the edge of the world.

A woman could be punished for not working hard enough when washing laundry with frozen hands. She could be punished for swearing, or falling asleep in chapel, or eating more than her share of bread, or sharing her sleeping hammock too enthusiastically with another woman.

Talking was discouraged too. Visitors to the prison remarked on how the women and children moved about the place in silence, like ghosts.

While the story disturbed her, Bess longed to see a ghost. Or a bunyip or a UFO—anything unearthly and hard to explain. She'd always been drawn to the colourful side of life, to anything whacky, creative, and eccentric. That was why she had moved to the kooky small town of Port Bannir three years ago—to work in a quirky gallery and live in a tiny house in a field.

But then her lovable boss had been killed and the gallery taken over by new managers who didn't like Bess at all. A year ago, they'd transferred her to the promotions team in their Melbourne office.

While city life was convenient in some ways, Bess knew her employers were sidelining her. After months of spreadsheets and Zoom meetings, her spirit felt starved. She missed her old job. She missed her beloved chickens, now living with her brother. Most of all, she missed the sense of adventure she used to feel every day.

This trip around Tasmania might help. Bess needed wilderness and beauty and strangeness in her life again.

The guide held up his lantern. "Through here were the nurseries. Hundreds of babies were kept crowded inside, neglected and half-starved. Those who survived were snatched from their mothers and sent away to the orphan school. They say some nights, when the wind blows down from the mountain, you can hear the screaming."

Bess pulled her coat tighter, her skin creeping. Maybe she didn't want to meet the spirits of this place after all. Could suffering, despair, and anger be so strong that they left an imprint on the locations where they occurred?

The guide began to talk about the women who'd been imprisoned here—thieves, poisoners, arsonists—and the sinister matrons who controlled them.

"You see where that cell is marked on the ground at the end? Once we had a blind visitor whose guide dog refused to go inside. And over there by the staircase? People complain that the photographs they take of that spot don't turn out. All they get is a dark image." The guide lowered his lantern. "I brought my daughter here when she was five. I left her alone while I went to fetch something. When I came back, I found her crying. She said a woman in black had been angry with her. But there was no one there but us."

A door banged. The woman beside Bess jumped and let out a muffled shriek. The guide's lantern swayed, light and shadows lapping across the walls. Footsteps rang out against the flagstones.

The guests bunched up together like an anxious herd. Those footsteps were coming closer. People whispered, "Is this part of it?"

Bess stepped forward. She didn't want to miss anything.

The gate to the yard flew open. A black silhouette stood against the gloom. She was tall and lean, and the air around her seemed to hum with a strange energy.

In the dim light, her face appeared as white and angular as fresh-cut marble above her black clothing. Her features were strong with a certain stark beauty; her eyes were shadowy, her hair jet black. Her long fingers flexed as if searching for a neck to wrap around.

She stepped forward. Her gaze swept the crowd, her dark eyes glinting malevolently. "Would the owner of a blue Nissan Pulsar, numberplate XIR679, move it immediately, as it is taking up two spaces."

Bess bit her lip, fighting not to laugh.

"If you'd done that at *my* museum, you would have been banned," Margaret Gale said.

"You missed a good start to the tour while you were parking the car," Bess told Margaret. The group, slightly shaken, had moved on to examine the matron's cottage. "Thanks for dropping me at the entrance."

"I wouldn't have needed to, if certain people had learned basic driving skills."

"Do you think it could make a good topic for a gallery exhibition? Haunted prisons of Australia?"

"Plenty of source material." Margaret brushed a speck from her long black coat. She knew a lot about colonial relics, having once run a museum full of them.

Bess and Margaret had loathed each other back in Port Bannir when they first met. They were professional rivals with very different views on how to manage a gallery. Bess had thought Margaret a snarling control freak who needed to move with the times, while Margaret had considered Bess an incompetent, irritating hippie. It had taken them some time to recognise how much they both looked forward to their arguments and how much they really had in common.

"Haunted prisons are a scam, though," Margaret said now. "When I was locked up for murder, I didn't meet any ghosts."

A pleasant-looking family turned around to stare at her.

Bess rushed to explain. "It was a false accusation; she was released…" It was hard to sum up quickly what had happened in Port Bannir.

The parents hurried their children away.

Unperturbed, Margaret examined the cottage door. Her indifference to what other people thought of her was a quality Bess found both attractive and maddening.

Someone's phone sounded, disrupting the guide's speech.

"They should bring back the punishment cells for that." Margaret did not bother to lower her voice, despite Bess mouthing, "Be friendly!"

Margaret's refusal to compromise and play nice was another thing that frustrated and occasionally delighted Bess.

As the group moved forward, Margaret said, "You're still thinking about new exhibitions for that gallery of yours, then?"

"It's not mine." Bess pursed her lips. "My manager hasn't let me make any decisions about exhibits in months."

"Which is why all their recent shows have been abysmal." Margaret might be bad-tempered, but she had always been loyal.

"Thank you." Bess took her hand, ignoring the way Margaret stiffened and seemed to stop herself from pulling away. Margaret never minded when people thought her odd, but public acts of affection were foreign to her. It was one of the things they'd agreed to compromise on, just as Bess had agreed to respect Margaret's detailed systems for bookshelf arranging and sock folding.

She squeezed Margaret's long, cool fingers, touching the nails which were filed back smooth. "Are you enjoying our holiday?"

"I'm enjoying the ruins."

"Wait till you see what I've got planned." Bess knew she sounded overeager, but the past few months had been hard.

When she and Margaret had got together at last after many misunderstandings and some dangerous adventures, Bess had assumed they'd earned their happily ever after. Instead, real life had intruded once again: frustrations at work, changing living arrangements, family tragedy. She didn't regret any of the time they'd spent together, but she wished it could have been smoother sailing.

They needed a break, a reset. Bess was determined that they would enjoy it. "I've got our itinerary planned. There's lavender ice cream, llama walking, a petting session with Tasmanian devils, a honeybee encounter…"

"As long as I don't have to do all four at once." Margaret looked as if she would be happier lurking around another crumbling old prison, but Bess wasn't having that. Ghosts were interesting, but life had to be lived too.

She gripped Margaret's hand tighter, willing the warmth from her own skin to flow into her partner's.

They followed the tour group outside again.

The guide explained, "Over there is the site of the old infirmary. It was freezing, dirty, and damp—you were more likely to catch a disease than be cured of one. Sometimes, on a still night, you can hear the sound of nails being hammered into wood as if someone were making a cheap coffin…"

Bess flinched and glanced at Margaret, who didn't seem to react. Until a message beeped on Margaret's phone, cutting through the quiet.

People turned to stare.

"Seriously?" Bess hissed as Margaret turned her phone to silent, the muscles in her face working in repressed embarrassment.

"It may have slipped my mind," Margaret whispered without moving her lips.

"Who is it?"

"Hmm." Margaret frowned at her screen. "Not a number I recognise."

The guide finished and invited everyone to explore the compound. "But be sure to leave before ten because that's when I lock up. And trust me, you don't want to spend the night alone in here."

A group of tourists ventured over and asked with big, hopeful smiles if they could take a picture with Margaret.

"No," said Margaret. She stalked off to look at a display of historic manacles.

Smiling as hard as she could, Bess was left to explain to the tourists that Margaret was just another visitor, honestly, and not an actor playing a ghost at all.

Margaret could barely see the road. Her headlights lit up a few metres of bitumen rolling out like a conveyor belt, but there was no telling what lay beyond. A fallen tree? A car accident? A kangaroo springing from the bushes about to hit their windscreen? She cursed herself for agreeing to a late-night tour and a motel outside of town. She'd grown up in the country and should have known better.

The road was lined by murky shapes: bracken, tree stumps, dead animals swept aside by logging trucks. This island was lush and beautiful, but it was also the roadkill capital of Australia.

"You're smouldering again." Bess turned up the heater.

Margaret's fingers began to thaw. "I'm concentrating."

"I know a smoulder when I see one. It's like I'm travelling with Lord Byron, if he used colour-coded packing cells in his suitcase and wiped down the whole motel room with disinfectant."

"Do you know what people do in motel rooms?" Margaret shuddered. "You'll thank me when you don't get giardia. I can't believe you nearly drank out of one of their mugs."

"Your flying tackle to stop me was impressive," Bess said. "You're a great loss to women's rugby."

"Thank you."

"Please tell me you're enjoying this trip a little."

"I always enjoy your company." How strange to think that she had once considered Bess the most aggravating woman she'd ever met. Nowadays, Margaret could not imagine being without her.

She thought back to a hike they'd taken yesterday near Cape Raoul at the southern end of the island. Bess had led the way to the lookout point over the jagged cliffs. The sea foamed and churned far below.

Yelling "Wow!", Bess had scrambled over the rocks to get closer, until a massive gust of wind blew her coat out like a sail and Margaret had to haul her to safety, Bess laughing in delight. Her freckled cheeks were pink, her red curls damp under that ridiculous Viking hat, her buxom body panting from exertion.

Margaret wondered yet again where this woman got her energy from. *It's not like me to be this lucky.*

It reminded her of the way she'd felt when she and Bess had first got together two years before. A startled, unexpected joy, a sense that the future might indeed turn out to be better than the past.

Then new problems had come crowding in, and little by little, that lovely optimistic feeling had been tugged away. Could she recover it again out here?

Bess said, "How about that sea yesterday? Majestic!"

Margaret didn't dare take her eyes off the road. But she breathed deeply, inhaling the scent of the other woman's organic shampoo, a light herbal aroma. Bess always smelled like a garden.

Her tone a little too casual, Bess added, "I wouldn't mind being buried at sea. To return to the elements, become part of that wild, primal energy… When you think about it, it's the most spiritual way to go."

"Humph." Margaret knew what Bess was hinting at: a brass urn sealed in plastic and stowed with care in Margaret's locked suitcase.

She wasn't sure why she had brought the urn with her, except that she didn't like to leave it at home. You heard of burglars breaking into houses while the owners were on holiday and trashing everything. And Tasmania wasn't such a bad place to take someone's ashes. Her family had gone on a trip here once when Margaret and her sister Deirdre were children and their mother was still alive, before things went wrong for the Gales once and for all. Margaret couldn't remember much about that holiday, but she thought Deirdre had enjoyed it.

Still, she wasn't prepared to have the conversation Bess had been dancing around, about what to do with Deirdre's ashes. Knowing Bess, the conversation would involve a lot of talk about workshopping, healing, and radical acceptance. Probably with some moonstones and rose quartz thrown in.

Margaret didn't scorn the idea as she once would have. Actually, it gave her a kind of tender pain to know that Bess cared. But she couldn't think about those things now. She'd spent enough time organising Deirdre's funeral, managing her will, closing her bank accounts, paying her medical bills, sorting through her belongings...all the bureaucracy of death. She couldn't give any more time to that tonight.

Changing the subject, Margaret said, "Not a bad tour this evening, despite the silly ghost talk. Some of the displays needed updating, though."

Bess sighed. "You must miss your own museum."

"I never think about it." Margaret cringed at the obvious lie. That museum had been her life's work: a bluestone nineteenth-century courthouse filled with artefacts from sailing ships, the whaling industry, and Antarctic voyages. She'd devoted each day to the history she loved and the tourists she hated, and it had given her life structure and discipline. When developers had forced her to sell the place, she had managed to negotiate a good price, but it left her feeling like she'd lost a limb.

As if she'd heard Margaret's thoughts, Bess said, "Do you think that's why you struggled when you went to work for that antiques auction house?"

"I did not 'struggle'." Margaret sniffed. "If I told people the truth about what their grandparents' old junk was worth, and if I refused to sell preposterous figurines of television characters, that wasn't struggling. It's called having professional standards."

"I thought it was called getting sacked." Apparently even Bess could only put up with Margaret's snapping for so long.

"I was not sacked. It was a mutual separation."

But where she would head next, Margaret had no idea. Changing careers at her age? And right now, when all the world apart from Bess seemed so foolish and irritating, so poorly run and badly designed and...grey? Her vision blurred and she blinked hard. *Don't you fall asleep.*

Something burst from the darkness and shot across the road. Margaret stamped on the brake.

The car screeched to a stop, jerking them forward and back.

Bess gasped.

The bushes waved on the side of the road as a long tail slipped inside and vanished.

"God." Margaret squeezed the steering wheel. "Are you all right?"

"I'm fine." Bess loosened her grip on the seatbelt.

Recalling Bess's history with car accidents, Margaret berated herself for her carelessness. "I'm sorry. It took me by surprise." Her voice shook. "What was it—a cat?"

"A possum, maybe." Bess pressed her face to the window, but nothing moved in the darkness.

"Terrible driving," Margaret said, angry with herself. "I put you in danger. I should have hit it."

"No, you shouldn't." Bess gazed out into the night. "Do you think it could have been a quoll? Those spotty animals with the fluffy tails and the pretty little faces?"

"I've no idea." Margaret got the hire car moving again, driving slower than before and scanning the road until her eyes watered. The rush of adrenalin had left her jittering.

No more country driving after dark, she decided as she turned into the motel carpark. It wasn't safe.

Still, as she climbed out of the car, she felt a rush of dizziness so intense she had to clutch the door handle. She'd been so lifeless for so long. Was it possible that what Margaret secretly craved was not healing and peace but a little bit of danger?

In the motel room, Bess gathered up her silver spotted pyjamas and cruelty-free toiletries while Margaret checked her phone. There was an email from a neighbour who'd been collecting her mail: two more bills had turned up in Deirdre's name. One was from an insurance provider who explained they could not close her account until the account holder contacted them personally. Margaret gritted her teeth. She would call them tomorrow and ask if they had a Ouija board. The other bill was from a phone company whom Margaret had informed about Deirdre's death. Their computer system had addressed it to "The Deceased".

And she had a missed call and voicemail from that unfamiliar number again. They must have come through during the ghost tour after she'd switched her phone off.

"Everything all right?" Bess stood in front of the bathroom mirror, brushing out her thick, wavy red hair.

"Another call." Margaret studied the number. "Has Deirdre's oncologist thought of one more charge to add to the bill? Or are her cretinous in-laws ringing again to ask how much money she left them?"

"At this time of night? Probably a wrong number." Bess took out her toothbrush. "Hey, I've been thinking: do you reckon we should get an Asian-style squat toilet installed at our place?"

Margaret put down her phone. "What are you talking about?"

"I've been reading this amazing book about gut health and good bacteria, and it says the best position is actually—"

"I withdraw the question. And absolutely not."

"You're so conventional," said Bess around a mouthful of toothpaste. "Well, do you think I should become a foster mother for rescue goats? I've been reading about that too."

"Oh, that's easier." Margaret checked their maps for tomorrow. "No."

Bess spat out her toothpaste. "Have it your way." She arranged her vegan cosmetics along the sink, nudging too close to Margaret's toiletries.

"We said you would keep your things on the left-hand side."

"Fine." Bess moved everything farther away, although she made a point of leaving her cactus and kale recovery lotion next to Margaret's toothbrush.

Margaret narrowed her eyes. "Are you trying to provoke me?"

"Play your cards right..." She grinned, then pulled Margaret down for a kiss.

Margaret stiffened in surprise, then returned the embrace.

Bess pressed her warm, full body up against her, sliding her arms around Margaret's waist.

The tension in Margaret's muscles began to seep away, as though she were sliding into a soothing bath. She felt Bess's lips moving as she smiled, felt the laughing flutter of her breath. Her kisses were often like this: light-hearted, joyful. Disarming.

That was not a thing Margaret was used to—not a thing she had ever wanted before she met Bess. Could one person change you that much?

A few minutes later, while Bess sang Dolly Parton songs under the shower, Margaret decided to stretch her legs. She should check that message too.

The night sky was clear, the air crystal-cold and scented with eucalyptus. In the bushland behind the motel, things rustled and crunched and squeaked.

"Margaret?" She didn't recognise the woman's voice in the recorded message. But there was something about it—an alto pitch, crisp consonants, a slight breathiness—that made her listen hard.

She thought she had heard that voice before, a long time ago.

"I hope you're the right Margaret Gale," the voice said. "Otherwise some poor stranger is about to be confused…" A quick note of laughter, like a bird's cry. Margaret frowned. Again, there was something familiar about it.

"You might remember me," the voice went on. "We met on graduation night, 1997. Vivienne Bolt."

Margaret froze. Her breath hung in the cold air.

"I'd love to do all the what-have-you-been-up-to-all-these-years guff," said the voice, "but Ivy, my grandmother, has fallen asleep at last and I don't know how long I'll have. So I'll cut to the chase."

Margaret gripped the phone. She remembered that voice now, with its rounded vowels and hint of an English accent, although Vivienne had been born and bred in Australia.

Back on graduation night when they'd met, Margaret had asked Vivienne about her unusual way of speaking. "Snobby relatives," was Vivienne's reply, "and the most God-awful elocution teachers at boarding school. Two-hundred-year-old harpies who hit us with walking sticks—truly! God forbid we should sound local." Her white-blonde hair blew in the night breeze, the black shapes of trees in Melbourne's Alexandra Gardens behind her. In the lamplight of the gardens, Vivienne's pale skin had an eerie glow. "I'm not from any country," she laughed, and Margaret had thought of sprites, of mermaids.

Now Margaret stood motionless as the past returned without warning, slicing through the present.

Vivienne's message continued: "I looked you up online and phoned your employer. By the way, their silly receptionist really shouldn't give out phone numbers to any nicely spoken lady who calls claiming to be an old friend. I wanted to ask your advice about something, but they said you'd left and were travelling here, and I thought: perfect!" That laugh again. "For me, I mean."

She cleared her throat. "Margaret, I need a favour. My grandmother is ill and I'm staying at her house at seven Renfeld Lane, outside a town called Mount Bastion. You won't have heard of it; it's rather a dump. But… Well, strange things have been happening."

Margaret held her breath. Strange was right. Vivienne Bolt calling her? Vivienne, whom she had imagined long gone, whisked away twenty-five years ago? How could Vivienne be here in rural Tasmania of all places?

The voice said, "I'm afraid this will sound completely barking, but I promise I'm compos mentis. It's just… I think someone is trying to harm us. My grandmother has a large antique collection; all her money is tied up in it. Ghastly things, but valuable. I'm trying to sort out her finances to make sure she's looked after because she'll need to go into care soon. She's getting worse, poor old girl, and there's only so much I can do."

A pause.

"But things have been going missing. A silver-plated Art Deco cigarette lighter, a porcelain nymph, an amber paperweight. Things small enough to slip into a pocket. I noticed it this week when I was cleaning her disaster of a house. And now I wonder how many other things have been swiped!"

Vivienne took an audible breath. "It's not just the thefts. Someone scared away the two carers I hired to help look after Ivy. One of them left after her car tyres got slashed three times in our driveway, and the other quit when she found a piece of glass in a sandwich she'd left for herself in our kitchen! And— Look, I know it's a drafty old building and perhaps I'm letting the atmosphere get to me, but sometimes I swear I hear noises. Something moving around in the house. It makes my skin creep."

She laughed again, this time a little desperately. "I don't dare report it. Ivy would have a fit if she knew; she's so ill, and she's devoted to her collection. And this is a small town. Ivy relies on the local businesses for groceries, medication, transport. If the police started questioning her neighbours, things could become very difficult.

"Listen, Margaret, I'm thoroughly embarrassed to call you out of the blue and drop this in your lap, but I remembered how you said you planned to start your own museum one day, so I did some research into you. I hope that's not too intrusive, but you must know there are intriguing stories online about a museum you used to run. It's clear you know a lot about antiques, and you're a—a friend of mine. Could you stop by? Look over Ivy's collection, help me do an inventory, figure out the extent of the loss, advise me on what to do? It would be ever so useful. And perhaps…perhaps with your brains, you might be able to figure out what's happening."

Vivienne exhaled. "Listen to me blathering on! Are you still listening? I know I've got no right to ask you for anything after all this time, but…I've got nowhere else to turn, Margaret."

A computerised voice took over: "To return call, press two. To replay message—"

Margaret hung up and stared into the night.

A bloodcurdling screech ripped through the darkness, making her jump. There must be a masked owl in the bushland nearby. It was a sound that had always made her think of witches.

Chapter 2

"BUT WHO IS THIS VIVIENNE?" Bess asked the next morning.

Margaret's jaw was firm as she drove, her eyes narrowed in concentration. But since that was her resting face, it didn't tell Bess much.

"I met her at university in Melbourne. Or rather, the night after I graduated from university. She'd done her honours in fine arts and was about to head to Rome on a scholarship."

"Nice work, if you can get it."

"We skipped the graduation party because everyone else was drunk and obnoxious," Margaret said. "We went for a walk around the city and along the Yarra River instead. Then we went our separate ways and I never heard from her again. Strange that she would contact me now."

Bess thought there was something curious about Margaret's tone. Did she sound distracted? Vague, even?

Still, Bess was determined to make the best of things. "Well, it's a mystery. Let's go and solve it! I'm always up for an adventure, and I like meeting new people. It puts water back in my well."

"Here we are." A sign directed them off the highway towards Mount Bastion.

This town had not been on Bess's list of places to visit on their Tasmanian holiday. As they pulled onto the main street, she could see why. Some parts of Tasmania were heaven for tourists, with breathtaking views, fluffy native animals, fine wine, and gourmet food, but Mount Bastion was not one of those places.

Instead, the town had a general store, two dilapidated pubs, a tatty-looking Chinese restaurant, and a community centre whose sign said OPEN MOST TUESDAYS. No school or doctor's surgery. Whatever industries had once sustained the area were long gone. Port Bannir had been like Manhattan compared to this.

Incongruously, there was an antiques shop in an old Edwardian building. She wondered where they found customers.

As they drove down the quiet street, two locals turned to watch.

"Shall we find somewhere to have lunch? Or did your friend invite us to eat with her?"

"She's not my friend," Margaret said. "I told you, it's been twenty-five years. And no, the message about theft and sabotage didn't mention lunch. But given the broken-glass-in-the-sandwich story, I'd suggest we buy something in town."

One pub was shut. The other bore a sign: KITCHEN CLOSED DUE TO ILLNESS.

Seeing Margaret raise her eyebrows, Bess said, "Let's try the general store."

When they pushed open the doors to the shop, the people inside turned to stare. Bess saw their own reflections in a fridge door. Margaret was tall and thin, her short dark hair slicked back. She was clad in black, including black leather boots and matching gloves. Bess was short and plump, and wore cats-eye glasses, a jacket in psychedelic patterns, and a hand-knitted hat in the shape of an octopus with tentacles streaming down her back.

The place fell silent. If a piano had been playing, it would have stopped.

Bess took two juices from the fridge and made a point of smiling as she approached the counter. After all, the energy you put into the world was the energy you got back. Most of the time.

"Petrol station's down the road," someone blurted out. "They sell maps, if you're lost."

"Thank you." Bess kept smiling. "But we are exactly where we want to be."

Margaret ordered a sausage roll in a less friendly tone. Then she said quietly to Bess, "Do you mind us stopping here? I don't know what's happening with Vivienne. But we won't stay long."

"Of course I don't mind. I love new places, new people…" Bess turned to the woman behind the counter. "Are any of your pies vegetarian?"

The woman stared at her as if she'd ordered peacock tongues in jelly. "No."

Well, maybe not all new people. Bess ordered a pasty that looked fossilized, her tone a little less perky now.

She turned back to the counter. "We're looking for number seven, Renfeld Lane. Do you know—?"

"Nope." The reply came before she'd finished asking. The woman busied herself at the register. When Bess looked over her shoulder, everyone else seemed engrossed in other things.

While Margaret paid, Bess studied the community noticeboard near the door. There were ads for sheep dip, pest exterminators, mental health crisis lines, and a Rotary Club dance scheduled for that night. And a large poster, tacked over the top of several others. It showed a portly man with long silver curls, a leather Akubra hat, a swirling scarf, and a smug look.

"Dorian Visser LIVE. Local writer in residence reads from his critically acclaimed work, *Crossroads House: Inside Australia's Most Haunted Homestead*".

She was about to call Margaret over when a message sounded on her phone. "Oh wow."

"Good news?"

"Yes!" Bess caught herself. "Well, no. Our chief curator has broken both legs skiing, just when his second-in-command went away on maternity leave."

"My sympathies to them both."

"But it's left the gallery short-staffed." Bess chewed her lip. "And they need to start planning next season's exhibitions."

"Really? Perhaps now they wish they hadn't spent months turning down your ideas and inventing meaningless tasks to keep you busy."

Bess studied the message. "This could be my chance."

"After how they treated you, they don't deserve to benefit from your hard work and talent."

"Maybe not, but I can't quit right now, can I?" Bess spoke without thinking, then regretted it. She didn't mean to make Margaret feel as if her own unemployment was forcing Bess to stay in a job she hated just to pay the bills—although there was some truth in it.

"If I could get one more strong exhibition under my belt, I could leave on a high note," she continued. "It would look great on my résumé, and it would make me feel better about my time there. Plus it would make those bozos realise how wrong they were to take me for granted." It wasn't good karma to dwell on bitter thoughts, but you had to give yourself permission to be imperfect sometimes. "So stuff 'em."

Margaret shifted from one pointy-toed boot to the other. "I am…sorry. The way your employers have treated you has been unacceptable. And it started because of me."

When Bess's previous boss, Leon, was stabbed to death in his own gallery, many people in Port Bannir had assumed Margaret, his business rival, was responsible. Bess's new employers had been happy to go along with that explanation, and they had not liked it at all when Bess had believed in the woman's innocence and set about proving it.

She grasped Margaret's arm, feeling the sinewy strength there. "Totally worth it."

Through the shop window, she sensed several people staring as she craned up to kiss Margaret firmly on the mouth.

And stuff you too, she felt like calling back over her shoulder. But she managed a big, joyous smile instead. Living well was the best revenge.

"Now let's go and meet Vivienne. I can't wait."

"Oh boy," Bess said fifteen minutes later as they pulled up outside a set of high iron gates that must have been elegant a hundred years before. Now they were half swallowed by creepers. Welded into the gates were the words CROSSROADS HOUSE.

The property backed onto a national park and was framed by blue gums, blackwoods, and silver banksia trees. The grounds of the house must have been pretty once, but now the lavender bushes and hollyhocks were fighting for survival against blackberries and weeds.

Bess felt sorry for places like this. They made her want to jump the fence with some garden shears, a shovel, and a sack of organic mulch.

"What...?" Margaret stared, her mouth hanging open. "She can't live *here?*"

The house was a ramshackle old mansion with sagging gable windows, moss covering the roof, and paint peeling off the pillars that held up the front porch.

Trying to stay positive, Bess said, "Well, it's got character."

"It's got termites."

"Come on, it's interesting." Bess always defended the downtrodden, even houses. "What would you call that architecture?"

"Criminal?" Margaret winced. "I can see it's been altered a few times. Stolid Victorian manor farm meets Edwardian new money, meets Art Deco hangover, meets whatever they were thinking when they added those gargoyles."

"But if the owner fixed it up, it could be worth a lot of money." Bess led the way through the gates. "I wonder why she hasn't?"

"Perhaps I got the address wrong." Margaret hung back. "Vivienne wouldn't live somewhere like this."

"Don't be silly. It's just a building." Bess pressed forward along the gravel path that was overgrown with flatweed. As she neared the entrance to the house, she said, "Places only seem good or bad because of the meanings we attach to them. If we can let go and just breathe into the moment—"

"In that house? We'd breathe in black mould."

"—then we can calm those judgemental thoughts and accept things as they are," Bess finished, pitching her voice loud enough to cover Margaret's disbelieving snort. "Try a one-minute meditation with me."

"No, thank you."

"You can't spare one minute?" Bess had reached the front steps but saw no reason to rush. She shut her eyes and spread her arms wide. "Right now, I'm wriggling my toes and noticing the ground underneath me." The awareness made her smile. "I'm becoming conscious of my breathing and how each breath is different from the last, like the moments of our lives." She shook her shoulders to loosen any tension. "And I'm repeating to myself, 'I am safe, I am loved, I am forgiven'."

She knew Margaret would dismiss this as hippie nonsense, but Bess wished she would not. If Margaret could bring herself to believe those things, surely she would be happier.

Finishing with a big, delicious exhale, Bess spun around to demonstrate how much better one minute made her feel. She caught her foot in a rabbit burrow, toppled, and sat down hard on the gravel, crashing into a heavy object that tipped over, drenching her in something wet, cold, and smelly. The object hit something else, which shattered.

Water soaked through her clothes; she had fallen over a birdbath. Evidently no one had cleaned it in a while, and she was spattered with pond scum and slimy leaves. The birdbath had broken in two when it hit the other object, which looked like it might have been a garden statue. A nymph maybe? There wasn't much of it left.

Margaret helped her up. "Are you hurt?"

"I'm fine." Bess looked down at the broken items. "But that's not good."

"I'd say you did a few hundred dollars' worth of improvements."

The front door of the house opened. Two women appeared in the doorway, one in a wheelchair. The younger one was slender with piercing green eyes and long white-blonde hair pulled back. She looked to be in her forties, but her skin was flawless and very pale as if she had never been allowed outdoors. There was a delicate air about her, but her sharp cheekbones and pointed chin hinted at a kind of strength.

The other woman must have been past ninety. She was stick-thin, her body shrunken and hardened as if life had drained the juices out of her. Her brittle white hair was yanked back and skewered to her skull with an expensive-looking silver pin. Matching silver pendant earrings dragged her withered earlobes down towards her shoulders. Her hands, gripping the arms of her wheelchair, were gnarled and veiny but looked like they had once been strong.

The two looked like a very old but powerful witch and a sad fairy held prisoner by her spells. They stared at Bess as she stood next to their broken ornaments, drenched and dripping slime from her octopus hat.

In a voice that sounded like a deep croak, the older woman said to the younger one, "Get rid of them. You know I won't have *people* here."

The younger woman flinched as if she knew the rules only too well.

Margaret felt as if she'd put her weight on a step that wasn't there. The younger woman was Vivienne?

For twenty-five years, her memories of Vivienne had run on a loop in some darkened cinema at the back of her mind. Vivienne smoking French cigarettes without filters, her hair gleaming like platinum under the wet streetlight. Vivienne talking about the Louvre, the Tate Modern, the Uffizi, her young voice world-weary as she explained that they were all right but not what they used to be—now, the Buchmann Galerie in Germany, that was interesting, cutting edge. She wouldn't mind going there.

She and Vivienne had walked along the wall of the moat outside Melbourne's National Gallery, looking over the darkened city with cheerful disdain. Below her in the water were hundreds of coins tossed in for luck, now wearing away. "People are such sheep," Vivienne had said. "You have to make your own luck." The wall sloped higher until her lace-up high heels were level with Margaret's heart. Margaret had held out her arms to help her jump down.

How could Vivienne be *here*?

During those twenty-five years since graduation night, she had wondered sometimes what Vivienne was doing. The young Margaret had pondered the question while she struggled along in junior curator jobs whose pay mocked her education and ability. And later on she'd wondered about it again as she worked to set up her maritime museum while battling a hostile town and caring for an ageing, angry father.

It had cheered her up in a strange way to picture Vivienne poring over medieval manuscripts at the Vatican or restoring seventeenth-century folios of Shakespeare's plays in the British Library. Still looking poised, chic, and somehow otherworldly as if these expert jobs would suit her well enough until a better opportunity arose. Perhaps to become an advisor to some top-secret government agency or marry into minor royalty.

Never would Margaret have imagined Vivienne living in a rotting old house in a town much shabbier and lonelier than Port Bannir, caring for an elderly relative who seemed worse than Margaret's dad.

This was all wrong.

She felt thrown off balance and, quite unreasonably, betrayed.

"Please don't feel dreadful," Vivienne said for the fifth time.

Bess, who believed you should apologise for accidental breakage once, then pay for repairs and move on, longed to reply *I don't, but clearly you think I should.*

The visit was not going well.

Breaking those garden ornaments had been a bad start. Vivienne had insisted on lending Bess some dry clothes, which was nice of her, in theory. Then she fossicked through her wardrobe, pulling out size-eight garments that wouldn't fit before handing Bess a frilly pink robe ("antique Edwardian peach lace," she'd said) which clashed eye-wateringly with Bess's red hair.

Not that Bess believed in body anxiety or restricting women's colour choices. But she suspected that Vivienne did.

If Vivienne was subtly unwelcoming, there was nothing subtle about her grandmother. When Ivy wasn't squinting at Bess through cloudy eyes and barking loudly, "Who's the blob with the red hair?" and "Why did you let her break my things?", she was grabbing at Vivienne and snarling, "Who are you anyway? Where's my Viv?"

"I'm sorry about her," Vivienne whispered to Margaret. "Her pain medication makes her confused."

Which was terrible, of course. Bess tried to feel pity for them both.

Despite its rundown exterior, Crossroads House was neat and functional inside. It needed repairs—there were patches on the walls covered in rough plaster, and the furniture looked at least eighty—but the two women seemed to live here comfortably enough. There was a stairlift installed against the wall by the staircase to transport Ivy up and down.

Bess spotted an alcove in the wall at the top of the stairs. It held a display pedestal with some item in a glass box. She squinted. "Is that an animal's skull?"

But her companions had walked on.

The walls of the entrance hall were decorated with black-and-white photographs of the property in its heyday. Cattle grazed in sunny fields while workers hurried around, filling carts with timber and stone. In those pictures, Crossroads House was new and ostentatiously wealthy—every roof tile and brick seemed to gleam. People posed in the driveway next to vintage cars: men in three-piece suits and waxed moustaches, women in Edwardian lace and enormous hats.

Where had it gone, all that bustle and success?

Ivy snapped at Vivienne, "Why would you invite strangers here? You know we don't do that."

Bess wanted to ask *Why don't you?* But after the birdbath incident, she didn't think she should cause further tension.

Maybe Ivy was worried about protecting her antiques. The place was full of them. Delicate brass and enamel carriage clocks bonged on the sideboard, and blue and white Chinese vases sat on occasional tables. Dainty porcelain shepherdesses peeped out from glass cabinets.

Bess knocked over two brass statuettes and an umbrella stand. She wasn't really clumsy, but she was used to living in a tiny house furnished with sturdy, brightly coloured things she'd made, knowing that if they got broken, she could mend them or turn them into something else.

What was the point of living in a gigantic house and tiptoeing around your own belongings?

Still, she could have stayed positive about Crossroads House. It was Vivienne's behaviour that Bess found hard to excuse.

Their hostess had barely asked Bess a single thing. She was too busy questioning Margaret and listening intently to her replies as if preparing to write Margaret's biography.

When Margaret described running her own museum, Vivienne clasped her hands, saying, "I knew you would do something distinctive. You were always one to follow your own passions and to hell with everyone else."

Vivienne raised her perfect eyebrows when Margaret talked about the difficulties of managing staff, suppliers, and visitors. "I can't image how you did it, Margaret—every single day? I simply can't bear dealing with *people*."

And she waved a dismissive hand when Margaret mentioned leaving the auction house where she had worked in the city. Vivienne declared, "Most people who work in those places are cretins. If they didn't have the brains to appreciate you, you were right to withdraw."

Listening to the conversation as she trailed behind, Bess could not help comparing Vivienne's responses to her own. Back in Port Bannir, she had ticked Margaret off for being too hard on her staff. She had urged Margaret to wait and reflect instead of leaving that auction house in a huff. And the first time they met, Bess had gotten into an argument with Margaret over an antique dildo and told her crossly that her maritime museum was cold, unwelcoming, and dull as dishwater.

Was she, Bess, the negative one here? The idea disturbed her.

On the other hand, she wanted to roll her eyes at Vivienne and say, *Come on. You can't think every single thing Margaret's done is that damn impressive.*

And what about Margaret herself? Her manner was strange. Gone was her usual haughtiness, her sharpness and air of authority. Instead, she seemed awkward, almost baffled, and she kept darting nervous glances at Vivienne as if she could hardly believe this was happening. What was that about?

With an effort, Bess told herself to cheer up and change the subject. Breaking into their conversation, she said, "So, Vivienne, tell us about this house. It must be an amazing place to live."

"Oh!" Vivienne looked startled, as if she'd forgotten her second visitor. She'd walked ahead of Bess; now she turned to look back. Her hair, held back with a clip, swayed between her shoulder blades in a single gleaming curl. "Well, I suppose it is. Some parts of the estate date back to 1837."

"Really?" Bess thought about mentioning the poster she had seen in town which claimed that Crossroads House was haunted.

But Vivienne was speaking to Margaret again. "Of course, it needs major repairs. More than we can afford right now."

"What's she saying?" Ivy demanded. "Money? You're not getting my money, missy."

"I don't want your money, Ivy." She never called the older woman Gran or Nanna, Bess noticed.

"What would you know about money?" Ivy said. "Burrowing away in a library all your life like a little mole? Reading books for a living? Ridiculous. Why aren't you married?"

"I restore and preserve rare volumes at the State Library in Hobart," Vivienne reminded her.

Ivy just snorted. The job sounded interesting to Bess; under different circumstances, she would have asked Vivienne about it.

"But when Ivy fell ill..." Vivienne continued.

"I'm not going into any bloody nursing home, missy, so you can stick that idea where the sun don't shine." Ivy clawed on a side table. "Where are my glasses?"

"You broke them this morning, remember? We'll get them replaced in the city." Vivienne said, adding tiredly, "Heaven knows when."

Then she turned to Margaret, and the energy rushed back into her voice. "You got my message. Perhaps we could talk?"

"Certainly."

Vivienne hesitated, glancing at Bess. "It's delicate."

Are you for real? Bess felt like demanding. She'd had enough of this. She imagined flinging off this frilly pink robe and stomping out of here in her underwear.

Instead, she took three deep breaths and waited for the moment to pass. When it did, she realised she didn't care. Why was she getting upset? They were only here for the afternoon, and most likely she would never see either of her hostesses again. She trusted Margaret, so what did it matter how anyone else behaved?

"I might take a walk around your garden." Fresh air would do her good.

As she left, she saw Vivienne lay an imploring hand on Margaret's arm.

To say Margaret felt dismayed would be an understatement. If she weren't so averse to melodrama, she would have said her past had been violated. How could Vivienne Bolt be living like this?

This woman was Vivienne but not Vivienne: a faded negative of the girl from graduation night. She had Vivienne's ethereal beauty, her sharpness, her sarcastic drawl that seemed to draw you into a private joke against the rest of the world. And like on graduation night, she behaved as if she and Margaret had known each other for years.

But where was her optimism, her ambition? Where was that air of certainty that she could go anywhere and do anything if she deemed it good enough for her? Where was that sense of fun that had radiated from the young Vivienne as they'd strolled down St Kilda Road in a light mist of rain past the well-dressed crowds outside the theatres, with Vivienne expertly pretending to be a noisy American tourist, an expensive callgirl, a Russian spy? And the young Margaret, who rarely laughed at anything, pressed her lips together and shook with suppressed mirth.

What had happened to all of that?

"Sorry to leave you stuck here." Vivienne nodded around the sitting room as she wheeled Ivy out the door for her nap. "Won't be long."

The old woman complained, "Who's stuck? Why are you here? And who's that long streak of misery in the black coat?"

Margaret shrugged. She'd been called worse.

Walking around the room, Margaret wrinkled her nose at the smell of damp that air fresheners couldn't quite cover. She didn't care for this place. Yes, Margaret liked historical relics, but her passion was for seafaring history with its importance to the rise of the modern world, its stories of peril and desperate endurance, its grim majesty. Scrimshaws carved from whales' teeth, wheelhouses lashed by briny waters, surgeons' kits, powder kegs, battered old maps, medals from battles on the high seas. Artefacts that even now seemed to carry a whiff of seaweed, rum, and blood.

Those items made Margaret feel invigorated. Ivy's fussy ornaments and dark, stuffy rooms had the opposite effect.

Returning, Vivienne asked, "Are they any good? Ivy's poured so much money into this wretched collection. At the expense of the rest of the house, as you can see. I hope the antiques she chose are actually worth something."

"I've not had a chance to look closely. But I'd say, put together, they would make a nice little nest egg."

"That's a relief. Come and see the spare room; there's more in there."

Despite the size of the house, Vivienne and Ivy only seemed to use a few rooms. The east wing was shut up completely, Vivienne told her, pending repairs they couldn't afford.

Vivienne led her upstairs and opened the door to a bedroom at the top. "Ivy bought these years ago." Margaret looked inside and reeled.

The room was full of dolls. Porcelain dolls with leather bodies and hoop skirts, naked Kewpie dolls with wings, clown dolls with ball-joint bodies and sheepskin hair, World War I soldier dolls, character dolls with faces like real children and blue glass eyes. They were lined up on the bed, the windowsill, the top of the wardrobe. They peeped out of drawers and boxes. Some sat on little swings hung from the ceiling.

"Ivy says there's ten thousand dollars' worth." Vivienne wrinkled her nose. "Repulsive, aren't they? Come in, though. We won't be disturbed here."

"Are you sure? It looks disturbing to me."

Vivienne shut the door behind them.

"You haven't told me yet what you've been doing these twenty-five years," Margaret said. How strange that all of their earlier conversation had been about Margaret herself.

"Oh, don't worry; I haven't been locked up here for a quarter of a century." Vivienne sighed. "Although it feels like it some days."

"When we said goodbye, you were about to head off on a scholarship to Rome."

"Yes, magical stuff. The blue Italian skies, the ruins, the art, the carbohydrates..." Vivienne shrugged the way she'd done on graduation night as if to say, *It's more amazing than most people could imagine, but it's nothing special to me.*

"And what about after that?" Margaret pressed, still trying to reconcile this Vivienne with her own memories. "You talked about going to Cologne, Seoul, Tokyo..."

"All that and more." She flashed a crooked smile. "I'll tell you the full story one day. But for now, my time is dictated by Ivy's medication regime and dodgy bladder, so I hope you'll forgive me if we cut to the chase."

It was dismissive, but Margaret couldn't blame her. She had looked after dying people; she knew the score. She'd never imagined Vivienne, the ultracool loner, having to do it, though.

"In your message, you said someone had been stealing from Ivy and harassing her carers. And you thought somebody had been inside the house."

"Yes." Vivienne hesitated. "Well, perhaps. It's hard to tell. By the time Ivy called me and I travelled down here, she was already really ill. I'm not sure what might have gone on before I arrived. Even if she remembered, she might refuse to tell me out of sheer bloody-mindedness. Still, I need to do the right thing by her. I know she's rather an old nightmare, but she's been on her own too long."

Intrigued, Margaret said, "A property this far out of town... It's an interesting choice for a thief. You've never noticed strange cars coming and going?"

"No."

"Do you have visitors? Employees? Carers?"

"No." Vivienne played with her strand of pearls. "Not after what happened to the last two. The district nurse visits occasionally, and there's a girl who looks after the garden."

Margaret tried to hide her disbelief.

"Well, I didn't say she was good at it. It's hard to get help here. As for visitors... Ivy said Alan Moore from the antiques shop used to visit, offering to buy and sell things, but he stopped coming last year. Maybe she offended him. Then there's that Visser man: a local historian."

"Visser?" The name rang a bell.

"I don't remember his first name. Ivy said he used to stop by, asking peculiar questions about the house. From what she said, I thought he sounded like a crank, but she seemed to find him amusing. She has an odd sense of humour. And then there's Janine Jones. She's from the historical society, and she's phoned up a few times to talk about displaying some of Ivy's antiques. She seemed pretty insufferable, and Ivy wasn't well enough to talk, so I put her off."

"What about friends? Relatives?"

"I don't think there are any."

"What's wrong with Ivy, anyway?"

Vivienne didn't seem to mind her blunt phrasing. "Take your pick. Heart murmur, infections, arthritis. She had cancer two years ago; she didn't tell me until recently. I'm sure it's back now." Vivienne let out a breath. "I'm no doctor, but I'd say she has a year left at most. And whatever her feelings about nursing homes, she'll have to go into care soon; I'm barely managing."

"I'm sorry." If Margaret had been a more demonstrative person, she might have hugged Vivienne. Instead, she said awkwardly, "You have my sympathy, but I'm not sure how much I can do. I don't know how to track down a thief or a saboteur." She moved towards the window, wishing she could let in some air. The panes were grimy, the wooden frames starting to rot.

"It's good to see you again, Margaret."

She turned to find Vivienne standing closer and gazing up at her. Her eyes were bright green, like moss.

"I've been harping on about my problems," Vivienne said, "but this must have been a hellish year for you. I told you I'd been Googling—I hope you don't mind, but I saw the funeral notice for your sister. I'm sorry."

"Well…" Margaret was never sure how to reply to condolences. Not that many had been offered.

"Cancer, wasn't it? Was it you who cared for her?"

A muscle twitched in Margaret's cheek. "Yes. Until—until I couldn't any longer."

"Changes your perspective on things, doesn't it? No wonder you stopped going along with silly workplace politics."

"Perhaps." Through the murky glass, Margaret could see Bess in the garden below. She was talking to someone: a woman with chestnut hair cut short like toothbrush bristles and a ring through her eyebrow. The woman wore a khaki shirt cut off to show arms that were tanned and muscular.

Was this the gardener who didn't do much gardening? She was leaning on a shovel and grinning at Bess.

Margaret frowned, wishing she were down there now.

"Look, Vivienne." Normally, Margaret would have had no trouble saying, *I can't help you.* But this time, the refusal wouldn't come. It was the cancer talk, perhaps, or the mention of Deidre. Or maybe it was the shock of seeing Vivienne trapped in a miserable situation. She had remembered Vivienne as a sort of heroine, and heroines weren't meant to end up like this. "I can take a look at your grandmother's collection. I'm not sure I can help with anything else."

"Oh, that's perfect!" Vivienne grasped her hand. "You don't know what this means to me."

"Well…" Margaret shifted uncomfortably.

In the garden, Bess must have said something funny because the woman with the shovel laughed and gave her shoulder a playful push. Margaret imagined lobbing an antique doll at the gardener and knocking out her stupid eyebrow ring.

Vivienne was still hanging onto Margaret's hand. Her fingers were cool and soft, curling like the spirals of a fern.

Bess was starting to feel better about the frilly pink robe.

"Makes you look like one of those *Downton Abbey* chicks," said the gardener, Ty, leaning on her shovel and giving Bess an appreciative once-over.

It didn't really, and Bess wouldn't have liked Ty much even if Bess had been single. She was too cocky and kept glancing at her reflection in the house windows as if to check that her hair was still good.

Still, Bess didn't believe in refusing a compliment. If the universe saw fit to send positive energy your way, why not accept it? She'd been feeling down on herself after that meeting with Vivienne, and that wouldn't do. She'd put in a lot of work over the years to achieve good self-esteem, and she didn't intend to give it up now.

"You've got a big job here." Bess gestured around the neglected garden.

"Hell, yeah. Couch grass, bindiis, purple morning glory, milk thistles. Topsoil needs replacing. Couple of trees have got to come out before they fall on someone. Aphids. Mites. Rabbit burrows."

Not that Ty seemed to be in a hurry to start work. She ran a hand through her short chestnut hair with a gesture that caused her shirt to ride up, affording a glimpse of tanned, muscular torso. Bess wondered if she practised that move in the mirror.

"It's sad that some gardens are allowed to get that way," Bess said. "They deserve better."

"Yeah, well." Ty nodded towards the house. "Lady Face-ache never gave a stuff about people. So I s'pose it's a bit much to expect her to care about plants."

"Who—Vivienne? Or Ivy?"

"The old biddy. Horrible woman. You know her family used to own half the town, right? Back when it was worth owning."

"This used to be a wealthy estate, right?"

"Yeah. Both my grandfathers worked here. They reckoned the Bolts were mean as cat sick even then. And a bit funny in the head. But Mr Bolt had shares in every business in town and knew everyone who mattered. Course, that was a million years ago, but the old girl still orders everyone around." Ty rolled her eyes. "You seen all her stuff in there?"

"The antiques?"

"Yeah. And that skull, whatever it is." Ty screwed up her nose in distaste. "I don't like dead things."

Bess tried to sound casual. "What's Vivienne like? Her granddaughter?"

"I never saw her till a few weeks ago. She lives in Hobart. Came back to look after the old lady."

"That was good of her." Bess admired anyone who gave up a career to care for someone they loved. Still, it made her uncomfortable to compare Vivienne's sacrifice for her grandmother with Bess's own family relationships, which could be described as mixed.

She imagined quitting work to care for, say, her mother, Yvonne. The thought made her shudder—not a reaction she was proud of. To make amends, she shut her eyes and did a quick three-breaths meditation, sending loving intentions towards Yvonne and wishing her a lifetime of very good health. And she meant it.

Ty rubbed the back of her neck, drawing Bess's attention to a feathery tattoo of a dream catcher there. Noticing Bess looking at it, she said, "It's my own design. I create original artworks." She made it sound naughty. "Check me out on social—I'm LadyGardener96."

This woman was shameless. "I'll think about it."

"Give me your contact details and I'll send you a sample. No obligation to buy."

"Another time maybe." Bess nodded at the house. "Striking building, isn't it?"

Looking disappointed, Ty said, "Creepy old dump, you mean. When we were kids, we'd ride our bikes out here and dare each other to touch the gates. You know there were murders in there, right? Like, a hundred years ago or something, when the place was new."

"Is that right?" Bess followed Ty's gaze towards an upstairs window. Something was moving behind the dingy pane. A dark figure. She was fairly sure it was Margaret.

"Bad vibes," Ty said. "Maybe that's what turned the old lady so evil."

Somewhere nearby, a twig snapped. Ty swung around.

At the end of the garden where the property backed onto the national park, a clump of rhododendrons was waving.

"Hey!" Ty picked up her shovel and took a threatening step towards them. "This is private property!" The bushes stopped moving. "I know you're in there! Piss off!"

"What's going on?"

The bush sprang forward and back as if elasticised. A row of conifers flailed about, suggesting an intruder was pushing through them.

Bess caught a glimpse of khaki clothing and a clump of foliage moving above the bushes. Was it attached to someone's hat?

A wire-link fence separated the garden from the bushland behind. The top of the fence vibrated above the treetops, like someone had shoved through an opening. Then everything went still again.

"What was that?"

"A pain in my arse." Ty rolled her eyes. "Nutjobs."

"Really?" Bess's ears pricked up at any hint of the unusual. "What kind?"

The back door opened. Vivienne emerged, holding up Bess's clothing. Margaret stood beside her wearing a scowl that seemed to inform Ty she'd better get back to work.

Ty grabbed her shovel and hurried into the lavender bushes without saying goodbye.

Chapter 3

MARGARET WAITED OUTSIDE THE BATHROOM while Bess changed back into her clothes. Bess had looked less than thrilled when Margaret asked if she would mind waiting while she looked through the old lady's collection.

But all Bess said now was, "I hope it's doing you good, seeing an old friend. Reminiscing."

"Hmm." Was Vivienne an old friend, really? She had appeared out of nowhere twenty-five years before by the side of a darkened river. Margaret remembered everything about it. A crowd of people shoved and squawked drunkenly around her, people who had rejected or ignored her for years. Amid their jostling bodies, Vivienne stood still. Her hair shone.

Vivienne talked about Tintoretto, quoted Catullus, and moved like a dancer. She said that the elite boarding school she'd attended was a dump, that their university was so parochial, that Australia was a wasteland. She spoke to the awkward, intense unpopular young Margaret as an equal, as someone who deserved to escape too.

But the next morning, Vivienne had vanished, and after one failed attempt, Margaret never went looking for her. She was no expert on friendship, but she didn't think it worked like that.

Margaret craned around the half-open door and saw Bess wriggling as she adjusted her skirt around her substantial hips. Then she buttoned her cardigan, leaving a hint of plump cleavage.

The sight made Margaret soften with desire and gratitude. "Thank you," she told Bess, referring to this visit and other things. Bess's kindness, her optimism, her ability to understand the things Margaret could not put into words. "I know Crossroads House wasn't on your holiday itinerary."

"As long as you're happy here."

"Well…" No, Margaret wasn't happy. It was strange trying to match her youthful memories of Vivienne with this woman who was both familiar and unfamiliar, and who seemed determined to introduce more problems into Margaret's life.

Still, she couldn't refuse to help. After what Vivienne had done for her on graduation night, Margaret owed her.

It was hard to explain those things, though, and Margaret worried it might make her sound weak, conflicted, or confused. She'd had to rely so much on Bess's loving compassion and patience over these past few months. And she was thankful for that, more than she could say. How she would have coped without Bess didn't bear thinking about. Still, part of her felt humiliated at needing so much help. It wasn't her style. Bess must have found it dull or frustrating sometimes, and surely it was time for Margaret to pull up her socks. Go back to handling her problems herself.

So she just said, "I'm not thrilled at the prospect of looking through Ivy's collection. But I suppose I should use my skills while I have them."

Margaret had applied for a couple of jobs back in Melbourne, but so far she hadn't even got an interview. At least Vivienne thought she was good for something.

"I'll try not to take too much time," Margaret added. "I don't want to waste your holiday."

"*Our* holiday," Bess reminded her, a slight edge in her voice. "You deserve a rest. You've done a lot for other people this year."

By other people, she meant Deirdre. Margaret stared ahead down the shadowy corridor. There were dark patches of damp on the ceiling.

Suddenly, she forgot it all: their Tasmanian holiday, her adventures with Bess, Vivienne's presence, the ghosts of graduation night. Other memories seeped into Margaret's mind instead: shower chairs and pureed food, bedpans and disinfectant smells. Her sister's hoarse breathing, every inhalation an effort, while her hand lay limp in Margaret's.

That wasn't doing a lot, though. If she'd really done a lot, she would have noticed Deirdre's illness sooner and done something to stop it.

"You need a break," Bess insisted. "It's okay to feel sad, but it's also okay to relax, do things you enjoy. It might help you gain some perspective. Decide how you want to honour Deirdre's memory and what you want to do next." She touched Margaret's arm.

Everything she said made sense, Margaret supposed—but it didn't really help. She didn't feel sad, just tired and guilty, and she didn't think any number of beach walks or winery lunches was going to change that. Perhaps grief was another thing she had failed to do correctly.

"We won't stay long." Margaret stared out the window into the overgrown grounds.

As they descended the stairs, Bess asked, "Do you think she'll mind if you don't get through the whole collection?"

"Hmm?" Margaret seemed distracted.

"Vivienne. Will she be disappointed if you don't manage to value everything?"

Bess tried not to let any unpleasantness enter her voice. She was opposed to jealousy; it was a patriarchal construct, and all it really revealed was the jealous person's own need for confidence and spiritual growth. Surely.

"I can only do what's feasible. I'm sure she'll understand." Margaret's old firmness returned, and Bess was relieved to hear it. Perhaps she had imagined Margaret's strange manner around Vivienne before.

Margaret added, "I know how to say no to people, don't I? I'm not a soft touch. Once I sacked a man on his birthday when he'd just had his wisdom teeth out."

"You did?"

"He persisted in mislabelling exhibits in my museum." Margaret scowled at the memory. "Who confuses a recording of the mating cry of an elephant seal with one of a walrus fight and then argues about it?"

Bess smiled. That was the old Margaret. Maybe there was nothing to worry about. She tried not to dwell on the memory of tiny, delicate Vivienne hovering around Margaret, almost vibrating with enthusiasm, like a hummingbird searching for nectar.

But no, Bess was not going to obsess about that. It wasn't healthy. "Do you mind if I don't hang around while you're valuing the antiques? I think

I offended these women, breaking their things, and it's not like they know me. I might take a walk instead."

"All right."

The good thing about being with someone as socially unusual as Margaret was that she didn't mind when you weren't very polite to people. In fact, she didn't seem to notice.

Bess didn't love the idea of leaving Margaret alone with Vivienne, but she could be an adult about that. She trusted Margaret, after all. However difficult and odd she might seem to other people, Margaret had always been loyal to Bess and loved her.

And what a relief it would be to stroll in bushland instead of sitting in that house, striving not to move a muscle in case she broke something else. She let herself out the front door, walked back through the gates, and found a track she'd noticed earlier that cut into the bush. It was just wide enough for a car.

Wallaby grass brushed against her legs and stringybark trees loomed above, their tough, fibrous bark looking like it had been shredded. Leaves crackled underfoot, cobwebs glittered between the bushes, and birds chortled. The air smelled of eucalyptus. She breathed deeply.

How she had missed this, cooped up in her city office. Her employers had messaged her today, demanding a briefing paper she'd already sent them a month before, wanting the code for the photocopier which she had stuck on the machine before she left, and asking if the hummus in the fridge was hers. (It wasn't.) Evidently, they did not respect Bess's holiday any more than they respected her work.

She was determined to quit, but it wouldn't be easy, especially with Margaret unemployed. If she could pitch one last successful exhibition, surely that would allow her to leave on a high note and find something better. She mused over the idea; she'd always had a preference for Australian-themed shows. Kooky art, forgotten histories, exhibits that celebrated this weird, wild country.

Something growled nearby.

Bess swung around. Not growling—humming. A wasp's nest? She scanned the bush, getting ready to run.

Something red showed through the trees. Frowning, she stepped off the track, crunching through the undergrowth. The humming grew louder.

Tied to a tree, suspended in midair, was a joint of meat. A sheep's leg maybe? The skin was stripped off, the flesh crawling with flies.

Someone was trying to lure something to this place.

She swivelled around. A minute ago, she'd been blissfully alone in nature, but now that feeling had gone. Was she being watched?

A bird gave a strangled warbling cry. It was a big black currawong, its sharp beak pointed straight up. The flies droned on.

Then something flashed in the sun. A small square camera in camouflage colours was strapped to a tree, its glass eye trained on the hunk of meat.

The hairs on Bess's arms prickled.

A few steps farther, and she spotted a large aluminium frame draped in canvas and camouflage netting, tacked to the ground with tent pegs. It was half-hidden by branches and uprooted shrubs piled around it for concealment or to muffle sound.

Bess lifted the flap. Inside, someone had left a folding chair. There was a vent in the fabric wall with a tripod set up in front of it, waiting for a camera. She crouched in front of the gap. It afforded a clear view of the hanging meat.

Something streaked past. She swallowed a gasp, her body tensing. But it was just a pademelon, a small fat fluffy creature—like a kangaroo that had shrunk in the wash.

Her breath escaped in an anxious laugh. Bess shuffled out of the hide and made her way back to the track.

Who had set this up? What were they after? How many animals here could eat a piece of meat that size? A family of Tasmanian devils maybe? A spotted-tailed quoll? A bird of prey?

Had that camera caught her image? The thought made her uneasy.

The track reached a fork. The main path, broad and flat, continued into the national park. But another trail curved off to the left. It was much rougher, just thick, lumpy grooves cut into the ground by the tyres of a 4WD. Mud had spattered the undergrowth. The tracks looked recent.

Bess hesitated, twitchy from the sense of being watched. Probably she should go back to Crossroads House and let this remain a mystery. Be sensible, live cautiously. Just like she had been doing for months in her city office, feeling her soul grow smaller with each little grey day.

To hell with that. She followed the rough trail deeper into the bush.

For the next hour, Margaret worked. It had been weeks since she'd been asked to value antiques, and it felt good to limber up her mental muscles again.

She looked at sterling silver thimbles and tortoiseshell hair combs. She examined crystal letter openers, a scalloped china oyster plate hand-painted with purple wisteria, ivory lace doilies crocheted with butterflies, and a Victorian horsehair fly swish with a handle made of carved bone.

Vivienne made notes to check against her grandmother's inventory later to see if anything was missing. If Ivy would tell Vivienne where the inventory was, of course. That wasn't guaranteed.

Margaret tried to ask Vivienne questions about her work and life in Hobart, but they couldn't speak for long. Every few minutes, Vivienne hurried away to answer shouts for assistance from her grandmother. Ivy needed the toilet, another blanket, the curtains pulled, a cup of tea— "But not like that one you made this morning; that tasted like it had been through a horse!"

Vivienne never complained, but her delicate jaw seemed to clench tighter each time. It wasn't pleasant to see a free spirit trapped like this.

Mostly Ivy sounded like a bully, but once or twice she seemed bewildered and scared, crying, "What's happening? I don't know what's happening!"

At last, the cries stopped. Ivy must have fallen asleep.

Vivienne said, "Fancy a stroll outside?" She smiled, but the frustration in her voice was unmistakable.

They set off on a lap of the outside of the building. Noticing a thirty-year-old BMW parked at the end of the drive, Margaret said, "That's an interesting old car."

"It's rather a nightmare, actually. Has a fit of the vapours every few months. I bought it second-hand from a colleague, so it would feel too rude to get rid of it."

That statement baffled Margaret. She would have parked that defective piece of junk across the colleague's driveway and demanded her money back. So would Bess, although she would have used more compassionate words.

Vivienne added, "The car won't start at all now. Inconvenient, under the circumstances."

"Do you need help?"

"A man from the garage said he'll come next week. I'll manage until then."

"It must be difficult here."

Vivienne sighed. "I hadn't visited in years. Ivy discouraged it. She never seemed to want to see anyone. When she got really ill, she called me back. I nearly fainted when I saw the state of the house." She touched Margaret's arm. "Thank you for examining her collection."

Margaret shuffled away a little. All that touchy-feely business was far too common nowadays. Like those frightful people who tried to greet you with cheek kisses—ugh. "Well, it looks valuable, and I've not found any fakes or problems yet. But I'm afraid someone else will need to complete the task. I can't finish it today, and we'll need to leave soon."

"Oh." Vivienne stopped.

"As I explained, I'm here with Ms Campbell, my partner. We're on… holiday." The word sounded unseemly to Margaret. She didn't take holidays, and to take one now when she was out of work seemed the height of indulgence. As if she'd bought herself a Lamborghini. Still. "I can't disrupt Ms Campbell's plans. We have bookings, deposits…"

Vivienne stepped closer. "If they're only Ms Campbell's plans, surely she could manage without you for a couple of days?"

Margaret frowned in confusion. "Well…no. Ms Campbell and I are together." Margaret might not be very interested in wombat feeding, cider making, or jam tasting, but she didn't intend for Bess to do those things alone. She liked being there to see Bess's exuberance, her wholehearted enjoyment of all things Tasmanian.

"I see."

"Apologies."

"I understand. It was selfish of me to assume you could drop everything and come to my rescue." Vivienne braced one hand against the side of the house. Her fingers were so pale they seemed almost translucent, her nails perfect little pearly-pink ovals.

"There are plenty of antiques dealers. You could invite someone…"

"Here?" Vivienne gave a sad chuckle. "I might as well ask them to come to the moon. But it's all right, Margaret. I'm not incapable—"

A creaking, cracking noise. They looked up.

The air whistled as something huge and heavy plummeted from above. Margaret recoiled, one arm flying up to shield her face. The object hit the ground, sending splinters and metal screws flying.

It was a shutter from the upstairs window. Its mate was hanging by one hinge. Margaret grabbed Vivienne's elbow and hurried her away. Her narrow arm felt fragile as if the bones might snap.

"Good God!" Vivienne shook.

"It didn't hit you." Margaret wasn't very good at comforting people. Cautiously, she moved to examine the fallen item. The wood was rotten, the paint peeling, the hinges eaten away by rust. "You'd better call a handyman."

"Somebody pushed it." Vivienne's voice was level, but her eyes had grown huge. "They…they tried to kill us."

Margaret stared. "This is a decrepit old building. I'm sure it drops parts like a leper."

"I saw someone!" Vivienne pointed up at the window.

"There's no one there."

"I saw an arm." Vivienne managed a laugh, but it sounded desperate. "Oh, I'm sorry, do you think I'm making it up?"

"Well, no, but… Wait here." She hurried around to the front door.

The foyer was empty. Margaret paused, listening, then jogged up the stairs and opened one door after another until she found the right room. It must have been the old nursery; there was a small ancient bed draped in mosquito net and musty-looking children's books in a cabinet. Nowhere for a person to hide.

The window was open, though. Yellowed lace curtains moved in the breeze.

A stair creaked, followed by a thump on the floor below. As if someone had leaped down and landed on the carpet? Margaret rushed out and leaned over the banister in time to glimpse the side door slamming shut.

She dashed downstairs, hauled the door open, and looked outside. The garden was wild here: black wattle, she-oaks, a choking tangle of blackberries merging into the bushland beyond. A person could have reached it in seconds, scrambled inside, and vanished.

The wind tugged at the door, almost tearing it from her grasp. Maybe it had been open when she arrived and had simply blown shut?

Returning to Vivienne, she said, "I didn't find anyone. There were a few sounds, though. I can't swear someone didn't leave the house." Margaret's cheeks were warm, her heartbeat cantering.

In a strange, flat tone, Vivienne said, "They'll come back." She walked shakily to a garden bench and sat down.

"Who are 'they'?"

Her hostess tried to laugh. "I wish I knew. Whoever has been doing this: the thefts, the noises, the damage. It seems they know that I've been talking to you, that I'm trying to stop them. Clearly, they're not happy."

"Now, now. We don't know that anyone was there. Pull yourself together." Margaret made herself pat Vivienne on the shoulder.

Vivienne shot her hand up to grab Margaret's arm. Her fingers dug in hard. She drew Margaret down until they were face-to-face. "I'm not making it up. Someone has been coming into the house. And I can't do anything! Ivy refuses to leave. I'm stuck here..." Her voice cracked, and Margaret saw tears in her eyes.

She remembered the first time she had looked into those eyes. A bridge over the river at night with the darkened shapes of city buildings and the sky clouded over so that no stars were visible.

Margaret had been in danger. In her shock and fear, everything had seemed to stand still.

And then Vivienne had appeared. Illuminated by the lamppost above them as if standing in a spotlight, her eyes were as large and green as a cat's. She'd laughed and asked, "Do you need my help?"

"Yes." And in that moment, Margaret had felt a strange sense of having entered into a bargain. What would Vivienne ask in return?

Now she sat down beside Vivienne. "Don't be upset. I don't know what's happening, but there's bound to be a rational explanation." Some consolation seemed to be required, so she gave Vivienne's shoulder another stiff little pat.

Vivienne's head drooped in exhaustion, a warm tear splashing onto Margaret's hand.

Bess followed the dirt track deeper into the wilderness. Gumnuts crunched underfoot, and she was wary of snakes. This landscape called for desert boots, thick hiking socks, and trousers with lots of pockets. Not a skirt, tights, and funky zebra print ballet flats.

Something rustled in the undergrowth: an echidna, its golden-brown spikes bristling, its snout probing the soil for insects. As she drew closer, it curled itself into a ball of spikes. She smiled. It made her think of Margaret. Exotic and defensive to the rest of the world, but strangely cute to Bess's eyes.

The track turned into a clearing. There was a caravan and a dusty red 4WD, the remains of a campfire, properly extinguished, and a well-worn swag in army green. No rubbish scraps, cigarette butts, or dogs running loose. Evidently, these were experienced campers. But this was not a legal campsite.

Bess could call out. Say hello, ask casually what they were doing here. But she had listened to too many podcasts about serial killers to go chatting with strangers in the outback. Besides, there was no one around.

A tree bough groaned in the wind. She crossed the clearing, feeling way too visible in her bright teal cardigan and matching tights. At the caravan door, she stopped, glanced over her shoulder, then knocked.

No reply.

She tried the door and found it unlocked. Tensing, Bess pushed it open and slipped inside.

The interior was gloomy, the curtains drawn. She clicked the door shut, then squinted in the dim light. The bed and seats were folded up into the walls. A collapsible table took up most of the floor space. It was covered by a map held down at the corners by binoculars, a compass, and a hiker's drink bottle. The map showed green spaces, tracks, contour lines. Someone had added circles, crosses, and notes on sticky labels. The light was too faint for her to make out the writing.

She opened a cupboard. It was crammed with tinned foods, bottled water, toilet paper, bags of rice. Not the sort of packing for a weekend camping trip.

The beam from her phone's torch hit the far wall, illuminating pieces of paper pinned to a corkboard. There were old yellowing newspaper clippings and printouts of articles. Faded black-and-white photographs. Pictures drawn by hand.

Next to all that was a poster with an image of something that looked like a weird-shaped rug. She leaned in. No, it wasn't a rug but a skin, curled and leathery at the edges, splayed out where the limbs would have been. Bess trailed her fingers down stripes of deep brown, honey, and grey.

Footsteps.

Bess dropped her phone with a crash. Swearing silently, she groped on the floor, grabbed it, and switched off the torch. Then she crouched, holding her breath.

From outside came the sound of boots tramping through the undergrowth.

Should she stay here in case they went away? Open the door and brazen it out? Arm herself with something?

As she tried frantically to decide, an explosion catapulted her to her feet. A gunshot!

She wrenched open the caravan door and half-tumbled down the folding stairs. The sound had come from her right. She took off to the left and plunged into the bush.

Gasping for breath, she crashed through the dried ferns and button grass, the air rushing in her ears. Her sturdy legs and arms pumped as she shoved branches aside and hurtled over fallen logs.

No one was following. After several minutes, she stopped and doubled over, clutching a stitch in her side. Her face was scorching. Where was she?

All around were trees. Bess struggled to slow her breathing. Leaving the trail was arguably more dangerous than confronting the person with the gun. People went missing in the Australian bush every year, and some were never seen again.

Oh, this isn't good.

There wouldn't be much phone reception out here. Would she wander around in the wilderness until she died? Would she end up in one of those vaguely sneering newspaper headlines? *City woman with no hiking experience found dead in the bush fifty metres from the road...*

Bess looked down at her teal tights and zebra-print ballet flats, now covered with dirt and animal droppings. The coroner's report would make her sound like an idiot.

A noise. She listened hard. Rumbling, then a heavy rattling whoosh. A logging truck! She was near the road! Bess took off towards the sound until she glimpsed bitumen through the trees. The road was familiar—it led to Crossroads House.

It took her several minutes' walking to recognise the feeling that rushed through her with every clanging heartbeat. It wasn't just relief or fear. It was elation.

Margaret left Crossroads House and pulled the gates shut behind her, flakes of rust and dirt dropping around her feet. The gates wouldn't shut all the way, and the lock was clogged with spiderwebs. Margaret's own house had an alarm system, deadlocks, and sensor lights, but it seemed Vivienne couldn't keep anyone out.

She leaned with both hands on the roof of her car, her pulse throbbing in her temples. A bird called nearby with a screech like a siren.

When was the last time she'd felt like this? Her breathing fast and shallow, her muscles taut, her senses sweeping the surroundings for every sound and movement. Primed for danger, awake and alive.

Margaret's thoughts raced back to Port Bannir, to everything that had happened there two years ago. She heard the smash of glass as a fanatical woman beat her way into the museum, determined to attack her. She saw the two policemen who'd loomed up in front of her to arrest her for a murder she hadn't committed. She tasted the salt between Bess's breasts as Bess leaned back against Margaret's car, her white skin glowing in the freezing night air. Her laughter and sighs as Margaret ran her hands and adoring mouth all over her—

A touch on her shoulder. "Margaret?"

Bess's red hair was tangled, her shoes muddy, her cheeks flushed. Margaret grabbed her face in both hands and kissed her hard.

Bess laughed breathlessly. "What's gotten into you?"

Margaret grasped her around her waist. They both burst out at once: "You're not going to like this—" and "I have a favour to ask."

Bess laughed again. "You go first."

"Well…" *Ridiculous*, Margaret scolded herself. *Pull yourself together.*

45

She should hustle Bess into the car and drive them both away from here, away from this excitement that made her hands shake. She should drive them back to their regular lives where Margaret could go on hunting for jobs, cancelling Deirdre's loyalty cards and library memberships, and fielding calls from third cousins ringing to check that her sister had really died. All those things she should be doing.

Instead, she blurted out, "Would you mind if we stayed a couple more days? I know you don't like this place and neither do I, but—"

"No, that's what I was going to ask you!" Bess started to smile, then looked perplexed. "But why do you want to stay?"

"I—" How could Margaret answer that? *Because there are things I can do effectively here, things I can fix? Because being in danger for a second made me feel fully alive again?*

Rejecting that, she said, "It's silly, but Vivienne is convinced someone is stealing from the house and trying to…to hurt her." It seemed melodramatic to say *kill*. "It could be all in her head. But there's a chance something is happening, and either way, she and her grandmother are very isolated. They need help."

Bess frowned. "Is this dangerous? For you?"

"Not at all." She banished the memory of that falling shutter. "I would finish valuing Ivy's antiques, identify anything missing from the inventory, and try to connect Vivienne to some assistance. I imagine she'll persuade Ivy to sell some items to pay for care in a nursing home. That's all."

Yes, that was all she was proposing to do, and there was nothing especially strange about it. No need for her to feel so agitated and thrilled. She asked Bess, "But why do you want to stay?"

"Well, you know I wanted to pitch one last exhibition to the gallery so I can leave my job with a recent success. I think I've found the perfect topic for a show here in Mount Bastion!"

"Oh yes?" Margaret tried to focus. "What sort of show would you make about this place? Rural potholes of Tasmania?"

"No." Bess's eyes sparkled with excitement. "I think I've found a cryptozoologist living in the bush. And he's hunting the Tasmanian tiger."

Chapter 4

"I DON'T KNOW WHO'S MADDER," Margaret said the next morning as she sat down at the table outside their motel room. "Some genetically challenged fantasist who's living in a caravan in the bush and looking for Australia's equivalent of Big Foot—or you for wanting to talk to him."

"Don't be so grumpy." Bess blew her a kiss as she unrolled her yoga mat. "You were in a good enough mood last night."

The memory made Bess's cheeks glow and her insides feel like warm caramel. Last night... How sweet it had been.

Margaret had pressed her up against the motel room door and kissed her with a heat and urgency that took Bess by surprise, then laid her down on the crisp white sheets, kneeling between her legs and leaving traces of dark lipstick all over her. She had shown such intense focus on Bess, such dedication to her pleasure. It was like the way things used to be before the sadness and disappointment that had settled over them since the loss of Margaret's job, the stalling of Bess's career, and the death of poor Deirdre. Perhaps they were coming out the other side.

But this morning, Margaret had withdrawn, seeming to retreat once more to a chilly little island inside her head. A place where she spent a lot of time nowadays.

Bess knew she couldn't force it. Things always got better eventually. She stood up straight on the mat, touched her hands in front of her heart, closed her eyes, and breathed deeply.

Margaret said, "I don't like this."

"Morning yoga is part of my self-care. It's nonnegotiable." Bess rolled her shoulders, reached to the sky, then lowered her elbows into a cactus pose. "And I have to do it out here; there's no space in that room." She bent forward and swayed from the waist, letting the blood rush to her head.

"I'm not talking about you tying yourself in knots in a car park."

Outside the manager's office, a couple of locals were smoking. They turned to gape at Bess on her yoga mat. Margaret glowered at them.

Bess waved and called out to them, "You're welcome to join me!"

Margaret rapped the table. "I'm talking about you breaking into some hillbilly's cabin in the woods, then wanting to go back and introduce yourself! Have you lost your mind?"

"I've told you why I want to do it. You know my work situation."

"Of course, and I sympathise. You're right to take the initiative and design a new exhibition. I'm sure you'll do it well. Just pick a different topic."

"Why aren't you more excited about this?" Bess lowered herself to the mat. "The Tasmanian tiger is legendary!"

"The Tasmanian tiger is long gone."

"Or is it?" Bess buzzed with excitement. Last night, while Margaret was dropping off to sleep, she had snuck out to the car, done some preliminary research, and hammered out a draft one-page pitch. If her hunch proved correct, she might send it to her employers tonight.

Recalling what she'd read, Bess said, "The tiger was a remarkable animal: a large marsupial carnivore unique to this part of the world. It looked like a striped dog, but it carried its babies in a pouch and was barely related to canines at all. Convergent evolution: the process by which two separate species evolve independently to look like each other due to filling the same ecological role in a similar environment. Isn't that incredible?"

"Marvellous. But the last Tasmanian tiger died in 1936."

"How did you know that?"

"I know many things." Margaret opened her laptop, took out her disinfectant wipes, and began cleaning the keyboard. "Anyone who thinks that animal is still around must be—"

"—a very special type of person," Bess finished, although she doubted those would have been Margaret's words. "That's my angle for the show! It's not just about the tiger; it's about the people who search for it, who still hold onto hope. Imagine the passion and commitment it would take to go out into the wilderness and chase a dream like that."

"I'm imagining someone who looks like the Unabomber, smells like a compost heap, and spends his evenings posting videos on Facebook about government conspiracies. You cannot go back there."

"Imagine if I found lots of tiger hunters and made a show about their lives." Bess raised herself into a cobra pose, then cascaded down again. "It would be fascinating."

"He fired a gun at you!'

"*Near* me." Bess pressed up into a plank. "And I never actually saw him. He might not have known I was there."

"Oh, so he was shooting at someone else? That's all right, then."

"Relax, I'm not going back into the clearing."

"Thank goodness." Margaret began tapping on her laptop. She'd said she planned to do some research about Ivy's antiques.

"I thought I'd just put up some friendly signs around town, asking him to please meet me for a coffee and a chat."

Margaret looked up incredulously. "There's no coffee shop. And don't even think about bringing him here." She held up her hand. "But go ahead; put up posters if you like. It'll do no harm. I don't imagine this person can read."

"Why are you being like this?" Bess rolled up into a warrior pose and glared. She wanted to centre herself, focus on her core, and set an intention for the day, but Margaret didn't make it easy.

Margaret growled. "Because I don't want you getting hurt again." Her gaze travelled down to the jagged white scar on Bess's forearm.

Bess looked at it too. The scar had faded over the last two years, but it would never disappear. Nor would her memories: hard ground underneath her and the smell and frenzied sound of a killer's breath on her skin as she fought in vain to throw him off. Fought to stay alive.

But Bess had stayed alive—with the help of a carload of teenagers and a loyal rooster—and she was not going to be kept prisoner by her own memories or her own fears.

Nor was she going to spend her life doing things she didn't care about. This was her chance at something better.

Reaching up into a palm tree pose, she lengthened her spine and stretched her fingertips towards the sun. "I won't do anything dangerous, I promise. But I won't hide in a motel room while you play *Antiques Roadshow* with your ex-girlfriend either."

"Vivienne's not my…" Margaret looked astonished and rather appalled by the word.

Remembering their passion last night, Bess shook off the idea and laughed. "Don't worry; I trust you."

"I'm sorry if I seemed overexcited yesterday." Margaret wrinkled her nose in embarrassment. "My imagination ran away with me. I don't really think I'm stepping into some great mystery here. Ivy's missing items could well have been misplaced, the slashed tyres were probably the work of local teenagers, and the glass in the sandwich— Well, I wouldn't be surprised if Ivy did that herself to get rid of the poor carer."

Bess winced. "I can picture that too."

"I shouldn't have become so agitated. Really, I'm just doing a favour for Vivienne."

"I don't mind you getting agitated. Or…overexcited." Bess glanced through the open door into the motel room. "When do we need to leave? In half an hour?"

Margaret bit her bottom lip and swallowed hard. Her gaze lingered over Bess's rounded figure in singlet and leggings, the healthy pink glow that the cool air and exercise had brought to her skin. The intensity of Margaret's stare made the heat rise in Bess's body all over again.

"Half an hour sounds"—Margaret snapped her laptop shut—"workable."

Her phone rang. She glanced at the screen. "Vivienne." She hesitated before switching it to mute. Then she held the door open for Bess and flipped the sign to Do Not Disturb.

After half an hour exactly—Margaret was nothing if not punctual—they drove out of Mount Bastion towards Crossroads House. Bess had already drawn some flyers and hurried around town taping them to utility posts. The signs read: "We almost met at your campsite yesterday. I know what you're looking for and would love to get your story out there. Promise I am not taking the piss. I want to believe."

She had included her phone number and drawn some tiger stripes.

"For heaven's sake." Margaret might have said more, but their time together this morning had improved her mood.

The road out of town was almost empty. Margaret drove smoothly, looking out for potholes and animals. Her country driving skills were coming back. Perhaps other things were returning too: her ability to work, to deal with people, to love Bess as she deserved to be loved. To build a future together. The muscles in her neck and shoulders loosened. Maybe Bess's relentless optimism would turn out to be catching.

The road wound through thick trees and hilly terrain. They were almost at the house before she saw the police car blocking the drive.

Margaret pulled over. She was always calm in a crisis, but her fingers locked around the steering wheel until her knuckles whitened.

Bess leaned forward. "What's happened?"

Margaret switched off the engine. Through the front windows, she could see people moving around in the house.

She reached for her jacket on the back seat; her phone was in the pocket. She'd forgotten she'd switched it to silent earlier.

There were half a dozen missed calls from Vivienne and a text which she must have sent later, after she realised Margaret wasn't going to pick up.

Please come over. I need help. Ivy is dead.

Chapter 5

Bᴇss ʙᴜᴛᴛᴏɴᴇᴅ ᴜᴘ ʜᴇʀ ᴄᴏᴀᴛ. It was hard to get warm. Margaret kept working her jaw as if she'd swallowed something nasty.

"What did the police say?" Bess asked.

There were no other pedestrians around as the two women walked along the main street of Mount Bastion. A car slowed as if the driver were looking at them.

As they approached the community centre, a hand flipped the sign over to Cʟᴏsᴇᴅ. And somebody had torn down Bess's posters.

"Ivy was found dead at home sometime before dawn. That was all they would tell me." There was no inflection in Margaret's voice. The presence of death made her quiet and calm—far too quiet and calm for Bess's liking.

"How awful. If the police were called, does it mean there was something…wrong?"

"Not necessarily. I assume she had some sort of accident. But I told them what happened when we were there yesterday, in case it was relevant."

"And?"

"And the police thanked me for speaking to them." Margaret shrugged. "It probably means nothing. All I witnessed was the shutter falling."

"That's true. And you have to remember, it's common for isolated elderly people to become paranoid and think people are stealing from them and plotting against them." Bess shook her head. "It's sad. A caring society would value its elders, keep them connected to community."

"It wasn't Ivy who thought people were stealing and plotting; it was Vivienne. She must be with the doctors or the funeral directors. Perhaps she'll call later."

"Oh, I'm sure she will." Bess's voice came out sharper than she'd intended. Of course, she felt sorry for Vivienne. But it had not escaped her notice that one of Vivienne's first moves had been to ring Margaret several times. After twenty-five years of no contact, was that a normal thing to do?

With an effort, Bess brought her attention back to what had happened. "Poor Ivy. She seemed a very vibrant and strong personality. A colourful character."

"You mean mad, rude, and cranky?" Margaret hunched her shoulders against the wind. "But you're right. The old woman's life couldn't have been much fun, but she did seem keen to hang onto it."

Was she thinking of Deirdre? A memory flashed through Bess's mind of Margaret's sister breaking down in tears one day towards the end and saying, "This quilt cover is so grubby, and I'll never get to the dry cleaners again, will I?"

Margaret, sorting Deirdre's medication, had tried for a grim joke: "That place? Mr Wilmot has BO, and he overcharges you every time. Is it really so bad?"

Bess had fetched Deirdre a glass of water and tried to smile, but she knew that, yes, it was so bad.

Now she took Margaret's arm and breathed deep, concentrating on the smooth fabric of Margaret's coat and the warmth of her body beneath it. "There must be something we can do to help. Maybe I should have got my sage sticks and done a cleansing ritual for Ivy."

"Maybe I should have rung a solicitor before I talked to the police." Margaret frowned as Bess took out her phone. "What are you doing?"

"Making a donation in Ivy's memory to an Alzheimer's charity." Bess tapped in her credit card details and sent off the money. Then she searched online for the nearest newspaper. "Here's the local *Gazette*: I'll post a sympathy notice. Do you think I should describe Ivy as a friend, a valued colleague, or a memorable acquaintance?"

"That's kind of you. You don't need to do that for someone you barely knew."

"It's good to do something." Bess finished her notice. "Now let's try the general store. We can put together a care package for…Vivienne." She managed to say the name in a friendly tone.

The shop counter was unattended. Passing the noticeboard, she saw the poster advertising the local historian Dorian Visser, who claimed that Crossroads House was Australia's most haunted building.

Surely that couldn't be true. If the place had so much supernatural activity, she would have heard of it before, like the Monte Cristo homestead or the Old Melbourne Gaol. Still, she noted that Mr Visser was due to read from his book at the regional library on Thursday night.

She found the confectionary aisle and checked out the chocolate, searching in vain for an organic fair-trade brand. The flap to the storeroom swung open, and a woman in an apron wandered to the counter, not noticing Bess or Margaret. Another customer entered.

"Millie."

"Kate. Carton of Winnie Blues, thanks."

There was a pause. Bess craned her neck and saw Kate searching through the cigarettes behind the counter.

Millie sighed loudly. "Heard what happened?"

"Mrs Bolt? Course."

"Hell of a thing." Millie hunted in her purse. "My Tina cleans the police station. They're saying she broke her neck."

"That right?" Kate's tone gave nothing away.

"It's what they're saying. That she got up in the middle of the night, made it as far as the stairs, then…"

"Well"—Kate rang up the till—"shouldn't have been on her own, should she?"

"Isn't there a granddaughter?"

"Humph." Kate made change. "When did she ever come home to visit? I'd never clapped eyes on her before. Only turned up when the old lady was dying."

"Was she?" Millie tore open the packet and drew out a cigarette. "Dying?"

"Cancer. My Terry does the deliveries for the pharmacist."

"Hell of a thing," Millie said again. "Maybe she was better off going the way she did."

Bess flinched. She hoped Margaret had not heard that.

"Yeah, well," said Kate. "You reap what you sow."

Millie fiddled with her lighter. "It wasn't all her fault. Losing her son like that... Of course she went funny."

"Say hi to Tina for me." Kate turned away.

When Millie had left, Bess gathered up the ingredients of a care package: chocolate, fruit tea, bubble bath, and a sympathy card. When she walked up to the counter, Kate stiffened at the sight of her.

"Help you?" The words came out like a bark.

"Just these, thanks."

Bess didn't want to be inquisitive about poor Ivy. She had dragged Margaret along on this holiday to get away from death, away from all the dark, sad, debilitating things that had drained them for months. To bring fun and sunshine and optimism back into their lives.

And yet somehow she couldn't help saying, "I met Mrs Bolt yesterday. She was an interesting woman. How did she lose her son?"

"That's three dollars change." Kate smacked the coins down so hard they rolled onto the floor. She did not offer to help pick them up.

"Were Ivy and Vivienne close?" Bess asked as they resumed walking down the street. "When she was young?"

"Not that I know of. Vivienne told me she grew up in boarding school and didn't go home for the holidays. She said her family were all dead, mad, or sick of her."

Bess frowned. "You didn't think that was strange? Sad?"

"Not really," said Margaret. "I didn't stay in touch with my own family when I was young. I'd left Port Bannir behind and couldn't wait to forget the place. Never mind anyone I abandoned in the process."

Two deep lines appeared between Margaret's brows. Bess knew she was brooding again over her sister's fate. Poor Deirdre, left behind in the care of an angry father and a dangerous husband, her mind falling apart a little more with each passing year.

Bess squeezed Margaret's shoulder. "The way I heard it, you were virtually run out of town when you were still in your teens. And I'm sorry for how people treated Deirdre, truly, but she made her own choices. Flogging yourself over it now doesn't help."

Margaret sighed. "You're right. As usual." She smiled reluctantly, as if she couldn't quite manage it. There had been a time when Margaret disagreed with everything Bess said on principle. For a moment, Bess found herself missing those old days of conflict. Things had seemed simpler then.

She cleared her throat. "Have you thought any more about how you would like to lay her to rest?"

Margaret's expression shut down. "Not yet. I'll get onto it."

"I'm not hassling you. But it might help—give you some closure."

"Yes, doctor. I'll sort it out."

Realising the conversation was going nowhere, Bess decided to drop it for now. She checked her phone instead. Work had messaged her back: they were interested in her proposal for a tiger exhibition but wanted a more detailed outline.

"Hmm. And I haven't heard from the tiger hunter yet."

"You don't really think he's going to call?"

"You never know. Sometimes the more secretive someone is, the more they secretly want to tell their story."

Margaret looked as if she might disagree. But they were distracted by someone yelling "Fuck" in the antiques shop.

The sign on the Edwardian building read MOORE & PARTNERS. Hurrying towards it, Margaret said, "Didn't Vivienne mention an antiques dealer called Alan Moore?"

They peered through the open shop door. The place was higgledy-piggledy, crammed with vases, clocks, bureaus, tapestries, hat stands. There were button hooks and cheroot cases, gilded birdcages, a harpsichord, and a stuffed crocodile. Behind the counter, surrounded by drifts of paperwork, sat a large untidy man in a cheap-looking brown suit. He was hunched over the phone, running his free hand desperately through his hair.

"I've bloody told you," he snarled into the receiver. "We're done, all right? All I want you to do is stay the hell away. If I see you around here, you'll wish I hadn't!"

He slammed the receiver down, missed, and knocked a cup of coffee flying.

"Fark!" It sounded like the bellow of a dying mastodon. Coffee dripped down his suit and pooled on the desk. It soaked through a pile of what looked like overdue bills, judging from their angry red lettering. He must

have paid them at last, though, for they were stuck through an old-fashioned bill spike.

If this was Alan Moore, he didn't seem like Bess's idea of an antiques dealer. His accent was broad Aussie, and he was dressed like a not very successful, not very honest car salesman.

"He must be having a bad day," she said. "He probably wants to be left alone."

"Probably," Margaret agreed, and marched into the shop.

There were no other customers. The air smelled of furniture polish and dust.

"Gary, I told you to bring the deliveries around the back." The man wrestled out of his ruined jacket and threw it aside. Then he looked up. "Oh! Sorry." He seemed unused to customers. "G'day, I'm Alan. What can I do for you?"

"Just browsing." Margaret glanced at a Royal Engineers officer's sword strapped to the wall in its leather scabbard. "Business headaches?" She nodded towards the phone, letting him know they'd overheard.

"Sorry about that." Alan tried to smile. His shirt was wrinkled, and he wore a Daffy Duck tie that looked like a Christmas present from 1995. "You know how it is."

"Not really," said Margaret. "When I ran my own business, I never needed to raise my voice."

For heaven's sake. Bess poked her and mouthed "Be kind."

Margaret mouthed back "Why?"

Despite months of coaching from Bess, prosocial behaviour did not come naturally to Margaret. It drove Bess crazy now and then, but secretly she wouldn't have wanted her to change too much. Her tartness added flavour to their lives.

Seeing Bess looking at an inkwell, Alan said, "Little beauty, isn't it? Edwardian, 1903. Solid silver base, cut glass body, Chester hallmark. Sweet condition. Don't get many coming onto the market these days."

"I would hardly call them rare." Margaret sounded suspicious, as if she expected him to cheat them, although Bess had no interest in buying it. "I've handled a few. At Élevé Auction House in Melbourne. Margaret Gale." She flicked a business card from her wallet and showed it to him without handing it over. It wouldn't do for him to call the number and find that the auction house had dispensed with her services.

"Élevé?" Alan swallowed. "They've never sent someone in person before. Are you buying or selling?"

"Neither." Margaret's gaze was fixed on his face where a nervous sheen had appeared.

"Oh." His smile looked desperate. "Then can I ask what...?"

"We visited Crossroads House yesterday. Then this morning we heard about the...tragedy."

"Right." Alan wiped his palm on his trousers. "Poor Mrs Bolt. Such a sweet old lady."

"Was she?"

"Oh yeah." Alan seemed to check himself. "I mean interesting. A real character. Not that I knew her well."

"Her granddaughter said you used to visit." Margaret stepped closer.

"No, no... Not exactly. I called a couple of times, but I call at all the old places in these parts." He rubbed the back of his neck. "If you visited her, maybe she showed you her inventory book?"

"I can't discuss details of a meeting." Margaret evaded him coolly.

"Right." Alan tugged at his earlobe. "Did, ah, did Mrs Bolt mention me?"

"Why do you ask?"

"No reason." He cleared his throat. "Is the granddaughter having visitors yet? I haven't met her in person and I don't want to intrude, but it would be nice to, you know, pay my respects."

"I couldn't say."

"Right." A memory seemed to brighten him up. "Hey, did Mrs Bolt show you her Tassie tiger skull?"

"Her what?" Bess put the inkwell down.

He grinned, growing animated. "She used to keep it in a glass box on the landing. Weird-looking thing. She swore it was real, although I couldn't tell a thigh bone from a knee bone myself."

Bess thought back. "I did see it! Although I didn't realise what it was."

"If it's genuine, it'd fetch a bit. Especially these days, with all those mad scientists trying to use DNA to bring the tiger back from the dead."

Alan fossicked behind his desk where a dozen old framed photographs were stacked, apparently waiting to be sorted. "Check this out."

It was a black-and-white shot from the early 1900s, Bess guessed, to judge from the clothing. A group of men posed in a hunting party surrounded by things they must have killed. Foxes, deer, Tasmanian devils…and a striped object, half-hidden, which might have been a tiger. Bess winced. She hated killing, and killing for fun struck her as especially cruel.

"Is that Crossroads House in the background?"

"Yeah. I got the photo from a local bloke; he found it in his gran's house. I tried to sell it to Mrs Bolt, but she said she wouldn't pay for pictures of her own relatives." He smiled hopefully. "I could do you a deal on the picture plus the inkwell, if you like?"

"I'll just take the picture." Bess negotiated a price, ignoring the incredulous look on Margaret's face. As Alan wrapped it, she explained in a whisper, "It'd be good for the exhibition I'm planning. The gallery will reimburse me."

"Make sure they pay extra for your trouble," Margaret grumbled.

Making a sale seemed to cheer Alan up. "Got much on for the rest of the day?"

"We might return to Crossroads House." Margaret was still glaring at him. "To check on Vivienne Bolt."

"Ah." The look of discomfort returned to Alan's face. When the phone rang on his desk, he dived for it, seeming relieved. "Sorry, ladies, I need to take this."

"We'll be in touch." Margaret escorted Bess out of the shop.

"It's nice to see you amusing yourself," Bess said when they were out of earshot, "but I wish you could do it without tormenting people. Why were you having a go at him?"

"I was not 'having a go'. I was taking an interest." Margaret chewed her lip. "Strange man. He didn't seem happy that someone from a big auction house was visiting. You'd think he would have been eager to do business."

"You're not from a big auction house," Bess felt obliged to say, but Margaret didn't seem to hear her.

"Why do you think he wanted to know what Ivy said about him? And why does he want to visit Vivienne, if he wasn't a friend?"

"I don't know." Bess frowned. She felt sorry for Ivy and Vivienne, but she didn't like the way Margaret seemed preoccupied with them. What happened to Ivy was terribly sad, but elderly people did have accidents and pass away.

Bess didn't set much store by Vivienne's talk of thefts and sabotage. It sounded silly to her, just the paranoid fear of a woman who had been isolated and stressed for too long. Or maybe a woman who wanted Margaret's attention. Either way, they shouldn't dwell on it.

"I'm sorry this happened," she said firmly, "but what does it matter what relationship Alan Moore had with Ivy? It's none of our business."

"Mm?" Margaret seemed to awake from some thought. "No, I suppose not."

She took Bess's arm as they walked. The photograph bumped against Bess's side, the smiling hunters and their pile of dead creatures hidden beneath the paper wrapping.

That evening, Margaret threw herself into her usual motel room routine. She disinfected the light switches, the TV remote, the fridge door, and the sink. The cleaners had been through earlier, but that didn't reassure her. She'd seen a documentary once about the things cleaners did in motel rooms, and it haunted her to this day.

Most evenings, cleaning calmed her down, but tonight it wasn't working. She felt restless, the exposed-brick walls closing in.

Bess was stretched out on the bed reading a book called *The Aboriginal Tasmanians*, about a people still very much alive, whatever the world thought. Earlier she had recorded a video diary for the exhibition she was planning, describing how she had wandered into an antiques shop in a country town, seen a photograph from the time of the tiger's destruction, and learned that she might have been feet away from the remains of a tiger the day before. She was a good storyteller, although Margaret wished she would find a different topic—one that didn't involve going after a reclusive lunatic with a gun.

Her phone rang. She grabbed it.

Bess looked up.

"Margaret?" Vivienne's voice quavered. "Thank God."

"Vivienne. What happened?" Remembering Bess's lessons in empathy, Margaret said, "Pardon me. I meant to say we were very sorry to hear about Ivy's passing."

"That's generous, since she was so utterly vile to you." Vivienne sniffed. "Sorry. I'm all over the place."

"It must have been a shock."

"I thought I was going to have a heart attack and join her. I was asleep and got woken by this almighty crash. I thought someone was breaking into the house. I rushed out waving a bedside lamp—it was comical, you should have seen me—and I…I found her."

"Did she fall?"

"Yes." Vivienne paused. "Well, I think so. Although the police don't seem too sure."

"What do you mean?" Margaret sat down on the bed.

"The police kept me with them all day. They've looked at the house too. I think they think—or at least they're wondering"—she made a noise between a laugh and a sob—"whether I might have…you know. Pushed her."

Margaret's mouth fell open. "That's absurd."

"Try telling them that." Vivienne sounded tearful but relieved to say it out loud. "You should have heard the questions. Was Ivy very difficult to look after? Did I find it too much? Did I think she deserved to be put out of her misery? Did she leave me everything in her will?"

"Did she?"

"Goodness, I don't know. I've never seen her will. It's no surprise if her property goes to me, since I'm the only relative, but I never asked for it. You think I *want* this house? You've seen the place—it's horrible. I hate it here! I just want to get away!"

Bess must have heard because she opened her laptop and started watching a YouTube video. *"The Tasmanian tiger, or thylacine, a shy and mysterious forest-dwelling creature…"* She kept the sound low but loud enough to signal that she was trying not to eavesdrop.

"Vivienne, I'm sure the police are just making routine checks. No one could believe you would do anything like that."

The Vivienne whom Margaret had met twenty-five years ago had been a sharp personality, certainly—cutting, sarcastic, and merrily rude—but the thought of her throwing a helpless old woman down the stairs was ridiculous. The young Vivienne would have thought violence was barbaric and too, too tacky. And she had helped Margaret, not hurt her.

"Anyway," Margaret added, "why would you do a thing like that? Even if you had found it impossible to look after your grandmother, you were about to put her into care. And she was dying already, wasn't she?"

Possibly Margaret should have used a kinder, more Bess-like phrase: *Reaching the end of her earthly journey* or something.

But Vivienne didn't object. "Of course. And if I was planning to do something heinous, I don't suppose I would have invited you to visit."

From Bess's laptop, a solemn voice said, *"Accused by farmers of killing their sheep, the tiger was hunted ruthlessly…"*

"The police didn't arrest you, did they?"

"No. They just told me not to go anywhere. As if I could. I've got a"—Vivienne's voice cracked—"a funeral to organise."

"Is there anything we can do?"

The video went on: *"Later, it was revealed that most of the sheep had been killed by wild dogs. The tiger had been destroyed for nothing."*

Vivienne seemed to pull herself together. "I can handle the arrangements. But maybe… Maybe you could come around tomorrow? I don't want to be alone in the house or face this town by myself. I can imagine what people are saying."

"Hmm." Margaret could imagine that too. "We'll come tomorrow and help out."

"Oh, Margaret. I wish you'd been here when it happened."

Margaret said goodbye and stared at the threadbare carpet. Surely the police didn't really suspect Vivienne of causing Ivy's death. Margaret had looked after an elderly father and a dying sister. She knew how stubborn sick people could be, refusing to admit their own weakness, and how illness, pain, and drugs could make them become confused, take risks, and have accidents.

She knew all too well what it felt like to be falsely accused of a serious crime, to be judged guilty without a trial or even evidence. Just because certain people had always disliked you, or because you stood in the way of their own ambitions, or because they were bored and liked to spread rumours. And the sick feeling when you realised that the authorities were on their side. Margaret would never let herself be helpless like that again.

Her restless energy intensified and gathered around a sense of purpose. In a strange way, it felt good: she had something to do now. "This isn't right. We must help her."

She wondered why Bess did not rush to agree.

Chapter 6

It was a quiet drive to Crossroads House the next morning. Bess stared out the window as the houses of Mount Bastion gave way to fields, then bushland. She told herself they were doing the right thing by going to help. Vivienne was probably feeling very alone, shocked, and vulnerable. It would go against Bess's values not to help her.

And yet secretly, Bess wished Margaret would turn the car around.

Did that make her a bad person? She sighed. Maybe, but she'd had such plans for a beautiful, relaxing holiday, a chance to rejuvenate and cheer themselves up. They didn't need to get dragged into someone else's sad situation.

Especially when that someone else was a virtual stranger who, for some reason, thought it was okay to pour out her troubles to Margaret.

They pulled up at the property. The police were gone, but a hefty woman in her sixties was tottering down the driveway in high heels, shoes unsuited to this terrain. She wore an electric-blue blazer and skirt, a string of pearls, and coral lipstick, and she carried a massive wreath of pink and white flowers.

"Ah!" She waved them over as if they were waitresses slow to take her order. "Do you know when the granddaughter will be back? I've been knocking. Really, she should have left a note. After a bereavement, friends are bound to pop by."

"Good morning," said Margaret in the voice she used for telemarketers. "I don't believe we've been introduced. I'm Margaret Gale, and this is Bess Campbell. We're visiting Ms Bolt."

"Oh." A lanyard hung around the woman's neck read, Mount Bastion and Districts Historical Society. And, in much bigger letters, Janine Jones, President.

"I'm sorry; I thought you must be from the funeral home." She gestured at Margaret's all-black outfit. "I'm Ivy's friend, Janine Jones." She pronounced her surname with an affected French accent so it sounded to Bess like *Jeans*.

"I expect Ivy mentioned me?"

"No."

"Oh." The visitor looked miffed. Then she managed an unconvincing smile. "Well, she had her little ways, didn't she? But she was a wonderful woman. From one of the oldest families in the area."

"Yes, I heard," said Bess.

After an initial horrified glance at her Viking hat, Janine refused to look her way.

"I saw pictures of the house in its heyday," Bess continued. "It looked very elegant."

"Indeed?" Janine turned towards her at last and, with a mighty effort, seemed to decide to overlook the Viking hat. "Well, it's nice to meet someone interested in local history. I'm afraid most people here don't care about their own heritage, but it's our job to educate them. I'm from the historical society." She touched the sign on her lanyard modestly, then reached out to shake their hands. Her hand was surprisingly meaty, her grip strong.

"Was Mrs Bolt a member of your society?"

"She wasn't well enough to attend, but I presented her with an honorary membership as her family goes back six generations in the area. They ran sheep out here before there was a town. Pioneers—but the right kind, of course."

Bess guessed this was a reference to the convict labour that had built so many of the original houses, bridges, and roads in the district.

Janine asked, "What brings you two here?"

"Friends of the family."

"Oh? I don't recall Ivy mentioning you." Janine managed another thin smile. "Well, as I say, there's no one answering at the house, and I must get on." She laid the wreath by the letterbox. "If you do see the granddaughter, remind her to give me a call, won't you? Ivy must have so many things to sort through, and I'm very happy to help. It's the least I can do for an old friend." She smiled again, this time almost anxiously. "You will tell her?"

"Sure," said Bess.

Janine stumbled off down the rough driveway in her bright blue heels, turning around at her car to wave and call, "Toodle-oo!"

After a moment's silence, Bess asked, "If you were a local resident, would you want her educating you?" She made air quotes with her fingers.

"I would not. Ivy had an interesting taste in friends."

They reached the house, and Margaret knocked on the front door. It was surrounded by stained glass panels showing birds, orange trees, and blooming flowers. Symbols of spring, but they were so caked in grime that Bess had to squint to see the patterns. Two panels had been broken, and pieces of plywood were nailed across. It gave the doorway a grim look, like a face with its teeth smashed in.

No one replied to Margaret's knock. She rang Vivienne's number. "No answer."

"She must be busy." Bess wondered if it would be insensitive to suggest leaving.

"I told her we'd visit. You don't suppose the police are giving her a hard time again?"

"I've no idea." Bess glanced up at the porch ceiling, which was clumped with old wasps' nests. Ropes of greyish cobwebs dangled. The wind shook the door in its frame, and Bess flinched. Silly, but it felt like that breeze blew from inside the house as if some force were bottled up in there, rattling to get out.

"Do you get a bad vibe from this place?" Bess asked. "Like there's a psychic imprint of something that happened here?" She didn't just mean Ivy's death either.

"I don't believe in vibes," Margaret reminded her. "Or psychic imprints. Or ghosts, or hobbits, or elves..." She tried Vivienne's number again.

"Suit yourself." Bess tried not to get irritable. "Let me know if she picks up. I'm going to stretch my legs."

She stepped out into the garden and strolled over to where Vivienne's old BMW was parked. She wondered what sort of bumper stickers Vivienne would have working as a rare books conservator. *My other car is a library trolley? Archivists do it in the stacks?*

But there was nothing except a sticker from the last garage to service the car. Not very well, apparently, as Margaret had told her it wouldn't start.

Talk about dull. Bess knew she was being petty, but what sort of person didn't have bumper stickers? She'd had them when she didn't even own a car, proudly adorning her bicycle with *Magic Happens* and *Hens are Friends*. Was Vivienne too cool, too chic, too much of a grownup to do that?

Bess jumped when, from the other side of the car, a voice blurted out, "What do you want?"

She tiptoed closer and saw short chestnut hair. Ty, the gardener, was crouched there, whispering into her phone and stealing glances down the driveway as if she were worried about who might arrive. She didn't look over her right shoulder to where Bess stood.

"We said no phone calls." Ty, who had been so cocky before, now sounded anxious. "You were the one who wanted to call it off, remember? What if someone checks?"

The voice on the other end must have asked a question. She huffed. "No, I don't know where it is, all right? Now piss off. I've taken enough risks." She hung up.

"What risks have you taken?" Bess asked.

Ty rocketed out of the grass like a startled bird. "Christ, it's you." She wobbled with relief, then tried a spot of flirty eyebrow work. "Bess, yeah? Looking good today."

Bess wondered if this was Ty's default setting or if the young woman was trying to distract her. "I was sorry to hear about your employer."

"Who? Oh yeah, Mrs Bolt." Ty sounded out of breath. "Poor old biddy. Nasty thing to happen." She glanced towards the road again.

"Are you waiting for someone?"

"Hmm? Nah, who would I be waiting for?" Ty ran a hand through her hair. "Why? Is there anyone new in town I should know about?" She winked as if to say *Anyone hot?*

But somehow Bess got the sense that wasn't what she really wanted to learn. "We're from out of town, so we wouldn't know."

"Right. You're stuck talking to me, then." Ty leaned back against the car, hands in the pockets of her tight khaki shorts, her tanned, muscular legs on display above her desert boots. She had a tattoo on each ankle—a Tasmanian devil on one, a Tasmanian tiger on the other.

"That's a nice car."

"Looking to sell it, actually. Less for cash, if you're interested."

Bess stared. "Well, since I know it's broken down and it's Vivienne's, let's say I'm not."

Ty chuckled. "Just mucking around. But hey, if you do want to buy one second-hand, I've got a mate who could help. Let me know what you're after, and I'll sort one out with him. There's just a small finder's fee."

"No, thanks." Bess couldn't help being intrigued by Ty. She'd never met anyone so obviously shonky and so unembarrassed about it. "Who were you talking to before?"

"Mind your own."

"Well, what will you do for a job now? Will you stay here?" She glanced at Crossroads House. It looked like a heap of grey slate against the clouded sky.

"Not if I can help it. Told you, that place is haunted." Ty grinned again but with a flicker of unease in her bright blue eyes. "Can't you feel it? You look like the sensitive type."

"I am, actually."

Vivienne appeared from the other side of the property wearing a filmy white dress and a plaintive expression. She hurried over to the porch where Margaret waited.

Bess nodded farewell to Ty and hurried back to the house.

No, she didn't believe in jealousy, but this time she didn't want to leave Margaret and Vivienne alone.

"Come in," Vivienne said.

Margaret glanced at the staircase. She wasn't someone who gawped at accidents, but she would not be intimidated by them either.

The stairs themselves looked undamaged; Ivy's stairlift was still at the top. But two balusters had been knocked out as if someone had crashed into them at full force. And there were marks on the stair carpet and stains on the dingy wallpaper, which Margaret was fairly sure had not been there last time they visited.

Bess glanced in the same direction, a look of pain crossing her face.

Margaret touched her arm, knowing other people's suffering affected Bess deeply. She was rather relieved not to be so empathic herself, but she didn't like seeing Bess sad.

Vivienne didn't look. "Come through and sit down."

The sitting room was hot, and Margaret peeled off her coat.

Noticing, Vivienne said, "I'm awfully sorry. There's some problem with the furnace; I can't adjust it, and I can't bear to have it off altogether. Ever since…since it happened, I've been feeling the cold." Her complexion seemed whiter than ever, the delicate bones pronounced in her heart-shaped face.

"Maybe you should put on a cardigan," Bess said.

Margaret might have been imagining things, but it seemed to her that Bess's tone was not quite as compassionate as usual.

The two guests sat on an ancient horsehair sofa. There were half a dozen places on the walls where pictures had obviously once hung. They had been taken down, leaving squares of wallpaper paler than the rest.

Vivienne said, "Ivy meant to update the décor. I suppose she didn't get around to it."

While Margaret had told Bess she didn't believe in vibes, those empty squares gave her an uneasy feeling as if she were looking at old windows that had been bricked up.

"I'll make us some hot chocolate." Vivienne hurried from the room, not seeming to hear Bess, who called out behind her, "A herbal tea would be nice, if you have any."

Bess muttered to Margaret, "Or an ice cream. This heat…"

Margaret nodded, tugging at the high neck of her black sweater and pushing up her sleeves. But when Vivienne returned with a tea tray and set down three fine bone china cups, her hands still looked blue and stiff from the chill outside.

She sank down into an oversized wingback in burgundy leather, its armrests too high for her elbows. Her slight figure looked elfin surrounded by all that gleaming dark red hide. It made Margaret think of an open mouth that might snap shut and swallow Vivienne whole.

"How are you?" Bess asked. She sipped her hot chocolate and grimaced.

"You don't like it?" said Vivienne. "I'm sorry. I've been told I make them too sweet. An old boarding school trauma, I'm afraid. They used to ration our sugar, and I've been compensating for it ever since. But I might have some coffee beans somewhere. I could—"

"No, no, this is lovely." Bess smiled and took another sip. "You must need a rest."

"I wish I could sleep." Vivienne forced a smile, tears brimming in her eyes. "You should have seen me after it happened, jumping and jittering."

"A terrible thing to happen."

"I still can't believe it," Vivienne said. "I was asleep, and I heard—*felt*—this awful thump." She tapped her foot manically against the rug. "I keep hearing it…"

"That's normal when you're in shock," Bess assured her. "It will pass." She put her hand to her mouth, stifling a yawn.

Margaret couldn't blame her; the warmth was suffocating. She wished she could kick off her boots.

"It's the behaviour of the police I can't understand," Vivienne said. "Of course, they have to do their job. But they didn't care that I was shaken and devastated at losing Ivy. They were so aggressive; they clearly thought I'd done something dreadful."

"I'm sure it's just protocol. Try not to take it personally." Margaret sipped her hot chocolate. It was too sweet, spicy, and watery for her, like some kind of nectar.

Vivienne wrapped both hands around her cup and drank the contents in one long swallow. "I can't think what made her get up in the night and drag herself all the way to the stairs…" She shuddered. "Perhaps I didn't look after her as well as I should have. But to be suspected of hurting her… I know it's childish, but I keep thinking this is so unfair!"

The light bulb in the ceiling buzzed, then went out.

"It's always doing that." Vivienne switched on a table lamp. It cast a thin pool of light. With the dark furnishings and the heavy curtains pulled closed, it could have been midnight.

In a glass case on the mantelpiece were the taxidermized bodies of native birds: a pink robin, a rainbow lorikeet, an electric-blue fairy wren. They were posed on twigs and branches as if trying to take flight.

"I was afraid they wouldn't let me out," Vivienne said.

"Margaret was falsely accused of killing someone," Bess broke in. "She was arrested and imprisoned for a while. Did you know that?"

There was something odd about Bess's tone, Margaret thought. Almost…suspicious? Accusatory even? Those qualities weren't like Bess at all.

But Bess's expression had grown weary, and her eyelids were drooping. She yawned again. Perhaps she had not meant to be rude; perhaps she was just tired.

Margaret squeezed her hand, hoping to signal that they would not stay too long. She assured Vivienne, "Don't worry. My experience was quite different. That was a murder case. But your grandmother's death was an accident, as I'm sure the investigators will agree."

Vivienne stared into her empty cup.

Her confidence wavering for a moment, Margaret ventured, "You're not still worried about…those concerns you raised yesterday, are you?" She remembered Vivienne's fear as she spoke of thefts and damage, and her belief that someone had been inside the house.

"You mean, am I worried that someone came into the house and killed Ivy?" Vivienne spoke defiantly now. "Actually, no. Not really. I woke up and ran to her as soon as she fell. If someone had been there, I would have seen them or heard them running away. Wouldn't I?"

"Yes." Margaret nodded in relief. "I would assume so."

"Mind you," said Vivienne, "if I'd had fewer morals and more sense, I might have told the police I *did* see someone. It might have distracted them from accusing me."

"Trust me: lying to the authorities after someone has died is a bad idea."

"I suppose." Vivienne heaved a sigh. "But I didn't tell you the other thing the police asked about. You see, Ivy used to tell people that there was one item in her collection more valuable than the others, an item no one knew about."

The room seemed to be getting hotter and darker. Bess was sliding down against the couch cushions as if the energy were draining out of her.

Margaret blinked, trying to clear her head. "What was it?"

"She wouldn't tell me. She said she would never sell it, but if she wanted to, she could charge whatever she liked. Goodness knows what she meant. She might have made the whole thing up."

Vivienne's foot twitched, her slim body rocking faintly back and forth. She reminded Margaret of a puppet in a spotlight.

"But the police had heard the story too," Vivienne continued. "Evidently, they suspected that this item—whatever it was—gave me even more of a motive for wanting Ivy gone. You can imagine the scenarios running through their minds: maybe I got angry with Ivy because she wouldn't leave the item to me, or maybe she caught me stealing it… It's crazy. But what if the police can't find this object because it doesn't really exist—or because whoever stole the other antiques took this one too? And what if they decide that I must have taken it, and I must be guilty?"

"That's enough." Margaret made herself sit up and speak with authority. She wasn't worried about the scenario Vivienne described—it sounded nonsensical. But she was troubled by Vivienne's agitated movements and frenzied expression. That wasn't how Margaret remembered her.

In her best museum director voice, she said, "You are describing a fantasy. There is no evidence to support it. Even if the police are prejudiced against you, they have no evidence. I realise your grandmother's death was a shock, but you must pull yourself together."

She stood. "Now, let's get to work, shall we? I'll assist you to keep going through Ivy's collection and appraising things. Once we find her inventory book, we'll be able to tell if anything was stolen. If it was, you can report it and make a claim on her insurance. If nothing is missing, you can get started sorting out her estate. Either way, it's better than sitting around." She nodded towards the door. "Shall we?"

Vivienne looked up, her eyes swimming with tears again. "Oh, Margaret. Of course, you're right. I'm jumping at shadows. Thank you."

"Let's start with the next room." Margaret touched Bess's shoulder. "Bess? Will you come with us?"

"Mmph." Bess shook her head. Her eyelids drooped; her voice was thick with tiredness. "I'm zonked; I need to nap. You go and do your… valuation…" She shook off Margaret's hand.

"Very well." Margaret felt a twinge of abandonment but told herself not to be silly. She didn't need Bess for everything, did she?

Vivienne opened the door, letting in a welcome gust of cooler air. Margaret hesitated, then followed her out.

Bess woke to what felt like the worst hangover of her life. Her mouth tasted foul, and her skull seemed to be full of cement. She dragged herself upright and looked groggily at her watch. Two hours had passed.

Voices sounded from across the corridor. There was Margaret's low, crisp tone explaining that a Victorian armadillo-shell handbag would have actually lost value in recent years, and Vivienne's higher voice crying, "Oh, Ivy would have been cross! She cherished that ghoulish thing. She wouldn't even let me dust it. You're so knowledgeable, Margaret."

Apparently, they hadn't missed her, then.

Bess got to her feet, suddenly wide awake and angry. She had been trying so hard to support Margaret these past few miserable months, but did Margaret really appreciate it? And Bess could admit it to herself now: she didn't trust Vivienne one bit.

Not that she thought Vivienne had actually harmed her grandmother. Bess knew that murders were very rare, despite her past adventures in Port Bannir. There was no real reason for their hostess to hurt Ivy, and it was hard to picture flouncy little Vivienne getting up the nerve to swat a fly.

"No," Bess muttered to herself, "she'd ask Margaret to do it for her."

That wasn't very kind, but Vivienne's poor-me act was getting on Bess's nerves. It was so obvious she was playing on Margaret's sympathies, Margaret's memories of her own unjust imprisonment, and Margaret's need to be an expert and a protector.

How could Margaret not see that? Most of the time she was so sharp, the cleverest woman Bess had ever known. What was wrong with her today?

Bess crossed to the window, yanked open the curtains, and looked out onto the grounds. In the bushland behind the property, a flowering gum tree was shaking. She pressed her nose to the dusty glass. The flowering gum shook again. Something was moving out there.

She recalled Ty chasing some unseen person off the property, growling about nutjobs.

Should she go across the hall and tell Vivienne? It might distract her from Margaret. Unless Vivienne started bleating again about how frightened she was…

Bess knew she was being harsh now, but she did not need to see Margaret striding outside to confront someone for scaring poor little Vivienne. Ugh. Bess would rather check things out for herself.

She would not take any risks; she would just look from a distance. It was probably nothing anyway, just a bird shaking the branches. But she'd prefer to be out there than in here, waiting for Margaret and Vivienne to finish. She pictured herself glaring like a pathetically jealous girlfriend while they chatted about Edwardian fob watches and Victorian silver sugar bowls.

"Stuff that." She rubbed the sleep from her eyes. If Margaret came back and found her missing for a few minutes—well, so be it. It wouldn't hurt her to worry about Bess briefly. The last few months, Bess felt like it had mostly been the other way around.

She walked out of Crossroads House and shut the door quietly.

The bushes at the back of the property were so dense she had to bend branches and tread on vines to get through them. She reached the wire-link fence. It had been damaged, possibly by wire cutters. There was a hole large enough for someone to squeeze through, which Bess did.

The bush closed around her, cocooning her in a hundred shades of green and grey. Insects buzzed. Twigs scraped her face and snagged her clothing. She took several steps, then looked back to see Crossroads House disappearing behind the trees.

"Not too far…" From the garden, it had looked as if the flowering gum were just a couple of metres away, dead ahead. But here in the scrub, she couldn't see it.

Six more steps, she promised herself. If she hadn't spotted it by then, she would turn around and walk a straight line back.

Ahead were scraps of bright pink, blossoms of the flowering gum. A tiny creek ran beside it, water flowing sluggishly through mud. Something flashed, making her jump.

Not sunlight. More like someone taking her picture.

All around were bushes, bracken, and fallen branches. Was someone there?

An inner voice reproached her for being so reckless, charging out here on her own. Why had she done it? Just to see if Margaret would notice she'd gone?

Then she spotted it: another camouflaged camera, like the one she'd seen the other day. It was strapped to the flowering gum, its lens pointed at the little stream. Had someone been adjusting it earlier, causing the tree branches to move? Were they keeping this area under surveillance?

She reached towards the camera, and it flashed again. An infrared sensor maybe. She ran her fingers over it, feeling for a latch to open the mechanism. There might be some sort of memory card inside with her picture on it.

Impatient, she reached for the strap binding the camera to the tree. That memory card would hold more than her picture; it would also contain footage of anyone else who had been past this spot. She began unfastening the strap.

"*Oi!*"

A shove sent her flying into the undergrowth.

Branches cracked under her, bark scraping the skin from her knees and hands. Gasping, she rolled over to face her attacker.

A figure loomed up out of the bracken. It was long, gaunt, and greyish brown, with strips of ragged bark like leprous skin, dangling broken twigs, and winter leaves hanging over it. The strange cloak swayed in folds between the creature's raised arms. It had no face, only a hood that hung low, obscuring the head in shadow.

Bess stared, her mouth open in horror. Poking out from under the hem of the cloak was a pair of battered old desert boots.

The creature pointed at her. "Hands off!"

The undergrowth rustled and shivered. Dumbfounded, she watched as more shapes made of twigs, bark, and dead leaves began to rise up out of the bracken.

One shape cried out to the first, "Stand down at once! What did we agree?" This new figure was small and round with a rich, plummy Shakespearean voice.

"She was only nicking the bloody camera!" the first creature yelled back. It had a voice like sandpaper, an old-time smoker's voice. "And you know what they cost!"

"I saw the flash!" A third creature erupted out of the bushes, another strange woodland cloak flying out around it. This figure was taller and thinner than the others. "What happened?"

"Nothing," snapped the rough-voiced creature. "It's just that nosy redhead from the other day." The figure turned on Bess. "Are you bloody stalking us?"

"I... No," Bess squeaked.

"Enough." The shape with the posh voice seized the other two and hauled them away. "For pity's sake, do you want to bring all that trouble from the house out here? *Move!*"

They took off through the scrub like three great tumbleweeds borne along by the wind. The short, fat tumbleweed was booming, "I'm shocked by your conduct! Shocked! What did we agree about remaining hidden?"

The tall, thin tumbleweed was chattering in a fast monotone about megapixels and flash ranges and a trigger response of four-tenths of a second.

And the cranky swearing tumbleweed kept repeating, "Three hundred bucks we paid for that bloody camera! Three hundred bucks! And weirdos come along and help themselves..."

Their voices faded, leaving only the cheeping of insects. Bess clambered to her feet.

"*I'm* the weirdo?" That seemed more unfair than being thrown into a bush.

She brushed herself down, trying to make sense of things. It wasn't just the arrival of the three strangers, who must have been her tiger hunters lying in wait for their quarry. And it wasn't just their strange appearance. After a few seconds, she'd realised they were wearing camouflage cloaks. The cloaks resembled dead foliage but were probably made from ordinary fabric and polyester.

No, what amazed Bess were the voices of the hooded figures. The rich, fruity voice, the high-pitched, rapid voice, and the rasping, cursing voice... They had all been female. The tiger hunters were women.

"She doesn't care much for me, does she?" Vivienne said as Margaret pored over a copper-plated nineteenth-century ear trumpet. "Your friend, Ms Campbell."

"Pardon?" Margaret looked up. "Ms Campbell is my partner; I specified that before. And of course she likes you. She sees the best in everyone. It's one of her more mystifying qualities."

Still, she paused. It was true: Bess did seem less enthusiastic about Vivienne than about most new people.

"Perhaps she thinks I'm working you too hard," Vivienne said. "Asking too much of you."

"Nonsense." Margaret disliked the suggestion that she wasn't up to doing her job. Surely Bess didn't think that. "I'm perfectly capable."

They had been looking through Ivy's antiques for ages, sorting through coin collections, cases of butterflies, Chinese lacquered tea caddies, cowrie-shell snuffboxes, and a rather horrifying hundred-year-old leather monkey. There was no sign of a special, exceptional item, and Margaret was inclined to think that no such item existed.

"Perhaps Ms Campbell just doesn't like my face, then," Vivienne said lightly. "After all, she doesn't know me."

"Well…" Concentrating on her work, Margaret spoke more frankly than she intended. "I don't know you well myself. It's been twenty-five years since your vanishing act."

"Vanishing act?"

Margaret straightened. "You gave me a false address on graduation night. I walked you back to that fashionably shabby old terrace house in Carlton where you told me you lived with a troupe of artists and poets, and you stepped through the gate and closed it behind you. But when I returned the next morning, the students who lived there—who worked at McDonalds, by the way, and were not poets—swore they'd never heard of you." She looked hard at Vivienne, who shifted in her seat. "Nowadays I believe the young people call that 'ghosting'."

"All right." Vivienne sighed. "I lied about my address. The truth is, I lived in an ugly little house in a boring, beige part of town with a couple of elderly sisters who made me go to church with them and walk their horrid incontinent dogs, and they wouldn't let me have visitors. I was broke, and I didn't want to tell you. I was headed off overseas anyhow, so I told myself a little harmless deception didn't matter. I wanted you to remember me as a bohemian free spirit, not some sad little drudge from the suburbs."

"As if I would have cared how much money you had or where you lived." Margaret was stung. "I wasn't that shallow."

Although perhaps she had been, a little. She hadn't cared about Vivienne's wealth, but she'd certainly been drawn to the world Vivienne came from: her stories of poetry readings, gallery openings, and archaeological digs. Her anecdotes about meeting indie film directors and fashion designers. Even her childhood tales of boarding school food, ballet classes, and being bullied by the daughters of bankers and prime ministers.

It had sounded so glamorous to the young Margaret, whose own childhood had involved public school canteen food, rough country netball games, and being bullied by local yobbos. Shaking her head, she said, "I would have admired you no matter where you lived. You were so poised and accomplished, and you gave me such clever advice."

"Did I?" Vivienne laughed. "I had an opinion on everything, but I doubt much of it was useful.'

"Of course it was." Margaret was dismayed at the thought that Vivienne might not realise how significant that night had been. "Don't you remember? You told me what I should do to…to make the best of myself."

Twenty-five years ago, Margaret had been a sullen, awkward, tongue-tied young woman from a country town. Her years at university built her brains but not her social skills. Try as she might, she was still an outsider. Her efforts to dress fashionably were embarrassingly clunky—the memory of her crushed-velvet dress and choker necklace on graduation night made her cringe even now. Her posture was stooped as she tried to shrink herself down to the height of the popular girls.

Every time she attempted to break into people's conversations, she would blurt out the wrong thing, then shrink back, glaring at her classmates and despising them for being shallow and silly, all the while yearning for their approval.

Vivienne saw through all of that straight away. But she didn't mock Margaret for it. Instead, she lit up another French cigarette and said, "Listen, Margaret, you're going about this *entirely* wrong. Stop trying to loosen up. Stop trying to dress fashionably, make the right jokes, or have the latest hobbies because you're never going to manage any of those things."

Smiling to soften the blow, she said, "Face it, Margaret, you're an odd duck. But you could make that work for you. If you looked more severe, if you stood taller, if you walked faster and made people scurry to keep up with you. If you learned to use that voice and those eyes of yours to intimidate everyone. If you held yourself aloof and stayed silent on purpose until people squirmed with fear, wondering what you might be thinking…" Vivienne smiled. "Well, *then* you could make an impression." She'd waved her glowing cigarette at Margaret like a magic wand. "Think about it, won't you?"

Now Margaret said, "I did think about it." That night had been the beginning of a new Margaret Gale: firm, cool, black clad, and masterful, able to reduce people to quivering blobs with a single, singeing glance. Her transformation had taken time and effort, yes, with one or two missteps along the way, but it had started with Vivienne's advice.

And in spite of Vivienne's disappearing act, Margaret had been grateful to her ever since. "I made something of myself because of you."

Vivienne shook her head. "Margaret, I'm touched. No one's ever said that to me before. I'm amazed you trusted my judgement—I was such a pretentious young fool—but I'm glad I was right."

"Of course I trusted you," Margaret said. "After what you'd done for me already that night. When we first met."

"Remind me?"

"You haven't forgotten?"

"Of course not." Vivienne raised her eyebrows. "I want to hear you tell it. That's all."

"You know what happened." Margaret felt almost embarrassed, now that they were speaking about the event at last. "I'd gone down to the river with our graduation class for that awful student booze cruise. I was trying to fit in. We were queued from the quay all the way up the stairs to the bridge across the river. I didn't want to be there, but I sat up on the railing to get a better view."

She gazed into the distance, remembering. "There was a group of boys who'd started drinking early. A scuffle broke out. One of them got punched backwards and flew right at where I was sitting. I was knocked back, lost my balance. I started to slip."

It flashed in front of her again: the black river far below and the concrete structures that jutted out from underneath the bridge. Which would she hit first?

"Then you appeared," Margaret continued. "Out of nowhere, it seemed. The boys hadn't noticed—they were scrapping with each other. But you grabbed my arm and leaned back hard to balance me. I didn't know your name; I'd never even seen you before. You asked me if I wanted your help."

Margaret brought her attention back to here and now, to the Vivienne who sat opposite her: twenty-five years older but with hair still glowing like a beacon. "Remember?"

"I'm glad I was there. Glad I could help."

"It's funny…" It wasn't like Margaret to speak so openly, especially to someone she barely knew in any objective sense. But part of her was still back on that bridge, hanging in the balance between life and death. "You disappeared after that night. But part of me always thought I would have to pay you back some day."

Vivienne smiled, her eyes wide and green, just the way Margaret remembered from that evening on the bridge. "Guess what day it is."

Chapter 7

MARGARET SAT STILL. THE SPACE around her seemed to flicker as if someone were switching a light off and on again. Switching between this dark, hot room and a riverside twenty-five years ago.

The one thing that didn't change was Vivienne.

As she looked into Vivienne's eyes, she had a sense that all she needed to do was move towards her, reach out, and she would be transported back to that riverside. Back there permanently, so she could do everything over again. Do the last twenty-five years over again, this time without making mistakes or neglecting anything that mattered. A second chance…

But if she had done everything differently, she would not have met Bess.

She turned away.

Desperate to change the subject, Margaret asked, "So… When the police stop being obstructive and you inherit Ivy's collection, what will you do with it? Especially if we find one antique more valuable than the others?"

Vivienne watched Margaret for a moment. Then she stood, walked to the bookcase, and ran her finger along one shelf, leaving a clear trail in the dust. The bookcase was the one thing in the room they hadn't examined for its value as it only held photo albums. And as Vivienne had pointed out, no one would pay for her family's unhappy memories.

Brushing off her hands, Vivienne flopped into a carved wooden chair on Margaret's other side. "What would I do with this valuable thing if I found it? I'd sell it, of course! Along with this house and everything in here."

Margaret must have looked shocked because Vivienne laughed, chiming like a bird. Her high-backed chair was carved with oak leaves and acorns, framing her pale hair and her fine-boned, pointed face.

"Oh, Margaret, I told you: I have no love for this place or my grandmother's things. Why not sell them to someone peculiar enough to enjoy them and take my freedom? I suppose I shouldn't say this right after a bereavement, but I can't wait to get back out into the world and go travelling again. The Hofburg in Vienna, Saint Catherine's Monastery in Egypt, the Royal Library in Copenhagen…"

Then her gaze sharpened. "And what about you, Margaret? I'm grateful that you came here to help me, but I was astonished you were available. I thought you would be on the other side of the planet, doing remarkable things. You know, restoring the HMS *Victory* or sailing a replica tall ship around the Pacific. Not living quietly in Melbourne with no job and taking your holidays on this little island."

"Well…" Uneasy, Margaret took the chair at Vivienne's side. "I'm between employers at present, but that's only a brief setback. And I can't spend my time flitting all over the world. I have commitments, responsibilities."

Vivian smiled understandingly. "Of course. You're happily settled with your Ms Campbell. I'm pleased for you."

Did Margaret hear a hint of sarcasm? Or did she imagine it because deep down she knew that Deirdre's death had hacked away at her happiness and left her feeling more unsettled than ever? God knew, she loved Bess, but everything else…

"You mustn't think I'm not happy for you, Margaret. It's just… The Margaret Gale I met on graduation night didn't seem the type of woman to be tied down."

Margaret blinked. "I'm not. Why would you say that?"

"Oh, of course you're not." Vivienne shook her head. "Pay no attention to me. I'm a rotten person, really: spiteful, envious, sly." She raised her eyebrows as if daring Margaret to take it as a joke. "Try to make allowances. I've been cooped up for weeks in a place I thought I'd escaped from long ago. And it's just as I remembered, only dustier and smellier." She sighed.

"You think I'm awful, don't you, for speaking like this when Ivy's just died? You mustn't think I'm not sorry. For heaven's sake, I didn't *want* her to go like that!"

"Of course you didn't—"

"But I don't want to be stuck here either, dealing with the mess she left behind." Vivienne groaned and ran her slender hands through her hair. "I tell you, if that wretched car would start, I would jump into it now and take off, and to hell with everything." She looked at Margaret. "Or perhaps I'd make you chauffeur me around in yours."

Her teasing tone and the expectation in her eyes made Margaret tense. What did Vivienne really want from her? Baffled, she said, "Well, that wouldn't be possible. I'm here with Ms Campbell."

"Of course," said Vivienne silkily. "You have plans." Then she fell silent, apparently waiting for something.

Margaret couldn't think what. She might not be very skilled at human interactions, but she could tell this conversation had taken a strange turn. She was half-inclined to put an end to the whole thing—the whole visit, maybe. After all, she had come here to help out someone in trouble, not to engage in…whatever this behaviour was. Despite her limited experience, she suspected it was flirting.

And yet it was hard to get up and leave. Something was keeping her here in this musty room with its hunched furniture and hoarded antiques. And Vivienne sitting in the middle of it like some fairy-tale figure chained in a tower, begging to be freed.

It wasn't that Margaret wanted Vivienne, not the way she had always wanted Bess. Bess warmed and softened her, made her feel both vulnerable and hopeful, connected her to someone else at long last. She felt nothing like that for Vivienne, no impulse to touch her, kiss her, or speak words of love.

But the idea of breaking out of imprisonment, of being beckoned away by a will-o'-the-wisp—she couldn't deny it had a certain appeal. The thought of walking away from her own past, her disappointments, failures, guilt and regrets. Into the unknown…

The arms of their chairs were set so close together that their hands were barely an inch apart. Margaret looked down and saw Vivienne's fingers twitch, straighten, and stretch towards hers, like the stems of flowers moving in search of sunlight.

"Yoo-hoo!" The front door crashed open.

Vivienne leapt up.

Relieved, Margaret looked around as if she'd woken from a dream. What had just happened?

A voice bellowed down the corridor, "Hello-oo? Only me!"

Margaret recognised the voice as Janine Jones, president of the historical society and, apparently, no great respecter of private property.

Vivienne looked startled. Then she seemed to recognise the puffing and high-heeled clumping of Mrs Jones approaching. "That woman! She was out here first thing and threatened to return. I've been hiding from her."

Janine flung the door open. "Oh, you're here at last! I wasn't sure if anyone was home."

"It's sweet that you felt comfortable enough to come in anyhow," Vivienne replied.

It was the sort of thing Margaret might have said.

"Oh, your grandmother and I were great friends. I took her spare key from behind the shutter."

"Did you?"

"Never fear, the cavalry has arrived!" Janine stepped back into the hall to retrieve an enormous covered dish full of some kind of casserole. It filled the room with a hot cloud smelling of onions and gravy.

"Oh, that's very—"

"No, don't mention it. I have two more in the car. I'll take them through to the kitchen, and then we can get started."

"Sorry?" Vivienne wrinkled her forehead. "What are we getting started on?"

"The clear-out, of course! I know you must be devastated by your grandmother's passing." Janine made as if to pat Vivienne sympathetically but was hindered by the dish in her hands. She jostled Vivienne with her elbow instead. "But there's no sense in dragging things out. Best to sort through her belongings now, decide what to keep, what to donate, and what to throw away."

"That's what we're doing." Vivienne gestured around the room. "But—"

"Marvellous! Good girls, that's the spirit. You seem to have this lot in hand. Why don't I go through the study?"

"Ms Bolt and I can manage." Margaret fixed Janine with a steely glare. "We won't keep you."

Janine twitched, her face reddening.

"Actually," said Vivienne, "I could use some help to go through that bureau." She pointed. "If it's not too much trouble."

"No trouble at all!" Janine trilled. "I'll sort things out in the kitchen, then I'll be back." She shot Margaret a nasty look before bustling away.

Margaret raised her eyebrows.

Vivienne whispered, "I gather she's very influential in town. I've got enough problems; I don't need the postman to stop delivering or the supermarket to lose my order. Anyhow, I've seen what's in that bureau. If Mrs Jones wants to sort through paperclips and rubber bands, let her."

Which was all very well, but it meant they would be trapped with Janine for quite some time.

When she returned from the kitchen, Janine gave them the full history of her ancestors, the Flanders family, who'd arrived here as pastoralists and became one of the most prominent families in the area, setting up the agricultural association and serving on the local council and the Royal Society of Tasmania.

"But of course, you'd know about that," she prompted Vivienne. "I expect your grandmother told you."

"No." Vivienne smiled politely.

"No? But she must have mentioned my great-great-grandfather, John Flanders? He was a great friend of her own great-grandfather, William Ingham. John helped him set up this estate."

"That's interesting. But no, she didn't mention it."

"Oh? Well, she was ill." Janine returned to the bureau, although she wasn't doing a very thorough job of sorting it. She pulled out handfuls of stationery, balls of string, and newspaper clippings, tossing them aside with barely a glance before diving back in as if in search of something else.

Was Janine a sneak thief hoping to swipe an antique or two while their backs were turned? Or was she just a crashing bore? Janine told them about the committees she sat on, the school prizes she gave out, and the musical society she ran. Admirable, Margaret supposed, but they had not asked to hear about it. Nor had they asked for Janine's blow-by-blow account of how her great-uncle had set up the historical society exactly a hundred years ago and how she was planning their centenary celebration. The minister for the arts was booked to unveil the plaque. Margaret wasn't known for her compassion, but she felt a flicker of pity for the minister, whom Janine had cornered at a charity fundraiser.

"Of course, some of our members weren't happy about inviting him," Janine said. "He wouldn't qualify for membership himself, not being from one of the original pioneering families. But I said that's all the more reason to welcome the poor man, so he can learn about our history."

"Noblesse oblige?" Margaret snarked.

Janine nodded earnestly. "Exactly! Those of us with a proud heritage should use it to help those less fortunate. Anyhow, it's not as if I invited him to become a member. I would draw the line at that, obviously." She dusted off her hands. "Well, that's the desk emptied. I'll make a start on the bookcase."

"Is that the time?" Vivienne stood. "I must check on something. Mrs Jones," she said, politely using Janine's French pronunciation, "you've been so kind, but I couldn't possibly keep you. You're busy planning your centenary celebrations."

"Never too busy for friends!"

But Vivienne stood there until the visitor clambered reluctantly to her feet.

"Well, I'll pop by again tomorrow," she said, and left.

"Is something wrong?" Margaret asked Vivienne, wondering what was so important—unless it was the need to be free of Janine.

"No, I just need to call the solicitors. And I must check where our gardener has got to. She's meant to be cutting back the hedge, but she spends most of the day on her phone. You know what young people are like." Vivienne leaned in. "She likes talking to your friend too. Ty asked me all about Ms Campbell after you visited the other day. I saw them chatting again this morning."

"Did you?" Margaret wondered why Bess hadn't mentioned that.

Not that it was important. Margaret certainly didn't feel threatened by some fit and confident woman twenty years younger than herself who worked outdoors and was covered in obnoxious tattoos. Well, obviously not.

Bess followed the tiger hunters back to their camp. Yes, she had promised she would be careful, but she couldn't resist. And why did trios of eccentric women keep popping up in her life?

She crept over and hid behind a tree trunk, holding her breath as she peered out.

The tiger hunters didn't notice her this time—they were too busy arguing. They had taken off their camouflage cloaks. Looking at their feet, Bess recognised the woman in the desert boots who had tackled her before.

The woman was wiry and weather-beaten. She was dressed in well-worn jeans and a tattered flannel shirt. Her haircut looked like she had done it herself; it was shaved up the sides and flopped down to her collar at the back. She must have been sixty, but she moved like someone who walked many miles a day. And she was strong, judging by the boxes, spare tyre, and folding chairs she was loading into the back of the 4WD.

But every time she packed something, a second woman would wait until she turned her back, then haul the object out again.

The second woman reminded Bess of a grasshopper. She had gangling limbs, a long thin face, and eyes that seemed to bulge behind her thick bifocals. Her hair stood out in silver spirals, and she gave off so much nervous energy that Bess half-expected sparks to start flying.

The first woman noticed what she was up to. "The fuck are you doing?" she demanded in her gravelly voice.

The grasshopper woman grabbed a small portable camping toilet out of the car and hurried to a distance as if holding it hostage.

"We can't abort the mission!" the grasshopper woman insisted. Her voice was high-pitched, and she spoke so quickly that Bess had to concentrate to understand her. "I won't allow it!"

"Penny, put down the toilet and be sensible."

"Sensible?" Penny let out a cry like an angry mouse. "I'm the sensible one here! This is the most promising location we've found so far. Multiple witness testimonies, paw prints in the leaves which show a forty percent accuracy match, and thick undergrowth for animals to hide in. And something ate that pigeon you shot yesterday. There wasn't a scrap left!"

"Yeah, but since *someone* stuffed up the camera settings, there's no footage left either. It was probably a cat."

"If you're determined to be a denialist, Daz, I don't know why you're here."

"Don't give me that." Daz planted her rough hands on her hips. "You saw what happened back there! We're being spied on. The old lady's dead, the place is crawling with cops—"

"They haven't come here."

"They will. Someone in town will point the finger."

"Those people in town won't talk to the authorities. You know what they're like."

"I know I didn't come here to get hassled." Giving up on the toilet for now, Daz gathered the other items Penny had removed from the 4WD and loaded them back in.

"This is unacceptable!" Penny yelped. "You can't disrupt a research schedule we spent weeks perfecting just because you're nervous about something. It's irrational. Totally neurotic!"

"I'm neurotic? This from the woman who can't drink her tea if it's in the wrong mug."

"There is nothing strange about that! Studies have shown that a stable routine enhances intellectual functioning."

"Or eat her Rice Bubbles if they're too soggy."

"Studies have also shown that one in six people have heightened sensory sensitivities. Not that you would understand that, Daz, having all the sensitivity of a wombat's bottom!"

"I've had a gutful of this." Daz stomped back to the 4WD.

But as she did so, the third woman emerged from the trees, demanding in her booming voice, "What is the meaning of this? I could hear you two shouting from miles away. If you want to scare off the wildlife and draw attention to us, you're doing a splendid job."

The third woman was small and rotund with greying blonde curls piled on top of her head. She wore a safari suit with lots of pockets, and she strutted as if leading a parade. All she needed was a pith helmet and an elephant gun. The woman said, "I've checked the other cameras, and they're functioning correctly. Which is more than I can say for you two."

"Matilda, she's disregarding our research schedule!"

"She's stealing our toilet!"

"That's quite enough," Matilda glared at Penny and Daz until they both wilted. Despite her odd appearance, Bess had the sudden, definite sense that this woman had once been a school principal. She seemed on the verge of ordering them both to pick up rubbish during recess and think hard about what they'd done.

Instead, Matilda said, "Daz, you must accept that we cannot abandon this location when it has given us our best leads so far." When Penny looked triumphant, Matilda added, "And, Penny, you must accept that we can't remain here at present. Our operation depends on discretion and patience. So let's pack up sensibly, move to our backup place, and await developments." Matilda sighed. "Never mind. *Semper ad meliora:* always onward towards better things."

Penny handed over the toilet reluctantly.

"What about the cameras?" Daz asked.

"Leave them in place for now."

"And what if Little Miss Snoopy Pants comes back and steals the equipment? I dunno what her deal is, but I don't suppose it's the tiger she's looking for."

"Actually, that's exactly what I'm looking for," Bess said, stepping out from behind her tree.

Vivienne did not return. Margaret wondered what was keeping her. Was she talking with her solicitor? Or was she having trouble with Ty the gardener? Ty, who had taken an interest in Bess…

Don't be silly.

Moving out into the hall, Margaret wondered what she was doing there. Helping a distraught and persecuted Vivienne, she had assumed, but after hours of work, she wasn't so sure. If the police were really framing Vivienne for a terrible crime, surely she wouldn't be at home pricing antiques and talking to Margaret the way she was.

Margaret twitched with unease. Had she misread things? Made a fool of herself somehow?

From Ivy's study next door, she heard a rolling noise and a muffled clunk. It sounded like someone closing a drawer.

But she'd looked out the window ten minutes earlier and seen Vivienne on her phone, strolling around the side of the house. There should be no one here but Margaret.

She approached the study door, listened, then shoved it open.

"Oh!" Janine Jones clutched her chest. "You gave me a fright!"

One desk drawer was open. Janine shut it with her elbow. Her high heels were on the floor next to her stockinged feet.

"Can I help you?" Janine asked as if this were her study and Margaret the intruder.

"Yes. You could tell me why you're going through things that don't belong to you. Especially when Ms Bolt presumably believes you've left."

"Oh, she won't mind." Janine stepped back into her shoes as if everything were normal. "When old Mrs Bolt was alive, I was always popping in."

"Were you?" Margaret folded her arms.

Janine shifted uneasily. "As it happens, I remembered I'd left some old family correspondence of mine here. I'd brought it to show Ivy—we shared a passion for local history. It was from my great-great-uncle to her father's cousin, describing a trip they made through the bush to stake out new land for grazing. Do you know, he actually describes them stumbling across a litter of Tasmanian tiger cubs!"

"Oh yes? What did the men do next?"

"Well...killed them. But those were different times."

"Indeed. And did you find this edifying document in Mrs Bolt's desk?"

"Not yet."

"Well, let's have a look." Margaret strode over, beginning to enjoy herself, although she had no idea what was going on. "Perhaps in the next drawer down?"

But Janine blocked her way. "No! I mean, there's no need; I already looked there. Now that I think of it, perhaps I took the letter home with me after all."

"Ironic," Margaret said. "The president of a historical society having such a bad memory."

"Yes." The look Janine gave Margaret was pure poison, but she managed a smile. "Yes, it is rather funny, isn't it?"

"Well, let me see you out," said Margaret. "Again."

As Margaret shut the front door behind Janine, she wondered what could be so important that the woman would creep back in to get it. She returned to the study and sifted through Ivy's desk but found nothing except stationery and a key ring with half a dozen keys.

"Odd." Shrugging, she went in search of a bathroom. She paused by the foot of the staircase, looking at the spot where Ivy must have died. Then she straightened her shoulders and climbed up.

Margaret didn't believe in bad vibes or whatever Bess called them. Every old house must have seen a death or two.

Still, she tensed at the squeaking and groaning that greeted each footstep. The stairlift waiting at the top seemed to mock poor Ivy's memory. If she'd used it, she would still be alive.

But Margaret remembered her own sick father refusing to use a walking frame, no matter how many times he fell without it. Some people couldn't bear to do what was good for them.

On the wall just below the stairlift, a couple of steps down from the landing, there were marks in the wallpaper. She looked closer. Four little scratches. She held her fingers over them, curling them in midair to test the shape. Yes, it looked as if Ivy had flung a hand out, clawing desperately for something to hold onto.

The threadbare carpet gave off a sour, fusty smell as if things were growing inside it.

At the top of the stairs, set into the wall, was an alcove with a decorative pillar. On top sat a glass box containing an animal skull. This must be the one supposedly belonging to a Tasmanian tiger, the one Alan Moore had described in his shop.

Margaret was no stranger to controversial artefacts. At her old maritime museum, the whaling exhibits alone had received so many complaints that she'd had to set aside a drawer in her filing cabinet to hold them all. But surely there was a difference between a display in a museum meant to educate the public and a show in a private home. The latter felt unpleasantly primal to Margaret. There was a touch of gloating about it, a whiff of blood sports.

She walked along the landing, passing the old nursery, then a guest room evidently used by Vivienne. Her few belongings were arranged neatly, most of them still inside her open suitcases as if she were ready to leave at a minute's notice. The door to the next room was ajar. Margaret nudged it open with her foot.

This must have been Ivy's room. It was pristine, almost sterile, with no personal items and nothing on the bedside table except medical creams and a box of tissues. The curtains were shut, the bedclothes pulled up. There were grooves in the carpet near the bed where the wheelchair must have stood.

No antiques here. Vaguely uneasy, she backed away. It felt as if she had missed something, but she couldn't imagine what.

She reached the bathroom at the end of the hall. As Margaret washed her hands, she looked at her reflection in the mirror. A crack ran through the middle, cutting her face in two, and the glass was blackening around the edges.

It struck her that whatever Ivy had been doing when she died, it had not been a call of nature. The stairs and the bathroom were in opposite directions.

She turned the tap off. Somewhere in the building was the sound of metallic rattling and thumping. Dodgy old pipes, no doubt. But she had an unpleasant image of a family ghost shaking its chains.

As Margaret headed back towards the stairs, she heard a knock at the front door. Then voices. Vivienne must have walked around from the back garden.

Margaret peered out the window at the top of the stairs. A man and a woman in police uniforms stood below with Vivienne.

She fiddled with the latch on the window and eased it open, gritting her teeth as she tried to stop it from squeaking.

"…know your grandmother had been prescribed liquid oxycodone?" one of them asked.

"Of course I knew," Vivienne said.

"And sleeping pills?"

"Yes."

"Did you handle it yourself?"

"I gave her all her medication."

If Margaret had been down there, she would have advised Vivienne to take care what she said without a solicitor present.

"So," the other officer said, "can you tell us where those items are? The pharmacist says he filled your grandmother's script last week, but there was very little left in the house."

"That can't be right." Vivienne's voice faltered. "I measured it for her every time. I was careful. And she wouldn't have taken extra; she hated the stuff, refused to swallow it some days. She said she wasn't some disgusting drug addict. Sometimes she threatened to tip the whole lot down the sink." A little gasp. "Oh, that wretched old—" Vivienne stopped short. "I suppose she must have waited until my back was turned and poured it away."

"That was careless of you, Ms Bolt."

"I did my best with her." Vivienne sounded defensive.

"Any idea where that medication is now?"

"Down the drain, most likely. Perhaps you've already gone through our rubbish bins."

"We have."

"Well, test the town sewerage, then. I can't help you."

From her own experience with the police, Margaret could have told Vivienne that being haughty wasn't the best approach.

"So you have no idea what happened to those missing opioids?"

"I've told you—I didn't know they were missing."

"You didn't lock them up?"

"Why would I? It was only the two of us here." Vivienne crossed her arms. "If Ivy was determined not to take them, I suppose that was her right. And what does it have to do with her falling down the stairs?"

"We're interested in that too, Ms Bolt. We'll be in touch."

The tiger hunters stared at Bess. Then Daz and Penny turned away and went back to loading their belongings into the 4WD.

As if Bess couldn't hear her, Penny asked Daz in her rapid, breathless voice, "Why has that woman come back after you told her not to touch our things?"

"Dunno," said Daz. "We're irresistible, aren't we? Must be my hair."

Matilda stepped forward. "Young lady, I must ask you to leave."

Bess tried to process being called "young lady" at thirty-four. "Well, I'm pretty sure you don't own this bit of land, and you're not meant to be camping here."

Penny piped up, "Actually, parks and wildlife regulations are open to interpretation. Section 43b of the 2005 Act states—"

Daz elbowed her. "Save your breath. Bloody mainlanders always think they know better."

"No, wait!" Bess held up her hand. "I'm not here to cause trouble. I don't want you to leave. I think what you're doing is fascinating."

Matilda looked suspicious. "Is that so?"

"Oh yes. Why shouldn't the Tasmanian tiger be alive? There's so much about nature that humans don't understand. I could totally believe in cryptoids."

"We're not looking for the Loch Ness Monster," Matilda corrected her. "The Tasmanian tiger—or thylacine, to use its correct name—is a native species that lived on this island for thousands of years."

"And you think it's still here?" Bess asked excitedly.

"We think it's a possibility."

"About a forty-five percent possibility," Penny added.

Daz sniffed. "Of course it's bloody here. I've—"

Penny kicked her.

"Well, I think that's terrific," Bess said.

Matilda studied her warily. "Do you indeed?"

"Totally! I work for a modern gallery, and I'm thinking of creating a show about the tiger and the people who think it's still alive. Would you be interested in being photographed and interviewed?"

The women stared at her.

"Is this chick for real?" Daz asked, then went back to arranging the folding table, water cubes, and sleeping bags in the 4WD.

Penny said, "I don't think that's a good idea. I'm not confident I would interview well. I've been told that I talk rather quickly."

"You talk like a monkey on speed," Daz said. "But don't worry; we're not doing any bloody interviews. I'd rather set my own arse on fire."

Stepping in front of them, Matilda told Bess, "I'm afraid interviews are out of the question. Our operation requires privacy. We're only able to work here because the local people have so little to do with outsiders."

"I would keep your whereabouts a secret."

Daz sneered. "Sure."

Penny said in an anxious hiss, "But an expert viewer could still deduce our approximate location based on the terrain in the pictures and the background noise in the interview…"

"Keep your hair on; we're not being bloody interviewed. Grab that esky."

Matilda said to Bess, "I'm sure you would be discreet. But once an interview is in the public domain, people start to do their own sleuthing. And the more you tell them to stay away, the harder they will try to find us. *Nitimur in vetitum:* humans strive for the forbidden. Now, we can cope with naysayers, people attacking our reputations, and calling us mad—"

"Story of my bloody life," Daz grumbled.

"—but there's another type of person who's more worrying," Matilda said. "The type of person who would believe that we'd actually found something. If they thought we were closing in on the thylacine, they would show up here trying to kill the animal, or catch it, or feed it ice cream and take a selfie with it." Matilda's gaze turned steely. "And we cannot permit that."

"So…" Bess paused. "You don't want to do any of those things yourselves, then?"

Penny drew in a horrified breath. "Any one of those actions would be destructive to the species." She turned to Daz, visibly upset. "Why would anyone think us capable of that?"

"Don't worry about it," Daz told her. "Remember how we talked about people being meatheads?"

Matilda turned to Bess. "To answer your question: no. Should we manage to locate the thylacine, we would not harm it, capture it, or disturb it. On the contrary, we would do our damnedest to protect it."

"How?"

"Never you mind. We have our own strategies. Now"—she waved towards the path leading away from the campsite—"if you'd be so kind…?"

"You're not going to leave now, are you?" Bess said. "Honestly, there's no need. I won't tell people you're here."

"Well,"—Matilda glanced at her watch—"it is getting late. We never drive at night; it's dangerous to wildlife. Yes, perhaps we should hold off leaving till tomorrow."

"But you don't have to leave at all. I'll respect your privacy, I promise."

"Hmm." Matilda looked dubious.

There was something else niggling at the back of Bess's mind. Probably she shouldn't bring it up. God knows she didn't want to get dragged further into Vivienne's dramas, and she didn't want to think about poor old angry Ivy's death. But even so…

"What did you mean," she asked, "when you talked about trouble at Crossroads House?"

"What's that?"

"Before. In the bush when I…accidentally disturbed your camera."

This earned a buffalo snort from Daz.

Bess went on, "You said there was trouble at the house and you didn't want to bring it out here."

"Did I?" Matilda looked vague.

Daz and Penny busied themselves with hauling items out of the 4WD once more.

Penny said, "Be careful with that esky; it's got the scat samples for testing."

"What, in with my beer?" Daz slumped. "Fuck's sake…"

Guessing what kind of bait would get these women talking, Bess said, "You know there's a thylacine skull on show in Crossroads House, right? They keep it as a trophy."

Matilda scowled. "Given how much native habitat was destroyed by that wretched family over the years and how many thylacines they probably shot back in the day, I consider that to be in very poor taste. Not that I'm surprised. *Bellum internecinum:* a war of extermination."

"Horrible," Penny said, tugging at her fingers, "to keep a skull locked away uselessly like that instead of subjecting it to proper forensic examination."

"Yeah, well," said Daz, "I heard they had more than a tiger's skull in that house."

Bess looked around. "What do you mean?"

"I dunno. But people used to say the Bolt family had other things there. Things they weren't supposed to have."

"The Bolts and their ill-gotten gains are no concern of ours," said Matilda briskly. "Now, if you don't mind." She ushered Bess away up the path, not turning back until their camp was out of sight.

At the turnoff to Crossroads House, Bess found Ty. She was sitting on a rock and peeping towards the house as if she feared there might be someone on the property she didn't want to meet. Between glances, she fiddled with her phone. Reception was patchy, but it looked like she was searching for someone on social media.

"Hello," said Bess from behind her.

Ty leaped up and sent her phone flying. "Jesus!"

"Well, I always pictured him as a red-headed woman. But no, it's just me."

"Stop sneaking up on people." Ty hunted in the bushes for her phone. "I thought you were...someone else."

"Who?"

"Whoever. Anyone. Maybe one of those weirdoes who live in the woods."

"Weirdoes?"

"You must have seen them. Three crazy old witches in a caravan. They used to come to the house, you know. Scratching around in the bushes and taking photos of the garden beds. I told them I'd call the cops if I busted them again."

"And did you? Call the cops?"

"Me?" Ty laughed nervously. "Nah."

"Well, nice talking to you." Bess headed towards the house.

"Hey, don't run off. We didn't get to talk before." Ty smoothed back her hair. "What do you do for a living?"

"I work for a gallery. We have an office in Melbourne."

"Fancy. Have you got a house there, or...?"

"I live with Margaret," Bess said. "My partner."

"That right? She's a lucky lady."

"I know." Bess smiled politely and kept walking.

Ty hurried after her, still darting nervous glances around the property. "Hey, when are you leaving town?"

"Tomorrow, I think."

"I couldn't get a lift, could I? I've been driving my brother's ute, and he's taken it back cos he's a selfish prick."

Bess imagined the look on Margaret's face if she told her they would be travelling with Ty. "Where do you want to go?"

"Melbourne sounds nice." Ty winked. Did she think Bess was going to pack her in her carry-on luggage? "Nah, seriously, anywhere's good. Hobart, maybe?"

"I'll think about it." Bess wondered what this was about. "Does Ms Bolt know you're thinking of leaving?"

"Hff." Ty glanced up at Crossroads House. "I don't need her permission. But don't say anything to her. Okay?"

Margaret was still musing over what had just happened. Ivy's heavy medication was missing, and Janine Jones had basically broken into the house, hoping to steal something from Ivy's desk.

And there was something else too, something she couldn't put her finger on. Something to do with what she'd seen upstairs…

Frowning, she opened the door to the sitting room. It was empty.

"Bess?" She checked the other rooms on the ground floor. Bess could not have gone upstairs; Margaret had just come from there. Still, she hurried back up to look. No one there.

She tried Bess's phone but got no reply. She looked out the window; their hire car was still where they had left it.

Her chest tightened in anxiety. Surely Bess wouldn't have wandered off. She knew Margaret worried.

Back on the ground floor, she checked the rooms again. The corridor ended in a door with a Yale lock. She tried the handle, but it didn't budge. It must lead to the eastern side of the house, which Vivienne said they'd closed off as it was decrepit and unsafe.

From the other end of the corridor, the front door to the house creaked open.

She rushed back in relief. Bess stood on the doorstep. The gardener with the biceps and the stupid hair was behind her.

Had they been out walking together?

"Where have you been?" Margaret asked.

"And good afternoon to you too."

"I went into the sitting room just now and you'd vanished. No text, no note…"

"You only thought to check on me *now*?" Bess's tone was cool. "I've been gone ages."

"Why would I have checked earlier? You said you were going to take a nap." Margaret was baffled by this reaction. Why did Bess seem cross with her? Surely she, Margaret, was the one with a right to feel cross. "Really, you might have told me you were going out."

"I didn't want to interrupt you." Bess raised her eyebrows. "You'd left me in there for so long; you must have been busy."

"You've never minded interrupting my work before. You've interrupted me while I was working to tell me about a dream you had the night before, and to show me a video of a baby panda, and to make me taste your beetroot brownies, and—"

"Sorry to have inconvenienced you." Where was Bess's usual warmth, her look-on-the-bright-side attitude? Instead, her voice wobbled as if she were a bit angry and hurt.

Margaret couldn't see what she'd done to cause that. "You don't inconvenience me. I'm just saying—"

"Yeah, yeah, I should have left a note." Bess breathed out. "Are you nearly finished here? I'm tired, and I'd like something to eat."

"I… Of course. We can leave now."

As they moved into the house to get their things, Margaret glanced behind them. Ty was leaning against a veranda post, eavesdropping openly. And there was Vivienne, approaching from the back of the property with a curious expression.

Margaret wondered what her exchange with Bess had sounded like to those two and why they both looked so interested.

Chapter 8

DINNER THAT NIGHT WASN'T THE sort of gourmet feast they had planned for this holiday. They ate at the Mount Bastion Chinese restaurant, where the chef/waiter (whose name was Gary) served Margaret a dish of cabbage and seafood extender and Bess a plate of spring rolls full of raisins and shrivelled carrot. Olivia Newton-John played on the sound system. They were the only customers.

Briefly, they told each other what had happened that day, then lapsed into a tense silence. Margaret pushed her meal around, baffled by this change. They had never been short on things to say to each other before.

But Bess was frowning resentfully, which Margaret thought was unreasonable. Wasn't it obvious that she, Margaret, was the wronged one here? Bess had snuck out in secret to wander around in the dangerous woods with that gardener, leaving Margaret to worry, without even apologising afterwards.

All Margaret had done was price antiques as a favour to Vivienne. What was wrong with that? Bess was always saying "Look for the helpers" and "Be the change you want to see in the world". Well, Margaret had been helping, doing positive things for others, just as Bess wanted her to. Surely.

Granted, she could admit to herself that her mission to help Vivienne had been a bit of a letdown, that Vivienne probably was not in as desperate peril as Margaret had assumed. And yes, things had gotten a bit peculiar towards the end. She felt uneasy at the memory of Vivienne's moss green eyes, Vivienne's fingers stroking the air an inch from Margaret's, Vivienne's teasing voice saying, "Guess what day it is".

The thought made her flinch. None of that was supposed to happen.

But surely Bess didn't think Margaret was encouraging Vivienne's... close attention?

Still, perhaps she was reading too much into the whole situation— perhaps Vivienne spoke like that to everyone. Margaret was hopeless with social cues, as plenty of people had pointed out over the years. Either way, she hadn't done anything improper herself, and she didn't want to. There was no reason for Bess to be so prickly.

Giving up on conversation, they both checked their phones.

Bess left a voicemail for her employer, explaining that she wanted to pitch them a concept for a new show about tiger hunters and would send a written proposal later. She had met some hunters in person, she added, and they would be perfect subjects for a quirky exhibition, except for their reluctance to appear in one. But she was working on it.

"What if they keep saying no?" Margaret asked after she hung up.

"I don't know. Maybe I could still create an exhibition. I could interview the locals for any old tiger stories and see if the national museum would lend us a stuffed thylacine and some relevant artworks..."

"I'm sure you can craft a good show." Margaret hated to be childish, but she couldn't help envying Bess. She used to design exhibitions herself.

With a sigh, she checked her emails. There was one from Deirdre's podiatrist seeking two hundred dollars in outstanding fees, one from Deirdre's hairdresser (six heartbroken paragraphs; Margaret had no idea they'd been so close), and one from the florist who did Deidre's funeral, reminding Margaret to please leave an online review.

Her stomach clenched painfully.

"Messages about Deirdre?" Bess's voice was gentler this time.

"How could you tell?"

"You get a certain look. Like you're sucking a lemon."

"Can you blame me?" Margaret hit Delete with more force than necessary. "It turns out death isn't a blessed relief from earthly cares. People keep right on pestering you, spamming you, and sending you bills."

"That stuff is upsetting. But it's not how we have to remember people who've passed over. Have you thought any more about—"

Knowing she was going to ask again what to do with Deirdre's remains, Margaret snapped, "No, I haven't. But don't worry: it's on my list of things to do. Right after cancelling her Netflix subscription."

Margaret shouldn't have said that. She hadn't meant to sound so ungrateful and nasty. It had been totally unwarranted.

Bess only sighed. "It's your decision." Then she looked back down at her phone. After an unpleasant minute, she said, "Remember Dorian Visser, that local historian who wrote a book about Crossroads House? He's giving a reading tonight in the next town. We could go."

Margaret didn't want to, and Bess didn't sound keen herself. But what else was there to do? Go back to their motel room and watch television in silence?

"If you like."

As they paid the bill, she noticed that Bess didn't ask Gary for his life story, praise him for his unconventional approach to cooking, or tell him that Olivia Newton-John was a national treasure. She didn't say anything positive at all.

Bess must be feeling very unhappy indeed.

"Be warned," said Dorian Visser. "What I am about to tell you may frighten you."

Bess hoped so. A spine-tingling ghost story would be a welcome distraction from the grating atmosphere between her and Margaret. They sat stiffly in the back row of the library. The plastic chairs were set close together, but they both held themselves so their elbows and shoulders wouldn't touch.

Dorian Visser wore the same outfit as on his posters: Akubra hat, trailing scarf, silver-topped walking stick, and a look of great importance. Freshly printed copies of his book were piled beside him. They looked self-published. He had a loud, slow way of speaking as if he suspected them of not paying attention.

"Thirty-five years ago," he said, "when I was a young man—the youngest ever to run a successful real estate agency in southern Hobart—I was taking a well-earned break and driving through this part of Tasmania. Late one night, my car broke down on Renfeld Lane. This was in the days before mobile phones, so I sat there cursing the thought of walking into town, although I was in good shape and had recently completed a charity walkathon to raise money for victims of tinnitus."

Bess glanced at the clock. This might have been a mistake.

Dorian coughed ominously. "Then I saw a light. Through the trees, there was a crumbling old mansion, and the window of a top-storey room was lit up. In it, I saw the figure of a little girl in a blue nightdress. I saw her in the distance as clearly as you are seeing me now. I had twenty-twenty vision back then and a talent for observing all relevant details. The girl looked through the darkness at me and waved. Thinking what a godsend this was, I left my car and hurried to the house to ask the family I assumed lived there if I could use their phone."

He drummed his walking stick on the carpet.

"An old woman came to the door. She let me use the phone; luckily, I'd memorised the number of a roadside assistance company using a special cognitive retrieval technique invented by CIA agents."

He dropped into a creepy whisper. "But the woman was a widow who lived alone. She said there hadn't been any children in the house for years.

"As I waited by the car for roadside assistance to arrive, I was distracted by a white object moving through the trees. No sooner would it appear in one part of the woods than it would vanish and reappear in another. Was it darting so quickly that my eyes could not follow it? From a distance it looked like a dog, but when I moved closer, I saw the black stripes on its flank and realised this was no mortal animal. It was a ghost of the ancient creatures that once inhabited this landscape. Later, I heard a local story: that the tiger would lure travellers into the bush, enticing them to follow deeper and deeper until they became lost and vanished forever."

Bess sat taller, interested at last. A local myth like that would make a great addition to her show.

To her disappointment, however, Dorian moved on. "I continued with my travels and running my successful business, but I never forgot what I'd seen that night. After retiring, I resumed my studies, completing a doctorate by correspondence from the School of Paranormal Studies in Wichita, USA. I began touring historic buildings in my home state of Tasmania which were rumoured to be high in supernatural activity. For details, see my published works. But it was that first locale, Crossroads House, which started it all and whose mysteries I was determined to probe deeply."

"Gross," Bess mumbled.

Margaret's lips twitched as if she were amused but determined not to show it. They were still at odds, then.

Dorian Visser said, "Crossroads House was built in 1835, and horror is in its DNA. When the foundations were being laid, a young stableboy was cleaning a Smith & Wesson revolver nearby when it went off, killing him and spattering his blood and brains over the construction site. The labourers were horrified, but the cruel master of the house insisted they keep to their schedule and go on laying the stones and cement. And so the house came to be held together with the blood of innocents."

Margaret's throat must be dry, for she stifled a cough. Bess offered her a water bottle, then an organic sugar-free lozenge, both of which Margaret refused. While still coughing.

"Okay, what is wrong with you?" Bess muttered as quietly as she could. "I know why I'm cross, but I can't see why you should be."

"Can't you, indeed?" Margaret had the ability to speak through a clenched jaw. The angry words just projected from her somehow. "Perhaps it has something to do with you wandering off into the woods in pursuit of some people you knew were violent, armed lunatics when you had told me you wouldn't. Call me a stick-in-the-mud, but I don't think it was wise."

"The tiger women aren't violent, armed lunatics," Bess protested. "They just believe in something most people don't. They pushed me over once, and they have a gun for shooting pigeons. That's all."

"I stand *un*corrected."

A woman in the next row turned around. *"Shh!"*

They subsided into sulky silence.

Up front, Dorian continued. "Every generation that grew up in Crossroads House was warped by tragedy. In 1872, the lady of the house, a famous English beauty, Lady Jade Doyle, fell to her death from the attic window. Had she taken her own life in despair when she couldn't escape her husband, Charles, to be with her lover, Albert? Or had Charles killed her because he loved her too much to let her go to another man? They say if you sleep in the bedroom below, at the stroke of midnight you'll see a white shape flash past the window and hear footsteps running from the attic..."

Bess looked at Margaret, who was glaring straight ahead. Did she seriously think she was the aggrieved one? Under her breath, Bess asked, "If you're so worried about my safety, why did you leave me alone in that creepy old house?"

Margaret looked baffled. "You weren't alone. I was in the next room with Vivienne."

"Oh, right. Your ex-girlfriend slash drug dealer."

"I beg your pardon?" Margaret whispered loudly.

The woman in front turned around and glared at them again.

Bess waited until their neighbour had turned back around before whispering to Margaret, "Well, you said her grandmother's medication went missing while Vivienne was in charge. She wouldn't be the first person to sell the stuff."

"That is"—Margaret almost laughed—"preposterous."

From out front, Dorian said, "Then Jade's infant son died in agony of fire after a maid knocked a candle into his bedclothes. Afterwards, the maid went mad with guilt and hanged herself so the family would have justice."

Geez, this was morbid. Bess wrinkled her nose.

Margaret said in an undertone, "If anyone at that house has been stealing pills and selling them, it's your new friend, the gardener. She sounds as reliable as a nine-dollar bill."

Why did Margaret bring up Ty? Bess wasn't interested in her and was confident she hadn't done anything wrong in talking to her. But she was so cross with Margaret that she couldn't resist retorting, "Well, Ty is certainly a smooth operator. Very charming."

Margaret snorted.

"She asked me for a lift back to Hobart."

"Did she indeed? Well, why stop there? Why not give her the car keys and leave me to hitchhike back?"

"I didn't say yes, for goodness—" Bess bit her tongue. This was ridiculous. She pretended to listen to Dorian's speech instead.

He was flinging his arms around, apparently ready to tell terrible tales all night. "In 1900, Raewyn, the daughter of the house who was known to be simple-minded, got into trouble and gave birth to a bastard son. Her father was furious but relented to her pleas to keep the child—as long as no one ever saw him. So the poor boy was kept locked up in the cellar for fifteen years! Until one night he got free and burst from the house, leaving a trail of bodies behind him."

The ghastly stories were not helping Bess's mood. She pointed out to Margaret, "By the way, it wasn't just you and Vivienne in the house while I was asleep. According to you, there was also a stranger creeping around. And you still didn't think to check that I was safe?"

"Janine Jones?" Margaret rolled her eyes. "What would she have done—bored you to death? Vivienne must be in bad shape to put up with that woman. It's pitiful that she doesn't have the strength to kick her out."

"Hmm." Bess crossed her arms tighter. "And yet she's got the strength to keep you in."

"I don't know what that means. You're being tiresomely cryptic."

Unable to hold in her frustration, Bess said in a hiss that grew louder with each word, "Does Vivienne have no friends? Why are you the one doing everything for her?"

"What are you talking about? It was *your* idea to help her."

Bess flung up her hands. "I meant we should send her flowers and a card. Maybe a nice lavender diffuser to promote wellness. I didn't mean you should spend the entire day with her. Why don't you move in and be done with it?"

Dorian boomed, "This is intolerable!" He swiped his walking stick in their direction, nearly taking out the front row. "How much longer must I talk over this racket? Ladies, if you cannot bring yourselves to respect me as a historian, author, and paranormal expert, you might at least show some respect for the heritage of this area, to which you are strangers. Some people are here to learn."

Margaret scowled. "Well, they won't learn much from you." Picking a fight with her was never a good idea. Margaret rounded on the guest speaker. "Crossroads House was *not* built in 1835. The estate itself might have existed then, but the oldest parts of the building date to at least thirty years later."

"Yeah." Provoked, Bess glared at Dorian too. "And by the way, your framing of suicide, domestic violence, and disability is very problematic."

"The Smith & Wesson pistol wasn't invented until the 1850s," Margaret said, clearly warming up, "so it could not have caused a stableboy's death twenty years earlier."

As Dorian turned purple with outrage, she went on, "Moreover, the name Jade didn't come into popular use until the 1970s. So it's highly unlikely that the lady of the house would have had that name a hundred years before."

"Also, your stories also include too many irrelevant details about yourself," Bess threw in.

"And it's not possible to see the upstairs windows of Crossroads House from the road," Margaret finished in a ringing voice.

A vein pulsed in Dorian's forehead. *"Out!"*

The dark car park was shockingly cold, making Bess shiver and pull on her Viking hat. The two women looked at each other.

Margaret said, "I've never been thrown out of a book reading before."

"No. Who knew they had security guards?"

"Well, that was some of the most ahistorical, unscientific drivel I've ever heard."

"Yeah. Never trust a man who wears a hat indoors. It means he's got something to hide."

Silence fell. Bess supposed they should head back to the car, but the clear wintery air and the memory of being united against Dorian felt cleansing somehow.

Margaret coughed. "Look... I'm sorry I neglected you today. I was put out that you didn't want to look at the antiques with me—"

"I was just tired!" But having shouted out her frustrations at the ghost hunter, Bess felt calmer.

"I know. I was utterly unreasonable. But there's nothing...untoward going on with Vivienne. And she was never my girlfriend." Margaret wrinkled her nose at the word as if she found it frivolous. "We met once when we were young; she helped me out of a dangerous situation and gave me some good advice. That's all. I would never betray you, Bess."

Margaret's words seemed to hang like the pale cloud of her breath in the night air. Her face looked tense; her bottom lip was pinched between her teeth.

Bess was fond of that lip and didn't like to see it punished, didn't want Margaret to look so worried and despondent. She believed Margaret.

"All right." Bess sighed. "And I know it was reckless of me to follow those women today. I'm sorry about that. But I don't think they're dangerous, except to the odd pigeon." She looked hard at Margaret. "And you know I'm not interested in Ty, right? For Pete's sake, I saw inside her garden shed: she uses commercial pesticides and rat poison! She's not my type at all." Bess linked her bare fingers through Margaret's gloved ones. "Besides, I told her I'm already spoken for."

Margaret looked down at their joined hands, her face working with some tightly contained emotion. Then she leaned in until her forehead rested against the crown of Bess's Viking hat. "I told Vivienne the same thing."

Relaxing into their embrace, Bess inhaled the dark scent of Margaret's perfume and felt the heat of her breath, the only source of warmth in the cool air. Their lips brushed together lightly at first, then Margaret wound her hand through Bess's hair and pulled her in hard and close.

Bess wrapped her arms around Margaret's waist, pressing the full length of their bodies together. The rhythm of their kissing was sweetly familiar, but there was an urgency to it which took her by surprise.

Her belly fluttered with excitement as Margaret coaxed her lips apart with her tongue, her grip on Bess's head tightening. A melting sensation trickled deliciously down Bess's spine, and she moaned as Margaret flexed one leg between her thighs and tugged with her teeth at her bottom lip. She'd had girlfriends before Margaret, but no one else had ever touched her with such focus and intensity, such passion.

When they drew apart, her mouth tingled with the imprint of Margaret's kiss. "God, what are we doing here?"

"Apart from risking frostbite and making Mr Visser's book reading look far more interesting than it is?" Margaret raised an eyebrow. "Nothing."

"Do you want to go?"

"Oh yes."

Margaret locked the motel room door and backed across the narrow space to the bed, pulling Bess after her. They paused, shedding coats and shoes in between kisses. Bess stumbled and grabbed Margaret for balance.

Her companion's carefree laugher and loving touch made Margaret wonder why they had been out of sorts earlier that evening. What a foolish waste of time that had been.

"I want to tell you something." Margaret paused long enough to rip the cover off the bed and hurl it away. She refused to let those germ-ridden things near her person or her precious Bess.

"Mm?" Bess sighed as Margaret sank onto the bed and pulled her close, one knee nudging up between her legs, rumpling and lifting her skirt. "What is it?"

"I want…" Margaret pressed her mouth to her beloved's throat, kissing her fiercely. "I want to help you."

"Well, you're being very helpful now…" Bess combed her fingers through Margaret's hair, scraping close to the scalp with a firm pressure the way Margaret liked it.

"I mean it. I know I was helping…Vivienne." She pulled back and took Bess's face between her hands. "But please don't imagine I think that's more important than doing things for you."

A look of doubt crossed Bess's face, and Margaret pressed their foreheads together, hoping the closeness, the mingling of their breath would reassure her. "Let me prove it. Let me help you with your thylacine exhibition. I'll do anything."

"My…? You want to talk about that now?" Bess broke into a grin as she was pulled down to straddle Margaret's lap. It was clear she thought Margaret's timing curious, but unlike most people, she seemed to like the stranger sides to her. What a blessing that was.

"Whatever you need," Margaret vowed. "I'll source old photographs for you. Chase up copyrights. Negotiate artefact loans. Write object labels."

"You realise you're just describing things you like doing?"

"I'll even help you interview those mad women in the woods."

"You don't have to do all that." Bess gave Margaret a puzzled look. "What's gotten into you?"

"I want you to succeed. To do the things that matter to you. That… matters to me." Margaret looked hard at her, willing this woman to understand that, however bad she might be at expressing herself, she wanted Bess to be happy. Wanted her to triumph. "You know that, don't you?"

Bess smiled, the delicate pink shade of her lips making Margaret think of cherry blossoms. Then she leaned forward and kissed the swirl of Margaret's ear, tracing it with her mouth. Such a teasing sensation in a sensitive place… She bit her lip to hold back a cry.

Margaret made swift work of the buttons on Bess's sweater and blouse. She loved undressing Bess, loved using her hands and tongue to make Bess quake with need and then sigh in deep satisfaction. Taking charge was what Margaret excelled at. Often, though, she hesitated about letting Bess return the favour, never entirely easy about accepting the joy that another woman's touch could bring. It seemed a little too risky sometimes, a little too… personal.

But after so many passionate exchanges tonight, so many things thrown wide open, she did not feel the need to guard herself. What purpose did it serve when she knew she would be lost without Bess?

As she slid open the last few buttons and peeled off Bess's blouse, a hot pulse hammered between her thighs. With her cheek pressed against Bess's throat, she heard and felt her beloved hum with enjoyment. Then Bess squeezed one hand into the tight space between them, past Margaret's waistband and lower.

"Oh, you are divine." Margaret lowered her face into the luscious freckled curves of Bess's cleavage, burying a groan in all that lovely flesh. Bess's breath caught as Margaret snapped open the clasp of her lace bra and flung it aside. And this time when Bess unzipped Margaret's trousers and slid her hand right inside, Margaret didn't feel any hesitance at all.

She held Bess in place and kissed each taut pale pink nipple, applying a hot pressure while the surging rhythm of their bodies pushed Bess's fingers back and forth just where Margaret needed them. She arched closer, her own need dragging her hips forward, panting for more touch where it felt most tender, more connection with this woman who understood her.

Still, as Bess pushed gently at her shoulders, making to tilt her back onto the mattress, she resisted. Margaret couldn't bear to need so much straight away, to accept so much so quickly. Instead, she wrestled Bess out of her skirt and underwear before pulling her close once more until Bess's soft, sturdy bare limbs were wrapped around her. Margaret kissed her way down to her beloved's shoulder, then slid a hand underneath to cup and strum and caress her.

"Oh, you drive me crazy…" But Bess did not sound sorry about it. She flung her head back, her long, wild hair trailing almost to the mattress, accepting Margaret's touch without hesitation.

Margaret pressed her own thighs together, a wonderful ache spreading through her in response to the gasps and twitches of pleasure she was eliciting from the woman in her arms. She concentrated hard on caressing that slick, sweet place while Bess clawed at her back, crushing Margaret's shirt and digging desperate fingertips into her skin.

"I love you," Margaret moaned, just before Bess cried out and fell forward against her.

Expecting her to be exhausted, Margaret was taken by surprise when Bess revived almost immediately.

She pushed at Margaret's shoulders with determination, until Margaret gave in to Bess's wishes and her own and lay back.

Bess craned forward on one elbow, her hair tumbling across Margaret's face, her flushed cheeks and shining eyes taking up Margaret's whole field of vision. She pushed impatiently through her lover's clothing and took up where she'd left off, her wrist flexing against Margaret's quaking belly, her fingers massaging the woman beneath her with a slow, hard grinding pressure.

Margaret struggled to draw breath, unable to believe her luck at finding someone who understood that too much gentleness in that moment would have felt like cobwebs against her skin, would have made her flinch and jerk away. But this…

She gripped Bess's hips, relishing the ample flesh, the weight and substance of her. With each touch from Bess, Margaret's hips arched higher, her breaths hoarse and panting. Normally, she would not have given in to her own longing so completely, would not have permitted herself to be quite so vulnerable in another woman's presence, but those old restraints had dissolved. Now she was nothing but sensation, her whole body alive with it…until those feelings clenched into a single point of heat and light, then broke apart, cascading in a thousand pieces through the dark.

She collapsed back, Bess's arms and legs still around her, her sighs muffled in Bess's hair.

Chapter 9

LATER, AS THEY LAY BETWEEN the crisp white sheets, Margaret asked, "What's our plan of attack, then, for making your show a success?"

Bess laughed slightly and rolled her eyes. She'd held off from speaking as they'd changed their clothes and slipped into bed, trying to give Margaret space. She knew what had just passed between them was more intense, more high stakes than their usual intimacy, and she had wondered if there were other things Margaret might want to say. Other points of vulnerability she might wish to reveal at last.

But no, of course Margaret wanted to talk about a bloody museum display. It was a little exasperating but also endearing. Some people didn't change quickly.

She tickled Margaret's ribs. "You're serious about helping me with this show?"

"Of course. You didn't think I just said it to gain your favours, did you?"

"No, I don't suppose you would take advantage of a girl like that." Bess skated her fingers down Margaret's silk pyjama top, relishing the heat of her flesh that thrummed beneath it. The slippery fabric felt decadent against Bess's bare skin as they lay close together. She loved the feel of fresh sheets against her naked body, but Margaret never slept nude. As she pointed out, you never knew when there might be an emergency.

"Well, I can source material on the thylacine any time," Bess continued, "but right now I need to decide what to say about Mount Bastion and the people here." Suddenly energised, she propped herself up on one elbow.

"Have you noticed how many of them have some kind of tiger connection? Dorian Visser claims a ghost tiger lured him into the bush. Janine Jones broke into Crossroads House supposedly to find an old letter about her ancestor killing tiger cubs. Alan Moore has photos of tiger hunters in his shop. Even Ty has a tiger tattooed on her ankle."

"Confirmation bias," Margaret warned. "Become too focused on any topic, and you start to see it everywhere."

"Well, maybe, but what about poor Ivy?" Bess sat up suddenly at her new thought. "She had that skull on display near the staircase. What if she bumped into it and it caused her fall?" It was an awful thought, but it appealed to her sense of the dramatic. "Imagine: the last member of a family who led the extermination of the tigers in that district killed by the remains of a creature her ancestors probably slaughtered. It would be such a tragic illustration of humans' destructive relationship with the natural world."

"Very evocative," Margaret agreed dryly, "except that Ivy wasn't the last member of that family. Remember?"

"Oh. Right." But Bess didn't feel like talking about Vivienne now. Instead she said, "Obviously, I need to interview those women who are searching for the tiger; the footage would be great. But I could also weave in stories about this town and the way the tiger features in local people's lives. I could commission artists to create paintings or installations or…"

"Hold your horses. Not everyone likes being talked about. You don't want to get sued."

"Relax. We get legal advice for our shows. And I can fictionalise things a bit; we're an experimental gallery, remember?"

"Normally I would despise that approach, but in this case it might be best."

Bess nuzzled the curve of Margaret's neck, savouring her warmth. "You will help me, then?"

"I said I would." Margaret sighed in contentment as Bess slid a hand under her pyjama top and stroked her flat stomach. The muscles worked as she lifted herself a little. "I'm afraid we're stuck in this part of the island slightly longer anyhow. I didn't tell you earlier, but the police contacted me. They want formal statements from us tomorrow about our visit to Crossroads House."

"Oh." Bess frowned. "What does that mean?"

"I've no idea. It may be standard procedure. But it means we couldn't leave the area right away even if we wanted to." Margaret's words turned brisk. "So what do you need from me?"

"Well…" Trying not to dwell on Ivy's death, Bess returned to her idea for an exhibition. "While I might fictionalise the details about this town in my show, I'd still like to know the facts about the locals and their thylacine connections. That letter about Janine's tiger-hunting ancestor, for one thing. Why was it so important that she would break into a house to retrieve it? If that was her real reason."

"I could check out the local historical society," Margaret said. "They might have more tiger paraphernalia in their collection. And if the conversation happens to turn to their president and her housebreaking activities…"

"You think one of Janine's colleagues will gossip about her?"

"Someone that domineering and self-satisfied, living in a small town? If she doesn't have enemies, I'll eat your Viking hat."

"Perfect. Then there's Dorian the ghost hunter. I'd like to know why he said he saw a tiger spirit lurking around Crossroads House. Along with other ghosts, apparently."

Bess paused, thinking. While she'd seen nothing at Crossroads House that couldn't be explained, and while she suspected Dorian Visser was a liar, there was something about the house that made her uneasy. "I'll look for his books online."

"You're a glutton for punishment."

"And if he lives locally, I could reach out to him and apologise for disrupting his event."

Margaret curled her lip disdainfully. "Really?"

"Come on, we were pretty rude. I should say sorry. It's a karmic thing. And then if I should happen to ask a few questions…"

"Which he will answer, since he loves the sound of his own voice."

Bess grinned. "And I'd like to find out more about Alan Moore. He said he visits the old houses around here, and he knew about Ivy's family's tiger hunts and that skull on her landing."

"Well, I could contact some old colleagues in the antiques trade. Ask what they can tell me about Mr Moore and any association with tiger relics."

"And while we're at it," said Bess, "I'd like to know what's going on with Ty. Why is she still hanging around that house, looking so jumpy and talking about leaving town?"

"You could ask her. She seems to enjoy talking to you." But Margaret's tone was only lightly barbed this time.

"She never told me much." Bess thought back. "I could contact her brother. She called him a selfish prick; I assume they've fallen out. Maybe he'll tell me why she's acting so strangely."

"I'm not sure that's relevant." Margaret frowned. "She sounded untrustworthy to me, and her brother might be just as bad. If you insist on seeing him, I'll come too."

"Deal." Bess smiled, surprised to find Margaret being so accommodating. "And look, I'll take care what I say in public about Ivy's death. But if she did have tiger relics in her house, I'd like to know the details. And there was something Daz said..."

"Who?"

"One of those women in the woods. When I mentioned the skull at Crossroads House, she said, 'I heard they had more than a tiger's skull in that house'. She said there were rumours that the Bolt family owned things they weren't supposed to. What do you think that means?"

"I've no idea."

"You don't think Ivy could have had a tiger skin? Or a complete skeleton? Or a taxidermized one?" Bess wriggled with excitement. "I researched that stuff earlier; full thylacine remains in good condition are really rare. If she owned something like that, it would be amazing."

"That's a big if. You're basing this on a remark by some mulletted survivalist living in a caravan full of frozen faeces."

"She had a few sealed samples in an esky. For testing."

"To see if they were made by an animal that's been extinct for a century?" Margaret shook her head. "Well, if you want to know more about that skull and any other thylacine items owned by Ivy, I could take another look around Crossroads House. Ivy was supposed to have kept an inventory book for her antiques." She looked cautiously at Bess. "However, that would mean seeing Vivienne again."

Bess just smiled. She'd been wrong about Margaret and Vivienne, she decided. Vivienne might have her eye on Margaret, but surely it wasn't reciprocated. "I don't mind. But I'll come and help with *that*."

Margaret relaxed into a smile. "Thank you. A marvellous thing, teamwork."

"Amazing what you can achieve." Bess chewed her lip. "Listen... What do you think happened to Ivy's missing medication?"

Margaret started. "Why do you ask? It's hardly relevant to your exhibition."

"No, but I'm curious. Aren't you?"

"Perhaps, but it's not our problem. As Vivienne said, it's most likely Ivy threw the stuff away. If anything untoward happened—like that gardener stealing the stuff to sell it, for instance—it's a police matter."

"True." Bess pushed out her lower lip. "And you know the police will never tell us what they found."

"Does it matter?"

"It's a mystery," said Bess. "Of course it matters."

Margaret sighed. "If it's so interesting to you, I suppose we could make inquiries."

"About stolen opioids in Mount Bastion?" The thought made Bess laugh. "What are we going to do: ask people in the general store or get on the dark web?"

"No." Margaret rubbed her eyes, then rose and padded across to her phone. "But I know someone who could."

"Hillbilly heroin?" From eight hundred kilometres away, Zan tutted. "I'm disappointed in you, M. I thought we'd had the drugs talk."

"Yes, very droll." Margaret sat on the edge of the bed. Bess reached up to stroke her back. "Can you help me?"

Calling Zan late at night was never a problem. It was during the day that her burner phones went unanswered. Margaret had been careful to keep a number, knowing it might come in handy.

Back in Port Bannir, Zan and her mates, Tammy and Squid, had lived in shabby digs out the back of Zan's grandmother's house and made a living from being better and more ruthless with technology than anyone else in town. Whether you wanted a cyber-stalking ex out of your life or incriminating messages erased forever, the girls could take care of it.

Nowadays, they lived in the city and their flat was somewhat nicer (well, they had furniture), so Margaret assumed whatever they did now must pay all right.

Whenever Zan picked up the phone, you could count on hearing three things in the background: the hiss of a can of soft drink being opened, the *bleep* and *ack-ack-ack* of vintage video games, and the sound of Tammy and Squid arguing over which Hogwarts houses their favourite DC superheroes would be in.

"Diana Prince is in Ravenclaw, you total arsehead!"

Margaret pinched the bridge of her nose. "I do hope I'm not interrupting something important."

"Always," said Zan. "So you want us to find out where you can buy oxy in some weird little town in Tassie?"

"I just need to know who's selling it."

"Right. I'll ask them for their full name and star sign." Zan yawned audibly. "Usual rate?"

"I'll post the cheque in a birthday card. Quick as you can, please."

"M, I've told you before: never mind if the other kids tell you drugs are cool. Just say no."

"Goodnight, Zan."

"Hey, M?" It wasn't like Zan to sound worried. "You're not doing anything stupid, are you?"

"I live a quiet life nowadays. You know that."

"Right." She could almost hear Zan rolling her eyes. "And Squid's training for the triathlon."

Bess woke at four a.m. She never slept well in motel rooms; their walls were paper-thin, and the feng shui was atrocious. Margaret slumbered beside her. Bored, she reached for her phone and searched for the local library to see if they had a video channel.

"Yes," she whispered, plugging in headphones, then opening the file for Dorian's event. She skipped through to the point where she and Margaret had been kicked out. Then she watched the last ten minutes of the talk.

Dorian was waving his walking stick and exclaiming, "Imagine the horror I felt—even I, an expert scientist of the paranormal—to hear the news of Ivy Bolt's *murder*."

Bess sat upright in bed.

"Old Mrs Bolt was a brave woman and a dear friend who recognised the value of my work while refusing to be cowed by the malignant spirits with whom she was forced to share her home. But they got to her in the end. God knows, I'd warned her. The evil miasma that hangs over that house causes civilised people to do the most terrible things. Crossroads House has claimed another victim... And I fear she will not be the last."

Margaret rolled over, mumbling, "What are you doing?"

"Sorry." Bess gestured for her to go back to sleep. Not wanting to disrupt her further, Bess lay down again, but she kept staring at the screen.

Dorian's declaration had been the climax of the event. He took a bow, that superior smile back on his face.

Bess was gobsmacked. He'd just described Ivy's death as murder. With no proof and at a public event!

In the morning, she'd tell Margaret... And she supposed they'd better tell Vivienne. Bess didn't like or trust Vivienne, but the woman had a right to know what was being said about her family.

Why would Dorian say that? To sell books, perhaps? She wrinkled her nose. What an awful way to behave. Maybe Dorian could justify telling gruesome stories about Crossroads House in the olden days, but it was a different matter to cash in on the fate of a woman who had only died this week. And claiming she'd died by violence—well, that was totally unacceptable.

And untrue, obviously.

Bess put her phone down, trying to ignore the discomfort that crept through her. There was no reason to feel that way. All they knew was that a frail, elderly woman had suffered a fall at home and died. Sadly, that was not unusual. In all likelihood, there was nothing else to know.

Except for Vivienne's stories of thefts and noises in the house, of course. And the threats to Ivy's carers, and the falling shutter which Vivienne swore had been pushed. And Janine hunting through Ivy's things. And those missing drugs...

Bess rolled over. *Leave it alone.*

She and Margaret would make their statements to the police, and from then on, they would have nothing to do with any investigation into Ivy's death. They'd been caught up in a suspicious death once before, and while the experience had brought them together, she had no wish to repeat it.

Still, her brain whirled, and she wondered what Ivy had been doing out of bed that night. She could not have been headed to the bathroom; Margaret said it was in the opposite direction. Perhaps she was confused by drugs, but Vivienne said she avoided those. And maybe she'd had a touch of dementia—she certainly had said some odd things—but she had seemed sharp enough most of the time.

Bess thumped the pillow, trying to get comfortable.

Those tiger women had talked about trouble at Crossroads House too. *Stop. This. Right. Now.*

If anything was wrong about Ivy's death—and there was probably nothing—it was up to the authorities to sort out. Bess's only job was to plan an exhibition so she could leave her lousy job, jumpstart her career, and revive her relationship with Margaret. Weren't those things more important?

Of course they were. Bess rolled onto her side, shut her eyes, and breathed deeply, ordering herself to sleep.

Chapter 10

Margaret took a sip of petrol station coffee and shuddered at the taste of sludge and diesel. Still, it was stronger than the instant rubbish at the motel. When Margaret had left, Bess was sitting cross-legged on the bed, cueing up Tibetan chanting on her phone, explaining she was about to meditate on her intentions for a successful day. Margaret kissed her and wished her well but said she could achieve the same results with caffeine.

Now she took another mouthful, grimaced, and looked across the empty highway and the fields beyond.

On the horizon sat the mountain that gave Mount Bastion its name. The eastern side had been stripped bare by logging, leaving a bald wasteland scattered with broken branches. Margaret found it depressing and vaguely sinister. Nothing could be alive there now, not a single bird, snake, or insect. She thought of the women Bess had met, hunkered down in the remaining bushland, searching for an animal that was long dead, and felt a flicker of pity and annoyance. How could they think there was hope?

She shook her head, then picked up her phone. Bess had said that after she finished her meditation, she would write a formal pitch to her employers for her proposed exhibition. It would need some content.

"Margaret?" Even at seven thirty in the morning, her old colleague Maximillian sounded like he was wearing a bowtie and a three-piece suit. "Dear lady, what an unexpected pleasure."

"How are you, Max?"

"Frightful. Auction house so busy I might as well sleep there. My back's giving me grief. And Cleopatra has been pissing in the kitchen sink. She resents my working long hours."

"You knew Siamese cats were high-maintenance when you got her," Margaret said. "Listen, I'm sorry about this, but I need a favour."

"If you want me to ask Élevé to take you back, forget it. They still call you Cruella." Maximillian chuckled. "I enjoyed your dominatrix style, Margaret, but I was in the minority."

"How flattering." Usually Margaret rather enjoyed being reminded of her ability to scare idiots into line, but the memory of being sacked took the pleasure out of it. "It's not that. I just wondered: do you know anything about an antiques dealer in Tasmania called Alan Moore?" She crossed her fingers. Maximillian knew everything about everybody in the antiques trade. It made him a useful friend, if an untrustworthy one.

"Moore?" Maximillian took a sip of something. She guessed it was coffee of a far superior brew to the one in her own hand. Served in a gold-trimmed fine-bone Royal Albert mug too. "Alan Moore? Small town, cheap suit, rough trade?"

"Sounds right."

"Oh yes, I know Alan. I gave him his first proper job, in fact. Picked him out of our warehouse twenty years ago. He had a remarkable eye. Brought home delectable little pieces from op shops and garage sales and restored them beautifully. Completely self-taught. Never went to university, never fit in with all the yacht club, private school boys around here. I think his father built fences for a living." Maximillian tutted. "Alan always had a bit of a chip on his shoulder about that. Why do you ask?"

"I'm in a town called Mount Bastion in Tasmania, and he's here. Running an antiques shop."

"Ah yes. Alan was going to start his own place. He had grand plans to revive his home town and attract tourists, wine merchants, B&B owners. Well, why not? Other chaps managed it in other places."

"But Alan didn't?"

"No. Poor Alan. He overstretched himself on a loan and fell out with a business partner. Now I imagine he's broke and trapped there unless he sells at a loss. A damned shame. As I say, he was talented and loved his work. Still, that's no guarantee of success—as you know, Margaret."

She winced; Maximillian was merciless even towards his friends. "Do you know if Alan ever sold relics of the Tasmanian tiger?"

"Goodness, I've no idea. I don't recall him having much love for taxidermy, if that's what you mean. He was offered a stuffed chimpanzee once and refused it. Said he didn't want his shop looking like the Bates motel."

"Hmm." So much for that. "And did you hear of him having dealings with a collector called Ivy Bolt?"

"Bolt…" She heard a creak and pictured Maximillian leaning back in his exquisitely restored Victorian carved oak throne chair. "Not that old harpy in the haunted house? Tongue like a stockwhip? Bags of money but probably used old newspaper in the outhouse?"

"That sounds like her. She's just died."

"Well, a few collectors will be cheering. She was ruthless when she wanted something. I never heard of Alan having anything to do with her, though. She'd have eaten him alive."

"Did you? Have anything to do with her?"

"Me?" Maximillian chuckled. "Not my area of expertise, dear. Mrs Bolt had more…exotic tastes than I could cater to."

"Exotic? What does that mean?"

"Ask me no questions and I'll tell you no lies." His tone turned brisk. "You know me, I never gossip about my colleagues.'

Margaret frowned. "Max? Why the sudden attack of discretion?"

"Got to go, dear lady. Cleopatra is eating my butterfly orchid. Nice talking to you."

"Max—" But he'd hung up, leaving Margaret to finish her petrol slick coffee in silence.

"Thanks for coming on a stakeout," Bess told Margaret. They watched from their car as Ty left her house, strolled into the neighbours' place, and got a lift in the their hatchback.

"Where's she going?" Margaret asked.

"According to her Insta feed"—Bess refreshed the page—"she's headed two towns away to get her navel piercing redone. There are before pics, if you want to see them."

"I do not."

"It leaves the coast clear," Bess said. "Time for a word with her brother."

The family's house had not been difficult to find; the brother had an ad in the town's directory with the home address, where he ran his business. A sign on the lawn read, HANDY HAYDEN – NO JOB TOO SMALL!

A man emerged from the garage carrying a ladder over his shoulder.

Bess hopped out of the car and approached. "Excuse me," she called, then ducked as both man and ladder swung around, nearly knocking her head off. She thought that only happened in old Abbott and Costello films.

From where she was watching in the car, Margaret sounded a furious blast on the horn.

"Sorry, love, didn't see you there." The man strapped the ladder into the tray of his ute.

"No worries." Bess signalled to Margaret that she was all right.

Margaret looked capable of striding over and tearing a strip off the man.

Bess fibbed, "I'm looking for Ty."

"What do you want?" Hayden didn't seem to have listened. He tied a red rag to the end of the ladder.

"I'm here for Ty."

"Oh, you mean Tiffany. She's out, thank Christ."

"Sorry to have missed her." *Tiffany?* "I hope she hasn't left for good. She told me she might head to Melbourne."

"She can head to bloody Timbuktu for all I care. If you're here cos you loaned her money, love, you can kiss it goodbye. She still owes me two hundred for petrol." He growled. "Funny how she can still afford to bring home a games console and a new TV the size of a bedspread."

"Ty's been buying expensive things lately?" Bess kept her voice casual. "I'm surprised she can afford them on a gardener's wage, especially at that decrepit house. The old lady there didn't seem very generous." Bess had hoped this might prompt some discussion, but Hayden shrugged.

"How would I know where she gets her cash? Oh, but she's too poor to pay rent here! I've told her, if she tries to sweet-talk another cent out of Mum, I'm putting all her junk in the street, and she can go. I've had a gutful."

"So... She's changed her mind about leaving town, then?"

He strapped a tarpaulin over the vehicle's tray. "How should I know?" But he seemed aggrieved enough to talk anyhow. "Yeah, she was going to leave yesterday, matter-of-fact. Packed a couple of bags and wanted me to drive her to the city! I said forget it: I've got back-to-back jobs lined up. But she went on until I said 'Fine, I'll drive you one town over to Rusdown, and you can get the bus from there'."

"When was this?"

"Yesterday night. Bus leaves at nine. Anyway, I dropped her at the stop, and as I'm driving away, I see this taxi pull up. Tiff gets out and goes to talk to someone inside. I wasn't bothered; Tiff can look after herself. I get back home, and I've not been back an hour when my bloody sister barges in again! Said she's changed her mind and she's staying. No 'Sorry, Hayden, for wasting your time'."

"Why did she decide to stay?"

"What do I care? Whatever it was, though, she didn't look happy about it." That thought seemed to cheer him up. Then he looked at Bess. "Why are you after Tiff, anyway?"

"I met her the other day at Crossroads House. I noticed her Tasmanian tiger tattoo; it's really striking. We got chatting…"

"Christ, not another one."

"Sorry?"

Hayden shook his head. "My sister's always had women showing up here, crying their eyes out about how she did them wrong. Sorry, love, but it's nothing to do with me." He unlocked the ute, climbed in, and slammed the door.

Margaret didn't have to fake an interest in the Mount Bastion and Districts Historical Society Museum (*Open afternoons 1:00 till 4:00*). Their little collection might be smaller and shabbier than her beloved maritime museum in Port Bannir, but the atmosphere was familiar.

Some people would find it dull, she supposed—the dimly lit rooms with their glass cabinets full of medals from the Boer War, faded photographs of townspeople celebrating Queen Victoria's golden jubilee, old farming equipment, mangles, rabbit traps, hip baths, and crumbling mannequins dressed in soldiers' and nurses' uniforms from the First World War—but Margaret liked it. The flotsam and jetsam of the past. Reminders that human history was both real and fragile: so much lost and a few scraps surviving.

"Who knew you were such a romantic?" Bess had smiled when Margaret explained it, and squeezed Margaret's hand.

An old man at the desk adjusted his cardigan and set his spectacles on his nose. "Would you like a tour?"

Margaret said she would like that very much.

They had a display board about the Tasmanian tiger but no artefacts.

"I believe there was a stuffed one years ago," said Geoffrey, the guide. "But the bugs got to it, and it was thrown away."

"I met someone the other day who said her forebears used to see tigers in the bush," Margaret said. "You might know her. Janine Jones?"

Geoffrey flinched. "Yes, she's our society president. Did she tell you that story about her great-great-uncle tripping over a bunch of tiger cubs?"

"She said he'd described it in a letter…"

"I don't know about a letter, but it's one of her family anecdotes." Geoffrey looked pained. "She's got a lot of them."

"About tigers?"

"No, they're mostly about her folks laying the first stone at the council building, running the church group, discovering valuable minerals…"

Disappointed, Margaret said, "She mentioned your centenary celebrations were coming up."

"Tonight, actually. Come and see." He led her to the church hall next door and unlocked it.

The hall hadn't been renovated since the sixties, but someone had prepared it for the night's festivities. Every surface gleamed. A stylish new lectern sat up the front, and the tables were already covered by spotless linen cloths and place cards.

"Very nice. Janine did all this herself?"

"She *organised* it herself." Geoffrey's tone made clear that someone else had done the grunt work. "She's descended from half these blokes." He gestured at the oil paintings and black-and-white photographs on the walls: old councillors, town planners, and managers of the local football club. "She can tell you the story of every single one." Geoffrey's expression seemed to add, *Even when you beg her not to.*

"Janine must have been upset when Ivy Bolt died."

"Mrs Bolt? Yes. Sad news."

"Janine said they were friends."

He furrowed his brow. "I don't know about that. Janine might have hoped that the old lady would be generous to the historical society one day, but I never knew Mrs Bolt to put her hand in her pocket. When she deigned to show up to our dinners, it was Janine who drove her and paid for her ticket."

"Mrs Bolt just fancied a free night out?"

"And being fussed over by Janine and our committee. Guest of honour? Pride of place at the front table?" He sniffed. "She never even made a two-dollar donation." Seeming to catch himself, he cleared his throat. "Now, shall I show you our old surgeon's collection?"

"Please do." Margaret followed him back into the museum. "I'm sorry Janine was disappointed by Ivy after she'd taken so much trouble with her."

"Humph. Janine should have known better. Her family might have been successful, but they still worked for the Bolts, like my family and everyone's family. They might have been paid more, but as far as Ivy was concerned, they were still just staff."

Obviously deciding he'd said too much, he waved her towards the gallery. "Now let me show you the equipment the town's first doctor used for sawing off legs."

It took ten minutes of grovelling before Bess could persuade Dorian Visser to accept her apology. She admitted fault completely. She agreed that her behaviour at his book reading had been immature, offensive, and uncalled for. She told him she'd purchased his full set of e-books. But it was only when she admitted that she'd heckled him because she felt threatened by his fame and success that Dorian relented. He became quite gracious and even autographed her map of Mount Bastion for her.

Thank goodness Bess had told Margaret to go on without her. Margaret would not have played along with this.

It hadn't been difficult to find Dorian; his blog said he was "writer in residence" at the regional library, although Bess suspected he might have invented that title for himself. He worked on his laptop in a corner of the library, his possessions scattered around him.

To her disappointment, Dorian couldn't seem to tell her anything more about the ghostly tiger that supposedly lured travellers into the bush. He repeated the story he'd told last night, but it was virtually word-for-word.

"You said it was a local legend," she said. "Have other people in town seen it too?"

"Yes, of course. This is one of the most haunted parts of Tasmania."

"So who else...?"

"Oh, they won't admit it." He waved his hand. "People are in such denial about the paranormal that even those who've seen things will say they didn't. No point in asking, I'm afraid, dear. But my books will tell you everything you need to know."

"Uh-huh." Once again, she suspected Dorian's ghost hunting was nothing but a con. "What are you working on now?"

"A blog post." He didn't seem to mind her looking. It was headed, "House of death claims a new victim". There were several photos—selfies, apparently—of Dorian sitting with Ivy Bolt in the front room at Crossroads House. Dorian was beaming, one arm flung around Ivy's chair while she gave a crooked smile that hinted at some grim private joke. They were dressed differently in each picture. He and Ivy had indeed spent plenty of time together.

Bess craned forward to read the text.

"It was with grief that I learned of the death of my dear friend, Ivy Bolt, the latest in a line of innocent people to die violently inside Crossroads House, which, as I have demonstrated, is Australia's most haunted building. But while we mourn her loss, we also rise to action. The venomous power of this house is undeniable, and I've made a clear case as to why the building should be turned over to experts in the field of paranormal investigations. But the location's influence does not absolve individuals of responsibility for their actions. A genuinely innocent person would have left Crossroads House the moment she first felt its malignant forces beginning to affect her. But not all people are innocent, and not all people object to the things that places like Crossroads House encourage them to do. Those individuals know who they are. They must be held to account."

Bess read it again. "I'm confused. Why do you keep saying Ivy died violently? Didn't she fall down the stairs?"

Dorian tapped his thick fingers together. "Did she fall or was she pushed?"

"And who are the individuals you want held to account?"

"Use your head, dear. Who else was in the house that night?"

"Vivienne?"

"I never name names." He snapped his laptop shut as if he'd busted her snooping, despite the fact that he'd waited for her to read it twice. "I would like to think that anyone involved would come forward of her own volition."

"You'd better be careful. People could call this slander."

"I've said nothing slanderous." Dorian folded his hands across his substantial belly. "But I won't be silent about what I observed there."

"Ghosts?" Bess feared she sounded as scornful as Margaret, but really, Dorian Visser seemed like an old fraud. She prided herself on having an open mind but not an empty one.

To her surprise, he said, "Not only that. Oh yes, there was evidence of paranormal activity: cold, foul breezes inside the building, damp patches where nothing had been spilled, old furniture with *bite* marks in it. But I'm used to such things. What troubled me was this: Ivy was afraid of Vivienne."

Bess stared.

"Truly!" Dorian insisted. "And she wasn't a woman to be intimidated. But I was there once, months ago, when the phone rang. It was at my elbow, so I answered. The caller said, 'This is her granddaughter'. Well, Ivy, who could scarcely walk, positively flew over and snatched the phone. She listened for a moment, then shouted into it, 'Never call me again!' When she hung up, she was trembling. White as a sheet, poor thing. She never spoke of it afterwards."

He widened his eyes. "Then months later, out of the blue, Vivienne turned up, playing the dutiful carer, and before you know it, poor Ivy is dead. And Vivienne's set to inherit, no doubt."

Bess tried to take in what she'd just heard. Despite her dislike of Vivienne, she couldn't accept what Dorian was saying.

"I think you're jumping to some pretty strange conclusions. I visited them once, and Ivy didn't seem the least bit scared of Vivienne. It was the other way around, from what I could see."

"Ah, but how much did you see, really? Perhaps you saw what you were supposed to."

Dorian peered at her through watery blue eyes that all of a sudden looked surprisingly shrewd. It struck Bess that, for all his bluster and pomposity and the silliness of his ghost hunting, this was a man who'd built a successful career and who could persuade a roomful of people that his turgid book was worth queuing up to buy.

He leaned forward. "I spend my life travelling the country, talking to people about the spirit world. And do you know something I've discovered? When I empower people to speak about their experiences of the paranormal, all sorts of other revelations start popping out. I don't know why. Perhaps by opening a forbidden topic for discussion, I become a sort of father confessor?" He seemed to like the idea. "You'd be amazed at the things people disclose to me at my book readings and psychic tours. Crimes, phobias, incest, addiction. Domestic abuse..." He raised his bushy eyebrows. "Ivy Bolt was a vulnerable woman. An unscrupulous person might have taken advantage."

Still unconvinced, Bess asked, "Did you actually visit Ivy while Vivienne was there?"

"I was never invited. And that's suspicious in itself. Ivy used to have me around for a cuppa every week. It was as if someone were trying to isolate her. To keep her under control."

"Are you accusing Vivienne of harming her grandmother?" Bess had had enough of his hints. There was something slimy about Dorian Visser. "Because if you have proof, you should take it to the police, not the internet."

"How do you know I haven't?" He sat back to survey her reaction.

Bess turned away, not enjoying the pleased gaze of his pale blue eyes.

His car keys lay on the desk with a new-looking key ring reading LUXOR GOLF CLUB. It was hard to imagine Dorian as much of a golfer. She'd seen him limping around; his walking stick wasn't just for show. Maybe he was one of those men who just went there to drink in the clubhouse. As phoney a golfer as he was a ghost hunter.

As if sensing her disbelief, Dorian said in a wheedling voice, "Come now, dear, be honest. You've met Vivienne. I'll wager there was something about her that made you uneasy. Am I wrong?"

"I'll let you get on with your writing," Bess said.

"What?" Margaret stared at Bess over another petrol station coffee. They leaned against the bonnet of their hire car, watching as the freezing wind skated a chocolate wrapper across the concrete.

"You heard." Bess picked up the wrapper and put it in the bin. Even with the desolate logged-out hillside of Mount Bastion in front of her, she still insisted you had to do your bit for the planet.

Margaret found her determination both touching and perplexing. Bess never stopped caring about things. It was remarkable. How did she manage it?

"Ivy, frightened of Vivienne?" Margaret squirted hand sanitiser into Bess's palm. "When did we see any sign of that? Vivienne was scurrying about following her grandmother's orders."

"That's what I said. And if Dorian has any actual evidence that Ivy's death was suspicious, he didn't share it with me. I don't like to speak badly of people, but I think he's a nasty piece of work and he's making it up." Bess pulled a face. "God, is this even coffee?"

"It grows on you."

"You take me to all the best places."

"It was this or the seafood truck by the side of the highway. And we're a long way inland. So what have we learned that would be useful for your exhibition?"

Bess sighed. "Not as much as I'd hoped. We know Ty has been buying herself expensive presents, even though she owes money to people. She tried to leave town yesterday, but someone in a taxi came along and changed her mind."

"We know that Alan Moore has money troubles and professional disappointment," Margaret said, "but he isn't known for trading tiger artefacts, and he didn't have much to do with Ivy, whose tastes were more exotic. Whatever that means."

Bess took the lid off her coffee and examined its oily surface. "You know these cups aren't recyclable."

Margaret rolled her eyes, then said, "We know that Janine Jones tried to make friends with Ivy, but Ivy thought Janine was beneath her."

"And we know Ivy had some kind of friendship with Dorian Visser," Bess said. "I can't imagine why. And he is skating close to defamation by encouraging people to believe that Vivienne abused her grandmother or even killed her."

"That's about the sum of it."

Bess shook her head. "I think you might have been right about confirmation bias. None of this is relevant to a tiger exhibition, is it?"

"Well, no." Margaret touched her arm. "I'm sorry. It was a good idea, and we did try. For such an ethical person, Ms Campbell, you are surprisingly good at manoeuvring people."

"And for such a cunning person, Ms Gale, you are surprisingly sincere about sad local museums." She jostled Margaret playfully with her elbow, and Margaret jostled her back. "I'm not giving up yet. I'll make contact with the tiger women again and try to persuade them to be interviewed. I'll use all my charm. And if that doesn't work…" Bess seemed to deflate at the thought but drew herself up again. "Well, we can get on with our holiday."

"Next stop, a lavender farm?" Margaret smiled back. "Perhaps that wouldn't be so bad."

"Apparently they have lavender scones with lavender honey." Bess brightened. "And lavender martinis."

Margaret imagined Bess strolling through a field of lavender, her red hair lifting around her face in the breeze, surrounded by the sweet, sharp scent and the many shades of purple and blue. Yes, perhaps it was time for that.

She was about to say so when there was a screech of brakes. A battered Renault swung into the petrol station forecourt. It would have been a stylish car thirty years ago, but now it sported rusty patches and dents in the bumper bar.

The driver's window rolled down halfway, then jammed. Someone wrestled with it, gave up, and stuck the top half of his face out the gap. It was Alan Moore.

"Ladies, get in. We need to talk."

Margaret and Bess looked at each other.

Then Bess said pleasantly, "No, we're not going to do that. Get in, I mean. We don't mind talking."

"Not out here." He glanced around the forecourt. "Just get in. I've got an offer for you."

"And I've got a dozen true crime podcasts on my phone," said Bess, "and they all agree that you must never let yourself get taken to a second location."

Alan gaped.

Margaret said, "I'm not sure that car could make it to a second location. But I also decline to get in."

"For Christ's sake." He stamped on the accelerator, and the car coughed past them. He parked it, got out, slammed the door, and walked past without looking at them. "Might buy some snacks," he said in a weird, loud, and way-too-casual voice which would certainly have drawn attention, had anyone else been there.

The two women exchanged glances, then binned their coffee cups and followed him in.

They found him browsing through the snack foods. He was careful not to look up as they stood nearby.

"Which do you recommend, Mr Moore?" Margaret asked. "A local vintage of Fanta or a gourmet packet of Twisties?"

"Very funny." He spoke out the side of his mouth. "I've been ringing around about you. You don't work at Élevé Auction house. They gave you the boot."

"She chose to move on to the next stage of her professional journey," Bess corrected him loyally.

Margaret gave her a grateful nod.

Alan snorted. "Whatever. I know your career's in the toilet. And I know you've been sniffing around Crossroads House and the old lady's collection."

"What's your point?"

He looked nervously at the man behind the counter, then shuffled into the next aisle. Rifling through bottles of travel shampoo, he muttered, "I've got a deal for you. The old lady had an inventory book with a red leather cover. Get it for me."

"You want us to steal from a dead woman?" Bess stared. "You realise that's really bad karma as well as illegal?"

"Yeah, all right, I'll give it back. I just need a look."

"What for?" Margaret asked, interested in spite of herself.

"Now that Mrs Bolt's gone, her granddaughter will be looking to sell her stuff. And it's a big collection. If I knew in advance what would be coming onto the market, it'd give me an edge over the other dealers."

"An edge you need desperately, from what I've heard." Margaret studied him. His shoes, which must have been dapper when he bought them, now needed replacing. "It's none of my business, Mr Moore, but why not pack it in? Sell up and move somewhere with nicer weather. You might find it a relief."

"You're right. It *is* none of your business." But perhaps part of him wanted to talk because he said, "I'm throwing in the towel, all right? I was born in this town while my dad was sinking fence posts for the bloody Bolts. I worked my arse off to get that shop up and running, to show all the wankers in the industry and the snobby old squattocracy families out here that I could do it. That Ronnie Moore's son would buy and sell the whole bloody lot of them one day."

Margaret felt an unexpected twinge of sympathy. She remembered Port Bannir and her upbringing. She knew that feeling. Still, she wasn't one for reckless kindness. "And why would I do you a favour? I don't suppose you can pay."

Alan glanced around. "I could introduce you to some people. Private dealers and collectors who could put a bit of work your way."

"Who?"

"No one you would have met at toffee-nosed Élevé. These guys are a little more...maverick."

Margaret leaned against the drinks fridge. "I'll think about it."

"Think fast. You know where to find me."

Bess interjected. "When we met the other day, we talked about that tiger skull at Crossroads House. Do you know any more—"

But Alan didn't seem to hear. He grabbed an item at random off the self—a packet of Gastro-Stop—and hurried to the register. He left without waiting for his receipt.

Bess looked at Margaret. "You're not going to do it, are you? Steal an inventory book?"

"No. But I'm curious to see it. Aren't you? If Ivy did have other tiger paraphernalia, perhaps that's where we'll learn about it."

"Maybe. What do you think he meant by maverick dealers?"

"Probably people trading in stolen antiques. There's a market."

"Why doesn't Alan go and work for those dodgy characters himself, if he's broke?"

"Hmm." Margaret chose a new bottle of hand sanitiser and walked to the counter. "We don't know he hasn't."

Mount Bastion wasn't large enough to have its own police station, so they drove into the next town to make their statements. Thanks to Margaret's military scheduling, they arrived half an hour early.

"I saw a historic cemetery in the next street," Bess said. "Those places are interesting. Shall we look?"

"Go ahead. But I won't join you."

"Oh—" Bess wanted to kick herself. "I'm so sorry. Of course you don't want to after losing Deirdre."

"It's not that."

"I didn't think. I'm sorry."

"I don't mind."

"Let's go somewhere else."

"There's no need."

"But if this is triggering for you—"

"Oh, for—" Margaret wrestled visibly with her irritation. "Spare me the touchy-feely stuff. There is nothing wrong; I just don't feel like a walk. You should explore the cemetery if it interests you."

"And what will you do?"

"Answer emails in the car."

"You realise that's more depressing than walking in a graveyard."

"Have fun, Bess."

A rusted padlock held the cemetery gate shut, but it was so low Bess could step over it. The grass was long and yellow. Bindii prickles stuck to her socks, and bristly weeds scratched her legs. She walked past stone angels that had tumbled into the grass, past crumbling crosses and engravings obscured by moss.

Bess thought of Margaret's sister, Deirdre. Deirdre, who didn't have a monument, just an urn wrapped up inside a suitcase in a motel cupboard. That seemed wrong to her, like the natural order of things had been put on hold. Why was Margaret so reluctant to let her sister's spirit move on?

She walked until she found what she had only half-hoped to see here. A granite stone less ancient than the others. It was unadorned, and the lack of flowers suggested that no one had visited in some time. She squatted to read it.

Richard Henry Bolt
1954-1987
and his wife **Lorraine Henrietta Bolt**
1956-1987.

In God's hands.

Were these Vivienne's parents? Was Richard the son whom the women in the supermarket had gossiped about, saying it was no wonder Ivy had gone strange, losing her son like that?

The sound of movement made her look up. It was an older man entering the graveyard. He was tall, stooped, and stringy looking, his bald head marked with sunspots. He strolled to a neatly maintained plot nearby and set down a bunch of sunflowers.

Straightening, he gave Bess a nod that seemed friendlier than any greeting she'd had in Mount Bastion. "G'day."

"Beautiful flowers," Bess said.

"My mum. She loved 'em. Always bring her some when I come back."

"You don't live here, then?"

"Nah, not for years." He offered her a hand to shake over Richard Bolt's headstone and said his name was Ted.

"I'm visiting too," Bess said. "A woman called Vivienne Bolt. Her grandmother, Ivy, just passed away. She's not buried here, though."

"Ivy Bolt? Nah, they'd need to put a stake through her heart first." Ted shrugged. "Sorry. Shouldn't speak ill."

"You knew her?"

"Years ago. I was the police constable here. Fair to say the Bolts expected better service than the rest of the neighbourhood."

"Did you know Richard?" Bess nodded at the stone. "Her son?"

"Geez, I'd forgotten he was here. Yeah, I remember him."

"He was quite young when he died. The same year as his wife?"

"The same day." Ted grimaced. "I was first on the scene, as it happens."

"I'm sorry."

"Hmm." He stepped over to look at where Richard and Lorraine lay buried. Ted's friendly face tightened. "Stay down there, you prick."

"Pardon?"

"Sorry, love, 'scuse my French. But it's not a nice memory. Right before dawn, we had a call from a farmer who'd been driving past Crossroads House and heard a disturbance. I got there, went upstairs, and found them. Lorraine dead in their bed, Richard on the floor."

"What happened?" Bess breathed.

"Pistol. Lots of houses here had firearms back then. The Bolts sat on the board of the local rifle club, actually. Great shots, the whole family." Ted wiped his lips as if getting rid of something nasty.

"What..." Bess swallowed. "What happened to them?"

"Murder-suicide. Richard had always been a bit of an oddball, and Lorraine was planning to leave him. They'd had words about it the day before; the handyman heard them." Ted's face twisted as he added, "Although the handyman lost his memory miraculously the next day. At the same time, my crawler of a sergeant decided to declare the whole thing an accident and hush it up."

"You're joking!"

"Different times." He wiped his forearm across his sweaty bald head. "Ivy Bolt couldn't have her precious son's name dragged through the mud, could she? Official story: Richard was cleaning his gun when it went off and killed his wife, then was driven temporarily insane by the shock of what he'd accidentally done."

"Truly?"

"Yep. Bloody disgrace. I put in for a transfer a month later. Can't say I miss the place."

Bess stared down at the stone. Vivienne had lost her parents like that?

"What about their daughter? Her name was Vivienne. She would have been about ten?"

Ted crinkled his forehead. "Yeah, I think there was a kid. The family were visiting Ivy for their holidays, but I never saw her. Ivy wouldn't have let us interview her in case she let slip something we weren't supposed to hear. I think someone told me the kid got sent to boarding school straight after."

"Do other people in town know about this?"

Ted smiled without humour. "At the time, half of them worked for the Bolts. Nowadays... Well, there aren't many of us left to remember." He blew out a breath. "So Ivy's really gone?"

Bess nodded.

"There's an end to it, then." He nodded goodbye and headed back towards the road.

The police finished with Bess first. Waiting outside the station for Margaret, she did a short meditation and studied the street. Finally she gave in and did what she'd been tempted to do for days: she looked for Vivienne Bolt on social media. It felt grubby and she wouldn't like Margaret to know she was doing it, but she couldn't resist. Tragic though it was, the story she'd just heard about Vivienne's parents made her even more curious about what she might find.

Nothing.

She checked platform after platform, but if Vivienne was there, she wasn't using her own name. Bess tried the library where Vivienne worked, but aside from her name and title, there was nothing there either. Googling her just brought up pages of fashion accessories and locksmiths.

What had Bess hoped to find? Just some inkling of who Vivienne was when she wasn't at Crossroads House. Some hint at a relatable, normal life.

Not that Bess thought people were weird for staying off social media. Margaret wouldn't touch it with hazmat gloves. But still...

Having acted on her own curiosity once, she couldn't help wondering about something else that had been niggling: what had really happened in Ivy's home before she died? Remembering the stories of malicious pranks against Ivy's carers, she searched online for carers working in this region.

But no one came up. Either those women had been operating off the books, or they had found different jobs after whatever they'd experienced at Crossroads House.

She looked up to see Margaret approaching.

"Thank you for waiting," Margaret said.

"How was it?"

"The police were polite enough," Margaret said as she led her away. "But… It's possible Vivienne wasn't being paranoid when she said they suspected her."

"What do you mean?"

"They asked me lots of questions about Ivy's relationship with her granddaughter. How did they behave together? Was Ivy allowed visitors? Who controlled the money? Did I witness Vivienne withholding food or medication?"

"Jesus." A chill ran through Bess. "Did they get that from Dorian Visser? He implied he'd spoken to the police."

"Perhaps."

Bess wondered if Margaret was upset to hear a one-time friend accused like this. Margaret had been so eager to help Vivienne earlier, although she had stopped talking about it. But it could be hard to read Margaret's thoughts. Her pale chiselled face didn't give much away. Even when Bess had told her Ted's tale about Vivienne's parents, all Margaret had said was "Good God" before mulling it over in silence.

Bess said, "I wonder why Dorian made these claims. Is he whipping up drama to increase his book sales, or is he just a jerk?"

Or does he have a real reason to think it's true?

Trying to ignore that disturbing question, she took Margaret's hand. "This is a sad situation, but I'm sure it will turn out to be a misunderstanding."

Margaret nodded, seeming to return to the present. "There's nothing more we can do, is there? Now, let's see what we can find at Crossroads House to help with your exhibition." She squeezed Bess's hand. "Whatever's happening, you have a future to think of."

Chapter 11

WHEN THEY PULLED UP AT Crossroads House, the shadows were lengthening. A cold breeze tugged the car door from Margaret's hand and slammed it shut, the sound swallowed up immediately by the wild garden. Clearly, no further progress had been made to fix Vivienne's car; spiders had begun to build webs across the door handles. She thought the weeds had grown longer since yesterday.

Bess looked around. "What do we tell Vivienne about why we're here?"

"The truth, more or less. We're curious to see that inventory book. She can't object; she asked me to look for it."

"But will we tell her about the exhibition I'm planning?"

"I suppose we'd better. I'm not sure how she'll feel about her grandmother's death being referenced, however anonymously." Although Margaret suspected Vivienne might rather enjoy the idea and find it darkly amusing.

"And will we tell her that Alan Moore wants the book? Or what Dorian Visser has been saying about her?"

Margaret rubbed her eyes. "I suppose we should. How awkward." She didn't believe Dorian's accusations—grubby little man. As for Alan's request, goodness knows what he really wanted. She wondered if Alan was after that one item more valuable than the others in Ivy's collection.

She climbed the front steps, still musing. A roof tile must have fallen in the night; it lay shattered. Margaret squinted through the grubby windows, but there were no lights on inside.

She thought of what the old policeman at the cemetery had told Bess: that Vivienne's father had killed her mother and himself.

Vivienne had never told Margaret that. She must have been—what?—ten years old at the time.

Did she think of it often? Had she thought of it on graduation night when everyone else's parents had assembled proudly to celebrate their children's success? Margaret's had not—her mother was long dead, her father sulking in their home town four hours away.

Had Vivienne thought about her parents' deaths while she strutted along the edge of that fountain with the admiring young Margaret at her side, the very picture of art house cool, holding forth about painting and theatre and travel, making Margaret believe the future would be so much brighter than the past?

Margaret raised her fist to knock on the door, then paused. How well could you ever know someone?

She turned back. Bess was gently removing a spider that had dropped onto her octopus hat. She rehomed it into a rhododendron bush, murmuring some sort of encouragement. Looking up at Margaret, she asked, "What are you smiling about?"

"Were you telling the spider that the rhododendrons would make a nicer home?"

"Obviously." Bess straightened. "And that she could make friends with a bee and a snail and have adventures together."

Margaret smiled again. She knew Bess, didn't she? Bess didn't keep secrets.

She knocked, but no one answered. Checking her phone, she found she'd missed a text from Vivienne.

No word from you today. Assume you're not coming? Your loss: I'm having such fun. Off to solicitors now. They like to stretch their billable minutes, so Lord knows when I'll be back. Love.

"She's out," Margaret said while silently repeating *Love?*

No doubt that was just Vivienne being arch as usual, but it seemed an odd thing to write. Not *Love, Vivienne* or *Love to you both.* Just *Love.* "She's at the solicitor's office. About Ivy's will, I suppose."

"Oh." Bess slumped. "So much for finding that inventory book."

"Not necessarily." Margaret didn't feel like giving up. Besides, that "love" really irked her. Twenty-five years of silence, then Vivienne drags her into this weird situation and has the nerve to write "love"? Margaret looked behind the rotting shutters.

"What are you doing?"

"Just checking whether Janine Jones put something back... Ha!" Margaret held up the spare key. "Shall we see ourselves in, Ms Campbell?"

Bess grinned, then held out her hand for the car keys. "I'd better park farther down the street and out of sight. We don't want to be spotted."

"Good thinking." Margaret tossed her the keys.

"When we met, I would never have picked you for someone who would enjoy housebreaking."

"When we met, I had no one to encourage my lawless side," Margaret said.

Everything sounds louder inside a house when you're not supposed to be there, Bess thought. She crept down the hall, her senses humming with nerves, guilt, and excitement. She flinched at every squeak of the floorboards, tensed when Margaret opened the doors to the downstairs rooms, and jumped when an update pinged on her phone.

Vivienne must have switched off the furnace; Crossroads House was cold again. Icy breezes snaked through the cracks in the windows. The ceiling was speckled with mould. From inside the walls came a *drip-drip* and the scampering of rats.

Margaret strode forward without hesitation, her boots ringing against the floorboards.

"Can't you walk quietly?" Bess hissed.

"What for?" Margaret didn't bother to lower her voice. "There's no one here, and if someone does burst in, they'll catch us anyhow. Why worry?"

Bess huffed at her, finding Margaret's indifference both frustrating and thrilling. It reminded her of when they first met, when she'd been startled by Margaret's coolness in the face of risk.

They shouldn't be doing this; they could get in so much trouble. She touched Margaret's hand and allowed herself an anxious smile. This felt like a prank that could go wrong.

They looked briefly through the sitting room and study downstairs, Margaret explaining that she'd been through those rooms with Vivienne earlier.

Bess paused by the bookcase with its half dozen photo albums. She pulled them out on the off-chance that an inventory book might be hidden behind them. Nothing there. Bess shifted her weight, and the floorboards groaned.

"Any luck?" she asked Margaret, who was fossicking in a cupboard.

"No." Margaret dusted off her hands. "Nothing interesting. Certainly nothing about the tiger. Shall we try the study?"

Ivy's filing cabinets and desk held no inventory book either. Bess pulled the drawers out to check that nothing had fallen out before looking behind the desk itself. Between the desk and the wall was a cardboard folder. She retrieved it. It looked new and glossy with a logo reading GRAHAM & PRATT: LAST WILL & TESTAMENT.

"Hey, is this Ivy's will?" Bess scanned the legal waffle. "She signed it in January. Looks like she left everything to Vivienne." Bess read on. "Except for a couple of small charity bequests and a gift for Dorian Visser. The taxidermized platypus in the hall cabinet."

"Lucky Dorian." Margaret checked behind the bookcase. "But we're not looking for the will, remember."

"No, but..." Bess flipped the pages over. "How do you think it ended up behind the desk?"

"Slipped down, presumably."

"But it's an important document. Shouldn't Ivy have kept it in a safe or something? Would you lose a document you'd spent hundreds of dollars getting drawn up?"

"I would not," said Margaret. "But as I've often had cause to lament, not everyone is like me. You'd better put it back; Vivienne will get a copy from the solicitors anyhow, and we can't let her know we were here."

Bess dropped the folder where she had found it. "What does it take to get you excited about something?"

Margaret smiled. "I'm grateful you still want to know."

"Hmm." Bess shot her a teasing smile, appreciating a little flirtation. But something else was on her mind. "Remember how you found Janine Jones snooping in this desk? She said she was looking for that letter about her tiger-hunting ancestor. But what if she was really looking for this, and she dropped it when you arrived?"

"Why would she want it?" Margaret narrowed her eyes. "Besides, when I caught her, I got the sense that I'd interrupted her during a search. As if she hadn't found what she'd come for."

A metallic rattle sounded somewhere inside the house. It rose to a clanging sound which echoed, then ended in a *thump-thump-thump*.

"God." Silence fell, but it felt sensitive, ominous. "What was that?" Had it come from the far side of the building?

"It's the pipes." Margaret seemed unfazed. "I heard it last time I was here. Shall we keep looking?"

For the next hour, they searched through bookcases, cabinets, wardrobes, and storage boxes. Margaret even looked through an upstairs room full of old dolls, which made Bess rear back in horror. "I'm not going in there. Not without an exorcist."

"Don't be absurd." But Margaret didn't linger either.

Nor did they spend long searching Vivienne's room. There wasn't much to search. Vivienne's belongings were few, and her housekeeping was intimidatingly tidy. Her elegant clothes were folded symmetrically in her suitcase, while her bedside table held nothing but reading glasses and a copy of *Remembrance of Things Past*. The bookmark was two-thirds of the way through, but the cover was pristine, the spine unbent.

Bess had half a dozen battered second-hand books beside her own bed with titles like *Wild Women Warriors* and *You and Your Worm Farm*. She felt reproached and a little embarrassed.

"There's nothing here," Margaret said. "Should we give up? Perhaps there was no inventory book after all, or Ivy threw it away, or…"

Bess beckoned her out of Vivienne's room. It felt good to leave; snooping there had been a bad idea. She should do a cleansing ritual later to rid herself of the experience. She wondered if the shops at Mount Bastion sold sandalwood oil or moonstones.

Leading the way downstairs, Bess said, "We didn't try the kitchen. That was my gran's favourite place to hide valuables. She used to keep fifty-dollar notes in the biscuit tin."

The kitchen was cavernous, covered in cracked tiles and rough plaster. It felt five degrees colder than the rest of the house. Bess tried to think of that as clever nineteenth-century design rather than uncomfortable and creepy.

A shelf above the fridge held cookbooks, their covers stained and crusted with ingredients spilled half a century before. She flipped through them.

"Here!" Inside a smelly old tome called *Fifty Ways with Tripe*, she found a newer, cleaner book with a red leather cover. Pages nine to thirty of the recipe book had been torn out to make room for it. "Told you. My gran used to hide her old love letters in a recipe book too."

Margaret smiled in amazement. "Ms Campbell, you are remarkable."

"Thank you." Despite the freezing kitchen, Bess's cheeks warmed a little. That was the thing about someone as blunt as Margaret: when she gave you a compliment, you knew it was sincere. "What are we looking at?" Bess scanned lists of items, auction houses, dates, and prices, then passed the book to Margaret.

"Hmm. These look like the antiques I checked with Vivienne the other day. Nothing unusual, and nothing related to the thylacine."

The later pages were much the same. Margaret tutted. "Nothing special here. I don't know what Alan Moore was so keen to find, but—"

Her phone rang.

"*Shh!*" The sound seemed deafening in here. Bess flapped at her. "Turn it off!"

"Calm down. There's no one around for miles." Margaret answered it. "Zan. Any news?"

From the phone's speaker, Bess heard the faint sound of a young voice saying, "Nup. Waste of time, M."

"Would you care to elaborate?"

Bess picked up the inventory book and flicked through it again. She heard Zan say, "We've looked, but no one's selling oxy where you are. Although I know where you can get some *serious* botanicals. That's better for you, you know. More organic."

Bess held the inventory book upside down and shook it gently in case something more interesting was stowed between the pages. Nothing fell out.

"Zan, are you sure?" Margaret asked. "Did you check thoroughly?"

"Well, I posted a question on Facebook and no one answered, so…" A snort. "Course I checked thoroughly. But there's nothing being sold around Mount Bastion. This isn't the US; we don't have a big opioid problem in Australia. And you should stop assuming all depressed rural communities are full of drugs, you know. It's, like, offensive."

Margaret sighed. "All right, Zan. Thank you."

"Thank me not with words, M."

"The cheque's in the post."

"Choose life, not drugs, mate."

Margaret put her phone away. "Well, so much for our exciting theory about someone stealing Ivy's painkillers and selling them. Vivienne was probably right—Ivy just threw them out."

But Bess was staring at the book. When she'd opened it and shaken it upside down, the spine had bent outwards, opening a gap between the cover and the binding. Something was in there. Paper?

"Bess, are you listening?"

"Not really." She slid her little finger into the narrow space and poked the paper until it slid out the other end. It was a sheet of foolscap rolled into a tube. She unravelled it. It was covered in writing. The ink was the same watery shade of blue that Ivy had used in her inventory book. But this writing wasn't in English. There were lines, squiggles, and loops.

"What's that?" Bess asked.

"Pitman shorthand." Margaret took it from her gently. "They made all the girls learn it at my school in case we had to become secretaries for a while before we got married."

"Which century were you born in again?"

"We may have been a little behind the times in Port Bannir." Margaret photographed the page with her phone. "I'm not surprised Ivy knew Pitman, though. It was fashionable in the 1930s."

"What does it say?"

"Give me time; it's been decades since I've used it." Margaret pulled up a kitchen stool, sat down, and pored over the image of the shorthand on her phone, expanding it now and then.

Bess replaced the paper inside the book, the book inside the recipe collection, and the recipe collection back on the shelf. When she turned around, Margaret was biting her bottom lip so hard it almost vanished. "Are you all right?"

"I'm all right. This isn't."

"What is it? What did Ivy write?"

"I'm...not sure. It's been a while; maybe I'm misreading."

"You know I don't like cliffhanger endings. What does it say?"

"Just...give me a minute." Margaret put her phone back in her pocket as if she couldn't stand to look at it. "Come on."

"Come where? What's wrong?"

Margaret sprang down from her stool. "We have to keep searching this house."

Despite the cold, Margaret sweated as she led the way back to Ivy's study.

"What is it?" Bess asked again, hurrying behind her. "What did Ivy write in code?"

"I'm not sure." She quickened her pace.

"You must be pretty sure," Bess said as she puffed, "or you wouldn't be trying to break the four-minute mile."

"It's been years since I used shorthand. And it was hard to interpret."

"Okay, but what do you *think* you read?"

"Just let me...consider this for a minute." Margaret reached the study door and stepped in.

When faced with a puzzle in her professional life, she couldn't rest until she'd figured out the answer for herself. It had always been a quality of hers (she preferred not to think of it as a fault, although perhaps others did). And what she'd just read... There might be an innocent explanation for it, but if Margaret's suspicion was correct, it would mean Ivy had done things which many people would find shocking. Things which could prove disastrous for Vivienne if she were involved.

Things which might have provoked someone to murder the old lady?

Don't be absurd. There was no proof that Ivy's death had been anything but an accident. Although she had heard of people killed for far less compelling reasons.

She didn't like to think of what it could mean for her and Bess if they were the ones to uncover something like this. Probably she should stop now, delete Ivy's list from her phone, and pretend she never saw it.

But preserving the past was what Margaret did. She'd been doing it all her working life, from graduation night onwards. If she'd read that document correctly, she couldn't walk away.

"Margaret." Bess bumped her, none too gently. "What are you looking for?"

"Firstly, Ivy's keys." Margaret opened the desk drawers, remembering that she'd seen a ring of them earlier. "One of these might unlock the eastern side of the house. We haven't looked there."

"Looked for *what*?" Bess sounded really impatient now, but still Margaret hesitated to answer.

She didn't like to speculate. If she had read that document wrong, it would be beyond embarrassing. She would feel like an incompetent, hysterical fool, misinterpreting basic evidence and jumping to wild conclusions. Margaret prided herself on not making mistakes; she was the one who tracked down other people's mistakes and made sure they didn't get things wrong a second time. She had always hated being incorrect, especially on professional matters, but after the past two years of career failures, it seemed intolerable now. "I just need to check some things before I draw my conclusions. Help me get the east wing open."

Bess glared but, mercifully, dropped the subject.

Half a dozen keys failed before one fit the lock. The door had warped, perhaps from the damp. It took a hefty shove from Bess to get it open.

Margaret returned the keys to the study. Then they stepped into the darker side of the house.

There was a musty smell that made her think of compost: a smell of animal droppings and fungus. She didn't trust the electrics, so they used the torches on their phones. The thin beams swept over furniture stacked up and shrouded in dust sheets and empty bookcases linked by gleaming strands of spiderwebs. Their shoes left prints in the dust.

147

Not wanting to touch anything, Margaret pulled on her gloves. She lifted the sheets and opened the dressers, but they were empty.

"Can you at least tell me what to look for?"

Bess's whispering didn't seem silly any longer. Margaret lowered her own voice as she replied, "Anywhere you could store something."

They tried the room opposite. It was a laundry with cracked linoleum lifting up from the floor. The smell was worse in there, like clogged drains and dead mice.

A shutter crashed open, making Margaret's muscles clench and Bess yelp. The shutter swung closed again with a groan. Wind gusted through the slats in the window.

The cupboard under the trough was empty save for a few dead moths. Beside it stood a broom closet containing an old mop and bucket. Margaret glanced inside, then looked closer. The inside of the door was scuffed and scratched with little chunks gouged out of the wood. Had something been trapped in there? A possum maybe? She didn't tell Bess the animal lover; it would upset her.

Put off by the sight, she swung the door closed again. She noticed bolts on the outside, top and bottom.

From the corridor, Bess called in an undertone, "Margaret?"

Margaret hurried towards her and followed the line of her pointing finger. On the floor ahead, down the hall where they had not yet ventured, were footprints in the dust.

"Those could have been left any time." Margaret didn't believe in showing unease, let alone fear. She tried to ignore the unpleasant sensations slithering up and down her spine. "Vivienne might come here for some reason."

"Let's go. I don't like this."

"Let me look." Margaret swung her torch through the next doorway and found nothing but an ancient toilet with the window open and every surface black with grime. She wrinkled her nose. Bess was right; it would be better to go.

Still, she could not resist turning to the room opposite, the last on the ground floor. She pushed the door open with her foot.

On the bare floorboards stood a large cast-iron bed base without a mattress. A bedside table was on each side. Margaret opened the drawers and found them cleared out. Turning next to the large antique wardrobe against the back wall, she opened the doors; it too was empty. She held her phone higher. Was there something strange in there?

"Margaret?"

"One moment." She ran her hand over the inside surfaces of the wardrobe. Lovely polished Tasmanian blackwood on the sides. And at the back...

"Margaret."

She turned. Bess was standing close to the wall behind the bed, her phone held up for light. "What is it?"

Bess touched the air an inch away from the wall, showing what had caught her eye.

Margaret stepped closer. It was a bullet hole.

"Well"—she swallowed, determined not to betray her queasiness—"after that story you heard in the cemetery, perhaps we should have expected this." She looked away from the dark little crater and returned to the wardrobe.

"Seriously? Is that all you can say?"

"What is there to say?" Margaret touched the back of the wardrobe. The wood there was a different texture: cheap chipboard.

"I'm leaving," Bess hissed, "and I want you to come with me. There is something seriously wrong in here."

"You might be correct." Margaret reached into the corners of the wardrobe. She fiddled and pushed... "Ha." The false back came away; she lifted it out.

"What are you doing? What's that?"

Margaret held the light higher. It illuminated what had been hidden behind the false back of the wardrobe: shelves with objects on them. "Something seriously wrong."

The torchlight glinted off precious stones and silver figurines. It illuminated crockery and vases, faded paint hinting at their original brightness.

"More antiques?" Bess sounded confused. "Why did Ivy hide them here? Was she going funny after all?"

"I don't think so." Margaret gestured to Bess to hold her light up while she checked the shorthand list she'd photographed on her phone. "Hiding these things wasn't mad. Quite rational, in fact."

"Why? What are they?"

Margaret glanced between the coded words of Ivy's list and the objects on the shelves.

"Seventeenth-century bronze Shiva," she read slowly. "Southern India, 1981. Prehistoric stone bird figurine, Boroko, Papua New Guinea, 2004. Fifth-century BC, red-figure calyx bowl, Athens, 1973."

From the dawning dismay on Bess's face, Margaret sensed she'd guessed what was wrong, but she explained anyhow. "For thousands of years, thieves have looted antiquities from tombs, temples, graveyards, monasteries… But since the late twentieth century, most countries have tried to put an end to the practice. There is an international agreement that museums and dealers don't trade in any items stolen or illegally excavated after 1970."

"So why are these ones hidden in a wardrobe in Tasmania?"

"Why indeed?" Margaret continued down the list. "Ancient Mesopotamian lion-shaped stone amulet, Bagdad, 2003."

"How did Ivy get these?"

"Maximillian said she knew people in the industry who could cater to exotic tastes. No wonder he clammed up on the details." She read further. "Put your gloves on and look behind the first row, will you?"

"I'm not touching those things!"

"You don't have to remove them. Just check what's stashed behind."

Bess edged closer, clearly curious, despite her obvious unease. "These are spiritual objects. They shouldn't be here."

"That's not your fault, is it? Check what's behind the top row on the far right."

Bess reached in gingerly and shifted a pottery dish to look behind it. "Is that…?"

"Sauropod, late Cretaceous period, Henan Province, China." Margaret read from the list, then craned her neck to look at it. "A dinosaur egg."

"People trade those?"

"Illegal fossils are big business, if you don't mind the risk."

There was something different on the bottom shelf. A notebook. Margaret picked it up. Loose documents were shoved between the pages, and the whole lot was held together with rubber bands. Inside, the pages were covered in the same faded shorthand. She put it aside for the moment. Then she examined the list again and caught her breath. Surely not…

"Check the second row, far left." Margaret screwed up her eyes to better read her list.

Bess moved things aside. "I can't tell what's back here..."

Margaret looked up in time to see Bess reach in and lift something out. "No, don't—"

Too late. Margaret lunged forward to hold a hand beneath the object in case Bess dropped it.

But Bess was made of sterner stuff. She sucked in a horrified breath, but her grip remained steady as she placed the object back inside the wardrobe.

Margaret read out the item on her list. "Alexander Hudson," she recited, her tone flat with disgust that anyone would consider this an amusing collector's item. "Aged 42. Hanged at Hobart Gaol, 1857, for the murder of Isabella Brown. Body taken for dissection."

It was a skull.

"I'm leaving now." Bess strode to the door.

"Wait." Margaret hurried to replace the items in their original places and fit the false back in front of them. It seemed best not to leave signs that they had been here.

Bess stood in the doorway. "Are you coming?" The question did not sound friendly.

"Give me a moment." It was only after she'd closed the wardrobe doors that Margaret remembered the notebook lying beside her. "What do you suppose this is?"

"Why do you suppose I would care?" Bess spat.

Why was she so angry? Margaret looked at her, baffled. Granted, the discovery had been unpleasant, but that wasn't her fault. She wasn't the one who had stashed stolen icons and body parts in a wardrobe at Crossroads House. "I don't think there's any need for that tone—"

The sound of an engine nearby interrupted her. Car tyres rolled across gravel.

"God." Bess clutched her stomach.

Margaret waved at her to be quiet and, with no time to think, shoved the notebook inside her jacket. She ducked into the toilet opposite where the window was unshuttered. From here, she could see the driveway. A taxi idled while Vivienne paid the driver.

"Damn." Margaret returned to the bedroom, grasped the window sash, held her breath at the thought of the noise it might make, then hauled the window open and yanked at the rusted bolts on the shutters.

"Are you nuts?"

"She's on the other side of the house." The bolts slid loose, and she flung the shutters open. "Come on."

"What are we doing?"

"What you wanted to." Margaret moved to boost Bess up. "Leaving. Quickly."

Bess braced against the window frame, swung both legs over the ledge, and dropped down.

Margaret followed and pulled the sash down after her.

How would Vivienne react if she came around and caught them? Would she be shocked and angry at them for sneaking in and uncovering evidence of her family's crimes? Would she be distraught at what they had found? Or would she break into that crooked smile of hers and make a drawling joke about it, seeing some ironic side to the whole mess?

Margaret did not wish to find out. Her mind was racing as they dashed across the shadowed lawn and into the cover of the trees. She looked back. No lights glowed in the eastern side of the house. Had they gotten away with it?

Despite having discovered proof of someone else's crime, her pulse thudded as if she were the one at fault. The darkened windows made her think of that skull with its shadowy eye sockets.

Thank goodness they'd moved their car out of sight.

Without speaking, they hurried along the edge of the bush. Something thudded against her hip; she patted her jacket and felt the notebook.

What foolish impulse had made her take it? The same one that had led her through the house and into that cupboard in the first place. She'd wanted to know the truth, to outsmart whatever was driving all this mystery. To be on top of things at last. Instead, she'd gotten them both tangled up in a real mess.

They reached the car and climbed in, shutting their doors quietly. Afraid of how far the noise might travel, Margaret did not switch on the engine but instead released the handbrake and steered a slow, bumpy course out onto the road.

All the way down Renfeld Lane, they didn't speak. Bess broke the silence only when they reached the highway and Margaret turned left, back towards Mount Bastion.

"Where are you going? The police station is in Rusdown."

"The police station?"

"So we can report this."

"Ah. Well, that's…an option." Margaret's throat tightened.

"An *option*?" Bess sounded incredulous. "We just found stolen cultural artefacts in a dead woman's wardrobe."

"Yes, but—"

"Sacred spiritual objects."

"Probably. But—"

"*Human remains!*"

"Which we discovered while breaking into a house." Margaret clutched the steering wheel.

"That doesn't make a difference!"

"It's illegal, Bess. It's very illegal."

"That didn't bother you back when we were letting ourselves into the place."

"Well, it bothers me now. I've been in trouble with the police before. I don't want to go through that again."

It wasn't just the thought of the questioning, lawyers' fees, charges laid, bail, or media coverage, ghastly as those things would be. It was the thought of feeling the way she had felt the last time: helpless, cornered, disbelieved. At other people's mercy.

"Are you protecting Vivienne?" Bess spoke calmly, her voice strained.

"What?" Margaret glanced at her in surprise. "No. What is there to protect her from? She wouldn't have been involved."

"How do you know?" Again, Bess kept her voice level, but tension seemed to throb below the surface.

"Vivienne works with ancient items. She wouldn't risk her career like that. Anyway, she didn't use that part of the house."

The part where her parents died, Margaret added silently. No, she didn't believe she was protecting Vivienne, but the thought of Vivienne knowing Margaret had seen that room with the bullet hole in the wall made her feel queasy. They had invaded Vivienne's privacy back there, perhaps unforgivably.

"You barely know her," Bess said flatly. "You can't be sure what she might have done."

Which was true, of course. Margaret believed she would have no trouble telling the authorities if she believed Vivienne had been involved in a serious crime. Well, of course she would tell. And yet…

Her memory tripped back to graduation night. To the grip of Vivienne's hands and the unexpected strength in her slim body as she hauled Margaret to safety. What did you owe someone for saving your life? How did you know when the debt was paid?

"I'm not protecting anybody," Margaret said, "apart from the two of us. We don't need any more trouble."

"Are you seriously suggesting we don't report it?" Bess sounded appalled.

Margaret was glad to have the excuse of watching the darkening road so she did not have to see the look on Bess's face. "No, but… It's not an emergency, is it? And I doubt the one constable on duty in Rusdown specialises in artefact theft. There's no harm in leaving it until tomorrow, so we can…assess the situation."

"So *you* can assess it, you mean."

Margaret felt Bess's glare boring into the side of her head. "I beg your pardon?"

"You dragged me through that horrible house!" Bess burst out. "You refused to tell me what we were looking for, although you'd obviously guessed the truth. What am I: your dopey sidekick?"

"Of course not! I just wanted to be sure—"

"You took me into a *murder room*, Margaret!"

"I didn't know that."

"I picked up a skull."

"I didn't tell you to pick it up." Margaret had a sense that arguing over the details wasn't very wise, but her natural nitpicking got worse during anxious moments. "Anyhow, you had gloves on."

"A human skull!"

"It was old. And he didn't sound like a very nice human."

"It's still a violation—a desecration!"

"It's…not ideal." Margaret grimaced. "But you've worked in museums. You've handled sensitive items."

"Not stolen ones. And not body parts!"

"I think it's important to stay rational about this." Instantly, Margaret realised that this had not, in fact, been a very rational thing for her to say.

"Oh, do you?" Bess's voice filled the car. "Well, I happen to think that human remains are a sacred thing and should be handled with respect. Maybe that doesn't bother you—maybe you're happy to wander through Tasmania with them bouncing around in your suitcase, but—" Bess stopped short.

There was an awful silence.

"I'm sorry," Bess said. "I didn't mean that."

"It doesn't matter." The car was so quiet, Margaret could hear every bump in the road.

"Of course it matters." Bess shook her head. "It was a rotten thing to say. I'm sorry."

Margaret turned into the township. They didn't speak until they reached the motel.

As she switched off the engine, Margaret said, "I think there were some items missing. I counted about a dozen objects in that wardrobe, but there were around two dozen items on Ivy's list. What do you suppose she did with the other ones?"

It seemed a fair question to her, but Bess just shook her head as if to say *I give up*. Then she got out of the car and shut the door hard.

Chapter 12

BESS BELIEVED IN THE THERAPEUTIC power of knitting, but it wasn't working for her tonight. She had a pattern for a toy Tasmanian devil, intended as a present for a friend's daughter, but it kept losing its shape and looking like a lopsided rat. Sitting cross-legged on the motel bed, she unpicked her recent work and started again, her needles clicking angrily.

She did not look up at Margaret, who sat in the corner poring over the notebook she'd taken from Crossroads House. Bess could not imagine what she hoped to find there. The thought of that dark room made her want to brush herself down as if something might still be clinging to her like a spiderweb.

Still, she had made her position clear. Those stolen artefacts had to be reported tomorrow, and if Margaret wouldn't do it, she would. She had no problem doing things alone, did she?

Although since getting together with Margaret, she'd assumed she would not have to. They'd always backed each other before.

Hunched over the notebook, Margaret sucked in a breath. Perhaps she was hoping Bess would ask what she'd found. If so, she was in for a disappointment. How many times today had Bess asked what was happening, only to be ignored?

"You'll never guess what's in here," Margaret said at last.

"No, I probably won't."

But Margaret seemed too engrossed to notice her lack of enthusiasm. "Ivy had been writing down all the dirty little secrets of everyone in Mount Bastion. Going back decades. Births out of wedlock, extramarital affairs, arrests, feuds between families... Most of it is very old now, but there might still be people who wouldn't want the contents getting out." She tapped the book thoughtfully. "Between this and the stolen artefacts, I must admit... I'm starting to wonder about Ivy's death."

Bess did not look up. "I've told you what I think we should do about the notebook and the artefacts."

"Oh yes," Margaret said, a hint of snark in her voice. "I'll just tell the police I stole this very interesting book from a house I broke into, shall I?"

"There's no point arguing. You know what I think."

Margaret paused, then evidently decided to ignore that point. Instead, she mused, "Perhaps I'm getting distracted—these old scandals might have no relevance to what happened to Ivy. Perhaps it's Alan Moore I should be wondering about. He's an antiques dealer in urgent need of money, he was desperate to see a list of Ivy's possessions, and he said he had maverick contacts in the industry. Granted, Maximillian thought he wasn't capable of anything really untoward, but even Max makes mistakes. What if Alan sold those illegal artefacts to Ivy and then panicked about it? What if she was indiscreet or the police started asking questions? On the night she died, maybe he went to the house to warn her, and an argument started." Margaret chewed her lip. "What do you think?"

"I think you should share that theory with the police," Bess said, "when you report those stolen artefacts."

"I've explained why that would cause problems." Margaret said stiffly, as if she were hurt by Bess's unsupportive attitude. But how much support could she expect when she kept shutting Bess out of things?

Tears stung Bess's eyes, and she looked down at her knitting so Margaret wouldn't see. What was happening? They'd been having such a good time together earlier today.

Returning to the notebook, Margaret turned a page, stopped, and drew out a loose, folded document that had been shoved between the leaves. She unfolded it, read it, then sat back in her chair.

"Well, well."

Determined to ignore her, Bess kept knitting.

"This is quite a find."

Bess knitted harder.

"It concerns someone we both know." Margaret swivelled around. "Are you not speaking to me now?"

"If it's important to you to share what's on that paper, I'm not stopping you."

Perhaps realising this was the most encouragement she was going to get, Margaret held up the document. "It's one of those cheap DIY will kits, dated December last year. It leaves Crossroads House and all of Ivy's belongings to Dorian Visser!"

Bess looked up. "No way."

"It's signed."

"But we found Ivy's will at the house behind her desk. It was a proper lawyer's will, and it was dated January this year. So it must override that document."

"I assume so." Margaret traced the will with one finger. "Especially since someone—I suspect Ivy—has drawn a line through it and written 'Tosh' in big letters."

Bess looked. "Weird."

"And see the writing? Apart from the signature and the 'Tosh' part, this doesn't look like Ivy's hand. I'd say Mr Visser drafted it. For a while, he would have been set to inherit everything she had. And then he lost out to Vivienne." Margaret studied the document. "I wonder whether he found out that Ivy had changed her will and how he would have reacted."

"Crossroads House is falling to bits. Is it really worth inheriting?" Bess asked. "But land itself always has value, and those antiques would fetch a good price."

Then she caught herself. No, she would not get drawn into this. She refused to go back into that murder room even in her imagination. "Well," she said firmly, "that document suggests Dorian tried to take advantage of an old woman. Maybe he did something worse. All the more reason to hand it over."

"You're a broken record." Margaret thrust the paper back into the book. "I can't see why you're not more interested. Usually you're the one trying to get me excited about things."

"That's true," Bess said, stopping herself before she added: *And don't you think I get tired of that sometimes?*

Well, of course she tried to be on the lookout for the most interesting aspects of any situation, for those little moments in life that brought joy. But that approach took effort, and right now she didn't feel like it.

Margaret scraped her chair as she stood. "I need some air." She strode outside, taking the book.

Bess flung her knitting aside, fuming, telling herself she was not going to get involved. She wished she'd never had the idea for that dratted tiger show. It had brought nothing but trouble.

Still, curiosity got the better of her. She wanted to know what Dorian Visser had been up to.

Bess opened his blog, but there was nothing new there, apart from a post announcing that he would attend the centenary dinner of the Mount Bastion Historical Society that night, in case his fans wanted to get books signed.

Bess had bought his e-books reluctantly the other day. At the time, she had simply searched them for references to the Tasmanian tiger and, finding none, had given up. But now she picked up her Kindle and began scrolling through them again. There was a mixture of Dorian's anecdotes about his own achievements and grim stories from supposedly haunted houses.

She pored over the photo sections. They showed the ghost hunter standing with the owners of the properties, all of them elderly women. She searched for words like "owner" and "resident" and found mentions of Maud, Edith, May, and Colleen, all older women who lived alone. They were troubled by restless spirits, apparently, and thankful for Dorian's expert help and friendship.

"Hmm." Bess picked up her phone and punched Dorian's name into various search engines, along with the names of those homeowners. At last she found a match. It was a forum where several people had posted their own reviews of Dorian's ghost hunting.

"Disgusting," said one. "He got my mum to pay him $1,000 for some BS spiritual cleansing ritual. Then she handed over her mother's antique tea set as a thankyou—it was worth $2,000. He was gone before I realised or I would have kicked his arse."

"Total con," wrote another. "My gran had dementia, and he convinced her to give him her antique wardrobe worth several thousand. Said he'd trapped a poltergeist inside or some crap. What was really in there was my late grandad's set of golf clubs which cost a fortune. Police said there was nothing they could do. Can't we sue him or something?"

Another comment read: "WHEN I GET MY HANDS ON THAT THIEVING PRICK, I'LL STRANGLE HIM. Mum's sick with diabetes and all her friends are dead. Visser started hanging around, and she thought the sun shone out of his backside. She sold him her perfectly good car for a few dollars to 'help with his work'. We haven't seen him since."

There were more posts going back years, accusing Dorian of scamming vulnerable, lonely people. Sickened, Bess wondered what else he might be capable of.

Something else niggled: the mention of golf clubs. She remembered seeing Dorian's key ring from some golf course. What had the logo said? Luxor?

Another online search revealed that the Luxor Golf Club was a swanky-looking place in Melbourne. A few entries down, Bess found a news item about Luxor purchasing land in Tasmania and applying to the planning authorities to build a golf course, hotel, and restaurant there. Environmentalists were challenging the application in court because the land included a corridor of wilderness which Luxor wanted to bulldoze. The company insisted it needed the full area in order to have proper access to the road. The case was ongoing.

She searched for the location on her map. It was just outside Mount Bastion. And adjacent to the land where Crossroads House stood.

"Well, well," she said, echoing Margaret.

If the slippery Mr Visser had gotten hold of Crossroads House, he could have sold the land to the golf club and given them the space and access they desired. How much would Luxor have paid him for the privilege?

Then she felt cross with herself. It was up to the police to pursue things like this. She hadn't come here to get involved in local disputes.

And she had not meant to imitate Margaret either. She was not thinking about Margaret at all.

Margaret decided fresh air was overrated. She had tried walking around the motel forecourt, but the frigid wind stung her face and tangled her hair, making her crosser than ever. Giving up, she sat in the car.

The closed door to their room seemed to reproach her. She glared at it. Why was Bess being like this? Were they just having a disagreement, or was this the start of something worse?

"How should I know?" she murmured. It wasn't as if she had a rich history of past relationships to learn from. Bess was the first woman Margaret had been with in years. Margaret had assumed she would be the last.

The thought of losing Bess made her feel ill. Should she go back in and apologise, even though she couldn't see that she'd done anything especially wrong?

Her phone rang. *Vivienne.*

She hovered her thumb over the screen, then answered.

"Margaret. I missed seeing you."

"Pardon?" Margaret swallowed. God, had Vivienne figured out they'd been in her house?

"When I went to the solicitor. I drove through Mount Bastion on the way home, but I didn't see your car outside the motel."

"Oh." Margaret bit her tongue. "We, ah, we went out for dinner."

"Nice for you. I've been watching solicitors filling out paperwork at the speed of paint drying. It made me think of you."

"Sorry?"

"Graduation night." Vivienne chuckled in a sad tone. "All those marvellous things we talked about doing when we were properly grown up. The exotic travel, the exciting work, the fascinating people we were going to meet. The opposite to my day today. I hope you've been having more fun."

"Don't count on it," Margaret muttered before she could stop herself.

"Oh?" The energy returned to Vivienne's voice. "What's wrong?"

"It's nothing."

"Go on, Margaret. I've got the police treating me like some homicidal drug dealer; I'm trapped in a quagmire of death and paperwork; I've got a broken-down car, rats in the roof, and a fridge full of Janine Jones's casseroles. Tell me your problems. I could do with a laugh."

"It's nothing interesting." Should she confess their break-in to Vivienne and tell her what they'd found? But Margaret hadn't made sense of it herself yet. And it would be humiliating to admit to sneaking around like the cast of Scooby-Doo, especially to the cool, cynical Vivienne. Instead, and rather to her surprise, she replied, "It's silly. I've just had words with my partner."

"Goodness. What's the problem?"

Margaret rubbed her eyes. "It's nothing important."

"Oh, come along, Margaret, you have my full attention. You're speaking to a lonely single woman, remember? Make me feel better about my sad plight."

Was Vivienne joking or not?

"Is it money troubles? Clash of lifestyles?" Vivienne paused. "Infidelity?"

"Human ashes."

"Well, now I'm intrigued."

"Don't be. It's…foolish." Margaret slumped. "I, ah, I haven't disposed of my late sister's ashes yet. I should. I just…haven't. They're in my suitcase for safekeeping, and Ms Campbell implied that this was not the most respectful way to handle them." She leaned her forehead against the window. "Perhaps she's right."

"Nonsense. Your sister is long past caring what you do. Her ashes are yours now. If you want to put them in a snow globe or snort them in a nightclub toilet, it's nobody's business but your own."

It was brutal but lighthearted and sounded like Vivienne from all those years ago. It made her smile in spite of herself.

Vivienne continued: "If I had the remains of a sister to deal with, I'm not sure where I would put her either." She seemed to think on that for a moment. "Burial, probably. I'm more of a traditionalist than people realise. But I'm pretty damned sure I wouldn't want anyone else's opinion about it." Her tone softened. "You've lost a great deal, Margaret. I do know how it feels."

Margaret remembered that bedroom with the bullet hole in the wall. It filled her with sadness. "I'm sorry, Viv. Things must be hard."

"Don't worry. I've survived so far." Vivienne paused. "What are you doing now?"

Margaret looked around at the deserted forecourt, the closed motel door, and the notebook in her lap. "Nothing."

"Fancy a nightcap? I've found the key to Ivy's wine cellar. There might be some antique items in there that we actually like."

Margaret sat still. The car keys were in her pocket, their jagged shape pressing into her thigh. Her gaze flickered up to the rear-view mirror. She saw the black stretch of highway laid out behind her, framed by tall trees, stretching back into the shadows.

"No, thank you," she said at last. "Ms Campbell is waiting for me."

"You're so devoted," Vivienne said. "What a good little citizen you've become. And you used to be a real outsider."

Margaret flicked the lock on the car door open and closed. "Who says I stopped being that?"

A chuckle. "If you change your mind about that drink, you know where to find me."

"Goodnight, Vivienne."

After she rang off, the car seemed quieter than before. Margaret had sat in a car like this with Deidre outside the hospital when she'd got her diagnosis. Margaret had been frozen in horror, her fingers locked around the wheel. Deirdre, who'd always been so nervous and fretful about everything else, had smiled and told her not to take on so, had said she was not afraid.

Margaret shut her eyes. She hadn't cried since Deirdre went, not even at the funeral, and she wouldn't start now. Instead, she opened the notebook and studied it, using the torch on her phone. What had Ivy meant by squirrelling away her neighbours' secrets, their weaknesses and sins? Flipping through the pages, she found another item stuck inside. An envelope.

She opened it and drew out a sheet of paper. It was fragile and looked much older than the notebook itself. Probably she shouldn't examine it under these conditions, but she didn't feel like waiting, so she spread it with care on her lap and held the light over it.

It was a letter dated 1860, signed by someone called William Ingham. The name rang a bell from her conversation with Janine. Wasn't he Ivy's great-grandfather?

It began, "My dear brother", and gave an account of the running of the estate, his wife's health, and some dispute over the sale of a horse.

Then Mr Ingham went on.

"John Flanders has proven an estate manager of no common value. Indeed, I depend upon him for everything and hardly know any man in the district to equal him for diligence and initiative. There are few around here who know the truth about his origins, and I judge it best to keep my lips sealed, for I truly believe the poor fellow to be sincere in his repentance. Accordingly, I permit no joking talk of 'government

men' and take care that the name of Joseph Flannery never escapes me.
For while it may shock you, my dear brother, the truth is there are many
men of greater wealth and consequence in these parts whose own origins
could scarce stand up to equivalent scrutiny. Indeed, in many households
here it is considered most impolite to ask a man about his forebears or
his motives in travelling to the colony, for some memories are best left
undisturbed, and all agree that it is best to forget as soon as possible the
hated name of Van Diemen's Land."

Margaret stopped, then reread it. She knew that the government men
in the letter were the convicts brought to this island in its early days before
transportation was abolished and before the colony changed its name from
Van Diemen's Land to Tasmania in an effort to start again.

Had the writer been anyone else, she would have found the letter mildly
interesting, a relic of the island's colonial past and the deep shame people
had once felt about its criminal origins. But John Flanders? Surely that was
the name Janine Jones had quoted for her great-great-grandfather.

After working in museums, Margaret had become proficient at using
genealogy websites. A search found John Flanders' marriage and death
notices, but nothing about his birth. And a man called Joseph Flannery
had indeed arrived here in 1845, transported in punishment for stealing
some pigs. There was no record of his death.

If John Flanders was Joseph Flannery, what would Janine think?

Margaret chewed her lip. Nowadays most people wouldn't be ashamed
of convict ancestry; indeed, since the 1970s it had become positively
fashionable. But she thought of Janine's extreme pride in being descended
from respectable free settlers and local leaders. She remembered Janine
snooping through Ivy's belongings, looking for something. Janine wasn't
like most people.

In the old days at her museum, Margaret would have been thrilled
to uncover something unexpected and scandalous. The excitement of
stumbling across an unexpected nugget of history with contemporary
ramifications, the satisfaction of being the first person to know about it...
It would have made her happy once. But not now.

Not when Bess wasn't here to share it.

Chapter 13

THE HALL WHERE THE HISTORICAL society was holding its centenary dinner was only one street away. But Margaret walked the long way around, hoping to clear her head.

The doors to the hall were open, revealing dressed-up people seated at the tables, the remains of their meals in front of them. At the lectern, a Tasmanian historian was speaking; he'd been well-known twenty years ago.

He must be desperate, she thought, then remembered her own professional situation. All those ambitious plans she'd hatched with Vivienne on graduation night—had they dwindled away over time? Had they vanished when she lost her beloved maritime museum? Or had they died along with Deirdre?

"Margaret."

She turned around. Bess had come up behind her, her face a pale oval in the darkness, her hair whipping in the breeze. She looked beautiful.

Had she come to make up after their quarrel? Margaret took a step forward.

"What are you doing here?" Bess asked.

She had not come for a reconciliation, then.

Inside Margaret's chest, something clenched shut. Stepping back, she spoke coolly. "I discovered Ivy knew something disreputable about Janine Jones's ancestry. I thought of asking Mrs Jones about it." Glancing inside, she said, "And I see Alan Moore is in there too. But why did you come?"

"I found out Dorian Visser was conning old ladies." Bess seemed uncomfortable too. "His blog said he would be here."

"I see." Margaret looked away. "Of course, it would be rather foolhardy to confront several people whom we think might have broken the law. Especially if we suspect they might have had motives for—for wanting someone dead."

"Maybe," said Bess. "But it's a public place; there are scores of people. And we can't just do nothing."

"Hmm." Margaret thought about it. "If you are going to insist that we tell the police about the contents of that wardrobe—"

"We have to!"

"—then I would like some leverage. Some more information we could give the authorities to offset the embarrassing matter of us breaking into that house. If I could give them information pertinent to Ivy's death… Well, it might help our position. It might even persuade them to overlook our unlawful activities."

"That's not why I'm here. I want to know the truth." Bess sighed. "But yes, I suppose some extra information would help us too."

Margaret longed to say more, to break this pained silence and close the gap between them. But she couldn't think how. Their falling out had seemed so sudden to her, so unaccountable. But her inability to fix it made her wonder if the tension had, in fact, been coming on for some time, growing quietly in the darkness between them. She nodded towards the hall. "Shall we, then?"

As they entered, Janine was presenting a prize to the town's top year-twelve history student. Then the minister for the arts made a short speech, unveiled a plaque, and shook hands with Janine while a newspaper photographer took pictures.

Janine smiled, waved, and elbowed other people out of the shot. This evening might seem dull to some, but clearly it meant the world to her.

The ceremonies finished, and the guests began to rise, chatting and mingling. Margaret couldn't see Dorian or Alan, and she and Bess had not planned what to do next. Improvisation wasn't Margaret's style at all. She turned to ask Bess how they should approach this, but Bess wasn't there.

"Evening, folks." A familiar voice chimed over the sound system, causing Margaret to walk into a chair. How had Bess got to the front of the hall so fast?

The guests stopped talking and turned, confused, towards their new speaker. From the lectern, Bess waved to them.

"Sorry to interrupt," she said as Margaret stared in dismay, "but Ms Gale and I are new in town, and we just wanted to say that, like you, we think Mount Bastion's history is super interesting."

From across the hall, Janine goggled in outrage at this intruder. She set down her drink and bustled forward.

"Especially the recent history," Bess went on. "For example, we've been *really* interested to learn about the friendships Ivy Bolt had with your president, Janine, your ghost hunter, Dorian, and your antiques dealer, Alan. There was certainly more to those friendships than met the eye."

Janine looked appalled. She walked faster, clearly intending to drag Bess from the microphone.

Seeing Janine move, Bess sped up her speech. "We've got some good documentation about those friendships, but we'd love to talk to the people involved to hear their side of the story before we share what we know. We're here all night. Oh, and if anyone has lost a blue mitten, it's sitting on the fence outside." She strode back to Margaret, apparently unperturbed by the stares and whispers that followed her.

"What," Margaret hissed, "do you think you're doing?"

"Insurance," said Bess. "If Janine, Dorian, or Alan really did something wrong in relation to Ivy, they might decide to get heavy with us. But they'll think twice, now that the whole town knows we've got dirt on them."

"Or they might get ten times heavier!" Margaret glanced around. "And why on earth did you mention the mitten?"

"I saw it on the way in. And it only takes a moment to do a good deed."

Seething, Margaret said, "Then do one for me. Next time, *ask* me before you make wild, reckless decisions and drag me into them!"

Bess lifted her chin. "After what happened at Crossroads House, I could say the same to you."

"I see. Was that some sort of payback?"

"No," said Bess. "I've told you what it was: a tactic to protect us. And I happen to think it was smart. Now, excuse me. I'm thirsty."

She strode off to the bar, ignoring curious and disapproving looks from the guests. Under different circumstances, Margaret would have admired her composure.

French nails like talons dug into her arm. She turned to find Janine standing an inch away from her and looking unquestionably capable of murder. Janine leaned in until Margaret could see the mascara clumped in her eyelashes. "Kitchen. Now."

Looking around, Margaret couldn't find Bess in the crowd. Wondering how risky this was, she followed Janine into the kitchen next door.

Janine waved at the catering staff. "Out." They stared. "I said get out!" Her voice rose to a screech, and the staff scurried away. She slammed the door behind them.

Then she turned to Margaret. "So. Not content with harassing the Bolt family during their grief, you and your friend thought it would be funny to barge into our special night and make a scene." She pressed her lips together until they nearly vanished. "I could call the police."

"If you like." Margaret pulled her shoulders back. "And I can tell them about a certain document I found hidden in Ivy's house. I assume it was the one you were really searching for the other day. It's an old letter describing how Joseph Flannery won a free one-way trip to the colony of Van Diemen's Land. And how later he moved to Mount Bastion and changed his name to John Flanders."

The colour drained from Janine's face. "You're lying."

"Ms Campbell tells me I'm not very good at dialling up my emotional intelligence," said Margaret. "Whatever that means. But I can see from your face that you know I'm telling the truth."

Janine grabbed the door handle for support, looking like she might be sick. "All right. What do you want for it?"

Why did so many people assume Margaret was a criminal? She frowned. How could anyone think she seemed sinister? "Well, firstly, I'd like to know how you learned the truth about John Flanders yourself."

"From Ivy, of course." Janine spoke through gritted teeth. "God knows I tried to be a good neighbour to that woman! Meals, shopping, trips to the cinema. It wasn't easy with her demanding and complaining."

"Are you sure you weren't just trying to ingratiate yourself in the hope that she would leave her antiques to your historical society?"

"I will not dignify that with an answer," Janine said. "Anyhow, one day I was dropping around a casserole, and she wanted me to drive her to a solicitor's meeting in Rusdown. I didn't have time. I offered to call a cab, but she didn't like them. She got very pushy and insisted I drive her. I told her politely that I didn't appreciate her tone and I didn't work for her. To which she replied, 'Your family always worked for us, and you should be grateful we took you on!' I said I didn't know what she meant but I was disappointed she would speak to me that way. I said we prominent local families had a duty to stick together. And"—Janine flinched—"then she told me about John Flanders."

"Did you believe her?"

"Of course not! Until a photocopy of that awful letter showed up in my mailbox." Janine seemed to wilt. "Why did she do that to me?"

"Why do you think she did?"

"Spite, I suppose. She didn't like being disobeyed. And she hated people presuming they were equal to her."

The sight of a miserable Janine Jones made Margaret uncomfortable. She had almost preferred it when Janine was raging at her. Surely this was more of a Bess conversation, calling for compassion and sensitivity. In Bess's absence, Margaret felt obliged to say, "You know you were equal to her, don't you? Goodness knows, I enjoy Australian history, but there are limits. You're not accountable for what your ancestors did in order to get here two centuries ago. It doesn't say anything about you as a person. For heaven's sake, no one cares."

"People in this historical society care." Janine blew her nose. "You've no idea the work I've put in, the reputation I've built, the toes I've had to tread on over the years to get things done." She raised her voice. "How would you know what matters and what doesn't? You're a stranger here! My family's good name is everything to me, and that old witch was going to ruin it. She attached a note to that photocopy. It said she was thinking about sending the original to the local newspaper in time for our centenary."

"What did you do?"

"Rang her, of course. But her granddaughter had arrived by then, and she said Ivy was too sick to come to the phone. I drove over, but no one answered the door." She shook her head. "So I decided to tell the editor of the newspaper that someone was harassing me and that he should throw out any defamatory letters. I just had to hope he would."

"And later you tried to retrieve the original document from Crossroads House?"

"If you must know, yes. You saw me. But Ivy had died by then."

"Yes. And we don't know exactly how yet."

Janine's eyes widened. "What...?" Her face, so sickly a minute before, now turned beetroot-red with anger. "What are you suggesting?"

"Isn't it obvious?"

"You—" Janine spluttered. "How *dare* you? First you come in here blackmailing me over poor John Flanders—"

"Don't you mean Joseph Flannery?"

"*John Flanders*. Then you make up a wicked false accusation, and you think I'll pay you to keep quiet about that too? You disgust me! I will ring my solicitors as soon as you leave. Which will be right now, by the way!"

"You've misunderstood me," Margaret said. "I never attempted to blackmail you. I only wanted to know the truth."

"The truth is that John Flanders was a good man who just made a mistake, Ivy Bolt was a wicked old harpy, and I did nothing wrong except try to help a neighbour who didn't deserve it!" Janine flung the door open. "I am going to say goodbye to the minister. I will expect you and that red-headed disaster to be gone by the time I'm done."

She strode out and shut the door so hard that Margaret heard the yelp and smash of several guests dropping their drinks.

For all her bravado, Bess was having second thoughts about her stunt with the microphone. Had it really been a good idea? Not that she would have admitted her doubts to Margaret, who couldn't give her credit for any intelligence or initiative today.

Queuing at the bar, she looked around. Margaret had vanished. Had she walked out?

Her face hot with emotion, Bess turned back to the bar. Well, let her go. She refused to get upset now.

"Buy you a drink?" It was Alan Moore. Clearly it wouldn't be his first beverage of the evening. His tie was loose, his face flushed.

"Aren't they free?"

"Only for guests, and I'm pretty sure Janine didn't send you an invite. She never did like hippie weirdos from the mainland. No offence."

"None taken." Bess turned to the barman. "Do you have any guava juice?" He stared at her. "Or orange would do."

"Put it on my tab, Harry."

"You don't have a tab, Alan," the man grumped. "Actually, you still owe me—"

"Yeah, all right. Later." Alan handed over some coins. "Important business meeting with Miss Cameron here."

"Campbell."

"Yup." He hustled her away from the crowded bar.

"So, Alan, what brought you here tonight?" Having accused him in front of everyone, Bess now felt oddly compelled to make polite conversation. "Are you from one of Janine's pioneering families?"

"What? Nah. I'm sure my great-great-whatevers were just scumbags from the chain gang. But I bought a ticket. These people like antiques, and I need to sell a few." He picked up a half-finished glass of beer from a nearby table and downed it. "So what was all that bullshit about?"

"You mean what I said at the lectern?" Bess tried to look calm. "You asked us for an inventory of Ivy's antiques. You seemed eager."

"So?"

"Well, we found something better: we found the antiques themselves. All of them."

"You've lost me." But perspiration appeared across Alan's ruddy face.

"Okay," said Bess. "I'm not good at being mysterious, and I don't like manipulating people, so I'll just tell you what happened. We found some ancient artefacts that Ivy had been hiding. We're pretty sure they were stolen, and we assume you probably sold them to her."

Alan blinked heavily. "Come again?"

"We're going to report it. But I wanted to give you the chance to act first and turn yourself in. Those artefacts are beautiful and meaningful. They should be in a museum or with the descendants of the people who made them. Selling them to private buyers is really unethical as well as illegal. You should do the right thing for your own sake."

She thought she spoke compellingly, but Alan just gaped. He still looked sweaty, but she thought she saw something else there too, a look he hid quickly behind another glass of beer. A look of…relief?

He wiped his mouth. "Is that it? You think I was selling stolen goods to Mrs Bolt?"

"Weren't you?"

"No." He looked her in the eye. "I can honestly say I never did."

Bess scrutinised him. "So if the police were to trace the story of how those items got to Ivy's house, they wouldn't find you in between?"

"Correct." He put his glass down with a thunk, his movements looser now. To her frustration, Bess sensed again that he didn't mind her holding this theory, that he'd been expecting her to accuse him of something else.

"We are going to report it," she insisted. "First thing tomorrow."

"Fine by me." Alan glanced around the hall, then hitched up his trousers. "Reckon any of this lot would buy a Tiffany lamp? I need to shift a few. But don't worry; the paperwork's all kosher."

"That's it, then? You're maintaining you never sold any illegal items to Ivy Bolt?"

"Sure. I'd take a lie detector test just to shut you up." His expression hardened. "Who told you to point the finger at me? And how'd you find these so-called stolen artefacts?" When Bess didn't answer, he rolled his eyes. "It's not like I can't guess. You tell that little ratbag Ty the next time she tries to make trouble for me, I'll wring her bloody neck."

"Ty?"

He snorted. "Who's playing dumb now? Listen, everyone in Mount Bastion knows that girl. She's been in strife since she was in primary school. She came to me asking for a job. I told her to hop it, and this is her idea of getting me back. Sorry she dragged you into it, but here's some advice, if you're smart enough to take it."

He straightened his tie, brushed the crumbs off his shirt, and looked her in the eye. "Forget whatever this is and leave town. I'm prepared to forgive the odd bit of slander cos I'm an easygoing bloke, and frankly, I've got bigger problems than you two idiots. But not everyone in this town is as nice as me." He returned to the bar and didn't look back.

Disappointed and unable to see Margaret, Bess headed to the bathroom. She splashed water on her face and looked in the mirror. Were things about to fall apart between the two of them?

The idea brought tears to her eyes. However aggravating Margaret could be—obsessive, stubborn, spiky, secretive—Bess loved her. She was still intrigued by Margaret's intensity and solitary nature—still excited by Margaret's intelligence, tickled by her sarcastic humour, floored by her unexpected passion. But if Margaret kept shutting her out of things, Bess would have to wonder how deeply she was loved in return.

With an effort, she composed herself. Then she opened the door and walked into Dorian Visser. His bulky body blocked the doorway.

"What do you want?" Bess tried not to sound alarmed.

She could stay standing there, so close she could smell his breath, or she could back away into the bathroom where she might get trapped. She chose to stand her ground.

"That's a funny question from a young lady who saw fit to attack my good name in public." Dorian must have been taking advantage of the free drinks too, for his pale eyes had turned bloodshot. They had a pinkish tinge that made her think of rats. He fondled his walking stick. "I think you are the one who owes me an explanation, Miss Campbell."

Stay calm, she reminded herself. She could hear guests in the hall, clinking glasses and laughing. Someone was bound to come by soon. Surely Dorian wouldn't risk doing anything. And she could outrun this unfit older man easily—if she could get past him.

"How's your golfing handicap these days, Dorian?"

He squinted. "What?"

"The Luxor Golf Club bought all that land out here; I thought you might want to join. They might have given you a free membership, if you'd been able to sell them the land at Crossroads House. They need access to the road, and that pesky wilderness is in the way. If you'd sold the Crossroads property to them, it might have solved their problem and made you a packet. You must have been devastated when Ivy changed her will."

"What are you chattering about now?" But his grip tightened on the walking stick. It was one of those artistic ones made from gnarled wood. Up close, it looked like a club.

Bess dragged her gaze away from the stick and met his eyes. "You wrote a will for Ivy to sign. It's been discovered. How did you talk her into it? Was she losing her mind, or was she just lonely?"

Dorian glared. "I've told you: Ivy Bolt was perfectly sane and highly intelligent."

"But you would say that, wouldn't you? If you wanted to convince a court that her first will was legit." Bess pushed on, trying to ignore the dryness of her mouth and the clamminess of her palms. "Was that why you kept implying to people that Vivienne had come along and started abusing and controlling Ivy? To cast doubts about Ivy's second will—the will that cut you out and left everything to Vivienne?"

A new thought struck Bess. "It might have suited you if Vivienne had been found guilty of causing her grandmother's death. I'm pretty sure there's a law that says murderers can't inherit property from their victims."

Dorian's left eye twitched, and Bess realised she'd guessed right. *Wow*, she thought, *poor Vivienne*. Which wasn't a thought she expected to have.

How far had Dorian gone? Had he merely hoped to put Vivienne under suspicion, harm her reputation, blame her for what was probably an accidental death, and hope the authorities saw things his way? Or had he done more?

He looked at her through slitted eyes. "You should be careful what you say, Miss Campbell. There are laws against slander, and I won't hesitate to use them." He licked his lips. "I could do with an extra quarter of a million."

"Why—didn't you make enough money out of your ghost hunting? Ivy might have seen through you eventually, but I heard those other women with haunted houses were very generous. If you're worried about your reputation, you should see what their families are saying online."

"Show me one law I've broken." A nasty smile spread across Dorian's face. He seemed calmer now, but there was a glitter in his eyes that Bess didn't like at all. "Those ladies came to me for spiritual succour, and I helped them. If they wanted to give me something to say thank you, that was their choice. They were happy to do it."

He rolled his eyes. "God knows, I earned those presents. Do you have any idea what hard work it was, listening to the old dears wittering on about all the dead people they thought were hanging around their houses? Having to show an interest when they dragged out the photos and dry their tears when they started sniffling over dead husbands and kids and dogs, for heaven's sake? The number of times I felt like saying, 'There's no way your old man's still wandering around this place, darling—he was glad to die and get away from you!'" Dorian blew out his cheeks as if relieved to get that out. "But so what? No one got hurt."

"Ivy Bolt died."

"That had nothing to do with me."

"If it had happened a few weeks earlier, you might have inherited Crossroads House. Did you know she'd drawn up a new will?" And if he'd found out, how angry had the news made him?

"For someone who claims to have important information about me, you don't know much, do you, dear?"

He pushed his face closer to hers until she could see the broken capillaries in his cheeks and the yellow stains on his teeth. "There was nothing illegal about that will. Indeed, one day a sympathetic court might find that it reflected Ivy's true wishes before that greedy, manipulative granddaughter got hold of her." He stepped nearer until his large stomach squashed against her.

Bess felt sick.

"You've got nothing on me," Dorian murmured. "Now, run off home before you make me lose my temper."

"Bess Campbell?" A voice rang out. Dorian moved away, still smirking.

Dizzy with relief, she realised it was the same security guard who'd kicked her out of the book reading.

He said, "There's been a complaint about you disrupting this event."

Bess did a double-take. "Well, *I've* got a complaint about this sweaty creep lurking around the women's toilets and trying to threaten me!" She pointed at Dorian. "What are you going to do about him?"

"Miss, I've been instructed by the organisers to escort you and your friend off the premises. I am authorised to use minimal force."

If she hadn't been so eager to get away, Bess might have been outraged. As it was, she hurried to the guard's side.

As they walked towards the exit, she asked, "What is minimal force? Do you squirt me with fly spray or chase me with a broom?"

Margaret was waiting outside. When she saw Bess, she stepped forward as if in relief. But she didn't speak or touch her.

"Best to leave town, ladies," the guard said. "This is no place for holidaymakers."

People inside the hall stared out at the two intruders who'd been expelled. Then gradually they turned back to their conversations.

Janine stood by the lectern. Dorian clumped over to join her, leaning ostentatiously on his walking stick like a frail old man instead of the angry grifter who'd cornered Bess before. Then Alan strolled across, schooner in hand, and said something to them both. All three turned to look at Bess and Margaret.

Seeing them together, Bess wondered why it had never occurred to her that in a town this small, they must know each other, maybe quite well.

A woman walked past them towards the hall, having obviously been outside for a smoke. She noticed where Bess was looking.

"Ugh, those three." The stranger seemed friendlier than anyone else here. "Should have seen them at the Rotary Club dance the other night. Nabbed the best table, drank all the booze, and bitched together for hours, never mind the poor waiters cleaning up around them." She wandered off.

Margaret cleared her throat. "Did you discover anything in there?"

Bess thought back. "Not really. You?"

"Not really. But we did make some enemies." She shook her head. "That guard was right; it's probably time we left." Margaret strode off but glanced over her shoulder, seemingly to check that Bess was following safely.

They said nothing more to each other.

Chapter 14

THE RECEPTION AREA AT THE Rusdown police station was not a place Bess would have chosen to spend six hours.

The constable behind the desk kept sniffing. The plastic seats seemed to have been designed to cause lower back pain, and she had read all the posters on the noticeboard eighteen times.

Snacking on chocolate and soft drinks from the vending machine had left her with a furry mouth and a sugar headache, and scrolling through social media was melting her brain. Bess wished she'd brought her yoga mat. She could have done a stretching routine to perk herself up and given the man behind the desk something to sniff about.

"After what we told them, I thought they might put us in the cells," Bess said.

Margaret raised her eyebrows. "The cells might have been more comfortable."

They had driven to Rusdown that morning to make their statements. They'd kept it brief. Officially, they had gone to Crossroads House to see Vivienne and become concerned when she didn't answer. Having been told by Vivienne where the spare key was and knowing she didn't mind them visiting, they had let themselves in to check on her.

As for finding the stolen artefacts at the back of the wardrobe—well, they had been searching for Vivienne in that part of the house and become curious about the wardrobe's strange dimensions.

Then they had handed over Ivy's notebook. Margaret told the police they didn't know what it was exactly, but it seemed to contain a lot of inflammatory information, especially the letter about Janine's ancestor and the cancelled will that had left everything to Dorian. Since Ivy had died suddenly, maybe the police should look into those things?

Bess knew their story sounded peculiar, and the sergeant had squinted dubiously the whole time. But he'd just told them to wait here. A very long time ago.

"If we were men, we would have grown long white beards by now," Bess said.

At least she and Margaret had stopped arguing over whether or not to report what they'd found. They had both lain awake in bed last night, glaring at the motel ceiling, not moving in case they touched each other. But when they got up this morning, Margaret said in a curt tone, "Well, let's get it over with."

She looked up the number of a nearby solicitor while Bess worried about what to wear. The octopus hat might give the wrong impression.

Although they had stopped arguing, Bess didn't feel that they'd patched things up. Margaret said nothing for most of the morning, her posture stiff, her brow creased. It was clear she thought making this confession would go badly for them.

Much as she hated to admit it, Bess had begun to worry that she was right. Looking around the dreary waiting area, she wondered how bad the fallout would be. Would she get a criminal record? Would her employer find out? There were people at her work who'd be happy to see her sacked for bringing the gallery into disrepute. And where would that leave her career? It wasn't as if she could take her concept for a Mount Bastion tiger exhibition elsewhere, not with the tiger women refusing to be interviewed and the locals hating her guts.

She rested her head in her hands. It was hard to remember now why sneaking into Crossroads House had seemed such fun yesterday, like a daring childhood adventure. How she and Margaret had been in it together, urging each other on, enjoying each other's nerve.

Had that really been only a day ago?

Still, regrets were pointless, so she nudged Margaret and said, "Hey. We're doing the right thing."

"Hmm. And no good deed goes unpunished."

Margaret didn't like herself when she was this gloomy. She itched to get on with things, to tick off this disagreeable task and move forward. While she didn't enjoy confessing to breaking the law and answering police questions, what she really hated was being stuck here, watching other people bustling around doing their jobs while she listened to their phone calls and read their discarded newspapers. She flexed her toes inside her high black boots. Oh, to get away.

A message sounded on Bess's phone. "Oh no."

"What is it?"

"The gallery wants to know why I haven't fleshed out my proposal for the exhibition and why I haven't sent back signed agreements by the tiger women to take part."

"Because those women hated the idea?"

"I didn't tell my bosses that yet." Bess ran a hand through her hair. "But they're putting pressure on. If I can't send them something concrete by tomorrow afternoon, they'll drop my idea."

"Oh." Margaret hesitated, then touched her hand. "I'm sorry." Despite the coolness between them, she wanted Bess to be successful, to achieve the acclaim she deserved.

"Apparently, one of my colleagues—you remember Tarquin with the green hair?—has put up a rival proposal. An all-black room with a deep hole in the floor. He's calling it *Zen and the Concept of the Void.*" Bess slumped. "They think it could really get people talking."

"About health and safety risks." Margaret sniffed. "How absurd. You could do better than that in your sleep."

Bess managed a smile. "Thanks. You think I should have one more go at getting the tiger women onboard?"

"Why not?" Margaret thought those women sounded peculiar, but she knew Bess had a good eye for what would work in a show. And anything would be more appealing than Tarquin's void. "When we finish here, I'll drive you back to talk to them."

She avoided Bess's eye, though. The atmosphere between them wasn't right yet.

"Thank you." Bess's tone was a bit too polite.

Jess Lea

The doors slid open, and a young woman stormed in. She was pale and skinny, her dingy hoodie and tracksuit bottoms ready to slide right off her as she charged up to the desk.

"Where's Troy? I've been waiting for fuckin' hours! What've you pricks done with him?"

The constable behind the desk sighed as if this were a weekly visit. He explained that Mr Moffatt was helping the police with their inquiries, and would Ms Wilkie like to take a seat?

"No, I bloody wouldn't! Three hours I've been waiting! You lot are always picking on him. He's meant to drive my mum to her appointment today. I've got things to do, you know!" She noticed Margaret looking. "The fuck are you staring at?"

Having enough problems already, Margaret looked away. Still, the young woman had given her a sense of déjà vu. She hadn't met the agitated Ms Wilkie before, but she made Margaret think of someone else.

She tried to recall.

Of course: graduation night. She and Vivienne had strolled through the city, the office blocks and late night bars lit up, the night sky like velvet. Vivienne had gone to light another cigarette, her lighter had died, and Margaret had stepped into a minimart to buy her another.

As Margaret stood in the queue, she glanced out the window and saw Vivienne talking to a young woman, a scrawny, twitchy kid in a windcheater, a beanie pulled down to her eyebrows. She must have asked Vivienne for money, Margaret assumed. Vivienne must have refused because, when she moved away, the young woman gesticulated and grabbed at her arm. Margaret hurried out in time to see Vivienne push the girl and shout, "Leave me alone!"

Seeing Margaret there, Vivienne seized her arm and said loudly, "Let's get out of here. I'm sick of dealing with crazies. This city is the pits." She hurried Margaret away, her heels clacking, her nails biting into Margaret's wrist.

The girl in the windcheater didn't follow them. Margaret glanced back and saw her standing, bedraggled and white-faced with anger. Then the girl seized the arm of another student from their graduation class and accosted him instead. Vivienne hadn't looked back.

Now Margaret shook her head. Funny, how sentimental the memory could be. Her mind must have edited out that unpleasant moment from graduation night, a moment which didn't exactly show Vivienne at her best. Margaret still felt grateful to Vivienne for that night, but now she had to recognise that, no, the young Vivienne had not been as cool or as compassionate as Margaret had remembered.

Not that it should matter. Vivienne hadn't even been part of Margaret's life until a couple of days ago. But still, the realisation brought a strange sense of loss and unease.

What other memories might be missing?

"You're joking." Bess leaned across the desk in the interview room. "You found nothing?"

"Not a thing." The sergeant managed to look bored and suspicious at the same time.

Margaret nudged Bess's knee, trying to signal that she should not get them into more trouble.

But Bess seemed too shocked to notice. "You looked around Crossroads House, right? The east wing?"

"Yes, Ms Campbell, we managed to find it."

"And the artefacts weren't in the wardrobe?"

"There were no such items in the house."

"You did take the false back off the wardrobe? You looked properly?"

The sergeant shot her a scathing look.

"Well… Alan Moore must have moved them," Bess said. "He must have known where Ivy kept them, and he must have broken in last night and taken them away to resell!"

"Amazing coincidence, if he had."

"No, it wouldn't have been a coincidence." Bess frowned. "I did tell him last night that we were going to report the matter."

For the sake of loyalty, Margaret kept a straight face, not showing how dismayed she had been when Bess had told her earlier about that naïve decision.

When the sergeant looked incredulous, Bess explained. "Since it's a nonviolent offence, I felt it was only fair to give him the chance to do the right thing and come clean."

"Uh-huh." The sergeant looked at her like she was an idiot, and Margaret longed to tell him off. All right, Bess made some choices that were…eccentric. But she meant well.

"Ladies, what I was about to say was: it would be an amazing achievement if Mr Moore had managed to burglarise any houses last night, since he spent most of the night here in the cells. I was at the anniversary dinner and caught him afterwards, pissed as a newt and trying to start his vehicle. I offered him alternative accommodation for the evening."

"Oh." Bess faltered. "So… Alan couldn't have gone to Crossroads House?"

"Correct."

"Well… Maybe he wasn't involved, then. But we still saw those stolen items!"

"I can vouch for that," Margaret added. "I'm a museum professional, and I'm confident—"

"Did you get any photos of these amazing stolen treasures?"

Margaret glared. "Not as such."

Bess said, "We were too freaked out by finding that skull!"

"And we were impeded by the sound of a car arriving," Margaret said. "It, ah, startled us."

"Hmm." The sergeant could not have looked more sceptical if they'd claimed to have seen a live Tasmanian tiger skateboarding past the window. "That was Ms Bolt returning home?"

They nodded.

"Well, I've got good news for you about that."

Margaret sat taller. "Oh?"

"Yes. We spoke to Ms Bolt, and she confirmed that she told you where the spare key was and gave you permission to use it any time. So we won't press charges there."

Margaret kept her face still, but she was astonished. Why had Vivienne covered for them? They had broken into her house and then sent the police there at a time when Vivienne was already fending off other accusations.

"That's all very well." Bess did not seem as relieved as Margaret or as interested in Vivienne's motives. "But we're looking for some resolution about the stolen arte—"

"*However.* There is the matter of your conduct last night."

"Sorry?"

"We've had a complaint from Mrs Jones that you"—he looked at Margaret—"made a nuisance of yourself at her anniversary dinner. And we've had a separate complaint from Mr Visser, who alleges that you"—he pointed at Bess—"cornered him outside the toilets and used offensive and abusive language, causing him to feel unsafe." The sergeant seemed to be reciting the words from memory.

"*I* did?" Bess turned red. "He did that to me!"

"Yeah, yeah." The sergeant put his notebook away. "Look, ladies, this is a nice, quiet place."

"Not in our experience," Margaret couldn't help replying.

"And it's my job to keep it that way. This isn't official, but"—he scraped his chair back—"time you were moving on. Go back to your motel, get your things, and go."

"You've got no right—" Bess started.

Margaret kicked her.

"Tonight." The sergeant got up and opened the door for them.

Margaret pulled Bess to her feet. Unjust though this was, she was not inclined to stay and argue. In fact, while she hated to admit it, she was relieved. They'd gotten off easier than she'd expected.

Bess was not so willing to go quietly. "What about Ivy Bolt's death? We've shown you evidence that two, maybe three people had grudges against her. Are you even going to look into that?"

The sergeant narrowed his eyes. "I'd watch those manners, Ms Campbell. You might offend someone."

He escorted them back to their car as if to make sure they didn't talk to anybody on the way.

"Unbelievable!" Bess raged as they queued up for Thai takeaway in Rusdown. She was desperate for something that might have vegetables in it. "We tried to do the right thing, and we're being run out of town! What is this—Dodge City?"

Margaret glanced along the street. There were three kids on bikes and an old man on a mobility scooter. "Not noticeably. Which would you like: the tofu pad thai or the shredded bamboo shoot salad?"

"It's outrageous," Bess said. "We should make a complaint. The salad."

Margaret ordered, and they wandered outside to wait as the sun dipped lower.

"What did happen to those artefacts?" Bess persisted.

"I've no idea."

"Your friend Vivienne was the only person in the house last night."

"We don't know that. And if she was involved, why would she cover for us with the police? Surely a guilty person would have been happy to land us in trouble, to make our story about the artefacts even less plausible." Margaret shook her head. "Anyway, it makes no difference now." She took a breath. "Listen, I owe you an apology for bringing you here. If I'd ignored Vivienne's phone message, we could be dining at a winery tonight like you wanted. Or doing a treetop walk, or enduring a music festival…"

"You were trying to help someone," Bess reminded her a little stiffly. Truth be told, she wished Margaret had ignored Vivienne's message too, and not only because of the day they'd just had. "Now those beautiful, ancient artefacts have vanished, and no one cares."

"I'm not sure anyone believes they existed." Margaret shrugged. "I'm sorry. I know you have a low tolerance for injustice."

"Damn right I do. Why doesn't everyone?" Bess pushed back her hair. "I'm not letting this go. Maybe if we contacted the federal police?"

Another matter must have occurred to her. "Plus my tiger exhibition definitely won't happen now, since we have to leave the area." She kicked resentfully at the footpath. "No, stuff it. I'm going to have one last talk to the tiger women. Maybe I can persuade them to take part."

"We've had our orders to leave town, remember? We're being cheeky staying for dinner."

"Those orders were totally illegal." Bess hesitated. "I think. Anyway, no one's come along and thrown us into an unmarked van, have they?"

"Not yet."

"Then let's spend the night at Mount Bastion. It's getting too late to drive safely anyhow. I'll see the tiger women tomorrow morning. Then we can leave."

"I suppose that's reasonable. And it would give me a chance to see Vivienne and apologise." Margaret winced. "Goodness knows how I'll explain what we were doing breaking in. How embarrassing. And she lied to the police for us."

"We never asked her to." Bess tried not to speak sharply, but she didn't quite succeed. She might be furious at being kicked out of town, but getting away from Vivienne was the one silver lining, as far as she was concerned.

Margaret nodded, but her thoughts seemed to be far away.

By the time they got back to Mount Bastion, the sky was darkening and a cold breeze blew.

As they approached the motel, Margaret said, "I can't pretend I'm looking forward to this. Spending another night in that sad old shoebox, haunted by the ghosts of a thousand cigarettes…"

"It is a bit depressing," Bess agreed. Eating a proper meal together had taken the edge off their tension and they were speaking almost normally now. "But it's only one more night. And it's good to spend money in a struggling rural town. The business must be grateful."

They pulled into the forecourt, and Margaret trod on the brakes so hard that they jolted in their seats.

"Don't bet on it." She leaped out of the car.

Bess hurried after her.

The door to their room was ajar. All their belongings—suitcases, clothes, Bess's eco toiletries, Margaret's cleaning products—had been dumped outside. One of Bess's books—*How I Rescued an Orphaned Wombat and How She Rescued Me*—had been kicked across the concrete.

Margaret dashed over and grabbed her suitcase. "No!"

The contents were stuffed in higgledy-piggledy as if they'd been searched then replaced in a hurry. Margaret rifled through the mess frantically until she found Deirdre's urn, still in its sealed wrapping. She clutched it, breathing hard.

Bess charged over to the manager's office. The lights were off, and the door was locked. She thumped on it. When there was no response, she found some yodelling music online on her phone and played it at ear-bleeding volume until the manager appeared at last.

"What do you want?"

"What do *I* want?" For such a good-natured woman, Bess could be incandescent when people really pushed her. "I want a lot of things, Mr Brice. World peace, vegan cooking classes in schools, plus-sized leggings with inbuilt supports... But right now I want to know why you've gone through our property when we were paying you to keep it secure, then chucked it outside for anyone to steal!"

"Calm down, love," said Mr Brice, then flinched when Bess threatened to press Play on the yodelling again. "You have to go. We've had an official warning. Nothing to do with me."

"The police came here?"

He hesitated long enough for Margaret to sense that the warning had not come from them.

Bess must have noticed too. "It wasn't the police, was it?" She clenched her fists. "Was it Janine Jones? The unofficial mayor of Mount Bastion?"

"Couldn't say."

"But you could deny it, which you haven't. Who went through our things? You or her?"

"Nothing's missing," Margaret called. Even the tablet and laptop were untouched.

"Well, there you are, then," said the manager as if that resolved things. "Time you were leaving. We won't charge you for today."

"Are you joking?" Bess stepped forward. "We'll call the police about this."

"Oh yeah? Good luck with that." Before Bess could explode, he added, "Seriously, love, I'm not your biggest problem. Take a hint and hop it."

Then he darted back into his office and locked the door. Even a full five minutes of "Lonesome Yodel Blues" didn't bring him out again.

Bess stomped back to Margaret, who was dusting down their possessions before loading them into the car. "They are not getting away with this! I'm totally tweeting about it."

"If you like. But first let's find somewhere to sleep." Margaret pulled out her phone and confirmed that, yes, this was the only accommodation in Mount Bastion. Pacing around the forecourt, she called a motel in a nearby town. Then another and another.

Returning to Bess's side at last, she said, "This is beyond a joke."

Bess looked up from repacking her suitcase. "Don't tell me no one has a vacancy."

"Fully booked, apparently. Even the Rusdown caravan park, where it looked like every surface would be dusted with mouse droppings and meth."

"Is there some local event happening?"

Margaret snorted. "If you ask me, they've all been warned off taking our booking. Someone wants us gone."

"Janine?"

"Amongst others."

"You think she went through our luggage?"

"Why not? She's entitled enough to demand entry to any building in town. And if she was after that letter about her ancestor, she probably believes it's her rightful property and we stole it." Margaret shrugged. "Unluckily for her, we'd already given it to the police. Not that I imagine they'll do anything with it."

She hesitated. The sight of her upended suitcase had shaken her badly, and she couldn't help adding, "The ashes are still here, by the way. No sign of damage."

Bess, looking preoccupied, said, "Good. I suppose there wasn't much danger; you'd wrapped them up well, and Janine wouldn't have been interested in them."

Margaret sagged. What had she hoped for? That Bess would apologise for not thinking to ask about the ashes? That she would comfort Margaret for how stunned and guilty and sick she'd felt in that moment when she'd feared Deirdre's remains were gone?

Yes, perhaps Margaret had been hoping for that.

Rearranging their bags in the car, Bess added vaguely, "Still, it's a good reminder, isn't it? About the impermanence of things. Locking up our memories and keeping them hidden away might make us feel safer in the moment, but it doesn't really protect us from loss."

Margaret stared at the back of her head while Bess fossicked in the car. "Thank you for that." But Bess didn't seem to notice Margaret's icy tone.

Bess asked, "What on earth will we do? Drive until we find a town that will take us in? That doesn't seem very safe."

"Hmm." Lifting her phone again, Margaret turned away. She would not admit that their exchange about the ashes had hurt. Instead, she said, "I'll call someone else first."

It took six rings before Vivienne picked up. "Margaret."

Did she sound out of breath?

"Apologies for calling. I realise you might not wish to speak to me after what happened today."

"Sorry?" Vivienne seemed distracted. "Oh, the police visit? Well, it was a bit odd, but nothing I'm not used to these days. What with being a hardened criminal and all."

"I'm truly sorry, Vivienne. We had no right to invade your privacy like that. I had some queries about Ivy's collection. I intended to ask you about it, but when you weren't there, I'm afraid I became impatient and—"

"Don't sound so anxious, Margaret." Vivienne laughed. "If you find this old place interesting, feel free to let yourself in anytime. It's not my real home."

"That's good of you." Margaret coughed. "And it was good of you to… well, to cover for us when the police called."

"Don't mention it. The least I could do for an old friend."

From Vivienne's end of the call, Margaret heard a muffled crash, then quick breathing as if Vivienne were hurrying someplace.

"Everything all right?"

"Perfectly. And how are things with you, Margaret?"

"Actually, we have a problem." She paused. She had only called Vivienne to apologise. And yet from the back of her mind, a voice whispered, *Go on, tell her…*

Part of Margaret knew she was doing this because of the exchange she'd just had with Bess about Deirdre's ashes, because of her disappointment and hurt at Bess's response. She shouldn't react to those emotions, shouldn't take this any further.

Even as she told herself that, she was already blurting out the story to Vivienne about them being evicted from the motel and unable to find anywhere to stay.

"Come and stay here, of course," was Vivienne's reply.

Margaret shut her eyes. She'd known this would be the response, and she felt ashamed of herself. Bess would hate it. "No," she said uncomfortably. "I wasn't hinting…"

"I know." Vivienne sounded breezy. "But the country roads here have no lights at all. I don't like the thought of you driving for hours in pitch dark, looking for shelter. I know this house is hardly the Hilton, but I can make space. I'd be glad of the company."

Her tone was warm, and the invitation sounded quite innocent.

Margaret wondered if she'd misunderstood Vivienne the other night when she'd invited Margaret back for a drink. "It's very generous of you…"

"Not at all. What else would I be doing tonight? I'll make up the spare room." She spoke briskly, as if it were settled.

"Well, goodbye, then." Margaret grimaced as she hung up. She did not like herself very much right now. She liked herself even less a minute later as she explained their new accommodation to Bess.

"Crossroads House?" All expression faded from Bess's face.

"Well, I don't like the place either." Margaret knew she sounded defensive. "I'm sure it will be cold and smelly with the least comfortable beds in Tasmania. But it's our easiest option tonight. And it would allow you to speak to your tiger women tomorrow morning." She said the last line too eagerly, as if this had been a brilliant plan to help Bess.

Really, she knew it had been no such thing. It had been a stupid impulse on the spur of the moment because she'd been feeling hurt by Bess. And for what? Her not saying the right thing about Deirdre's ashes at a time when Bess was distracted and worried about other things?

Feeling ashamed, Margaret backtracked. "Look, maybe it's not really appropriate. I'll call Vivienne and tell her we're going somewhere else." She meant it. Margaret took out her phone.

"No." Bess stopped her. "No, you're right. I do want to speak to those women again."

There was something odd about her manner, though. A hesitance. As if she were hoping Margaret would argue with her further and insist on going somewhere else. But Margaret wasn't sure. She didn't feel confident interpreting people's unspoken needs at the best of times, and right now she was tired. "Well, then…"

They climbed into the car. Bess seemed lost in her thoughts as they pulled out of the motel and turned in the direction of Crossroads House.

Chapter 15

BESS DROPPED HER BAGS ON the floor of the nursery. "Well, this is… historical."

The narrow bed was draped with mosquito netting turned yellow and brittle with age. A mat on the floor had been woven from rags maybe a hundred years earlier. The foldout bed was newer: from the seventies, she guessed, with a wafer-thin mattress above lethal-looking springs.

Something groaned in the walls as if the house objected to their presence.

"Vivienne did offer us her room," Margaret said.

In fact, Vivienne had tried to insist they stay there, but they'd refused— Margaret presumably out of politeness and Bess because it was bad enough sleeping under Vivienne's roof. She wasn't about to sleep in her bed as well.

Why had she agreed to come? Bess might have been happier sleeping in the car, but it would not have felt very safe; the hostility of the police and locals had spooked her more than she wanted to admit. And there was a question of trust. If she trusted Margaret, staying the night with Vivienne should not pose a real problem, however much Bess disliked the woman. Right?

And she did trust Margaret—or rather, she had always trusted her before. It was just… Bess bit her lip. There had been times in Mount Bastion when Margaret had not seemed herself. And Vivienne was so conniving, and this house had such a nasty atmosphere… Maybe it was irrational, but Bess didn't want to be here.

Margaret stacked her bags neatly, took off her coat, and hung it from the hatstand. "Shall we go downstairs?" Vivienne had invited them for a drink.

Dreading having to hang out with their hostess, Bess stalled. "I need to freshen up first."

Margaret nodded and headed downstairs alone.

The window in the bathroom didn't close fully, and an icy breeze whistled through the gap. Bess brushed her hair, looking in the cracked mirror. How had they come to this? A month ago—heck, a week ago—she had trusted Margaret completely. She didn't want to feel any differently now, but something about this place made her question herself and doubt her own judgements.

The strip of light beneath the door flickered as if something had moved in front of the hall lamp.

She paused, one hand grasping her hairbrush as if that would somehow ward off an intruder.

Don't be silly. It was probably Margaret returning to get something. Although you could usually hear Margaret's military footsteps from miles away.

She flung open the door.

The hall was empty. Returning to the nursery, Bess snapped on the light. But the room was unchanged. She peeked into the other rooms— Vivienne's, Ivy's, the dreadful doll one—but everything looked normal.

The atmosphere must be getting to her. Shaking her head, Bess went back to the nursery to replace her toiletries in her suitcase. A glance out the window showed the jagged outline of the treetops against the night sky. Beyond this house were miles upon miles of bush, most of it untrodden by humans. The thought made her feel small and lonely.

A light flashed in the garden.

She pressed her nose to the glass. A narrow beam bobbed through the trees, moving away from the house.

Should she raise the alarm? But when the clouds drifted away from the moon, the light popped out from behind a bush, and three figures appeared: one short and stout, one tall and thin with wild hair, and one wearing the torch strapped to her head like a miner's helmet. What were the tiger women doing so close to the house?

She could open the window, shout down to them to wait, but she feared they would do the opposite.

Should she call Margaret? But if she did, Vivienne would hear too, and Bess didn't want the owner of the house confronting the intruders. It might scare them off.

If she could grab them before they disappeared, get them to come indoors or speak with her in the garden, perhaps she could persuade them to think again about being featured in a show. Heck, maybe she could even do some interviews right now.

Bess had not forgotten how quickly the women had packed up to leave the other day. The longer she waited, the easier it would be to lose them. And she wanted to be down there doing something interesting and useful, not stuck here waiting for the end of what seemed likely to be a very uncomfortable night.

She should tell Margaret what she was going outside to do. But that would mean telling Vivienne as well, listening to her la-di-da remarks about Bess's work and getting stuck in a long debate about whether she should be doing this now instead of waiting and trying to track down the trio in the morning... After a day of being thwarted by one person after another, she prickled with restlessness to get moving *now*, to get on with it.

Without hesitating any further, she changed into boots for the wet grounds, grabbed her coat, and hurried downstairs and out the front door. On the doorstep, she sent a text message to Margaret. She wasn't going far after all, just into the garden. Her professional future could be creeping around out there, and she was not about to let it go.

Margaret took a sip of brandy and fought not to shudder. Foul stuff—like cough medicine. She was strictly a red wine and vodka woman. But she'd arrived in the sitting room to find that Vivienne had already poured three balloons, and unusually for her, Margaret didn't feel able to say no. Not when she had apologising to do.

She cleared her throat. "Listen. About us letting ourselves in here yesterday..."

"Margaret, relax." Vivienne leaned back in the dark red leather chair and sipped her brandy. Her spindly legs were clad in green leggings, and she wore a loose white blouse made from some filmy material that billowed around her slender figure. With her white-blonde hair, she made Margaret think of a lily of the valley.

Vivienne added, "I told you: it doesn't bother me."

"And that's good of you." Margaret leaned forward. "But we found a cupboard full of rare and, I suspect, stolen items. Whatever happened afterwards, they *were* there." She forced down another mouthful of brandy and watched Vivienne's expression.

Could Bess have been onto something when she said Vivienne was the only person in the house that night—the only person who could have moved those items?

To her surprise, Vivienne nodded. "I believe you."

"Really?"

"Of course. I know you, Margaret; you're no more a crank or a fantasist than I am"—she raised an eyebrow—"whatever the police might say. You remember what I told you days ago: that items were going missing and I'd heard movements inside the house. If it turned out that someone—Lord knows who—had let themselves in and used the abandoned part of the building to store and trade stolen goods... Well, it's bizarre, but it wouldn't surprise me much." She smiled. "I've believed more impossible things. Haven't you?"

Margaret relaxed her grip on the glass. "But isn't it possible your grandmother knew about those items?"

In truth, after finding the inventory book, Margaret assumed Ivy must have known. But she didn't want to tell Vivienne about the book now. It wasn't very admirable of her, but Margaret feared that if she revealed the book with its details about Ivy's legitimate possessions, it would lead to Vivienne persuading her to spend the night checking through more antiques together. Which might lead in turn to more pleas for Margaret to stay another day and help out some more... And she no longer had any wish to do so. Let Vivienne find the book herself when she cleaned this place out.

Vivienne shrugged. "It wouldn't surprise me if Ivy knew. She loved buying coveted items, loved knowing she'd beaten another collector to the punch. She positively gloated about how angry she'd made some people. Sometimes I think that's the main reason she did it."

"But illegal items, though…"

"I'm not sure she'd have lost sleep over that." Vivienne crossed her legs. "Ivy said possession was nine-tenths of the law, and that if people really wanted to be ethical, they would leave old treasures in the ground or pay top dollar for them voluntarily, which no one did." Vivienne laced her fingers together. "Her words, not mine."

"Of course."

Swirling the liquid in her glass, her hostess mused, "When I was young, Ivy told me that she'd wanted to be an archaeologist when she was a girl. Some women did, you know, in the 1930s. But not out here, not even girls from the best families. Mount Bastion was a long way from Khartoum and Mesopotamia."

"True."

"Perhaps this was the closest she could get to her childhood dream." Vivienne gestured around at the hundreds of antiques locked away from the world.

"Or perhaps this was how she took her revenge," Margaret suggested, "because she never got to pursue that dream."

"Well… Yes." Vivienne glanced at her over the rim of her glass. "Revenge isn't a popular motivator these days, is it? Especially for women. We're supposed to forgive. It makes life easier for everyone else. But our primal instincts can't stay suppressed forever." She studied the last of her brandy. "Can they, Margaret?"

Matilda was shorter than Bess, but she managed to tilt her head back and look down her nose at the intruder.

"Young lady, I insist you leave. You are disrupting a delicate scientific investigation."

"And you're giving me the screaming shits," Daz said.

Matilda tutted. "Language!"

Bess said, "You know you're on someone else's property, right? I'm staying here by invitation. Technically, I could tell *you* to leave."

"As if we'd hang around here." The light strapped to Daz's forehead made it hard to see her properly. "We're just collecting something."

Bess looked around. Penny opened another camouflage camera, this one strapped to a banksia tree twenty feet from the house. She removed a memory card and swapped it for another.

"You've been watching Crossroads House?"

"Don't be absurd." Matilda sniffed. "We have no interest in the house. But there has been promising activity in this grid square. The rubbish bins outside the house have been tipped over several times and foodstuffs pulled out."

"You've been...inspecting their bins?"

"Obviously. *De omnibus dubitandum:* suspect everything. And something knocked over that bird bath and broke it."

Bess looked at her shoes. "Um…"

"And there've been noises around here," said Daz. "Buggered if I can trace them, though."

"What kind of noises?"

"Nothing verifiable," said Matilda. "We couldn't get a decent recording."

"Could have been squeaking or grunting." Daz scratched her head. "Maybe a yap?"

Penny returned. "Stop making noise! And why is *she* here?" She pointed a long twiggy finger at Bess.

"She's leaving." Matilda waved the other two ahead of her towards the hole in the fence.

"Wait." Bess stepped in front of them. "Hear me out. I want you to reconsider being interviewed. An exhibition about your research could be really valuable."

"Sure, for you." Daz sneered. "'Roll up and see the nutjobs who believe in leprechauns and the Loch Ness Monster!'"

"I don't think that. Hey, I've lived an alternative lifestyle myself. I know what it's like to be treated like a weirdo just because you don't want to spend your days in an office and your weekends in a shopping mall. Seriously, I think this exhibition could be beneficial."

Matilda folded her arms. "How?"

In a flash of inspiration, Bess said, "Have you heard of the Luxor Golf Club?" Quickly, she explained that Luxor had bought land out here and were fighting for permission to turn it into a golf course.

"All this bushland could be flattened by next year," she said. "They'll bulldoze it and put in a putting green."

"They can't!" Penny gasped. "A whole ecosystem would be lost! And if a remnant thylacine population has survived—"

"It won't survive much longer," Bess said. The thought was terrible. She wasn't convinced that tigers were still living here or anywhere, but lots of other animals were.

"We'll have done all this work for nothing." Penny sounded close to tears.

Daz prodded her. "Could be bullshit, babe."

"Google it," Bess challenged them.

Matilda was already on her phone. The glow from its screen lit up her frowning face. At last, she said, "She might be correct." Her voice was gruff; her expression stricken.

"Jesus fucking wept." Daz paused, then kicked a garden gnome. It flew through the air and landed in the bushes.

"But don't you see?" Bess said. "If we could tell the world about your investigations, it might drum up interest, gain public support. I know you can't prove the thylacine's existence yet, but you must have documented lots of other endangered species here."

"Naturally," Matilda said.

"Well, isn't it worth sharing?"

Penny was picking anxiously at her nails; Daz was looking around for something else to kick. In the light of her phone, Matilda looked tired. Bess had thought her about sixty but now she seemed at least ten years older.

Still, when Matilda spoke, her voice was steady. "We'll need to consider this. It's a serious matter." She beckoned to her companions. "Pull yourself together, Penny. Daz, stop kicking that shrub. We still have tasks for tonight, other cameras to check." She turned to Bess. "I appreciate you alerting us to this matter."

"Seems like you wouldn't have found out about it in time otherwise," Bess pointed out.

"Perhaps. But we cannot discuss our sensitive work with a stranger." She looked Bess up and down, then nodded towards the bush. The other two were headed back there. "Let's talk some more. And let's see what you're made of."

Bess started. "You want me to come with you? Now?"

"If you want to understand what we do well enough to make a show about it, you'll need to experience it. Mud, cold, darkness, bugs, leeches…" She raised her eyebrows. "Perhaps you're worried about breaking a nail?"

Stung, Bess said, "If you three can do it, I can." At least she had her boots on this time. "But what about getting lost?"

"We know the trail well," said Matilda, "and we've got torches, flares, satnav. Stick with us and you'll be safe. We'll have some questions for you, though, before we start answering any of yours."

"Fine," said Bess. "But wouldn't tomorrow be better—"

However, the three women were already headed away, apparently not interested in waiting for her. If she didn't follow, would they decide she wasn't worth their time?

Cursing, Bess had only a few seconds to decide. She dashed off another text to Margaret, then trotted after the torchlight into the trees.

Matilda didn't look around when Bess caught up with her. But Bess thought she saw her smile as she said "*Sapere aude:* dare to know."

Margaret had to admit the brandy was growing on her. Warmth seeped through her limbs, making her stretch and stifle a yawn. Vivienne must have fixed the heating, for the room was almost cosy. Granted, the pale squares of wallpaper where pictures had been taken down, the crumbling ceiling, and the grim horsehair furniture weren't exactly welcoming, but perhaps they had an eccentricity that she could accept, a Charles Addams quality. Perhaps Crossroads House wasn't so bad.

She wondered what was keeping Bess.

"So"—Vivienne topped up Margaret's glass—"what will you do when you get out of here?"

"When our holiday is over?" Margaret might have commented on how badly this Tasmanian trip had gone, but she felt placated by the warmth and the soothing effect of the brandy. "Return to Melbourne. Finish getting my sister's affairs in order. Apply for jobs I don't especially want." She looked at Vivienne through the bulging curve of the brandy glass; it made her look distorted, shimmering. "What about you?"

"I don't suppose I'll go back to work." Vivienne swept her hair away from her face. It spread across her armchair, fine strands of platinum against the red leather. "I was bored with it anyhow. There are only so many forms you can fill out and colleagues' birthday morning teas you can sit through. Once things are resolved here—assuming I haven't been thrown into a dripping, rat-infested dungeon for murder most foul—I'll sell up and leave." She glanced at Margaret. "I'd still appreciate your help with sourcing buyers for Ivy's antiques. I'd make sure you had a contract and a decent percentage, of course. I'm not asking to be your charity project."

By now, Margaret was relaxed enough to laugh. "I never pictured you that way."

Her thoughts drifted. Bess was taking ages to come down. Was she still in a strange mood? Well, perhaps it wasn't bad for them to have an hour apart. Travelling together could feel claustrophobic. "Once you've sold Ivy's things, what then? Where will you go?"

"Wherever I please," Vivienne said. "I know a man who's starting an archaeological dig in France, in the Vézère Valley. Palaeolithic sites: cave paintings, burial mounds, evidence of hunting and tool use. Perhaps I'll tag along. Live in the Ice Age for a while."

"Fine wine and woolly mammoths? Sounds interesting."

Vivienne said, "If you weren't spoken for, I'd carry you off there with me."

Why had she said that? Margaret bristled in irritation at this lazy bit of flirting. And just when she had been starting to think it was pleasant in here. "Well, I am spoken for. And I'm not one to be carried anywhere."

"Goodness, Margaret, I know that! You're so literal; I was only being funny." Vivienne kept smiling to show it was indeed a joke as she craned over to fill their glasses again.

"Why are you doing this?" Bess asked Matilda as the four women tramped around checking camera sites. The air had grown so cold, she fancied her breath might turn to ice crystals in the darkness. Their torchlight picked up a glittering spiderweb and the shining eyes of a possum as it leapt through the branches. The path narrowed until it was barely a foot wide. If they left her alone here, she wasn't sure she could find her way back.

She had answered what felt like a hundred rapid-fire questions from Matilda about her background, her education, her work in galleries, her interests, her views on conservation. She couldn't tell if she'd passed the test or not, but it was time to get some answers of her own.

Penny and Daz walked on ahead. When Matilda didn't answer, Bess said, "Come on, enough mystery. Why do the three of you live this way? You don't seem to be on holiday."

Matilda tramped another ten steps before she said, "No, it's not a holiday. We are working from a hypothesis: that the thylacine is still alive. Our living arrangements are geared to testing that hypothesis as rigorously as possible."

"It's a big sacrifice. What if you don't find anything?"

"It's no sacrifice at all. The amenities are basic, but the bush agrees with us."

"All right." Bess thought it over. "Hey, I told you: I used to live in a tiny house in a field, just me and my chickens. No TV, no car, no street lights. I sat out there every morning, watching the sun rise and listening to the magpies singing. In some way, it was the happiest time of my life."

Matilda shone the torch at her, scrutinising Bess's face as if assessing whether she meant it. Whatever she saw must have satisfied her because she nodded. "Well, perhaps you can understand."

"But back then, I had a job and friends in town. You three seem very isolated. Doesn't the loneliness bother you?"

Matilda gave a grunt of amusement. "I was a school principal for twenty years. I had girls, teachers, and parents pestering me nonstop." She shook her head. "Penny lived in some dingy little unit. Her relatives had bullied her into it; she isn't very good at making mundane life decisions. Her mind works on a different level. As for Daz, when I met her, she was sleeping on a bunk bed with her sister's grandchildren. Eight people in that small house. Before that, she'd lived in all sorts of rough places, sometimes as a guest of Her Majesty."

"The three of you seem like very different people." Bess had not expected this frank turn, but the darkness, the exercise, and the sounds of the bush encouraged confidences. "How did you meet?"

"I volunteered at a community centre. Free lunches for the over sixties." Insects danced in the beam of Matilda's torch. "Conversations happened around the tea urn. Penny needed a change of circumstances; she's brilliant, but she has her quirks. One of her chemistry experiments had started a fire in her kitchen, and people were muttering about calling the mental health authorities. Daz needed to get away from old associates and sleep on something other than Minnie Mouse sheets. And I was at a loose end. Enforced retirement."

"How so?"

Matilda sighed. "Irreconcilable differences with the school board: they insisted on going coed and abolishing Latin in the name of progress. Every woman has her breaking point."

"Why look for the tiger, though?"

"I was always fascinated by it," Matilda said. "It was unique and inconvenient. Falsely accused, eliminated like vermin. *Damnant quod non intellegunt:* they condemn that which they do not understand."

"Right."

Matilda worked her jaw. "There's old film footage of one of the last survivors in a zoo, trotting around and around in a bare little concrete cage while half-witted people tease it through the wire. Looking for a way out... And then when the species was declared extinct, everyone felt sorry and said what a tragedy it was. The hypocrisy was breathtaking."

"But most people do believe it's extinct, though, don't they? They would argue that if the species had survived, one would have been found by now."

"That depends on how far the animal retreated," Matilda said, "and how good it got at hiding." She lifted her torch, showing the vast, looming mass of trees. "Plenty of wilderness out there. And some things are worth taking a chance on."

The bush thinned out, and Bess realised they were back at the women's campsite. Daz began to rebuild the fire while Penny headed for the caravan.

Matilda said, "You should go with Penny—watch her check the footage. Imagine if we found proof tonight."

"I suppose Bess isn't coming down." Margaret glanced up at the ceiling. "She looked tired when I left her."

"I imagine you're a tiring person to live with." Vivienne refilled their glasses. This time she got up to do it, leaning over so that her hair fell in a gleaming curtain between them. Her perfume smelled of lilies. She sat beside Margaret on the couch.

"That's a bit hard, coming from someone who hasn't seen me in years." Margaret took a sip, then regretted it. Her head felt fuzzy. She hoped she wasn't slurring.

"Oh, *I* wouldn't find you tiring," Vivienne sounded amused and not tipsy at all. "But I'm frightfully lazy. I would leave you as you are." She tapped a fingernail against the glass. It chimed softly. "But Ms Campbell strikes me as the sort of woman who likes a project. I wager she's always trying to persuade you to do things, isn't she? Make more friends, get an impressive job, take a Pilates class, eat more kale…"

"Not exactly." Margaret frowned. "Well, what if she does? It's because she cares; she's a good person." Even now, Margaret found it hard to say *it's because she loves me.*

Margaret had been on her own for most of her life, regarded by most other people with suspicion or fear. She wanted Bess's love, felt the need for it deeply, but still had trouble sometimes accepting that she really had it.

"Of course!" Vivienne gave her shoulder a playful push. "Good people—I think I read about those somewhere." She relaxed against the couch, her fine-boned face tilted up towards Margaret. "It must get frustrating for her, though. Trying to fix someone."

Margaret lowered her glass. No, she didn't want any more. She regarded Vivienne's delicate face. Its triangular shape and wide eyes made her think of a fox. "What does that mean? You think I'm broken?"

"Lord, no! That's my point: there's nothing wrong with you. So don't you get tired of all the well-meaning fussing and nurturing? All the home-made salads and pep talks about gratitude?" She touched Margaret's sleeve. "Don't you long to get away?"

"No. I don't, actually."

Margaret wanted to say more, to retort that Vivienne didn't know Bess at all, that her comments were way off the mark. But the drink had slowed her down. And perhaps… Well, perhaps there was a secret, insecure part of her that feared deep down that Vivienne might be right about one thing: that Bess might indeed view her as sad and malfunctioning, in need of repairs. Bess was so delightful, so energetic and friendly. Could she really want Margaret just the way she was?

Angered by Vivienne's comments but struggling to reply properly, Margaret managed to snap, "You're the one who has reasons for wanting to escape from here. I heard about your parents."

Vivienne didn't seem to move. But the brandy washed against the sides of her glass, so her hand must have trembled. "People are still talking about that? I thought they must have picked the bones clean by now." She looked away. "What did they tell you?"

"Well..." Margaret felt a twinge of guilt for mentioning it. Had she been taking revenge on Vivienne for saying those things about Bess? Vivienne deserved to be reprimanded, but that had been a low blow. "They just said that your father was a disturbed man and that he... You know. Decided to stop your mother from leaving him."

"I see. Well, it's good to know my family's annihilation kept the locals entertained."

Margaret winced. "I am sorry, Vivienne. It must have been...well, a terrible shock."

Vivienne raised an eyebrow. "I don't know. I don't recall feeling shocked per se." She reached over and covered Margaret's hand with hers.

Margaret looked down at her long, strong digits and the other woman's dainty hand on top. What was Vivienne doing? However much Margaret admired her in a way, she didn't want Vivienne touching her, didn't want to be touched by anyone but Bess. She pulled her hand away. "Don't."

Why had that taken such a physical effort? Her body was becoming heavy and sluggish. Was she really that tired? "I told you: I'm with Bess." She wanted to say more, to tell Vivienne not to touch her again, but her usual sharp remarks wouldn't come. Her tongue felt like concrete.

"I know. Excuse me for reaching out for a little human contact." Vivienne sounded affronted, as if Margaret were the rude one. "I was only saying that I wasn't especially shocked by what happened to my parents. Some things are inevitable, aren't they? Terrible things...and good things too."

Seated in the caravan, Bess watched Penny scanning footage. "What is it you like about this life?"

Penny paused on an image of a wombat nosing the camera and made a note. "The rigour," she said, her eyes fixed on the screen through her massive glasses. "I worked in laboratories years ago, but I couldn't stay. There was so much interference, people wanting me to do things differently, and their reasons made no scientific sense. Here I can work properly. Do you really think this wilderness will be destroyed?" She rattled off the question without looking at Bess.

"There's a danger. I'd like to help stop it."

"We'll stop it." Penny sounded matter-of-fact now. "Bulldozers can be disabled, you know. So can the people who pay for them. I would only need a little time. Maybe your exhibition can buy that for us."

"I hope so," said Bess. "I'll need your participation. Starting with an interview."

"We're considering it." Penny's tone made it clear she would not be pushed further yet. "Matilda thinks you might be trustworthy."

Bess raised her eyebrows. "She said you blew up a kitchen once."

"Oh no, it was a very minor explosion. I had it under control. There was no need for all the shrieking and fire engines. People get so irrational. If I'd wanted to blow the building up, I could have done it easily." She pushed a container towards Bess. "Liquorice Allsorts?"

"Thank you."

"Oy, Nutty Professor." Daz appeared in the doorway. "One of your thermos-sensor whatsits is pinging. It's doing my head in."

"Oh good, it's working." Penny bustled outside.

Leaning against the door, Daz looked at Bess. "You'd better not be stuffing us about."

"I'm on your side, honestly."

"Huh. We'll see." Daz glanced at the screen. "Nothing?"

Bess shook her head. "Why do you enjoy this life? Penny likes the scientific quest and Matilda likes the symbolism. What's in it for you?"

Daz rolled her sleeves up. There were murky blue tattoos on her forearms. "I get to sleep under the stars and eat what I want. What's not to like?"

From outside came a kerfuffle and a deep, ferocious snarling. Penny yelped, "Something's in the net trap!"

Bess sat bolt upright.

Matilda snapped, "Another possum! We agreed not to use those blasted contraptions again. I'm not getting bitten this time; you let it out."

"That's not fair," came Penny's voice. "I have allergies! Do you know the percentage of brushtail possums infected with dermatitis?"

Daz rolled her eyes. "Fuck's sake." She yelled over her shoulder, "I'll get it!" Turning back to Bess, she said, "I've seen one, you know."

"What? A tiger?"

When Bess looked at her with curiosity rather than disbelief, Daz said, "Camping trip, five years ago. I went into the bush for a smoke around midnight, and it shot across the track in front of me. Close as you are now." She shrugged. "You don't believe me, do you?"

Before Bess could reply, Daz said, "Yeah, no one ever does. Except those two." She dropped down from the caravan steps and into the dark.

Left in front of their laptop, Bess glanced around. Memory cards sat in a box, marked in different colours. She recalled seeing Penny removing one from the camera pointed at Crossroads House. It had been marked in yellow.

She heard shouts. "Look out, it's biting through the rope!"

Bess turned back to the box. The memory cards had dates on them. She found a yellow one with the right date range and slotted it in. Then she searched for the night Ivy died. She didn't know what she expected to find. Goodness knows there were plenty of other things she should be worrying about. But this memory card was the one objective witness to what had happened at Crossroads House that night. And she wanted to know.

The camera was trained on the rubbish bins. Bess scanned the screen as she moved the timer forward. Seven o'clock, eight o'clock, nine o'clock…

Outside, Daz hollered, "Get off me, ya little bastard!" Branches crashed as if something had sprung into the trees. Then sounds of spitting and retching. "It ran up my bloody face and put its mangy foot in my mouth! This is your fault, genius!"

They would be busy for a while, then. Bess kept scanning: ten o'clock, eleven, midnight…

She hit Pause. Something had moved in front of the camera.

Rewinding, she saw a dark object cross the screen. It stepped back, taking shape. A man. A large man leaning on a walking stick.

Dorian.

Her mouth turned dry. Dorian, who had tried to throw the blame for Ivy's death onto her granddaughter and who may have believed he had a legal claim on the house… He was clumping back and forth, gesticulating. Was he talking to someone? As she cursed the lack of sound, another figure moved into shot. A bulky figure, weaving a little as if drunk.

Alan? Here at this house full of antiques which he had wanted first shot at? A house hiding illegal artefacts that Alan swore he knew nothing about?

The two men had what looked like a whispered argument. They only shifted when a third figure appeared, high heels sticking in the grass and a frilly evening dress flapping.

No way… It was Janine Jones, still in the outfit she must have worn to the Rotary Club dance. Janine, who had been desperate to retrieve that incriminating letter from Ivy.

Onscreen, Janine took the spare key from under the shutter and eased open the front door. She waved the two men over, and the trio edged into the house.

"The hell are you doing?" Daz's voice made Bess leap up. Her three hostesses stood in the doorway.

"Have you seen this?" Bess jabbed at the screen. "Three people from Mount Bastion broke into Crossroads House the night Ivy Bolt died!"

She stared from one woman to the next, but their faces had turned guarded and quiet, giving nothing away. Whatever that expression meant, it was not a look of surprise.

"Why didn't you report this?" Bess demanded. "This is a crime. And Ivy's death was suspicious!"

"We don't know anything about that." Daz's reply came so quickly that Bess sensed this was not the first dodgy incident she'd denied knowledge of.

"The police are investigating!" But was that still true? The authorities' interest in Ivy's death had seemed to wane in the past day or two. And when the police did ask questions, they had focused on Ivy's missing medication and Vivienne's treatment of her grandmother. They had not said a word about Alan, Janine, or Dorian.

"I'm confident the authorities will get to the bottom of whatever did or did not happen." Matilda touched Penny's shoulder as if cautioning her to stay silent. "They don't require our assistance."

"You can't be serious!"

But Daz just crossed her arms while Penny looked at the floor.

In a calm voice, Matilda said, "We made it clear to you: we have as little as possible to do with the outside world. As long as they leave us alone, we leave them alone."

"But this is a crime! Ivy could have been"—Bess realised she hadn't said it before—"murdered."

"You don't know that."

"You don't know she wasn't!" This was appalling. A few minutes ago, she had thought these women were intriguing, even admirable. How could they be so coldly selfish? "You have to turn this footage in."

"And turn ourselves in too?" Matilda jutted out her chin. "Be forced away from our work? Questioned, searched, charged with trespass and illegal camping? Cross-examined and exposed to the world? No. Perhaps we might have tolerated publicity to save the forest but not for any other reason."

Bess waved at the screen. "These three people had motives for wanting Ivy Bolt gone. Did you know that?"

The women glanced at each other as if this were indeed news to them.

"They broke into her house," Bess said. "What if there was a confrontation that led to her death? Hell, what if they went in there intending to kill her?"

"Then let the police do their job and figure it out," said Matilda. "Look, if we'd known at the time that a woman was at risk, we would have stepped in, but we didn't. Whatever happened that night is a fait accompli now."

Bess looked at her incredulously. "Don't you care?"

"You think *we're* the heartless ones?" For the first time, Matilda sounded angry. "How much do people care about us? The world wrote us off years ago. And when we took ourselves off the map for good, no one even noticed." Her voice trembled. "*Iacta alea est:* the die is cast. Now, I think it's time you left. Forget your exhibition. We'll find another way to protect this place."

"I can't believe this." Bess threw her hands up. "Fine, I'll go. But I'm taking this." She reached for the memory card, but Penny flew in front of her and snatched it.

Daz seized Bess in an armlock and thrust her towards the door. "Sorry, love. Nothing doing."

"Get off me!" But Daz's grip was strong as she wrestled Bess down the steps.

"Here." Matilda thrust a torch into Bess's free hand. "Stick to the 4WD track and you'll get back to the road safely. Don't wander into the bush. It isn't safe."

Released, Bess stumbled forward. The caravan door snapped shut with a click of the lock.

She pounded on it and shouted until she was hoarse, but it didn't open again.

Margaret moved away from Vivienne. She wasn't sure why she felt so muddled, so heavy and queasy, wasn't sure why it was so hard to find the right words. But she wasn't staying for any more of this. "That's enough. I'm going upstairs. To Bess." She pushed herself to her feet and hurried from the room.

What had just happened back there?

Yes, she had known that she and Vivienne had a connection, that they shared a memory of important moments long ago. But Vivienne's remarks about Bess, her closeness on the couch, the soft grip of her hand... No. Despite the ambiguous feelings she'd felt from Vivienne in the past, Margaret had not expected her to behave like that. And she did not want it.

Why hadn't Bess come downstairs? Margaret felt unreasonably frustrated as she climbed the creaking steps past Ivy's stairlift and the marks on the wall. What had happened with Vivienne wasn't Bess's fault, obviously. But if she had joined them for that drink as she'd said she would, the whole exchange would never have occurred.

She opened the door; the bedroom was empty.

"Bess?"

She wasn't in the bathroom or the neighbouring rooms. Margaret patted her pockets and realised she'd left her phone up here on the dresser.

There were two messages from Bess.

Tiger women outside. Going down to speak to them. Back in a minute

And:

Going walking with TW. Sorry but need to pin them down for this exhibition. Won't be long.

The messages had been sent over an hour ago.

Margaret felt like her insides had been clamped in a vice. She tried Bess's number but got no reply. She looked out the window. Nothing moved in the grounds. Why had Bess run off after those women alone in the dark? Her panic rose, but she felt indignant too. Did Bess care nothing for how worried Margaret would be?

She should rush downstairs, find a torch, start searching. But something caught her eye: her suitcase lay crooked on the floor, not lined up with the wall as it should be. And the top compartment was unzipped. Margaret never left zips undone; the very thought drove her mad.

She flung it open. One of her shirts was rumpled, and a book cover was creased. Someone had gone through her things.

Her chest tight with dread, Margaret went to the most important section. *Empty.*

Hands trembling, she shook everything out and flung it onto the floor, but there was no mistake. This time Deirdre's ashes were gone.

But how could they be? She clawed at her hair. She, Bess, and Vivienne were the only people in the house. And after showing them to their room, Vivienne had retreated downstairs. She had stayed there the whole time.

Footsteps sounded on the landing. "Margaret?"

She sprang to her feet. *Bess!* "Where have you been?"

Bess looked pale, dishevelled, and drooping.

Margaret rushed over. "Are you all right?"

A weary nod.

"What possessed you to go out there after dark? Are you mad?"

"Spare me the lecture. I feel bad enough already. You'll never guess what I found in the tiger women's camp. Footage of Alan, Dorian, and Janine sneaking into this house the night Ivy died."

"Deirdre's ashes are missing!" Margaret blurted. Under other circumstances, she would have been stunned by what Bess had just told her, but right now she could barely bring herself to listen. "Do you know where they are?"

"Did you hear what I just said?" Bess screwed up her nose. "And what are you talking about?"

"Am I not speaking clearly?" Relieved though she was to find Bess safe, she still shook with anxiety. "My sister's urn has been taken from my suitcase. And everything was in order when I went downstairs."

"Are you sure you haven't—"

"Misplaced it? Heavens, that never occurred to me. Of course I'm sure."

"Have you asked Vivienne?"

"She's been downstairs the whole time. And what would she want with it?"

"What would *I* want with it?" Bess planted her hands on her hips. "I don't much like whatever it is you're implying."

"I'm not implying anything! I just want to know what happened." Margaret dug her nails into the palms of her hands. "Why did you go outside anyway?"

"I told you: I went to speak to the tiger women. I thought I could persuade them to take part in the exhibition."

"You didn't tell me, actually. You sent me two texts, which I didn't see."

"Well, whose fault is that?" Bess wasn't shouting, but she was getting closer to it.

"Good question." Margaret's voice rose in volume to match. "You couldn't be bothered to tell me in person before you rushed off to risk your safety with those lunatics—again?"

"They insisted! It was my one chance to get them onboard; I wasn't going to give up. And Vivienne must have made you very welcome downstairs if you only just noticed I was gone."

"Oh, so you hoped I'd sit around for ages being worried instead?" Part of Margaret knew she should calm herself before she said something she would really regret. But her head was storming with the loss of her sister's remains, Bess's careless disappearance, Vivienne saying, "It must get frustrating for her...trying to fix someone..." She blurted, "Did you move Deirdre's ashes?"

Bess stepped back. "Excuse me?"

"You were the one who said I needed a reminder about the impermanence of things." Margaret grimaced, sensing she had crossed a line. But it was too late to take it back now. "Were you trying to make some kind of point?"

"Get stuffed!" Bess spoke loudly enough to be heard downstairs. "Of course I didn't." She looked incredulous. "You actually think I would do that?"

A rock plummeted into Margaret's stomach. "I... No, I suppose not."

She'd just made a mess of things, hadn't she? And badly this time. Perhaps she had believed for a moment that Bess could have moved the urn for some obscure spiritual reason that Margaret couldn't understand. But Bess wouldn't lie about it. Margaret stammered, "But no one else has been in here. I didn't know what to think..."

"No, you don't know what to think because you barely notice anything that's happening around you any longer!" Bess flung up her hands in frustration. "You're more focused on locking up those ashes and not laying them to rest anywhere because God forbid you should feel pain and move on!"

Flushed with anger, Bess added, "All right, have a look." She strode over to her pile of belongings, opened her suitcase, and emptied its contents onto the floor. "Look, no urn in here." She unzipped her toilet bag and rifled through her cosmetics. "Gosh, not here either."

"Bess..." Margaret winced. "You said you didn't do it; I believe you."

"No, wait, here's my work stuff." Bess opened her shoulder bag and hauled out her laptop, diary, and tablet. "Wow, it's not here—" Then she stopped. Carefully, Bess put the bag down on the bed.

Margaret looked. The urn was in there. Her throat dried up. She reached out for the urn, picked it up, and held it like a bomb.

Bess's eyes widened. "I don't know anything about this."

Her voice croaky, Margaret said, "How did it get in there?"

Bess stared. "You *do* think it was me."

"It couldn't have been Vivienne."

"You don't know that for sure! Do you seriously trust her ahead of me?"

"No, of course not. But..." Her thoughts were whirlpooling. She gripped the doorframe. No, she didn't think Bess had done it, but none of this made sense.

Her tone still angry but reasonable, Bess said, "I don't know what's going on, but you need to calm down and think clearly. Take some breaths; centre yourself; put things in perspective—"

"That's not going to help!" Margaret burst out. "Someone has stolen Deirdre, and all you can do is tell me how to—what? Be less dysfunctional? Vivienne was right: you do think I'm deficient! You are trying to fix me." Saying the words out loud felt horrible and satisfying at the same time, like vomiting up something foul. "I apologise for being so broken, but I won't take up any more of your time. Perhaps you'd be better off with someone like Ty. I doubt there's anything there capable of being damaged."

Bess stared at Margaret, her mouth open.

Margaret couldn't bear to look at her. "I need to get out of here." She left the room and didn't look back.

Bess struggled to catch her breath. Her eyes watered. What was happening?

She didn't know what stunned her more: the ashes in Bess's bag or Margaret's response. Did she really think that Bess believed her inadequate, that Bess wanted her to change? Did she have to stalk off rather than talk about it properly? Yes, apparently she did.

In a perverse way, that thought calmed her. No, she did not understand what was happening. But she knew she was not responsible for Margaret's insecurities, and she was not about to go downstairs to try and reason with her again when she was in this state.

Had Vivienne planted the urn in Bess's bag? That would have been Bess's assumption, but Margaret had insisted that Vivienne was downstairs. Had another person crept inside the house? Or was Margaret so keen to absolve Vivienne that she had revised her own memory? Bess didn't believe she would do that, but this night had become so strange she couldn't feel certain.

She had to get out of Crossroads House. Maybe she was paranoid, but even the air smelled wrong, like mouldy fabric and grime. She gathered up her belongings from the floor and began repacking.

Her shock wasn't only at Margaret's behaviour but also at the footage she'd seen in the tiger women's caravan. Dorian, Janine, and Alan had broken in here the night Ivy died, all of them with a grudge against her. Alan had wanted that inventory book; Janine, that letter about her ancestor. Neither of those documents had been found that night, but Bess recalled

Ivy's new will, slipped down behind the desk. Had Dorian found it, read it, and dropped it again, perhaps startled by something?

Bess pictured it: Ivy hearing a noise and tottering to the top of the stairs in her nightdress to investigate. The image was pitiful. So many people had described Ivy as a spiteful old tyrant that Bess had gotten used to picturing her that way. She had not fully considered how small and vulnerable Ivy had been that night. What had happened next? An accident, an unplanned struggle, or a deliberate murder?

If that thought was horrible, another thought was almost worse: there was a tiny part of Bess that felt disappointed that those three people must have been involved in Ivy's death because it meant Vivienne was innocent.

Of course, she didn't want Ivy's death to have been foul play at all, but part of her must have been willing to think the worst of Vivienne, and now it turned out she'd been wrong. Vivienne wasn't a criminal. Apparently, she was just someone Margaret sided with over Bess.

Don't dwell on that now. She made herself focus. She would tell the police about the footage, but after the business with the stolen artefacts, she doubted they'd take her seriously. The tiger women could be erasing their videos right now.

The thought made her want to scream. How could they refuse to come forward?

Bess hauled her suitcase upright and slung her bag over her shoulder. Well, she couldn't change other people's choices; she could only do the right thing herself. Tonight, she would sleep in the hire car—well, sit up awake and fuming, probably, waiting to see if Margaret would come to her senses, find her, and talk to her. And tomorrow Bess would make a report.

But what if Margaret didn't seek her out? The thought made her want to sink down on the bed and burst into tears. What would she do then? Take a cab to some grim motel in the morning and wait for Margaret to call? Go on with the holiday by herself, sipping local beverages and feeding wildlife while trying not to break down? Book herself a ticket home?

No, she would not think about that now. She breathed deep, wiggled her toes, and returned to the moment, however lousy this moment might be. For now she had one task: get out of Crossroads House.

Bess dragged her bags downstairs and along the hall. She walked normally; she wasn't going to sneak or hurry out as if she'd done something wrong.

Still, when she reached the front door, she hesitated. Margaret had jumped to conclusions and said hurtful things, but she was grieving, and the events of the past few days would have unsettled anyone. And this place… The very walls seemed to pulse with some malignant energy. She didn't feel good about leaving Margaret behind. Should she turn back, try one last time to persuade Margaret to come with her?

From down the hall came the sound of a cork popping. Then the trill of Vivienne's voice. "I'm so glad I caught you before you wandered out into the cold. I felt so foolish after how I behaved earlier; I needed to explain myself. And it looks like you could use a sympathetic ear too. Sit down…"

From out of sight, Margaret replied in a tight voice, "Well, just one drink."

Bess clenched her jaw. There was her answer.

She set off on an unsteady walk down the drive, her suitcase bouncing over rocks and weeds. As she neared the road, she heard a distant growl.

Headlights lit up the area as an engine cut through the quiet. A 4WD bumped out of the bush nearby and onto the road, a caravan rocking behind it. The vehicle turned, accelerated, and disappeared into the dark. The tiger women had abandoned their campsite.

Bess shifted her bag that was cutting into her shoulder and looked back at the house. One window glowed faintly behind drawn curtains. That must be where Margaret was sitting with Vivienne.

Her eyes stung. She had never felt so abandoned.

Margaret clutched her glass between unsteady fingers. She'd been meaning to go outside for a walk to let the chill night breezes blow the disorder out of her head and give her some clarity. Letting Vivienne persuade her back here instead had probably been a mistake, but she'd been tempted for a moment by the promise of a warm room and someone who would listen.

Her eyes swam as she stared down at the floor.

She'd ruined things with Bess, hadn't she? Whatever had become of those ashes, Margaret should not have let it affect her so, should not have lashed out at Bess when she was only trying to help. Just as she had been trying to help Margaret for months on end while Margaret—morose, brooding, stuck in the past—had been unable to accept it.

Had she been destined to drive Bess away sooner or later?

Vivienne rested a hand on Margaret's shoulder, her hair lying in vivid stripes across the dark sleeve of Margaret's coat.

"You will make sense of this," she said. "Soon everything will be clear."

But that didn't make Margaret feel better at all.

Chapter 16

Bess kept trudging towards the hire car. She didn't bother to use the torch on her phone. If she walked through a puddle, what did it matter?

Something bashed her knee and scraped the skin off her ankle. Hissing with pain, she switched on her light. It was a set of handlebars. Someone had thrown a bicycle into the bushes.

Weird. Surely nobody would drive this far out of town to dump rubbish. As she rubbed her ankle, she heard the purr of an engine from the deserted garden.

A car emerged, rolling forward without headlights. It crunched along the gravel towards her, changing gear, gathering speed.

Was it aiming at her? Bess darted sideways, her heart pounding as the brakes screeched and the vehicle jolted to a stop. The door flew open.

It was Vivienne's old BMW, the one that had sat in the long grass for days. Someone clambered out: someone with a thatch of stylishly dishevelled hair and a T-shirt tight enough to show off her well-muscled arms.

"Ty?" Bess gaped as things came together in her mind: the pushbike that would have allowed someone to approach the house without being heard, the stealthy movements she'd sensed upstairs, the urn moved from Margaret's luggage into hers. "*You* stole Margaret's sister's ashes? Why?"

Ty didn't seem to hear. She stared at the car instead, looking dumbfounded.

"Hey!" Bess pushed her. "I asked you a question. Why did you steal Deirdre's remains?"

"Calm down. I didn't steal them. Check your bag."

"I did! So did Margaret! And then she suspected me of taking them, and we had a fight, and…" Flabbergasted, Bess ran out of words. She held back an urge to pick up the bicycle and hit Ty over the head with it. "What the hell were you doing?"

"Never mind that." Ty pointed at the car with a shaky finger. "It drives fine. There's nothing wrong with it."

"But there's something wrong with you!" Bess was ready to explode. But Ty's shocked expression made her hesitate. "What's going on?"

"*She* told me that the car had broken down, that it wouldn't even start. That was why it was dumped here and no one used it." Ty had been so annoyingly cocky whenever Bess had met her before. But now she sounded scared as she said, "I got suspicious, thought I'd check… Bess, there's nothing wrong with that car."

"Did you hear that?" Vivienne turned towards the window.

Margaret sighed. Of course she had heard it: a car starting and accelerating down the drive. It was the sound of Bess taking the hire car and leaving. Abandoning Margaret—and who could blame her? If Margaret had been her usual self, she would have marched down there and blocked the exit, demanding that they make sense of things. But she couldn't do that now when she felt so disoriented, so clumsy and helpless.

Staring down into her glass, she decided she had been right the first time. She didn't like the taste of brandy at all.

Wait, though… Surely the engine shouldn't have sounded so close. She and Bess had left the hire car at the other end of the drive.

"Don't tell me your friend has gotten lost on our property." Vivienne sighed. "I'd better go and check. Technically, I'm still her hostess, after all." She hurried out.

Margaret was too groggy to think much more. It was an unpleasant feeling, like wading through mud. What was wrong? Alcohol didn't usually affect her this badly.

Perhaps moving around would help. She stood, but her legs wobbled, and black spots whirled before her eyes. She grabbed the couch for support.

Leaning over it, she took deep breaths while her vision cleared. Her gaze was in line with the gap between the sofa and the wall. She squinted. There was something there.

She reached down the gap until she touched a wooden object. Dropping into a crouch, she leaned in from the side to seize it— No, wait. There were several things there. She pulled them out.

Half a dozen framed photographs. She held one up to a pale square of wallpaper; the shape matched. Someone had removed these pictures from the walls and hidden them.

The pictures had been taken in a photographer's studio more than thirty years ago, to judge from the hairstyles. A much younger Ivy posed, hands locked together in her lap, a tight smile doing nothing to soften her features.

But the other people in the photographs... Margaret stared, her skin prickling with suspicion. Something was out of place here.

Bess didn't believe in aggression. Still, she fantasised about kicking Ty in the shins as Ty stared at the BMW.

"Never mind the car." Bess waved angrily to get her attention. "Why did you steal Deirdre's ashes?"

"I didn't. I just moved them."

Bess gritted her teeth. "Why, though?"

"She told me to." Ty nodded at the house.

"Vivienne?" Bess wanted to howl, *I knew it!*

But Ty hesitated. "Sort of. It's complicated." She grabbed Bess's arm. "Listen, you've gotta help me. I'm deep in the sticky stuff here."

Bess raised her eyebrows higher than they had ever gone before. "Why would I help you?"

"Cos you're, you know, a legit person." Ty gestured, taking in Bess's new suitcase, the keys to her hire car, her funky vintage coat. "You've got a good job on the mainland, you go travelling for your holidays, you speak in that fancy voice. You must have money. You probably know lawyers and people like that. I need someone to put in a good word for me. With the cops and the judge and all. If everything goes tits up."

Bess hadn't realized she spoke in a fancy voice, And what was Ty talking about? "And you think I would help you because...?"

"Cos I didn't do anything bad! Not really. I was only selling stuff."

Bess's head started to throb. "Ty, what's happening? What were you selling?"

"Ah..." Ty stood on one foot, then the other. "Look, it wasn't stealing, all right? I just got hold of some things, and I sold them."

"What things?"

Nervously, Ty ran her hands through her spiked hair until it looked like a squashed bird's nest. "Just some things from the house."

"From Crossroads House?"

"Yeah. At first it was a paperweight and a cigarette lighter, small stuff like that. Couldn't have been worth much, right?"

"You stole antiques from the house while you were working here, then sold them?"

"Not exactly." Ty jittered around as if ants were swarming inside her skinny jeans. "When I took them into town, he wouldn't buy them. He reckoned I must have nicked them from here."

"He?" Bess paused. "Did you try to sell stolen antiques to Alan Moore?"

"Told you, I didn't really steal them." Ty shoved her hands into her pockets, then took them out again. "Are you gonna help me or what?"

"Based on what I've heard so far, probably not. Why should I?"

"Cos the next part I was forced into!" Ty looked around anxiously. "He said I must have stolen those things, and he was going to call the cops! Those bastards have always had it in for me."

"Uh-huh."

"Then Alan said he would sell the little items, and he wouldn't dob me in if I would look around Crossroads House and find something else for him. He'd heard the old lady had some things hidden away, things she wasn't supposed to have."

"Like illegal artefacts? Dinosaur eggs? A skull...?"

"Ugh, gross. Yeah, that was the stash he wanted, but I never touched the creepy stuff. I just took him some vases and statues."

"There were a dozen objects left in that cupboard. You didn't take Alan everything."

"Nah," said Ty. "He didn't know exactly what the old lady had, and I wasn't gonna give him first dibs on everything."

Bess guessed that Ty had been smart enough to realise that if Alan wanted those artefacts, others might pay for them too. No wonder Alan had tried to persuade Bess and Margaret to get hold of Ivy's inventory book for him. Obviously, he hadn't trusted Ty.

"Alan must have known the objects were illegal."

"Yeah, but he needed the cash. He said he knew people who would buy them."

Again, Bess thought back to their conversation with Alan when he had bragged about knowing private dealers and maverick collectors. "Did he pay you?"

"A bit." Ty wrinkled her nose and added, "But he reckoned we weren't really doing anything wrong cos old Mrs Bolt must have bought those things from thieves in the first place. Alan freaked out when the old lady died, though. He was so scared that someone would go through her stuff and figure out what we'd taken that he wouldn't be seen talking to me, wouldn't take my calls. He told me to leave town! Then he remembered that Mrs Bolt used to have some antiques inventory book, and he started worrying that someone was going to find the book and realise what was missing. He changed his mind about not speaking to me then. He wanted me to go and steal the book! I told him where to stick that. I wasn't taking any more risks, not with cops hanging around the place."

"Wait…" Bess shook her head. "The night of the centenary dinner, Alan found out that I knew about those stolen antiquities. But he couldn't get to Crossroads House himself that night. Did he ring you?"

"Oh yeah." Ty rolled her eyes. "He wasn't happy. Wanted me to race over here and move those things to a better hiding place."

"*You* moved those artefacts so the police wouldn't find them?"

"Nah…" Ty drew on the ground with her toe. "Not really."

Bess massaged her forehead. "I've had enough of this. All you've told me is that you sort-of-not-exactly stole valuables from this house for Alan to sell. I can't see why you think I'd help you."

"Cos it wasn't my fault! They both told me to do it."

Bess took deep breaths to stay patient. "Who's 'they'?"

"Alan." Ty hesitated, then nodded at the house. "And her."

"*Vivienne?* Vivienne told you to sell Ivy's things?"

"It was her idea. The first things I sold—the small things—she was the one who gave them to me. She said she needed to get some cash together. We split the fee. And she knew all about those dodgy old objects in the cupboard. When Alan asked for them, she told me where to find them. Later, when Alan rang me in a panic and told me to move them, I didn't have to go to the house and do it. I just called her, and she stashed them somewhere else."

"Where did she put them?"

"Dunno."

Bess squeezed her eyes shut. "This doesn't make sense. Vivienne was about to inherit her grandmother's estate. Why resort to stealing individual items ahead of time? And Vivienne works in antiquities! How could she think it was okay to sell sacred objects and stolen artefacts and *skulls*?"

"Aw, will you shut up about that dusty old junk!" Ty thumped a fist into the palm of her hand. "You're not seeing the real problem here."

"You mean apart from you, Vivienne, and Alan breaking the law?"

"Christ's sake!" Ty groaned as if Bess were unbearably dense. "Don't you get it? *She's not Vivienne.*"

Margaret looked at the photographs. Why had they been taken off the wall and hidden? In her mind, possibilities drifted, swirled, then formed a clearer shape.

Ivy was seated in the centre of a photographer's studio like a queen surrounded by her courtiers. She was much younger, but there was no mistaking her pointed chin and haughty posture. Behind her stood a man with eyes like hers, a loud eighties tie, and a worried smile. He must be Richard, her son. A woman stood beside him, a woman with a delicate, heart-shaped face and white-blonde hair. She had to be Vivienne's mother, Lorraine. On her other side stood a little girl in a yellow party frock. She looked like Lorraine in miniature. The girl's smile for the camera seemed a little too eager, desperate even, as she hung onto her mother's hand. Vivienne?

Hard to say. Because on Richard's other side stood a second girl, perhaps a year younger than the first. She wore a blue party frock, and her hands by her sides were screwed up into tight little fists.

Margaret sank down on the couch.

She thought of Deirdre and herself at that age. Their mum had been gone by then. Had anyone made dresses for the Gale girls for special occasions? Had anyone taken their picture?

She couldn't recall. Doubted it. But if they had, she could imagine Deirdre looking as eager to please as the first little girl in this photo and herself looking as tense and resentful as the second. Deirdre anxious to make amends for angry little Margaret, Margaret angry at little Deirdre for being so anxiously obliging.

Sisters.

Bess stepped nearer to Ty. "What are you saying?"

"Her name's Antoinette." Ty held Bess's forearms in a desperate grip. "Look, it wasn't meant to be a big deal at first. This woman just came up to me when I was leaving work and asked if I wanted to make some extra money. Well, I always want that! She said she knew all about Crossroads House and could get inside and take things. But she had to keep a low profile—she didn't want people in town getting a proper look at her—so she needed someone to take the objects to Alan and sell them. I thought she was crazy until she showed me the things she'd swiped already. I wouldn't have had the guts to sneak in there myself at the time; the old lady never let me past the front door. She made me use their outside toilet! But Antoinette said she could get in without anyone noticing. And when Alan wanted the illegal antiques too, she got them out for me. We split the cash between us.

"Then a week ago, she told me we needed to step things up. She said Vivienne had been called back to Hobart to deal with some crisis at her work, and this was our big chance. The old lady was half-blind and half-mad, and people in town didn't really know Vivienne. Most of them had never met her. This woman looked a lot like Vivienne; she could pass herself off as her for a couple of days and get her hands on the old lady's full collection. Earlier, when she was inside the house, she'd overheard Vivienne making plans with some antiques expert who was going to visit and tell her what everything was worth. Antoinette said that if the woman showed up while Vivienne was away, it could work out well for us."

"Antiques expert?" Bess swallowed. "Margaret."

"Yeah. There was meant to be something in the house that was super valuable; she was gonna find it, and I would flog it to Alan. Then we'd split the profits and leave before the granddaughter got back."

Ty looked dubious. "I'm not thick. I asked why Vivienne had left her car behind if she was needed in Hobart. Antoinette said Vivienne had to leave in a hurry and the car was cactus, so she left it, took Jim's cab to Rusdown to catch the bus to Hobart.

"And then… Then Antoinette started wanting me to do weird stuff, like pushing a shutter off the side of the house so it nearly hit her. She said she needed to seem like she was in trouble. I told her that was risky, but I was in too deep with her by then; she didn't give me a choice. And then… Then the old lady died."

Ty let out a breath. "I was shitting myself cos I thought Vivienne would come back for sure for the funeral and realise what we'd done. I looked for Vivienne on social media to see if she'd posted about her grandmother dying and what she was going to do. But I couldn't find her. I wanted to leave town—I went to the bus stop, but Antoinette made me come back. She said we had to stay cool, that people would get suspicious if I did a runner."

Ty picked at her nails. "But she lied about that car. So now I'm thinking… If Vivienne's car didn't break down, and she didn't come home like a normal person when her grandma died, and I can't work out where she is… Well, maybe Vivienne didn't go to Hobart? Maybe there was no work emergency? Maybe Antoinette's been bullshitting me and something else…I dunno…*happened* to Vivienne?"

Bess's head swam. The real granddaughter had vanished? And *this* Vivienne wasn't really Vivienne but some imposter working with Ty to steal Ivy's antiques?

But how could an imposter know so much about the family, about Crossroads House? About Margaret?

"Ty, I don't understand. This woman who's pretending to be Vivienne— this *Antoinette*— Who is she?"

"I wouldn't worry your ditzy red head about that, dear," said a voice.

Ty jolted at the sound.

Heart thumping, Bess lifted her phone. The torchlight swept over the tangled bushes, the smashed statue, the flowerbeds choked by weeds…and Antoinette stepping towards them with a shotgun in her delicate hands.

I have to call Bess. Margaret leapt up from the couch and lost her balance again. She steadied herself, then made for the door. She couldn't keep this discovery to herself.

In all the time they'd spent together, Vivienne had never mentioned another Bolt girl. She had edited her past to remove her sister and hidden the evidence. Why?

Margaret made it to the doorway before her vision blurred. Was she ill? Her eyelids were heavy, and sweat was soaking through her clothes.

Move. She pushed forward towards the staircase, one hand braced against the wall. When had this hall gotten so damned long?

Leaving her phone upstairs had been a mistake. One of many mistakes she'd made tonight. She should never have spoken like that to Bess, should never have doubted her or made her want to leave.

And after finding those pictures and realising she'd been deceived, Margaret now felt certain someone had messed with Deirdre's ashes to cause trouble. What was going on?

The staircase seemed ten storeys high. She used the banister to haul herself up, her arms trembling with the effort. Her legs seemed to be filled with cement.

She would call Bess, ask her to come back and collect her. Beg, if necessary. Find out what really happened, get them both away from here.

Margaret reached the top of the stairs, made it to the nursery, and retrieved her phone. It took her several clumsy tries to get Bess's number.

No reply. She tried again. Was Bess ignoring her? But Bess was a communicator; she liked frank conversations, long processing sessions, earnest discussions about feelings with a lot of "I" statements. The silent treatment wasn't her style. The muscles in Margaret's stomach clenched with dread.

She moved back onto the landing. Perhaps she could get outside and down the driveway. Bess might not have gone far.

Her surroundings swam in and out of focus: the worn carpet, the tiger's skull in its glass box. The stairs seemed to roll down like an escalator.

She lost her balance and fell forward, banisters blurring, the floor far below, racing closer—until she caught Ivy's stairlift with one flailing hand and clung on for dear life.

Her body snapped back as if attached to a bungee cord, her arm almost wrenched from its socket.

Cursing, she collapsed on the step. Everything hurt. Thank heavens for that stairlift.

Margaret looked at the wallpaper beside the stairlift, scratched and gouged in several places. She extended her hand again and held her fingers over the marks. Ivy must have done the same thing—fell and clawed for support—but she had not been as lucky as Margaret.

Except... Something wasn't right. Blinking blearily, Margaret forced herself to her feet and examined the wall. Those claw marks were right next to the stairlift, directly beneath it on the way down. And Ivy had been smaller than Margaret, her arms shorter. If she had fallen from the top step—gingerly, Margaret acted the movement out in slow motion—surely Ivy would have either caught hold of the stairlift or missed altogether and fallen forward?

Tilting from the top step, simulating a fall, Margaret tried again to touch that patch of wallpaper. She couldn't reach it from here; the stairlift was in the way. That stairlift could not have been at the top of the steps when Ivy fell to her death. But Ivy must have ridden it upstairs to bed earlier that night, intending to take it downstairs again in the morning.

Someone had moved the stairlift to the bottom, imprisoning Ivy on the first floor. Then they had moved it back to the top later, covering their tracks.

Margaret tried to focus. If only she didn't feel so ill, so weary. She took out her phone and tried Bess's number again. No answer.

Bess was intensely aware of everything around her. The night breeze, an insect chirruping, her phone buzzing while she didn't dare reach for it. Every detail stood out. All those years she'd spent practising mindfulness— who knew you could get the same result from deathly fear?

She looked at this woman who was not Vivienne. Antoinette, Ty had said. She tried not to look at the gun. "Where's Margaret? What have you done to her?"

"Nothing permanent. Don't fret." A chuckle. "One good thing about having to babysit that evil old woman: she had a pharmacy worth of drugs. They've come in handy a few times."

Try as she might to focus on Antoinette's face, Bess kept glancing at the shotgun. It looked heavy and old, but Antoinette held it confidently. She flicked some sort of lever, and a spotlight attached to the weapon shone into Bess's face, making her screw up her eyes.

Antoinette said, "Phones, please."

Bess thought about throwing the phone at Antoinette's head and making a run for it. But what would happen to Margaret if she did?

God, she'd been stupid. She'd sensed there was something wrong in this place. She should have insisted they both leave. She should never have left Margaret alone here. Cursing herself, she tossed her phone onto the ground.

Ty's was already there.

"You stole Ivy's medication," Bess said. In a small way, she was pleased her voice sounded calm. "At first I thought you might have been selling it."

Antoinette smirked. "Good thought. I certainly wasn't going to waste too much of it on the old woman." A tremor ran along the barrel of the shotgun. "Why should she be spared any pain? But I couldn't sell it. I needed it for other things."

"That hot chocolate." Bess thought back to her second visit here when she'd fallen into a heavy sleep on the couch. "You knocked me out."

"Nothing personal, dear. I just needed some alone time with Margaret."

Bess's thoughts darted in circles, searching for escape routes, distractions, arguments that might convince Antoinette to put the gun down. But all she could think of to say was, "What do you want with Margaret?"

"Really?" Their captor sounded incredulous. "That's your question? Why do you care after how she treated you? I heard you two fighting. I expect they heard it in Hobart."

"Did you think that would be enough to drive me away?" Another piece fell into place for Bess. "Is that why you sent Ty to interfere with Deirdre's ashes—to separate me from Margaret?"

"Mm. A pity for you it didn't work."

Bess said slowly, "I know Margaret didn't react well, but you manipulated her. And I'm not going to let you hurt her."

"Oh, calm down." Bess imagined Antoinette rolling her eyes from behind the spotlight. "I've got plans for Margaret Gale; she's important to me." She pointed the shotgun at Ty. "Unlike you, you treacherous, thieving little scumbag." An aside to Bess: "I'm sorry about her. It's hard to get good help out here."

"Chill, babe." Ty's voice trembled. "I didn't tell her anything. Honest."

"Honest? I doubt you could spell the word. I heard your little confession before, so please don't insult me with more lies."

"Hey..." Ty gave a forced chuckle. "I can see there's some drama going on with you three ladies, but it's none of my business. I've done what you paid me for, and you know I don't dob." She edged sideways. "So I'll leave you to it—"

How did Antoinette move so fast? She sprang across the grass, swinging the shotgun in an arc from her shoulder. The butt struck Ty in the head with a thud, like meat on a butcher's slab.

Ty crumpled on the wet grass.

Bess doubled over, one hand clapped across her mouth to keep from screaming.

As Antoinette bent over Ty and jabbed her with the shotgun, Bess realised that her captor was distracted. This was her chance. She could run now. Could she make it to the house, barricade herself in with Margaret, plan their escape?

"Stay there." Antoinette kicked Ty, who groaned, then pointed the shotgun at her temple. She said to Bess, "Take another step and I'll finish this one off. I don't suppose anyone would miss her." A glance back at Bess. "You're not going to make me do it, are you?"

How Bess hated both of them in that moment. Ty was a crook and a coward who'd been prepared to slink off and leave Bess to her fate. Maybe she deserved this. Still, as Ty lay there with her teeth bared in pain and blood in her hair, Bess knew the answer.

"No."

"Good." Antoinette jerked her chin, summoning Bess over. "Get her on her feet."

It took several tries, Bess slinging Ty's arm around her shoulder, her knees teetering as she took the other woman's weight.

"Move."

Bess staggered forward, trying to match her pace to Ty's dragging footsteps. The gardener could barely stay upright. Breathlessly, Bess asked, "Who are you?" And when Antoinette didn't answer, added, "Please, let's talk about this. You don't have to do anything extreme."

Ty's head slumped onto Bess's shoulder, her blood trickling down Bess's arm.

"You can walk away from here," Bess urged Antoinette. "Stealing a few antiques isn't a serious crime, and I'm sure you had a good reason."

Where was Antoinette taking them? They seemed to be circling the grounds, headed towards the back of Crossroads House where the abandoned east wing stood.

Bess urged their captor, "You probably wouldn't even get prison time for the thefts since you're not a violent offender." She tried to ignore Ty's painful moans in her ear. "I know you didn't kill Ivy. I've got proof that Alan, Janine, and Dorian did it."

Did Bess still believe that? Until a couple of minutes ago, she had assumed it must be true; now she wasn't sure. Still, she prayed that pointing the blame at someone else would de-escalate things with Antoinette, encourage her to believe she had options. Options which didn't involve using that gun.

"Have you?" said Antoinette. "That's gratifying. I'd certainly like to see those three go down for something. Dorian, Alan, and Janine—ugh. They're appalling, aren't they? Greedy, selfish, light-fingered little nobodies. Like this one." She prodded Ty in the back with her shotgun.

Bess dragged Ty forward, trying to put distance between them and their captor.

Antoinette sighed. "But that's Mount Bastion: a sinkhole of a town. I can't tell you how relieved I'll be to get out of here."

"We can help you get out." Bess took deep breaths, her muscles protesting with each step. "We can prove you didn't kill Ivy, that those three did it."

"Oh, I knew they'd broken into the house," Antoinette said. "They woke me up. You should have heard them, crashing around downstairs, dropping things, and tripping over the furniture. Ridiculous. Cat burgling is not a career for the over sixties. I had half a mind to storm down and confront them, but I decided to listen instead. I prefer to keep a low profile; it was better that they didn't get a close look at me."

"Alan was searching for Ivy's antiques ledger," Bess said, hoping to keep a conversation going. They had rounded the house; the east wing loomed ahead. "Dorian was looking for Ivy's old will. Janine was looking for an incriminating letter."

"Humph." Antoinette sounded mildly entertained. "Eccentric of them. I'm sure it was the most fun they'd had in years. But it was annoying for me, having to lie in bed while those halfwits blundered around. They were so noisy they even woke Ivy. She called out."

"For help?"

Antoinette laughed. "Oh no. She bellowed out to me to fetch her gun. It shocked the life out of those clowns downstairs. I could hear them falling over and shushing each other." A pause. "They hated her, though. They wanted her gone. I heard them hissing to each other and calling her names."

"So then... They came upstairs after her?"

"What? No, they fled out the front door. No nerve whatsoever. Pathetic. It would be gratifying if those three were dragged to court and punished, but on the whole, I think it's better if Ivy's death remains an accident. Less bother that way." Her footsteps halted. "Stop." They faced the back wall of the house.

Sweat was running down between Bess's shoulder blades. Her muscles seared from holding Ty.

Antoinette said, "Step around those hydrangeas."

The bushes were damp and drooping, infiltrated with harsh, spiny weeds. Bess inched around them. Behind the bushes against the wall of Crossroads House was a staircase leading down to the basement level. It had a thick door with padlocked bolts.

"Ivy's wine cellar." Antoinette nodded. "Go take a look."

God, Bess didn't like where this was headed. Heart hammering, she glanced around. Was it too late to risk running? But Antoinette was directly behind her, the barrel of the shotgun pointed at Bess's torso.

Her own dry swallow sounded embarrassingly loud. Ty couldn't stand without her, so Bess had to help her down, one worn, slimy step at a time. A snail crunched to its death under her foot, causing her a moment's sadness.

"Leave that idiot against the wall," Antoinette said. "She's not going anywhere."

Bess propped Ty there, then flinched as Antoinette flung her a bunch of keys, saying, "Open it up."

The keys rattled in her shaking hands. Bess tried to fit them to the padlocks.

"Get a move on."

Everything else in Crossroads House might be old and malfunctioning, but the padlocks seemed disturbingly new. Each one opened with a smooth click.

"Leave them on that step." Antoinette motioned with the shotgun.

Bess obeyed, searching wildly for something she could say or do to stop this. Ty whimpered and began to slide down the wall, so that Bess was forced to grab her and support her again.

"Inside."

No shapes or movement were discernible within the cellar.

"I won't." The words creaked in Bess's mouth.

Antoinette tightened her grip on the shotgun. *"Move."*

They stepped through the doorway, and the darkness wrapped around them. There was a bad smell in here, like a blocked drain.

"What are you going to do to us?"

"Oh, probably nothing. I don't like mess." Antoinette ordered them forward, three more steps into the stinking darkness. "The house will take care of you."

With that, Bess dropped Ty. The young woman fell as Bess raced towards the door. But it had already banged shut, and from outside came the sound of bolts sliding across.

She kicked it, thumped on it, wrenched at the handle. "Who are you?" she screamed, but their captor had gone.

Stay awake. Margaret clung to the banister. The house rippled around her.

She took one step down, breathing strenuously. This wasn't illness; she had been drugged. She held her eyes open as wide as they would go. *Don't fall asleep.*

The front door opened, and she heard footsteps.

"Margaret? What are you doing?"

Margaret drooped over the banister. The world was losing its shape, turning to a weird, dark jelly. Her hostess dashed up the stairs towards her.

"Why are you here?" There was a forced cheerfulness to that voice, something brittle and false. "I left you napping on the couch, Margaret. You should have stayed there; you were exhausted."

"You're misremembering." She forced herself to speak. "I was awake when you left. But you expected me to be out cold by now, didn't you?"

Was she speaking properly? Margaret hoped she wasn't mumbling; it would be so undignified.

That white-blonde head bobbed nearer as the woman climbed the last few steps towards her.

"Someone moved Ivy's stairlift," Margaret added.

It wasn't clever to reveal what she knew, but she sensed she was finished already. And she was damned if she would be a fool as well as a loser. "Ivy was trapped upstairs that night. What happened to her was no accident. And I found…"

God, her mouth was parched, her muscles so weak. Margaret longed to lie down. "I found your family photos. The Bolts had two daughters, not one."

"I leave you alone for five minutes…" A tutting sound. "Very well, Margaret. I wanted it to be a surprise, but I suppose you're one of those people who hate surprises. It's a control thing; I understand."

The woman's features seemed to blur, shadows creeping across her face. "I'm Antoinette Bolt. I would say 'pleased to meet you' and shake your hand, but I'm not sure you're up to such physical exertions just now. And when you think about it, Margaret, we've gotten to know each other tolerably well these past few days."

She stepped up so that she and Margaret faced each other on the same stair. It occurred to Margaret that if Antoinette chose to push her now, she would meet the same fate as Ivy.

Antoinette gave a fluting laugh as if Margaret had spoken that thought out loud. "Don't fret; I'm not holding a grudge against you. Quite the contrary." She leaned closer, her voice tense and excited. "I know it's a lot to take in. But once you learn the full story, you'll see why I was right to do it; why I'm the victim here." She grasped Margaret's arm. "You'll see why this was meant to be."

Margaret's head was spinning into a million pieces as if someone had tossed her brain into a blender.

Then she saw the corner of something sticking out of Antoinette's coat pocket. A rectangular object in bright colours. She recognised the cover: it was made from plant-based materials, fully compostable, and decorated with pictures of endangered coral from the Great Barrier Reef.

Bess's phone.

Margaret panted with horror. "Where's Bess? And what do you mean? What was meant to be?"

"Us being together, of course." Antoinette smiled before the darkness came pouring in and Margaret's legs gave way.

Chapter 17

LIGHT SWITCH. BESS RAN HER hands over the wall. There had to be one. She couldn't think about what was happening, what Antoinette might do to Margaret, what horrors lay ahead. God, she and Margaret should never have argued like that, should never have walked away from each other—but no, she couldn't let herself plummet down into those painful thoughts. She had to stay calm, take one step at a time.

"Where is it?" Bess's voice echoed. "Where's the bloody switch? Who builds a wine cellar with no light?"

A groan. Ty was alive then. She mumbled something.

"What?" Bess groped closer, then stepped on something lumpy.

"Ow! My foot!"

"Sorry." Bess crouched beside her. "You sound a bit better."

"Feel like shit." Ty hissed through her teeth. "My head…"

"Here." Bess took off her scarf and passed it to her. "To stop the bleeding. Don't go to sleep."

"Geez, that'll be hard when it's so comfy in here."

Bess heard Ty wriggling around. "What are you doing?"

"Keys." Ty jangled them. "The bitch might have got my phone, but she didn't check all my pockets. Thank God for cargo pants, hey?"

"You've got the cellar door key?" If Ty hadn't stolen Deidre's remains and tried to abandon Bess with an armed lunatic, she could have kissed her.

"Nah, sorry, I don't have that."

"Then why the hell—"

"Pen torch on my key ring." She flicked it on.

It was a weak beam of light, but it gave Bess a rush of relief. She refused to think of the bigger picture, which was too ugly to contemplate. They had light. Things were looking up. "Find a switch."

The torchlight wobbled around the cellar, picking up the wine racks with their dusty bottles, the low ceiling, the locked door. In one corner sat an open box. Squinting, Bess made out a gilded statuette, an ancient red vase: the illegal artefacts she and Margaret had found upstairs. So this was where they'd been hidden. She shuddered: that skull must be in here too.

But where was the light switch?

"There has to be one! Give me the torch."

"No way, it's mine!"

"You're not looking properly!" Panic gripped her. What if Ty dropped the torch and broke it? And what if Bess ended up trapped here in the dark with no chance of finding a way out, no hope of getting back to Margaret?

She tried to snatch the torch. Ty pushed her and they wrestled, the puny light bouncing around.

"This is your fault! You're a crook—"

"Get off me, ya moll!" Ty elbowed her in the face.

Twisting her head to avoid her, Bess glimpsed a string with a toggle dangling from the ceiling.

"The light!" She pointed, but the beam flitted away. "Here! Shine it here!" She waved her arms over her head, feeling for the string.

"Bess…" Why was Ty pointing the torch the other way?

"Here, I said!" Bess looked in frustration where Ty was directing the light.

Against the far wall lay what looked like a bundle of rags. Was the smell coming from there? The torchlight crept over the fabric to a stiff white shape like a dead starfish. Was that a *hand*?

The light drifted upward, illuminating a mop of tangled, dirty hair. White-blonde hair in a familiar shade.

Feeling blindly above her, Bess touched a small plastic shape: the toggle at the end of the string. She seized it and pulled, lighting up the cellar.

The bundle of rags twitched and gave a weak cry.

"Oh God." Bess rushed over. "Vivienne?"

Margaret woke with a groan. Her back throbbed as if she had been dragged over rough ground. Or down a flight of stairs.

She tried to sit up, but pain ripped through her. Were her hands on fire? She twisted around to look.

Someone had zip-tied her to the bottom of the staircase in the same spot where Ivy had drawn her last breath.

"Ah, Margaret. Back with us, then?"

Antoinette Bolt had pulled up a chair at the base of the staircase. The floor around her was stacked with Ivy's antiques. The shotgun lay across her lap.

"You know…" Margaret felt like hell, but her mind had cleared. "If it's bondage you're interested in, it would have been polite to ask."

Antoinette smirked. "You might have said no."

"I might have said some other words too." Margaret managed to shuffle backwards until she was sitting up. Pins and needles prickled along her arms, and her wrists burned, blunt plastic sawing into them.

She fought to slow her breathing, to ignore the pain and think. What had this woman done with Bess? If she'd stolen her phone, surely that was a good sign in a way, an indication that Bess was still capable of trying to call for help. An indication that Bess was still alive.

She clung to that thought, refusing to consider any other possibility. Bess was determined and quick thinking; she had survived dangerous situations before. Yes, Bess was alive. She had to be. And it was up to Margaret to handle things so it stayed that way. She would do anything, tolerate any pain, any indignity, if it meant Bess would survive.

"What do you want?" Margaret was damned if she would show fear.

"Actually, Margaret, I want you to do your job." Antoinette waved at the antiques around her. "We never got to the end of Ivy's collection, did we? And I'm eager to get a complete valuation done."

"You…" Margaret stared at her. "You want me to tell you what those things are worth?"

"Since my future rather depends on the old eyesores, yes." Antoinette raised an eyebrow. "If you can spare the time."

"Well, I'm a bit busy being cuffed to a staircase, but my calendar is empty otherwise."

"Good." Her captor picked up a jewellery box, carried it over, and held it open under Margaret's nose.

Margaret shifted her gaze between the item and the woman holding it, who seemed calm for now. Best to keep her that way while Margaret struggled to think of a way out. "A nice set of vintage earrings. Art Deco. Screw fittings. Good condition. The sapphires are fake, though. Fifty dollars at auction."

Antoinette pouted. "Are you sure?"

"If you'd like a second opinion, kidnap a Sotheby's dealer."

"What about this?" Her captor brought over a blue and white porcelain item.

Margaret made herself focus. "Worcester China sauceboat. Mid-eighteenth century. Attractive Fitzhugh moth and doughnut-tree pattern. Five hundred dollars?"

"Humph. I'd hoped for better."

Margaret tried in vain to sit more comfortably. "Are all holidays like this? As a workaholic, I ask it as a genuine question."

"I wouldn't know," said Antoinette. "I've never taken holidays either. Most of my life has been spent in confined spaces. After I had to kill my parents, Ivy kept me locked up here for years." She carried the next antique over. "How about this?"

Margaret swallowed. "Harvest Ale jug. Royal Doulton, from their Lambeth factory, 1930s. Lots of them still around, though. Sixty dollars?"

"Thanks for nothing."

"You, ah…" Margaret tried to sound conversational. "You had to kill your parents?"

"It wasn't as bad as all that." Antoinette picked up another antique. "I only meant to kill my mother because she was planning to divorce Dad and take me and Vivienne to Adelaide with her." She crossed her arms. "I didn't want to go. I had the lead part in the school play, and everyone said I was going to be a star. And there was this boy who wanted to take me to the movies. He had a fight with another boy about me and broke his arm." Antoinette smiled in satisfaction at the memory. "Why should I have to give up all that?" She waggled the antique at Margaret. "Well?"

"Ah… Sheffield silver asparagus tongs, 1920s. Damage to the handle. About sixty dollars."

"So much for Ivy's brilliant investments." Antoinette sniffed. "Of course, I know I did the wrong thing when I killed my mother."

"Really?"

"Yes. I should have used poison. Neater. But because I didn't know any better, I made an awful mess. And Dad, who'd been taking an early walk outside, heard the noise and came in. He got all upset and kept yelling. He called me a devil child and a freak and a monster and said I'd be taken away and locked up. I didn't like him saying those things."

Antoinette shivered. "Then Dad started crying and saying it was his fault. He said the evil came from his family, that he should never have had children. He said he'd tried to help me before, made excuses for me when I did bad things, but there was nothing he could do for me now. He was quite hysterical. He said he couldn't handle it and he had to get out. Then he took the gun away from me and...he *left* for good."

Margaret's mouth fell open.

Antoinette held up a figurine.

"Um... Late Victorian shepherdess in gilded porcelain. Ugly, but in good condition. Seven hundred?" She cleared her throat. "Did Vivienne know what really happened to your parents?"

"Hmm?" Antoinette eyed the rest of the antiques. "No, she was staying off with some grotty family at the caravan park. She'd made friends with their children, but they didn't like me. Afterwards, Ivy packed her off to boarding school, and she never came back. Ivy kept me here."

Antoinette's cheek twitched. "For my own good, she said. People mustn't know what I'd done; it would ruin the family name. So she told lies to the education board, the social services, the neighbours back in my parents' home town. I was sickly, she said, and gone to live with relatives on the mainland. They were going to homeschool me, she told people. For all I know, she might have had someone else fill out the paperwork. I don't suppose you could get away with that nowadays, but it was all paper records back then; mistakes got made. And children weren't so important then. We'd only been visiting Mount Bastion for our holidays, so no one in town really knew me. After a while, people stopped asking. They just... forgot about me."

What could Margaret say? She turned to the next antique. "English oak and brass open-twist candlestick. Edwardian. Two hundred."

"Horrible object," Antoinette said. Her thoughts returned to her childhood. "You'd think somebody around here would have paid attention, but no one came to the house much. Ivy made sure of that." Her face darkened, tendons standing out in her neck.

Margaret wondered how she could have thought this woman delicate. Right now Antoinette reminded her of a thin garrotting wire pulled taut.

"I got new dolls when I behaved myself," Antoinette said, "and a night in the laundry cupboard when I didn't. *In the pen*, she called it. Ivy said if she left the house, no one would think to look in there."

A pause. "Don't get me wrong; sometimes Ivy was entertaining. She knew the nastiest secrets of everyone in town. It occurred to me later that perhaps she hoarded those secrets as collateral in case anyone ever figured out the truth about me. Mostly she hated me for the death of her son. Sometimes after a few sherries, though, she would tell me that my mother had it coming."

As subtly as she could, Margaret tried to twist her wrists inside the plastic ties to find a weak point. But they were too tight. Every movement was agony. Was Bess tied up somewhere in the same way or worse? The thought made her shudder.

If she was going to get out of here, she would have to talk Antoinette into letting her go. Which would require empathy, persuasion, and friendliness. What Bess called people skills. Skills Margaret Gale had always rather prided herself on doing without.

She swallowed. Right, then.

"Oh, no…" Bess ripped off her coat and wrapped it around the splayed woman, then tugged the gag out of her mouth. The woman was feverish, her lips cracked and bloodied. Someone had zip-tied her wrists to a water pipe on the wall. The ties were savagely tight, the flesh around them discoloured, swollen, oozing blood.

Bess turned to Ty. "Give us your jumper."

"Get lost. It's freezing in here."

"Do you want to get hit in the head again?"

Something in her tone must have told Ty that this vegetarian yoga enthusiast was in no mood to be trifled with. Grumbling, Ty peeled off her jumper.

Bess rolled it up into a pillow for Vivienne.

God, the poor woman reeked. Bess tried not to look at what she was lying in. If they did get out of here, she wouldn't ask for her coat back.

Vivienne croaked, "Water?"

"I'm so sorry." Bess shook her head. "We don't have any. How long has she kept you here?"

Vivienne blinked, her eyes unfocused. Was she wondering if Bess was real? Did she think she was being rescued?

"About…a week? I'd figured out someone else was in the house. I…I phoned Margaret. To come and help. Of course, I know now… It was Antoinette in the east wing. She'd broken in and was living there. For weeks, maybe. Creeping about, stealing, listening. She heard me on the phone to Margaret. I guess she saw an opportunity. My coffee tasted funny that night. Then I woke up at midnight with my hands tied and a shotgun in my face. I didn't believe it at first—that she could really be Antoinette, that the mad things she was saying could be true. I thought I must be hallucinating. But she remembered details about our childhood, our family. She said she had some questions."

"Questions?"

"About me," Vivienne said. "My life. My job. My interests. That's why I'm still alive. She kept coming back with new questions, wanting to know everything. If I gave her useful answers, I got to eat and drink. She could have written my biography by the end. Identity theft is the sincerest form of flattery…"

The prisoner's eyes were glassy and her voice hoarse. Even so, Bess could hear how successfully Vivienne's captor had imitated her. The same half-English accent, the same playful, cynical inflection.

"Look at me," said Vivienne. "Surrounded by some of the finest wines in Australia and unable to get even the tiniest bit blotto. Now that *is* torture. Cruel and unusual punishment…"

"Hey, happy to help." Ty scrambled to her feet with a painful "Oof!" and surveyed the wine racks. "Lucky my key ring's got a corkscrew too, hey?"

"Scissors would have been better." Bess examined Vivienne's wrists. She couldn't undo the ties; they'd bitten too deeply into the flesh. "I'm not sure alcohol's a good idea."

But a *pop* said Ty wasn't listening. She took a swig, then held the bottle to Vivienne's lips. Bess supposed it could hardly make things worse.

"I'm sorry." She smoothed Vivienne's dirty hair out of her face, feeling ashamed of herself. She had been thinking of Vivienne Bolt as some sort of femme fatale: the snooty, scheming glamourous fantasy woman of Margaret's youth. And all the while, the real Vivienne had been lying in a dungeon in her own filth, wondering when she'd be killed.

The pipe was fastened to the wall with metal brackets; they were loose in places. All those times she and Margaret had heard clanking and crashing inside the house—had it been Vivienne kicking at the pipe, struggling to free herself? And what about the tiger women? They'd said they heard noises they couldn't trace. Animal sounds.

Bess rounded on Ty. "Did you know about this?"

Ty spat out her wine. "Fuck no! I told you: Antoinette said Vivienne had gone back to Hobart. I thought we were just lifting a few things, getting some cash together. I don't do stuff like this. I'm not sick."

"Then stop drinking and help get us out of here."

Ty looked longingly at the bottle before putting it down. "Yes, boss."

Together, she and Ty tried the sturdy door: kicking it, shouldering it, trying to bore into the edges with Ty's corkscrew. It didn't budge. They took the bottles off one of the wine racks and charged the door with the rack like a battering ram, but all that did was break the rack.

"Bastard!" Ty kicked the door again, then hopped around swearing.

"There has to be another way." Bess thumped on the walls, then made Ty boost her on another wine rack to tap the ceiling. Solid surfaces everywhere.

"Stay calm," Bess said, mostly to herself. "My dad's a foodie, and he says wine has to be kept ventilated..." She checked the walls, her breathing shallow. *Do something, do something...*

She didn't want to stop and think about their situation, about what would happen if she didn't find a way out. If their captor never returned.

How long would the three of them last down here, their screams growing hoarser every day, their blows at the door weakening, despair driving them to madness? Which of them would die last, watching the other two succumb before her? From Vivienne's weakened state and Ty's head wound, she could guess the answer.

And what about Margaret? What if Antoinette was holding her prisoner somewhere, tormenting her with jibes about what was happening to Bess? Or what if Margaret managed to escape but didn't realise Bess's fate until it was too late to save her? Bess recalled how guilty Margaret had felt about her sister's death. Something like this would destroy her.

"Here!" Bess found an air vent, an opening no larger than a brick covered in a metal grille.

Ty scrambled over hopefully, then saw what she'd found and shoved her. "A mini vent? Oh, thanks, genius!"

"Stay positive; it's a link to the outside. Maybe we can make some noise through it. Raise the alarm. I'll think of something." She held out her hand for Ty's keys. Ty handed them over, then dropped to the floor and started drinking again.

Bess chose a key, wedged it into one of the screws holding the grille in place, and began to twist it loose.

Crouched on the bottom step, Margaret watched Antoinette and tried to ignore the pain in her bound wrists. In her mind, she repeated *people skills*. How would Bess speak to someone like this?

"It sounds like you had a very traumatic childhood," Margaret ventured. "Children deserve nurturance and care. It must have been heartbreaking to grow up without those."

"That's an understatement. And all because of one mistake I made when I was too young to know better."

Margaret tried to look supportive. "I'm sure what happened to your parents was just a misunderstanding."

"Exactly!"

Margaret added, "You must have been upset to be separated from your sister too."

"Hmm. I suppose Ivy told her the same story as everyone else: that my parents had died by accident, and that I was sick and had gone away." She curled her lip. "Vivienne shouldn't have believed that, though. She should have looked for me. A real sister would have."

Margaret repeated to herself: *empathy, empathy…* "You must have been lonely without her. The bond between sisters is…" She thought of Deirdre and faltered. "It's like nothing else."

"You don't know the half of it." Antoinette sat back. "When I got older, sixteen or so, I escaped from here. I went to the city and later the mainland. I had no money and no clue how the world worked or how to keep myself alive. But it was surprising how many men were willing to help."

Antoinette sneered. "Freedom wasn't as much fun as I'd expected. I knew I had a sister somewhere, and eventually I tracked her down. I found her in the city. It was the night she graduated from university. When I saw her, I couldn't believe how beautiful she was, how fashionable and chic she seemed." Antoinette's head snapped around. She looked at Margaret. "Do you remember that part of the night? The part with me in it?"

Margaret thought back. That scrawny, desperate-looking kid grabbing Vivienne in the street. Vivienne pushing her away, saying she was sick of dealing with crazies…

"Yes. I remember."

"I only wanted her to recognise me. Be pleased to see me. Help me." Antoinette tightened her hold on the shotgun. "But she wouldn't believe I was her sister."

"Perhaps Ivy had told her you'd died."

"That's no excuse." Antoinette's face twisted in anger and perhaps pain. "Vivienne should have known Ivy was lying. She was grown up and clever enough, wasn't she? No, I think she just didn't want me back."

Margaret didn't believe it. Vivienne had not seemed stonyhearted. But if the young Vivienne had ever suspected the truth about what happened to her parents, perhaps it would not have been surprising if she had not wanted to imagine her sister returning, if she'd rushed away from a strange girl claiming to be Antoinette.

"You must have been shocked by her rejection." *Compassion,* Margaret told herself.

Antoinette stroked the barrel of the shotgun. "I wanted to kill everyone in that street. Everyone in that city. Including you."

"I see." Margaret swallowed. "Understandable, but…"

"I knew your name." Antoinette leaned closer. "I asked the other students. I needed to know who this girl was, this girl my sister wanted to follow instead of me. She liked your company; I could see that. She listened to everything you said. She held onto your arm." Antoinette's eyes grew dreamy. "I could have gone after you that night."

Margaret didn't dare blink. "But you're a—a good person. So you didn't."

"Of course I'm a good person." Antoinette seemed to snap out of it. "But actually, my boyfriend came along and made me go back to where we were staying. He had things he wanted me to do, as usual. But after meeting Vivienne, I wasn't in the mood. I kept thinking about how she wouldn't talk to me, how she'd walked away with someone else. I couldn't get it out of my head. So there was a bit of a row, and he ended up getting hit with a lump of wood. And I went to prison for murder."

Margaret's mouth was dry. She made herself say, "Well… I'm sure you were justified."

Antoinette shrugged. "I thought I might get famous for that at least, but it was before social media, and there was hardly anything about it in the newspapers." The thought seemed to vex her. "Apparently, he and I weren't very relatable."

"I was put in jail once," Margaret offered. "I found the loss of control the hardest thing to cope with. And the loss of privacy."

"Don't forget the morons you're forced to socialise with."

"Did your family contact you?"

"Vivienne and Ivy? Of course not. By the time I was arrested, I think Vivienne had left the country; I'm not sure when she learned the truth. As for Ivy, I rang her this year when I knew I was getting out. It was time she did something for me since it was basically all her fault. When she refused to speak to me, I wrote to her instead. And she wrote back saying she'd washed her hands of me long ago. She told me she was dying and was going to leave everything to Vivienne. I think she wanted to upset me." Antoinette breathed hard. "That wasn't very clever."

"So you decided to—what? Impersonate Vivienne, kill Ivy, and walk off with the money?"

"Yes, obviously. Who deserved it more than I did? Hadn't I suffered to protect the family name while Vivienne swanned off and had a perfectly lovely life? That money should have been mine.

"I got into the house in secret and stayed there for a while without Ivy realising, just getting my bearings. I even took a few small items and got Ty to sell them to get money for food and essentials. But I wasn't sure how much the antiques were worth, and I couldn't figure out which was the most expensive item, the one Ivy had said was worth the most. I didn't want to be duped by some crooked dealer." She eyed Margaret. "Then Vivienne invited you here."

"You overpowered Vivienne, took on her identity, and welcomed me here to do the valuation?"

"Of course. It should have been a smooth transition. Ivy hadn't seen Vivienne much over the years, and she was half-blind and woozy from medication. Once I'd perfected my imitation of Vivienne and broken Ivy's glasses, I figured I was safe. And I recognised your name, Margaret. I'd never forgotten you."

Antoinette leaned back in her chair, looking Margaret up and down. "The girl my sister liked better than me. And it struck me"—she gazed into the middle distance as if reflecting on her own brilliance—"how perfect it would be if I not only took my sister's name and her inheritance but if I *also* took the person she'd abandoned me for. I watched the two of you together that night in the city, the way you gazed at each other like you'd just found God. If I could take that from Vivienne too, it would give her something to think about!" Her tone was buoyant now, as if she were positively delighted with herself.

Margaret had never heard anything so alarming. She thought about protesting that Antoinette had got it all wrong, that one intense evening twenty-five years ago didn't mean she was Vivienne's one true love. That her own true love was Bess and always would be. But it might not be wise to contradict Antoinette now.

Instead, keeping her voice level, she said, "I had no idea I meant so much to you. That's very…flattering."

"Yes, I suppose it is."

"I don't mean to criticise, but wouldn't it have made more sense to let me value all the antiques before you got rid of Ivy?"

"Obviously. I'm not an idiot." Antoinette sounded cross. "But it was out of my hands. Those three fools broke into the house and woke her up, and unfortunately, Ivy was more lucid than usual. When they left, I went into her room and thought I might as well try again: I asked her if the burglars might have found that one especially precious item.

"Ivy was sitting up in bed, furious about the break-in, but she snapped at me not to fuss, that she'd put that item where no one would ever think to look. Well, I was tired and frustrated myself, and I didn't think clearly. I blurted out: 'Where—in the pen?'"

Antoinette grimaced. "Turns out she'd never told her precious Vivienne, the good grandchild, about that. The second I said it, I knew I'd made a mistake. Ivy stared at me, and even without her glasses, she knew who I was then."

Margaret sensed that, while the timing might not have been what she had wanted, Antoinette still felt a grim satisfaction at the memory of Ivy's shock.

"My grandmother didn't grovel; I'll give her that. She even had the nerve to order me out of her house, which made me laugh. Then she tried to leave herself. Of course, I'd taken the wheelchair away, but she got as far as the stairs, blundering about and holding onto things." Antoinette tittered.

Margaret tried to push away the awful image of Antoinette following Ivy's every step, taunting and sniggering.

"I hit the controls so the stairlift slid away, but she tried to climb down. Can you believe it?" Antoinette sounded almost impressed. "So I just... gave her a bit of help."

Margaret forced down a shudder. "It must have been satisfying, taking revenge on someone who'd hurt you so badly." She took a breath. "You know, when my father died, I was rather relieved too. He was a harsh man who never showed us much affection. I don't think he saw the point in having daughters. It hurt, although I never said anything at the time."

Margaret had never said much about her childhood since either. How strange to be speaking about it now.

"It does hurt." Antoinette nodded. "A person can't help reacting."

"And I know..." Margaret didn't like what was coming next; she hated personal disclosures at the best of times. But Antoinette's face had softened a little with each kind word. Maybe this empathy business was working. "I know what it's like to do something regrettable by mistake. It was like that with my sister, Deirdre."

Margaret's muscles locked painfully. She didn't want to think about this, let alone discuss it with a murderer. But she forced herself to go on. "I knew Deirdre was married to a rotten man. I knew she wasn't well in her mind. I tried to help her, but I didn't try hard enough. She wouldn't accept my help, which frustrated me. Angered me." She spoke roughly, as if each word were being dragged out of her.

But Antoinette seemed to be listening. Her grip on the gun had loosened.

Margaret went on. "Then Deirdre became ill with cancer, and I didn't realise for months. I dismissed it as hypochondria. By the time the truth came out, it was too late." Saying it out loud made Margaret tremble. Her throat seemed to be full of glass. "I've never forgiven myself for that. It wasn't all my fault, but I let her down. And I miss her."

Margaret fought to collect herself. Her cheeks were wet, and she longed to scrub them clean. "So I do understand how terrible it is to betray one's sister. How...unforgiveable."

Was she going to die like this, trussed up and weeping pathetically? If so, perhaps it was no more than she deserved, a punishment for Deirdre's fate.

Except that Deirdre had never blamed her. Margaret screwed her eyes shut at the memory. Deirdre had loved her, had thanked Margaret for her care, had held Margaret's hand at the end and tried to comfort *her*.

The thought was agonising—but for the first time, Margaret felt something else too. A tiny suspicion, like a little green shoot, that maybe she should pay attention to Deirdre's version of events and not just her own. Deirdre would not have wanted her to get hurt, to end up like this.

And Bess wouldn't want it either. Bess, who was still out there somewhere, alive and needing help. She sniffed, then looked Antoinette in the eye. "Whatever you had to do to Vivienne, I can't judge you."

Margaret's voice was clear now. Calm and confident. "If you need my help to make things right, you don't need to hold me prisoner. I'll help you freely. Considering my own guilt, it's the least I can do."

Antoinette gazed back at her. "Well," she started, her tone wavering, "we do have a connection, don't we? I could tell from the start you liked my company."

"Yes. You were so witty, so stylish and cosmopolitan."

Her captor smiled. "Rather different to that brown-rice-eating, joss-stick-waving friend of yours."

"Very different." That was true, Margaret thought: the two women were certainly different. Bess was the best person Margaret had ever met, while Antoinette was a deluded killer who didn't deserve to clean Bess's organic hemp sandals.

But Margaret didn't let those thoughts show. She kept her expression relaxed and made herself say, "Actually, the relationship with Bess had been on the rocks for months. You did me a favour by getting rid of her."

"Finally, the penny drops."

Thinking fast, Margaret added, "It wasn't just that you were different to Bess. You were different to *her* too. Vivienne. Obviously, I assumed you must be her because you looked so similar and played her so well. But you were much more charismatic than she used to be, and your sense of humour was much naughtier."

Was this working? Margaret glanced at Antoinette with what she hoped was a shy look. "And I didn't remember Vivienne being so attractive."

Antoinette gave a cynical chuckle, but she did not seem displeased. The woman wasn't stupid, but perhaps she was narcissistic enough to believe that she really had become important to Margaret, so important that Margaret would betray two women to make her happy.

In a casual voice, Margaret said, "You know none of these antiques are worth much, right?"

Antoinette glanced at them in disdain. "I suppose not."

"But I had a thought…about that one valuable item Ivy boasted of. We never paid attention to the furniture, did we? But there is a wardrobe upstairs in the nursery. I didn't examine it at the time, but it was in the eighteenth-century French style. Carved fretwork doors and cocked-hat cornices."

"The wardrobe?" It was clear Antoinette barely remembered it.

"If it's genuine, it could be worth twenty thousand. They're highly prized. And one with signed Pierre Varnez ironwork sold to an anonymous buyer in Melbourne last year."

Antoinette pulled out her phone and thumbed in some letters.

Margaret tensed in anticipation. The story itself would check out; she had been there when the wardrobe sold. Not to Ivy—it went to a friend of Maximillian's—but that information wouldn't be online.

Her captor looked up, her eyebrows raised. "Well. Twenty thousand would be…useful."

"Find the signature; it'll be on the bottom of the unit. If you can manage to tip it over—"

"Do I look like a furniture removalist?" But Antoinette sounded more excited than annoyed. "Oh, come on, then."

She hurried across to Margaret, then paused and reached out to stroke her face. Her fingertips were soft. "This could be our future, Margaret. We can go away together. We would never have to deal with people again."

Holding the other woman's gaze, Margaret nodded. She even craned forward until her nose brushed Antoinette's and their breath mingled. She promised her captor, "We can be free."

She didn't dare move as Antoinette crouched beside her. Her hair tickled Margaret's nose as she worked the ties open.

Released, Margaret moved with caution, rolling her shoulders and wriggling her fingers to get some circulation back. There were raw grooves in her wrists, but she didn't dare examine them. She sensed it would be unwise to draw attention to the fact that she'd just been tied up at gunpoint. Better to pretend that incident, like the deaths of Antoinette's parents, had been nothing but a mistake, an unfortunate misunderstanding. That seemed to be how Antoinette remembered it already.

Antoinette beamed as she stood. "Let's go." She even held out a hand to help Margaret to her feet.

Stiff and unsteady, Margaret accepted her help. Then she seized Antoinette by the shoulders and pushed her as hard as she could.

Antoinette flew across the hall, smashed headfirst into Ivy's heavy oak hallstand, and dropped like a stone.

Margaret dived for the shotgun. She clutched it, adrenaline surging. God, had she killed Antoinette? The thought was sickening, not the least because she had no idea what the woman had done with Bess.

Antoinette's eyelids flickered. She moaned softly.

Not dead, then. Margaret fossicked in Antoinette's coat pocket and retrieved Bess's phone. Then she hauled her former captor into the hall cupboard, slammed the door, and dragged the nearest bookcase in front of it. She supposed she should revive Antoinette, get the truth about Bess. But the thought of waiting for Antoinette to recover, restraining her somehow, and trying to cajole or terrorise her into talking… No. She couldn't stay another second in this house, breathing in its stale air and vicious memories. Bess must be somewhere nearby; she had to find her and get away.

She took the gun and staggered out into the blessedly clean night air.

Chapter 18

W͏HAT WAS THE CODE FOR SOS?

Bess had managed to unscrew the grille from the air vent and squeeze her hand out. She blinked Ty's pen torch on and off, hoping she remembered the sequence and wasn't signalling *We're fine in here*.

"Who bother?" Ty slumped against the wall, finishing a bottle of riesling. "We're nowhere near the road. Who's gunna see?"

"A light aircraft?" Bess ached from crouching. "A helicopter? A hiker?"

If the tiger women were still camped out there, they might have seen. If they hadn't run away like cowards.

Ty held the bottle to Vivienne's lips again. "Sorry about this, hon. Worst rescue ever, hey?"

Bess hadn't been sure whether Vivienne was still conscious. She had told them the strange tale of her sister, Antoinette, before lapsing into silence. But she seemed to be swallowing the wine. She even smiled at Ty, which was more than Bess felt like doing.

"If you've got a better plan, I'm all ears." Bess flicked the torch again. How long till the battery died? "When it gets light, we can try calling out. Someone might go bushwalking nearby." Although she had never seen bushwalkers in Mount Bastion, and any noise might summon Antoinette.

Because Antoinette was still in the house. They hadn't heard a car leave. She was in there with Margaret. The thought made Bess feel clammy with horror. What did that woman mean when she said she had big plans for Margaret Gale? What was she doing to her?

Margaret could take care of herself, Bess repeated firmly. Margaret was sharp and suspicious of people, and she knew how to take charge. She never got duped or bullied into anything. Bess had seen Margaret interrogating a plumber about every item on the invoice. Ordering a foul drunk man out of a restaurant where they were dining. Ticking people off for dropping litter outside her museum and looming over them until they picked it up.

Bess had found those incidents pretty embarrassing at the time, but now she clung to the memories, hoping Margaret would squash Antoinette as well as she had those other unpleasant people.

Although none of those people had been holding a firearm.

The thought made Bess want to scream, to pound her fists bloody against the walls. She had to get to Margaret, to do *something*.

"I've got a better plan." Ty wobbled to her feet and bent over a wine rack.

The darkness in the cellar was thinning out while the air grew colder. Was dawn approaching?

The young woman whistled: "Ooh, Penfolds Cab-Shiraz, la-dee-da. There's champagne too, but I don't s'pose we've got much to celebrate."

Bess snapped, "If you're going to be totally unhelpful, do you think you could do it quietly?" Disgusted, she turned away.

Through the air vent, she could see overgrown grass and a few trees. A bird started to sing. Daybreak was coming.

Dry leaves crunched. Was someone walking out there? Her breath caught in fear—was it Antoinette? But hell, things couldn't get much worse. She swung the torch in the direction of the footsteps. Then...

"Margaret!" Bess's voice burst out like an airhorn. There was no mistaking that lanky, dark figure—and she was carrying Antoinette's shotgun. "Over here!"

With a cry, Margaret rushed towards them, but Ty shoved Bess away from the grille and yelled, "Get the bolt cutters from the garden shed!"

Margaret dashed away.

"See?" Ty planted an unwanted kiss on Bess's cheek. "Told you things would work out, didn't I?" She turned and started regaling Vivienne with stories of all the pubs they would drink in when they were rescued.

Bess nearly crammed her whole hand into her mouth to keep from shrieking. Was Margaret all right out there? Had she found the shed, or had some fresh disaster got in her way?

But no, here was Margaret at last, sprinting back. The sound of her wrestling with the padlocks, then metal snapping and pinging off the steps as the bolts were yanked aside. The door scraped open.

Margaret stood in the doorway, silhouetted by the grey half-light behind her.

Bess gasped with relief. She flew to Margaret and seized her shoulders. There was a weird smell about her, like booze and anxious sweat, and her short dark hair was a mess. But there were no signs of injury. Bess let out a trembling breath, clutching Margaret so hard she could feel her collarbones through her clothing.

Then Margaret gently pushed her to arm's length, looked her over. She demanded, "Are you all right? What did she do to you?"

"I'm fine—but I was scared to death for you."

"You know she's not Vivienne?" Margaret said.

"I know that now. I'm sorry I left you alone with that snake. I should have realised how upset you were about losing your sister's ashes; you weren't making good decisions."

"No, I'm sorry. I should never have doubted you, Bess. And I should have removed that ghastly woman from our lives the moment she started fawning over at me. Whoever I thought she was at the time."

"Are you really okay?'

"I am now." Margaret drooped as if in exhaustion, staring desperately into Bess's face. But when she began pulling her closer, Bess stopped her. "Not yet. We need those cutters in here." She moved aside and shone the torch onto Vivienne.

The sight of a semi-conscious woman tied to the waterpipe made Margaret flinch. But she recovered quickly and hurried over to cut the plastic ties from the pipe.

Bess held the torch steady and thought she'd better be polite. "Margaret, this is Vivienne. Vivienne, Margaret. I believe you used to know each other."

"Oh yes." Vivienne laughed deliriously. "I've been interrogated about that wretched graduation night so many times in this dungeon that I never want to think about it again!"

As she tried to find a way to cut the ties without hurting Vivienne, Margaret said, "That's all right. I've thought all I want to about graduation night too." She didn't sound sentimental or emotional. And while she handled Vivienne gently, her manner was no different to what she would have shown towards anyone in that predicament. If she had once cherished the memory of Vivienne, that memory had clearly lost its power.

The ties fell away. Rolling onto her side, Vivienne looked up at Bess. "Are you Margaret's partner?"

"How did you know?" Bess asked. Most people seemed startled to learn they were a couple.

"Antoinette said Margaret had brought a woman with her; she wasn't happy about it." Vivienne grimaced, then shuddered. "I'm glad Margaret found someone so resourceful and kind. She deserves it."

Bess smiled at Margaret over Vivienne's head as they both carried her outside and laid her on the grass.

Ty waved a fresh bottle at them and started tearing foil off it. "Hey, ladies, what do you reckon? Time we cracked open the champagne after all?"

"Don't try and be friendly." Bess glared. "I haven't forgotten how you tried to bail on me before. We're going to report you for all the stupid, illegal stuff you did." Then she sighed, looking at the blood clumped in Ty's hair. "But we'll call a doctor first."

"That reminds me," Margaret said. "I got your phone back."

"From Antoinette? What did you do with her?"

"Knocked her out. It was an accident, more or less."

"Make that two doctors, then." But Bess needed something herself first. She grasped Margaret's lapels, held her in place, and scrutinised her expression.

If she saw hesitance or doubt there, or that shut-down, closed-off look that had become all too familiar over the past few months—well, she might just walk away. Painful though the idea was and desperately relieved as she was to find Margaret unharmed, Bess was not prepared to go back to the way things had been.

But that wasn't what she saw. Instead, she saw tears in Margaret's dark eyes, her face slack with exhaustion, looking paler and older than ever before. She gazed at Bess as if this was the first and last time she would ever see her. All the energy she had left seemed to be concentrated in that gaze, and the emotion in her face—relief, fear, need—was so raw that Bess could scarcely bear it.

She pulled Margaret down and kissed her.

And Margaret's answering kiss—an awkward nudge of her lips at first as if she couldn't be sure this was real, and then a tight grip of her arms and a hot pressure of lips and tongue that felt like plunging into deep water—told Bess everything she needed to know.

Margaret buried her face in the warm tangle of Bess's hair and inhaled deeply. The familiar press of Bess's body against hers, the softness and strength of her was the most welcome sensation Margaret had ever felt. She shut her eyes against tears.

A second chance. How many times in life were you granted one of those?

"There you are!" wheezed a voice. Two older women were hurrying up the driveway. One was small and stout, a safari suit flapping around her, her face lobster red from jogging. The other woman had gigantic glasses and ran like a giraffe, spindly legs and arms flying about.

"What are you doing back here?" Bess sounded less than friendly. "Margaret, this is Matilda and Penny. They spend their lives worrying about an animal that's been dead for a century while refusing to care about a woman who's been dead for a week."

"Touché." Matilda bent over to catch her breath. "But thank heavens you're safe. We came as fast as we could, but we were far from Mount Bastion when we realised."

"Realised what?" Margaret turned to Bess. "Is she the one who fired a gun at you?"

"Near me," Bess corrected her reluctantly. "And no, that was Daz."

"She's parking the 4WD," Matilda said. "Look, we owe you an apology for slinking off like that. Not exactly our finest hour."

"I'll say."

"We acted rationally," said Penny. "We were guided by our strategic priorities."

"Did you come back to tell me that?" Bess asked.

"No, to tell you that we found new evidence!" Penny's spectacles glittered. "And it forced us to reevaluate."

"What she's trying to say is"—Matilda had almost got her breath back—"before we left our camp, we made one last visit to all our camera sites. We had dozens of them, and we didn't have the time to check them all every day. We had to prioritise the most likely spots."

"And...?"

"And as you know, we had one camera aimed at the front of Crossroads House, at the bin bay. But we also had another facing the back of the building." Matilda waved towards the east wing. "The visibility was poor there and we'd never seen anything interesting, so we tended to forget about that camera. But we collected it along with the other equipment before we left. And as we were driving towards Hobart, Penny watched the footage on her laptop." Matilda paused. "Footage from a week ago."

After a sleepless night, Margaret was struggling to follow. "If you've come to tell us you've discovered footage of the Tasmanian tiger—or more likely a shadow of the tail of something that might be a Tasmanian tiger but is probably a neighbour's dog—well, I'm sure we're very happy for you." Her tone was tart. "But we're busy, so—"

"No, no, girl. Keep up!" boomed Matilda.

Margaret reared back, unaccustomed to being ticked off. Before she could object, Matilda went on.

"The footage showed that blonde woman who lives here marching another blonde woman—this one"—she pointed at Vivienne—"down to the cellar at gunpoint with her hands tied!" Matilda shook her head in horror. "Well, you could have knocked us all down with a feather. We knew there was a bit of a question mark over Mrs Bolt's death, but we'd assumed it must have been an accident. Perhaps there had been a scuffle between some elderly people, but nothing worse. We never pictured this!" She turned to Bess. "And you were staying in the house with the woman who did it! So of course we came back."

"How nice of you." Bess folded her arms. "I thought this wasn't your fight."

"Well..." Matilda turned an interesting shade of flamingo-pink. "I trust we're all big enough to admit when we've done wrong," Matilda said.

"*Malum est consilium quod mutari non potest:* bad is the plan that cannot change." She cleared her throat. "I'm…sorry."

"Uh-huh." Bess looked underwhelmed, but as usual, she seemed determined to make the best of things. "Well, you can make yourselves useful and call emergency services."

"We called the police on our way back, but I'm not sure they believed us." Matilda grimaced. "Or even understood us. Perhaps I shouldn't have got Penny to call."

"I described that footage to them in detail!" Penny said sulkily. "I even estimated the make and model of the shotgun."

Bess glanced around, then asked Margaret, "Where is the gun?"

Margaret hesitated. It wasn't like her to forget things, but she had never felt tireder than right now. "I put it down outside the garden shed," she recalled. "I was hunting for Ty's bolt cutters. I'll go back and fetch it—"

"Ah…" Ty looked past them. She had twisted the wire from the champagne bottle, but now the wire dropped from her fingers, and she gaped in dismay. "No need."

Antoinette Bolt paced towards them. Her face was streaked with blood, her hair clotted black with it and plastered to one cheek. More blood bubbled out of her nose. Her knuckles were raw and her shoes scuffed, evidently from wrestling and kicking her way out of that cupboard. Her eyes were wild, but the shotgun pointed at them was disturbingly steady.

"I should have known you would abandon me again," Antoinette said.

Margaret wanted to grab Bess and run, but Bess was bent over the injured Vivienne, trying to drag her to her feet. Did she really think Vivienne capable of getting away now, or was Bess just too decent to abandon someone so helpless? Vivienne made it upright, then toppled and clutched Margaret for support.

"All right, young lady." Matilda held up a hand and stepped towards Antoinette. "That's quite enough. Pull yourself together."

"I'm as together as I'm going to be"—Antoinette squinted—"whoever you are." She looked at Vivienne and Margaret. "I should have known I'd find you two with each other. You couldn't resist betraying me again, could you? I suppose you thought you'd take the antiques and go off together."

"Excuse me," said Bess, "but I would have a few things to say if they did."

"Oh? Who asked you, you human mung bean?"

"I'm truly sorry about shutting you in that cupboard, Antoinette." Margaret paused for effect. "It should have been the oven on full blast."

Matilda held up a hand. "We've rung the police." Her voice was remarkably calm; she might have been ticking off a student for smoking in the bike shed. "Time you called it a day."

"Oh, the day's almost finished." Antoinette drew in a hoarse breath. "Bunch up together." When no one moved, she screamed, *"Now!"* and took aim at Bess.

Margaret blurted, "Wait!" and stepped in between Bess and their attacker. "We're doing what we're told. Stay calm."

Antoinette waved the shotgun at Ty and Penny until they moved nearer, Ty still clutching the champagne bottle. Matilda moved reluctantly over to join them.

A sickly sheen gathered across Antoinette's skin. "You want to lock me up again," she said. "You want to tell lies about me and have me locked away, and then pretend I was never here..." She pointed the weapon at Vivienne. "I won't let you."

Vivienne stared at her sister. "I never locked you up, Antoinette. I'm sorry for what Ivy did to you, but I didn't know. I thought you were dead. I'm sorry for everything that happened to you, but none of it was my doing."

"I don't care! You abandoned me!"

Penny whispered to Matilda, "It's possible our original retreat was actually the wisest course of action..."

Margaret searched in desperation for a viable idea—or any idea—but nothing came. She took Bess's hand and stood tall, her chin up.

"Into the cellar," said Antoinette. "All of you."

Penny and Ty started to inch in that direction while Matilda stalled and Vivienne began to cry. Margaret looked at Bess, committing her face to memory again in case this was the last time.

But Bess stared ahead, past Antoinette to the end of the garden. The bushes were moving.

A woman stepped out of them and padded across the grass, a shotgun held in one hand. A lean and leathery older woman wearing a flannelette shirt, jeans that looked like they'd been run over by a ute, and a haircut that looked like it had shorn by a lawnmower. Was this Daz?

The woman swung the shotgun up onto her shoulder.

"You heard me," Antoinette told the huddled group of women. "*Move.*"

"All right." Margaret spoke loudly to cover any sound Daz's footsteps might make. "We don't want any more trouble."

"It's touching that you think I still care what you want, Margaret." Antoinette scanned the group, checking for signs of resistance. Her gaze lit on Penny.

Penny hadn't moved, but she was staring at Daz, her eyes round and bright behind her glasses. Oh no.

Antoinette whirled around.

Margaret's heart clenched as Daz stopped and took aim while Antoinette grappled with her own weapon. Margaret yanked Bess's arm. This could be their last chance to run.

But Bess moved the other way, tugging free from Margaret's grasp, snatching the champagne bottle from Ty.

Antoinette fired, the explosion making Penny scream.

Daz ducked sideways, roaring at Penny, "Stand back!" She raised the shotgun again, getting Antoinette in her sights.

In the confusion, no one but Margaret noticed Bess shaking the bottle with all her might. Then she pointed the bottle at Antoinette and pushed her thumbs in hard.

The cork shot out like a missile, striking Antoinette in the back of the head. She flew forward, then fell face first onto the grass.

The tiger women flung themselves on her. Penny wrestled the gun from her, Daz stepped on her arm, yelling "Bloody settle!" while Matilda sat down hard on her legs.

Margaret stared at Bess. "I don't mean to criticise, but you could have just thrown the bottle."

"I'm still building my upper body strength." Bess looked dazed. "Ask me when I've done a few more years of yoga." The bottle was still in her hand, and warm champagne sloshed over their feet.

"Hey," said Ty, "don't waste it!" She directed the spray into her mouth before offering it to Vivienne.

Margaret wrinkled her nose. Really, some people were vulgar. But when she looked back at Bess, who was grinning and nearly sobbing with relief, she had never felt more like celebrating.

Chapter 19

Several days later, when they had finished with the police, doctors, and solicitors, Bess and Margaret returned to Crossroads House. This time, the doors and windows were propped open so that sunlight illuminated the dark wooden furniture. A cleansing breeze stirred the dust from the surfaces and drove out the smell of damp and rot.

And this time it was the real Vivienne who welcomed them at the door, battered and twitchy from her ordeal but determined, she said, to get things sorted out.

"Carrot juice?" Vivienne blended it in front of them, perhaps sensing that they might be uncomfortable accepting beverages served in this house. "Before I came here, I was on a health kick. I even thought about taking up micro gardening."

"Oh, I've got a book on that!" Bess said enthusiastically.

Margaret sniffed her juice. Still, she couldn't stay irritable for long. She looked at Bess, remembering last night.

They had found an Airbnb three towns over: a weatherboard cottage with a wood fire and a rose garden. Last night, they'd sat on the back veranda, listening to insects whirring and small animals scampering in the garden. Margaret apologised again for the mistakes she had made the past few days, and then they talked: about Deirdre's death, their regrets, their hopes for the future. The night sky was so clear, the Southern Cross and pointers so luminous that she could imagine how lost sailors had once used the stars to find their way home.

Bess snuggled up to her on the couch and they kissed, their lips and breath and tongues finding a rhythm they had missed for so long but still knew so well.

Stroking Bess's hair, nuzzling the velvety flesh of her neck and the plump, perfect lobes of her ears, Margaret thought how remarkable it was to be alive. To be doing anything was a wonder; to be doing this, a miracle.

"We should go inside," she'd murmured as Bess traced the crease on the inside of Margaret's trousers, up one long, taut thigh to a place where a restless heat was gathering.

"Why?" And Bess had kissed the hollow of Margaret's throat, pressing down harder until Margaret forgot everything but the luscious shape of the woman against her, the pulsing of her fingers, and the smell of roses.

Was she turning red remembering? Margaret hoped not; how gauche. But Bess caught her eye and smiled in a way that reminded her they couldn't hide much from each other now.

Vivienne coughed. "Thanks for helping me sort through Ivy's things."

"I've assessed plenty of your grandmother's possessions already," said Margaret. "Some of them at gunpoint. The rest shouldn't take too long."

"Oh no, I don't need to you value any more antiques. I'll hire someone for that later. Today I'm just picking a few personal items to take with me. For sentimental purposes." Vivienne sounded unsure about the idea. "How are you at labelling boxes?"

In the end, she filled four small boxes with paperback books, knick-knacks, brooches, and tea towels. And the framed photographs of her family.

"Are you processing everything?" Bess asked.

"Not even slightly," Vivienne said shakily. "Ask me again in thirty years." She put the photos in box and taped it shut.

"Well, you're not the only shell-shocked person in Mount Bastion." Margaret labelled another box. "I gather Alan Moore has gone to ground. Janine Jones is at home having a very noisy breakdown while the neighbours chew over her family secrets. And Dorian Visser has skipped town."

"Ugh, he's a nasty man," said Bess. "If the police don't catch him for breaking and entering, we'll get him another way. You remember my friend Matt who has the true-crime podcast? He's keen to do a season on Dorian, the ghost hunting grifter. He reckons it could be big."

"Excellent," said Margaret. "As long as I don't have to listen to it."

"Alan's in trouble, though. I assume he'll be charged with selling those illegal artefacts."

Margaret sighed. "If he can hand over the buyers, perhaps the courts will be lenient." She still felt a little sorry for Alan. She wondered whether, in a different set of circumstances, that could have been her.

"Meanwhile, Mrs Jones will probably get off with a warning." Vivienne looked grim. "In light of her unblemished character. After running you two out of town and lurking around here like the family ghost!"

"And still failing to notice anything funny in the cellar," Margaret added.

Vivienne arched her eyebrows. "That too."

Bess said, "It was generous of you to get Ty a solicitor."

"I didn't mind. She's rather a laugh." Vivienne bit her lip. "My real problem is organising Ivy's funeral. What will I say in her eulogy? Do I call her a murder victim? An eccentric recluse? A smart woman who never did much? A grandmother who abused her family while insisting she was protecting them?"

"I don't know." Margaret shook her head. "But it's up to you now."

Bess asked, "What will you do with Ivy's antiques?"

"Sell them." Vivienne didn't hesitate. "Not that I need the money. But I'm thinking of donating it to the fight to save the bush around here from being turned into a golf course." She paused. "And if that doesn't work, perhaps I'll offer to sell this property to the golf club so they'll have the road access they want. I would make it conditional on them leaving the wilderness alone. That should please Matilda, Penny, and Daz."

Surprised, Margaret said, "I didn't know you were a tiger truther."

Vivienne laughed. "I wouldn't say that. But I like this landscape, and I owe those women a debt of gratitude." She glanced between them. "Although not as much as I owe you."

Bess wrapped Vivienne in a hug. Margaret settled for an amicable but awkward nod.

It was good to renew her acquaintance with the real Vivienne at last, but the fascination Margaret used to feel for her had vanished. Graduation night, once a powerful turning point, had become a memory. It left Margaret feeling slightly bereft but also lighter and freer than she'd been in a long time.

Vivienne stood up. "Another carrot juice?"

"Yes, please." Bess handed over her cup.

"I've got plenty." Margaret waited until their hostess left before tipping it out the open window.

"Incredible," said Bess.

"I don't drink anything that tastes of compost."

"No. These." Bess had taken the photo albums from the bookcase and started flipping through them. "Check out the seventies hair."

It seemed no one had opened these volumes in years. Their covers were dusty, the pages stuck together.

"Will Vivienne want them?" Bess mused. "Family photos might upset her, under the circumstances."

"Well, it's that or throw them away. I don't imagine anyone would buy them."

Bess didn't answer for a long moment. Then in an odd voice, she said, "I don't know about that." She placed the open album on the table carefully. "Look."

It was a page of photos taken sometime in the seventies. There must have been a party at Crossroads House. A classic Holden Kingswood car was parked in the drive, and people with bushy hair and flared trousers milled around in the garden. A middle-aged Ivy, actually smiling, sat in a deckchair with a drink and a cigarette.

"What about it?" Margaret asked.

Bess pointed at the photo in the bottom right corner. "Here."

The picture must have been taken later on the same day, after the partygoers had left. The light had grown dim, and Ivy was standing alone in the garden, which was now strewn with drink cans and paper plates. And food scraps too, Margaret assumed, like bones and gristle, half-eaten sausages dropped into the grass, carelessly spilled dollops of sauce and gravy. At dusk, with the noisy people gone, the smell must have been hard to resist.

Ivy looked calm. Perhaps the photographer had planned to show her ruefully cleaning up. Instead, she gazed across the lawn at a creature that had slunk from the bushes to snuffle around in the long grass. A grey and biscuit-coloured creature with a long pointed head and a distinctive set of stripes on its flanks.

"Is that…" Margaret bent closer until her nose almost touched the page. "Is that real?"

Bess touched the photo album. "Remember what Ivy said? That she'd hidden her most valuable possession somewhere no one would ever look."

Wondering if this could be some very old practical joke, Margaret said, "The last thylacine died four decades before this picture was taken. If this is real, it would be explosive."

"You'd better get Vivienne." Bess took out her phone.

"Who are you texting?"

"Matilda."

Margaret made it as far as the door before Bess's phone rang. When she answered it, three voices burst out so loudly that Margaret wasn't sure they needed a phone at all. As she listened to shouts of "Describe it exactly!", "Don't touch anything! We're coming!", and "Fuck me dead!", she guessed the tiger women's adventure had only just begun.

The sea hit the rocks with a *boom*, the water bouncing off and hanging in the air before a cold blast blew it back into the women's faces. Light rain began to fall, mingling with the sea mist.

Bess stepped with care onto the slick rocks of the breakwater. She yelled over the buffeting wind, "Should we have chosen another day?"

"No." Margaret stood upright, her black coat billowing around her. She closed her eyes as if in relish at the slap of the wind.

The ocean frothed and hissed, grey green in some lights, indigo in others. If you travelled in a straight line down from here, you would hit Antarctica.

From under her coat, Margaret drew out Deirdre's ashes, which she had transferred to a new biodegradable urn. It was shaped like a pretty seashell, chosen by Bess.

"Wait a second." Bess slipped an arm around Margaret's waist and lined up a selfie.

"Is that necessary?"

"Yes. It's important to keep a record of things."

Margaret rolled her eyes. Then she kissed the top of Bess's head as the phone clicked.

"Do you really like the location?"

Margaret nodded. "Deirdre was trapped at home all her life, and it didn't protect her. Time she had some adventures."

She waited for a break in the wind, a rare moment of calm, and tossed the container into the waves. It bobbed a second before the water rushed in again, then it vanished from view.

Bess took Margaret's hand. "How do you feel?"

"Cold." Still, Margaret smiled slightly as she gazed at the horizon. "But this is beautiful." She led Bess back over the treacherous rocks towards the relative calm of the beach.

Bess poured from a thermos of coffee. "What do we do now?"

Margaret's eyes watered, perhaps from the piercing wind. "What if we stayed?" she asked. "Not forever and not in Mount Bastion—God forbid— but just in Tasmania. There's a project starting in Hobart, restoring one of the old icebreakers that travelled to Antarctica in the 1950s. They're looking for a historical advisor. The money's decent, and I promise not to pick fights with anyone this time." She shot Bess a nervous glance. "What do you think?"

Bess smiled. "Actually, I was going to suggest the same thing. I reached out to someone I went to uni with—she works at the museum here. They're planning an exhibition about convict women, and they want a researcher to find examples of the women's voices. You know, from court transcripts, newspaper articles, prison records. I said I loved the idea, but I wouldn't rush off on any new tangents without speaking to you first."

"Do it." Margaret toasted her with the thermos.

"Really?"

"They're lucky to have you."

"I haven't given up on my idea for a show about the tiger women," Bess assured her. "They've agreed to help now. It'll just take time to get it right." She paused. "And when we find a house here, it must have room for chickens. That's nonnegotiable."

Margaret smiled. "Understood." She sipped her coffee, droplets of rain trickling from her wet hair down her temples and making her skin shine. "I like it out here. It's...invigorating."

"Is that a polite word for freezing?" But Bess was delighted by this wild landscape too.

"You know what I mean." Margaret put her coffee down. "Bracing. Lively." She looked at Bess. "Freeing."

Bess held tight to her hands and pulled her in for a kiss. Their lips were almost numb from the wind, but their breath had lost none of its warmth, and their skin tasted of seawater. Of coastlines and oceans and journeys still to come.

Other Books from Ylva Publishing

www.ylva-publishing.com

A Curious Woman
(Murder Under the Gum Trees – Book 1)
Jess Lea

ISBN: 978-3-96324-160-4
Length: 283 pages (100,000 words)

Bess has moved to a coastal town where she has a job at a hip gallery, some territorial chickens, and a lot of self-help books. She's also at war with Margaret, who runs the local museum with an iron fist. When they're both implicated in a senseless murder, can they work together to expose the truth?

A funny, fabulous, cozy mystery filled with quirkiness and a sweet serve of lesbian romance.

A Heist Story
Ellen Simpson

ISBN: 978-3-95533-958-6
Length: 315 pages (113,000 words)

Life gets weird for Marcey Daniels when an art thief dies and leaves her a curious and much sought-after book. Suddenly a determined Interpol agent named Wei is sniffing around, along with the mysterious, flirtatious criminal, Kat. Everyone has their own agenda in this intricate suspense thriller. As the double-crosses pile up, can Marcey unpick the trap within the puzzle?

The Red Files
Lee Winter

ISBN: 978-3-96324-534-3
Length: 304 pages (103,000 words)

Ambitious journalist Lauren King is stuck reporting on the vapid LA social scene's gala events while sparring with her rival—icy ex-Washington correspondent Catherine Ayers. Then a curious story unfolds before their eyes, involving a business launch, thirty-four prostitutes, and a pallet of missing pink champagne. Can the warring pair join together to unravel an incredible story?

Driving Me Mad
L.T. Smith

ISBN: 978-3-95533-290-7
Length: 348 pages (107,000 words)

After becoming lost on her way to a works convention, Rebecca Gibson stops to ask for help at an isolated house. Progressively, her life becomes more entangled with the mysterious happenings of the house and its inhabitants.

With the help of Clare Davies, can Rebecca solve a mystery that has been haunting a family for over sixty years? Can she put the ghosts and the demons of the past to rest?

About Jess Lea

Jess Lea lives in Melbourne, Australia, where she started out as an academic before working in the community sector. She loves vintage crime fiction, the writings of funny women, and lesbian books of all sorts. Jess can be found writing in cafes, in parks, and in her pyjamas at home when she should be at work.

CONNECT WITH JESS
E-Mail: JessLeaContact@gmail.com

A Curious Visit
© 2023 by Jess Lea

ISBN: 978-3-96324-779-8

Available in e-book and paperback formats.

Published by Ylva Publishing, legal entity of Ylva Verlag, e.Kfr.

Ylva Verlag, e.Kfr.
Owner: Astrid Ohletz
Am Kirschgarten 2
65830 Kriftel
Germany

www.ylva-publishing.com

First edition: 2023

Credits
Edited by Lee Winter and Julie Klein
Cover Design and Print Layout by Streetlight Graphics